BONFIRE OF THE CALAMITIES

A BEAUFORT SCALES MYSTERY – BOOK 8

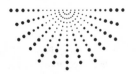

KIM M. WATT

For further information contact: www.kmwatt.com

Cover design: Monika McFarland, www.ampersandbookcovers.com

Editor: Lynda Dietz, www.easyreaderediting.com

Logo design by www.imaginarybeast.com

ISBN (ebook): 978-1-7385854-7-2

ISBN (Amazon PB): 978-1-7385854-8-9

ISBN (Ingrams PB): 978-1-7385854-9-6

First Edition: December 2023

10 9 8 7 6 5 4 3 2 1

CONTENTS

To the Toot Hansell Auxiliary,
for always keeping the magic alive.
Thank you, lovely people. There's no one I'd rather share dragons with.

ABOUT THAT GUY ...

"Remember, remember,
The fifth of November,
Gunpowder, treason and plot ..."

- English Folk Verse, Circa 1870

Bonfire of the Calamities takes place in the depths of the Yorkshire autumn, in the lead up to Bonfire Night (November 5th), which is also known as Guy Fawkes Night. It's a traditional celebration that commemorates the foiled Gunpowder Plot of 1605, where a group of Catholics, including Guy Fawkes, attempted to blow up the Houses of Parliament and so assassinate the Protestant King James I. Their plot was foiled, but ever since it's been marked by fireworks displays and bonfires, on which effigies known as guys are burnt, because that's not creepy at all.

There is, of course, a whole lot more to the history, involving upheaval, religion, politics, and more burning things, but that's a bit beyond the scope of this note, which is mostly just to ensure no one thinks the Toot Hansell Women's Institute were carting around some hapless individual called Guy in their wheelbarrow.

Speaking of that, something else that might be helpful to know is that in the lead-up to Bonfire Night, children would traditionally create guys (sort of like scarecrows) and wheel them around town in a barrow, asking for "a penny for the guy". It's not so common now, but it was a way for children to collect money to contribute to fireworks or community bonfire celebrations, and the guy would later be burned on the bonfire.

And finally, some regions in the UK observe Mischief Night. This falls on October 30th in some areas, but in Northern England it's the night before Bonfire Night (the 4th of November). And I think you can guess what that night's all about.

And thus ends a very little bit of background knowledge which it might help to know, if you're unfamiliar with it.

Now onward to dragons!

Happy reading!
Kim

1

MIRIAM

The trees were flushed with orange and gold, the sky a deep violet at the edges, and the air was so bright with the promise of frost that Miriam could almost see it gathering on the edges of the day, waiting to creep in like the year's first exhale. Lights were on in the houses that lined the narrow streets, casting warm tones over the fading flowers, and the whiff of woodsmoke spoke of deep chairs and hot kettles. She took a deep breath, then coughed as the chill stung her throat, and pulled her scarf up a little higher.

"Ooh. It *is* coming in cold tonight."

"Are you sure you should be out, dear?" Alice asked. "That was a nasty cold you had."

Miriam made a face. It *had* been a nasty cold, and she never wanted to see another mug of lemon, ginger, and thyme infusion again, even if she was quite sure that was what had sent it on its way, rather than the Lemsip.

"I'm quite alright. It does me good to have some fresh air. I almost forgot what it felt like."

Alice smiled, and tugged her hat a little more snugly down over her ears. It was felt, a tasteful sage green, and Alice's silver hair emerged from underneath in a smooth and rather attractive wave.

Miriam was quite aware that her own hair was pinned in place by a startlingly orange knitted creation, strung through haphazardly with bits of glittery brown wool, and the curls that emerged from under the heavy stitching were sticking out in a riotous tangle which had as little style as the hat did. She wasn't even sure where the horrible thing had come from, and she was certain she had a whole collection of better ones somewhere, but the only other she'd been able to find that evening was hot pink with green flowers appliquéd on it, which would hardly have been an improvement. But, she reminded herself, she *had* just been sick, and, to be honest, did still feel a little off. One couldn't expect her to be at her best.

They skirted the village green rather than cutting across it as they would usually have done. That summer there had been a unanimous vote to allow a certain portion of the green to become a wildflower meadow, which had delighted everyone except a small yet vocal collection of residents who had declared the long grass and nodding flowers an eyesore. There had been much back and forth about it, but the majority had held firm.

Then someone – and Miriam was fairly sure she knew who, as there were only two ride-on mowers in the village, and since Mr Peters had been one of the most enthusiastic supporters of the rewilding initiative, it had hardly been him – had mown the budding meadow down in the depths of an early June night, just as it was getting going. There had been quite an outcry, and before the evening cricket crowd (who had been a very active part of the vocal minority) could retake the area for their sundown series, the designated wildflower portion had been firmly chained off by person or persons unknown. It was re-seeded, and had started to come back rather well, until another night-time mowing incident had occurred, and the discarded chains were found scattered in a furious arc around the duck pond, still slicked with mud.

The second attempt at protecting the struggling meadow had involved chains which encircled a significantly larger part of the green than previously, plus padlocks attached to trees and the one lamp post on the corner. Unfortunately this had not been cleared with the local council, and only a couple of weeks later they had turned up to trim the grass. The man on the mower was quite happy to leave a large chunk of the green wild, but it ended up being rather more than planned when, chatting on his mobile, he ran straight over a length of chain that had been lurking unseen in the long grass, quite a distance from where any of the barriers *should* have been.

The resulting damage was loud and expensive, and with blame being thrown back and forth between the village and the council, no one had replaced the mower. Of the owners of the two ride-on mowers in the village, well. Mr Peters refused to use his, since he rather liked the idea of an overgrown green (Miriam wasn't even sure why he *had* a ride-on mower, since he lived in a terraced house with a paved patio, but she thought it might be to do with the fact that he had lost his driver's license due to terribly poor vision and often took the mower into the village centre rather than walking. A mobility scooter might've been more practical, but, as he pointed out, he wasn't *that* old yet). The other mower had been mysteriously and permanently disabled, and Miriam was rather sorry that they'd had such a busy summer she hadn't been able to follow the story more closely. Even so, she had an idea who might have disabled it, just as she had an idea who might have left the rogue chains. But family is family, and she didn't tell tales, even if she'd recognised the profile that had posted a picture of scuffed chains lying in the long grass with a caption reading *Victory!* in the local Facebook group.

However, all of this meant the *entire* village green had become somewhat of a wildflower meadow (she wasn't quite sure how the rest of the usually neat green grass had somehow been seeded with wild grasses and flowers, but she suspected the same person who may or may not have sabotaged the mower). It had been excellent for the birds and the insects, and children and dogs and picnicking couples looking for a little privacy had enjoyed it very much in the summer, other than the odd inevitable bee sting, but it was a little long to walk through on a crisp November evening. One would get more than one's ankles wet.

And now the grass rose still and brown across the green, the flowers having bloomed their last. The duck pond was quite hidden behind it all, but Miriam could hear a distant muttering that might have been the geese or might have been Nellie, the rather disgruntled sprite who lived in the pond. She was still insulted by the chains being dropped in her waters, and the geese were particularly feral as a result.

"The grass really shall have to be cut before Bonfire Night," Miriam said as they skirted it. "Unless we're going to do the fire someplace else."

"It will have to be cut," Alice agreed. "It was rather nice while it lasted, though, wasn't it?"

Miriam gave Alice a startled look. "I shouldn't have thought you approved of such things."

"Why? Because I keep my own grass well-trimmed?" Alice had a young man who came every two weeks in the summer to mow the lawn and do things like prune the taller trees. Miriam knew, because Carlotta and Rosemary made it a point to drop by Alice's whenever he was there, especially if it was a particularly hot day. Miriam felt somewhat sorry for the young man. It must be quite stressful, having someone as exacting as Alice as an employer, and then to have to deal with Carlotta and Rosemary competing to bring you cold drinks.

"It doesn't quite seem like your style," she said now, nodding at the meadow. "A little untidy, perhaps."

"I wouldn't choose it for my own garden," Alice said. "But I think such things are very important. Encouraging the native plants and insects. Where would we be without them?"

Miriam nodded, then said a little carefully, "They do need all the help they can get. I have a portion of my garden set aside for just that."

Alice looked at her, a slight smile tugging at the corners of her mouth. "Your whole garden is somewhat like that, dear."

"Well, as you said, it's very good for the wildlife."

Alice nodded. "Quite. And it's very good of you to think of them."

Miriam puffed air over her lower lip, fairly sure that Alice was deliberately missing her point, but it hardly mattered. She doubted Alice's garden would dare descend into disorder, even if its owner did consider allowing it to. There was just something about Alice that willed anything around her into order. She tugged at the front of her purple coat, and noticed she'd lost a button at some point. *Most* things, she amended.

❧❧

JUST BEYOND THE GREEN, the lights of the village hall were lit, glowing warmly and painting patches of its garden in brighter hues as the evening crept in. Alice led the way through the little wooden gate set into the low stone wall and up to the main door, and Miriam trailed in after her, already pulling her hat off in anticipation of the warmth inside. She rapidly replaced it, though.

"It's so cold! Why isn't the heating on?"

"There you are." Gert marched up to them, swaddled in a bright yellow puffer jacket that made her already large frame look like a child's drawing of the sun. "That cranky old boiler's finally died on us."

"Oh dear," Alice said. "That's unfortunate timing."

Miriam shivered, sinking deeper into her coat. "We can't use the hall like this. We'll all freeze!"

"And it's made such a mess," Jasmine said. She was mopping up a puddle of orange-tinged water rather inefficiently, the mop in one hand and Primrose, her nippy little Pomeranian, under her other arm. The dog was wriggling and huffing and baring her teeth at everyone. "It's a good thing we got here when we did. The floor'll start lifting if this gets under it."

Miriam looked at the old laminate wood floor, which was scraped from the passage of chairs and tables and boots, and chipped in places where things had been dropped, ladders or plates or some long-forgotten tins of paint from the last time the hall had been redecorated. The paint tins had left their own traces splattered on the boards, but it was all solid enough. Replacing it would be terribly expensive, and the boiler was going to be quite enough of a problem.

She padded over to Jasmine, keeping a wary eye on Primrose, who was growling irritably, and took the mop from her.

"I'll do it. You keep hold of Primrose."

"I *am*," Jasmine said, stepping back and shifting her grip on the dog. "She's very upset. I think she can feel that we're all rather stressed about this."

"She's not upset. She's *rabid*," Priya declared, coming out of the kitchen with a bucket and a large sponge. "She bit me!"

"She did not," Jasmine snapped. "You scared her!"

Priya pulled her skirt up and brandished a smooth brown leg at Miriam. "Look!"

Miriam inspected her leg dutifully. "Um … there?" she suggested, pointing at Priya's ankle.

Priya dropped her skirt with a huff. "*No.* It's going to bruise, though."

"I *told* you she didn't bite you," Jasmine said, cuddling Primrose closer. The dog's growl intensified into a heart-felt rumble, and her teeth flashed small but fierce in the hall's mellow lighting.

"Why don't you put her down," Miriam suggested, taking a step back. "She looks uncomfortable."

"She keeps trying to drink the water."

Miriam looked down at the wet floor. "Well, it's just water," she said, and Jasmine gave her a horrified look.

"Have you seen the colour of it? It's *orange!*"

"I suppose the tank was very rusty," Miriam said, trying to remember if she'd ever filled the kettle from the hot water tap. She hoped not.

Alice had picked her way around the puddle to peer into the cupboard, where the boiler usually huffed and grumbled its way through their evening meetings. There was nothing dramatically wrong with it that Miriam could see, although she thought its cover, which had been hanging on by one clasp for as long as she could remember, looked a little sadder and saggier than it had before. But that was how the whole evening felt, really, and she wondered if it was just the weight of the fading year. She hoped so.

"Well?" Gert asked, directing the question at Alice. "Not much to see, is there?"

Alice looked up from her inspection of the cupboard. "There doesn't seem to be any power to it."

"I switched it off at the fuse box," Gert said. "Last thing we need is the bloody place going up because the water shorted it out or something."

Alice nodded, and stepped back from the door, closing it gently as if to leave the boiler in peace. "Good thinking. It really is dead, then?"

"Seems so," Gert said. "Not like it hasn't put in the hours."

Miriam squeezed the mop out into the bucket. "I'm surprised it lasted this long. Some of the noises it was making, I've been expecting it to blow up for the last five years."

"Horrible timing, though," Jasmine said. She was still trying to keep hold of Primrose, who had stopped growling but was wriggling enthusiastically, trying to get down. "*Ow.* Primmy, stop it!"

Gert put her hands in her pockets and frowned at the ceiling. "I suppose we can get one of those fancy new ones now. All environmentally friendly and so on."

"And until then we can freeze," Priya said, just as the hall door banged open. They looked around as Rose marched in, a diminutive form bundled up in a khaki outdoors jacket with an enviable array of pockets and some mysterious stains on the shoulder. Angelus, her Great Dane, sloped in after her, his head almost as high as her chest.

"Sorry," she said cheerfully. "What're you all doing, standing about? And who's off with the guy?"

"What guy?" Priya asked.

"Our guy. For the bonfire. I didn't think we were collecting donations tonight."

"We're not," Alice said. "You must be mistaken."

"Then where is he?" Rose pointed to the corner of the hall, where the guy should have been slouched in his wheelbarrow, safe from the weather, with the collection pot for this year's charity (a local food bank) nestling under one arm and a pumpkin under the other, straw poking out of his ragged coat sleeves and his blank face grinning at the night. "I thought it was you, Miriam. They had your hair."

Miriam shivered. "Not me." She could only blame the lingering effects of her cold for her failure to notice the guy was gone. They always struck her as a little creepy, so she certainly would have noticed if he was there. She sneaked a look at Alice, but she looked equally nonplussed.

"I thought someone must have moved him due to the leak," Alice said, frowning.

"What leak?" Rose asked.

"No one moved him," Gert said. "I was first in, and he was already gone. I was more worried about the boiler than the guy, though."

"What's happened to the boiler?" Rose asked, but no one answered her.

"What's the guy doing on the green, then?" Jasmine asked. "If it's not one of us?"

There was a moment's pause, then Miriam said, "Did we empty the collection pot?"

No one answered. The collection pot had been heavy with coins when she, Pearl, and Carlotta had got back from the village market earlier in the day, and there had been five-pound notes and even a few ten-pound ones tucked into the guy's sleeves and neckline. The Toot Hansell Women's Institute were nothing if not persuasive when it came to fundraising, and it was amazing how many people found themselves digging deeper into their wallets when confronted with Pearl's wide blue eyes and guileless smile, or Carlotta lecturing them on how every country was built on community. She wasn't sure if they *guilted* people into donating, exactly, but she was also fairly sure there wasn't a lot of free will involved on the part of the donors.

The not answering seemed to grow in weight, then Miriam said, "*Oh. Oh no.* It was me. I was ... I'm so sorry! It's this awful cold! I took some paracetamol, and I *never* feel right when I take that. I forgot to pick up the tin. Oh *no!*" She clutched the front of her coat, the hall suddenly dark and cloying, and Alice patted her arm.

"It's done now. You shouldn't have been out at all, Miriam. I did say."

Miriam opened her mouth to apologise again, and Gert talked over her. "Rose, you saw the barrow on the green *now?*"

"Just as I was coming up."

"Well, let's get after him, then!" Gert launched herself toward the door, and Rose skipped out of the way, but Angelus gave a howl of fright and bolted out into the crisp evening.

"Angelus!" Rose shouted, and ran after him, narrowly dodging Gert as they rushed for the door together.

"*Ow!*" Jasmine yelped, and dropped Primrose, cradling her hand. "*Prim!*"

The Pomeranian shot out of the hall, and Priya picked up her skirts, jumped the puddle and sprinted after the dog, shouting, "*Get back here, you mutt!*"

Miriam and Alice looked at each other, and Miriam said, "I'm so, *so* sorry. I'll pay it all back."

"Everyone makes mistakes," Alice said, which Miriam thought was rather generous. She couldn't imagine Alice forgetting something as important as the collection tin.

"I can't believe I forgot," Miriam said, then frowned as Alice turned and headed for the kitchen. "Where are you going?"

"I don't think we're going to catch them. They'll have made themselves very scarce now that they've seen we're here."

"And so ...?" Miriam asked, following her into the little, low-ceilinged kitchen.

"We should find out how they got in, for a start."

Miriam peeked over her shoulder, back into the hall, as if the thief might still be lurking behind the curtains, hoping for a chance to grab the chairs and make off with them. "Half the village knows the key's on the windowsill under the ceramic frog."

Security had never been a terribly great concern in Toot Hansell, and especially not at the village hall. There was hardly a lot to be stolen, unless one were keen on the eclectic mix of donated clothes and costumes in the storeroom, or a jar of rarely touched instant coffee.

"I would hate to think that anyone who knows the village well enough to know where the key is would steal from a charity collection." Alice had given the windows a cursory inspection and now she opened the door and stepped out into the night. "Come on. Let's have a little look at the garden."

"Really?" Miriam asked.

"Absolutely," Alice said. "I'm sure they're long gone, but we may find some sign of who it was."

Miriam wondered if being press-ganged into a hunt for thieves was her punishment for being so careless as to forget the donation tin, but she hefted the mop and stepped after Alice into the damp-scented garden. The last of the evening light had all but vanished, and the churchyard beyond the hall was deeply shadowed. There could be entire armies of thieves out there, and she'd never see them. The darkness seemed to creep in a little closer even as she looked, and she shivered, tasting a sudden, aching sorrow that was nothing to do with her cold.

Alice hurried to the stile where the hall joined the churchyard, leaning over it to peer into the long shadows of the old trees beyond. She turned back to Miriam. "I find it very odd that they took the guy and the barrow rather than just the tin. The barrow will be very difficult to get across the green, too."

"How did they even know about the donation tin?" Miriam asked. "Have they been *watching* us?"

Alice didn't answer, just looked into the deepening dusk beyond the stile again, then said, "It is possible. They may have followed you from the market." She started across the garden, heading for the corner of the hall.

Miriam shuddered so hard that the mop splattered water onto her shoulder. She grimaced. "Where are you going?"

"To see what the others have found. You go the other way, Miriam. Just in case there's any sign of how they got in, or if they've dropped anything on the way. I imagine they hid back here when we started arriving, which is why Rose just spotted them leaving now."

Miriam had a sudden image of stumbling across the grinning, staring face of the guy lurking in the shadows, and wanted very much to express just how intensely she didn't want that to happen, but the lost donation tin was weighing on her rather heavily. Plus Alice was already striding around the corner of the hall, her back alarmingly straight and her stick gripped in one hand by the leg rather than the heavy silver handle. Miriam made an uncertain little sound, then padded off in the opposite direction, eyeing the shedding rose bushes warily. None of them seemed big enough to hide a thief or a guy, but she couldn't seem to shake that deepening sense of unease. Of course, she was hunting miscreants through the autumn dusk while armed with nothing more than a mop. A little unease was more than reasonable, as was reconsidering the whole situation, but she kept going anyway, with a tight grip on the mop and a close eye on the shadows.

A shout went up from the front of the hall, and Miriam broke into a run. She rushed through the gate and to the edge of the pavement, waving the mop wildly, and discovered Pearl and Teresa jogging up the street from one direction while Rosemary and Carlotta approached from the other.

"Have you seen anyone?" Gert shouted.

"Anyone with our guy," Rose added. "They nicked off with the whole barrow!"

"Someone took the guy?" Pearl asked. "Why?"

"Thieves!" Jasmine shouted.

"*Guy* thieves?"

"No—"

"We haven't seen anyone come off the green," Teresa interrupted.

"Or us," Carlotta said.

"Then they're still in there," Gert said, jabbing a finger at the long grass. "We need to get after them!"

"Because of the *guy*?" Rosemary asked, a disbelieving note in her voice. "Really?"

"The collection tin won't have anything in it," Pearl pointed out. "Miriam was looking after it."

"Um," Miriam said.

"They've got it," Priya shouted. "They've stolen our guy *and* the donations!"

"*What?*"

"*How?*"

The women surged toward the green without waiting for the questions to be answered, and somehow Miriam found herself joining them, racing across the road, with her mop raised fiercely over her shoulder. She plunged into the wild grass, her cold and her unease both forgotten as the long growth whipped around her legs and the moon rose over the trees, and somewhere in the darkness a bird screamed.

Autumn was here, and the hunt was on.

2

ALICE

Alice hadn't expected that everyone would be *quite* so enthusiastic about chasing the wheelbarrow and the donation thief across the road and into the depths of the long grass on the green. Even for the ladies of the Toot Hansell Women's Institute, who were admittedly rather enthusiastic about many things, it seemed excessive. She wondered if Gert had been giving out testers of her sloe gin already.

Gert herself was currently skirting the green, her hands cupped around her eyes as if it'd help her see better in the light washing from the one streetlamp on the corner by the hall. She kept bobbing up on her tiptoes, looking for movement in the long grass. Pearl, Teresa, Carlotta, and Rosemary had positioned themselves strategically along the road that encircled the hall side of the green, Pearl pointing into the long grass while she addressed her ancient Labrador, Martha. Martha, rather than looking like she had any intention of following what were likely instructions to *sic them*, slumped to the ground and put her head on her paws. Teresa had bundled her silvered braids out of the way and was in a half-crouch with her arms spread, as if she expected to be tackled at any moment, and Carlotta and Rosemary had put their Tupperware containers down on the village hall's low wall so that their hands were free, presumably for grappling with the thief.

Priya, Jasmine, and Rose, however, along with Primrose and Angelus, had taken to the green. Jasmine was still shouting for Primrose, Rose was ordering Angelus to heel, and Priya had come to a sudden stop, trying to extricate her skirt from a particularly clingy patch of growth.

Miriam had plunged into the long grass, but quickly ran into the same difficulty as Priya. She pulled her skirt free, retreated to the edge of the green, and looked at Alice. "Can you see anything? The grass moving or something like that?"

Alice had a momentary vision of the thief – or thieves – crawling across the green, the dry grass waving over their heads like lions creeping through the savannah. "They've probably gone out past the duck pond," she said aloud. There were plenty of ways on and off the green, after all, as long as one wasn't too intimidated by the geese.

"Well, that's good," Miriam said, but didn't lower the mop. "Um – should we go in and help, do you think?"

Alice regarded the green. Rose was only visible from the chest up, and Angelus was bounding around her like he was having delusions of being a kangaroo, his ears flopping in delight. Rose had given up trying to get him to heel and was waving a biscuit at him instead. Jasmine gave a shout of triumph and dived into the grass, then straightened up with a wriggling Primrose clutched firmly to her chest.

"Got her!" she shouted.

"Joy," Priya said, and poked the vegetation with a stick. "Did anyone see which way the barrow went?"

"We didn't see it at all," Carlotta said. "Are you sure you saw a barrow, Rose? It's getting quite dark."

"I can see perfectly well," Rose said. "*I'm* not the one not wearing my glasses."

"I've got my contacts in."

"Well, you must have them in upside down or something. They

were there." She pointed in a waving motion that took in most of the green.

Carlotta huffed. "Well, did anyone else see them?"

"No," Rosemary said. "But I was too busy watching to see who Miriam was going to behead with the mop."

Everyone looked at Miriam, who lowered the mop hastily and said, "Well, they might've been dangerous!"

"They stole a guy and a donation tin from an empty hall," Alice said mildly. "It seems opportunistic rather than dangerous." She didn't add that Miriam and her mop were looking rather more threatening than anyone else around the place.

There was muttered agreement to that, and Gert put her hands on her hips, frowning at the green. "Why take the guy, anyway? Why not just grab the tin and run?"

No one had an answer to that, and finally Rose said, "It was definitely the barrow. Maybe they were going to use it to try and solicit more donations or something."

"It was a very good guy," Pearl said. "I think we rather outdid ourselves this year."

"It was the ball gown that did it," Teresa said. "No one can resist a guy in a ballgown."

Alice wondered just where that piece of wisdom came from, and said, "There's not much we can do about it now. We shall just be glad no one interrupted them and ended up hurt."

"That's very true," Carlotta said. "They could have been waiting to *do things*, after all. A whole hall full of ladies."

Alice thought the thieves might have rather misjudged the situation if they'd had those sorts of ideas, and said, "Does anyone want to host the meeting? The hall's far too cold."

"I'd say come to mine," Rose said. "But I decided to re-tile the kitchen, and seem to have got a bit sidetracked. It's not really fit for a meeting. Or anything else, for that matter," she added. "I've had to put the microwave and the kettle in the living room."

Priya made a sympathetic noise.

"What about reporting the theft?" Rosemary asked. "The police need to come and dust for fingerprints and all that."

"We'll do that straight away," Alice said, watching Jasmine struggling across the green with Primrose still fighting to get free. "Jasmine, dear, can you call Ben and do it that way, perhaps?"

Jasmine made it onto the pavement and stood there breathing hard, her fine hair hanging softly in her face. "If he has time. I barely even see him these days."

"Well, I shall just call Skipton station, then," Alice said. "I doubt we'll get anything back, but they may still catch who did it and stop it happening again."

"I'm so sorry," Miriam said again, apparently to the ground. "I'll make it up."

"What about the boiler?" Priya asked. "We're going to need to get it replaced before Bonfire Night. We need to be able to use the hall, and it'll be impossible in there with no heating."

"We shall have to put it to the council," Alice said.

"We can't wait on them," Gert said, the phone already to her ear. "It'll be next summer by the time they get sorted. I'll get our Maurice on it. He's my sister's brother-in-law's second cousin's stepbrother. He'll get a good price on one, and we'll just tell the council it's a done deal." She turned away from them. "Murph? I need you to get on something."

"It goes through the council," Alice said firmly, and looked around at everyone. "Shall we go to the pub?"

Everyone stared at her, even Rose and Priya, who were still mired in the green.

"The pub?" Miriam asked. "Really?"

Alice tucked her hands into her pockets, feeling the twinge in the knuckles that crept in on the cold air. "Yes. Why not? Otherwise we shall just have to traipse around to someone else's house, and no one planned for a meeting. Unless someone wants to volunteer?" She could, of course, since her house was in very good order, but she didn't fancy having both Angelus and Primrose loose inside, and it was too cold to imagine asking either of their owners to leave them outside. Martha she was quite willing to have in the house, as the old dog did very little other than sleep and eat, but with Angelus and Primrose there'd be running about, and noise, and the risk of breakages, plus Thompson the cat would protest, loudly and vocally, and she really had very little patience for it right now. Besides, she rather fancied a gin and tonic, unseasonal though it was, and she had no tonic at home.

The other ladies looked at each other, then Miriam said, "The pub would be rather nice. The fire'll be going."

That raised a murmur of agreement from the group, and in very short order they were circling the green, still clutching their Tupperware, as they headed for the nearest of the village's selection of pubs. For such a small place, Toot Hansell still supported three of them. Two were on the village square, one a gastropub with disturbingly modern furniture and so much white paint and pale wood that Alice had been tempted to wear sunglasses the last time she went into it. The second pub had no such problems, as the dark green, vaguely sticky carpet and worn red upholstery were lit as dimly as possible, presumably so no one could see the stains on either. That particular pub still had the signs for ladies' and gentlemen's lounges hung over separate doors, and Alice had a suspicion that the owner retained a certain nostalgia for such times and situations.

The nearby pub, though, was all thick-paned windows, low ceilings, and heavy wooden beams, the whole place stuffed with cosy chairs and deep sofas clustering around tables that had never even heard of a flat-pack. It was as old as the village, and sported a priest hole by the fireplace, as well as a secret tunnel that connected it to the church. The owner was always rather keen on telling everyone about it, and the pub's Facebook page featured at least as many photos of the tunnel and his attempts to map it as it did nicely framed shots of sticky toffee pudding and roast lamb shanks.

As they pushed through the door, a wash of warm, smoke-scented air rushed out to greet them, and everywhere were low lamps casting golden light, and old framed photos of the village, and just enough bits of derelict houseware and small farming implements to be interesting rather than cluttered. A young woman behind the bar gave them an alarmed look as they filed in, and put her shoulders back as Gert strode over and slapped one hand onto the polished wood of the counter.

"Evening," Gert said.

"Good evening," the young woman said, and shot a glance across the room, to where an even younger man was studiously not looking at them as he laid a table for dinner. "Um – do you have a reservation?"

"Unfortunately not," Alice said. "The village hall's heating is out, so we wondered if we might have our W.I. meeting here. It's not dinner yet, is it?"

"No, but we will start filling up soon."

"On a Tuesday night?" Gert asked. "Surely you can spare a table for us."

"You can have some of my macaroons," Rosemary said, waving a Tupperware.

"Macarons," Carlotta said.

"No. These aren't those silly little French things. They're proper biscuits."

"You English and your proper biscuits."

"Is Manchester not in England, then?"

"We can try to be quiet," Alice said, without much conviction, and at that moment a tall and slightly bony man in a corduroy jacket and jeans hurried through from the back rooms.

"Alice!" he said, and to Alice's alarm he clasped both of her hands in his, then kissed her cheek. "And Miriam!" Miriam got the same treatment, which at least meant Alice got to reclaim her hands. When had people become so *European* about things? Surely a decent hand-shake was enough.

"Hello Bryan," Alice said. "You're looking ..."

"Skinny," Rose said, and handed him a Tupperware. "Eat that."

Bryan gave the tub a puzzled look, then said, "It's been very busy, what with ..." He trailed off, swallowed hard, then continued. "What with Thomas gone."

Miriam patted his arm. "Ignore them," she said. "It's good to see you smiling."

Bryan gave her a grateful look, then waved at the young man, who appeared to be refolding some napkins with studious care. "Jared, put a couple of tables together for the ladies, would you?" He turned back to them. "And I'll donate some wine to the cause. It's the least I can do after you were all so helpful last year."

"I don't think we need wine," Alice started, and Gert talked over her.

"Everyone alright with red?"

"I like rosé," Pearl said.

"White," Teresa said.

"Depends on the red," Priya added.

"Do you have anything Italian?" Carlotta asked.

"Are you quite sure about this?" Alice asked Bryan. "We don't want to disturb your customers."

"It's fine," he said, and ducked behind the bar. "Why don't I set you up with drinks, and by the time we've done that your table will be ready."

"It's very kind of you," she said, and there was a moment's silence as Bryan clattered around with bottles. She wondered if she should ask how he had been keeping, but the answer to that was in the way his shirt hung loosely from his shoulders. Losing his husband had been a terrible blow, she imagined. Unlike when she had lost hers, but then he had been a most unsatisfactory husband. Thomas had been rather lovely.

Then Priya said, "How's the mapping coming along?"

Bryan looked up, a grin lighting his face, and Alice suddenly saw how a much smaller Bryan would have looked on a Christmas morning, wrapping scattered across the room. "I found another passage!" he said. "I'm telling you, there's a *labyrinth* under our village. Do you want to see the map so far?"

"*Absolutely*," Priya said, and grinned back at him.

Alice had never heard the other woman profess the slightest interest in tunnels of any sort, but Priya leaned on the bar with her forearms folded on the old wood and the gold stud in her nose glinting in the warm light, nodding seriously and *ooh*ing now and then, and Alice smiled as she picked up a bottle of wine and took it to the table. This was why one had friends. One person alone cannot be very good at everything, but the right people together can make the most beautiful whole. And know when to ask questions about tunnels.

ALICE TAPPED the disconnect on her phone and went back to the table, where the volume had gone up by a couple of notches in direct contrast to the levels in the bottles of wine placed strategically along its length.

"What did they say?" Miriam asked. She was looking very pink-cheeked, but Alice had an idea that was the heat. Miriam had been nursing the same mug of hot water with lemon slices since they arrived, even when Bryan had offered to top it up with a little nip of whisky.

"The young man on the desk asked me if I was sure it was gone and I hadn't just misplaced it," Alice said, sitting down next to her.

Miriam gasped and covered her mouth with one hand, but a small snort of laughter still escaped. "What did *you* say?"

"That I was old enough to be forgiven for asking silly questions, but he wasn't, and that I wanted to speak to someone else." She smiled slightly and had a sip of her gin and tonic, which she'd insisted on paying for. Bryan couldn't be subsidising the whole of the W.I.

"And what did *they* say?"

"There wasn't anyone there, apparently, so I said I'd call DI Adams myself. He said that he'd get someone out here within an hour, so I assume DI Adams scares him more than I do."

"It's just because he hasn't met you," Miriam said in a comforting tone, then took a hurried gulp of her lemon and honey as her cheeks flushed an even brighter pink. "I mean, he wouldn't be accusing you of asking silly questions if he knew you!"

"I'm sure he wouldn't," Alice said, tapping her fingers lightly on the table. The meeting hadn't really come to anything – everyone was too busy speculating about the stolen guy to bother themselves with such things as stall bookings and refreshment plans. Not that it mattered terribly. Bonfire Night was always a small and local affair, not like the big summer fête or the Christmas market. There was something insular and wild about Bonfire Night, with its guys and flames and raw-edged shadows, shouting in the face of the looming, frost-edged spectre that was the oncoming winter.

"It's just plain ageism," Miriam said. "Or maybe sexism. Both, probably."

Alice looked at her and wondered if she had taken the nip of whisky after all. "Are you feeling alright, Miriam?"

She plucked at her jumper. "I think it's the paracetamol. Plus it's very *warm* in here. Or my fever's come back."

Alice nodded. "It is quite toasty. Shall we go outside for some air?"

Miriam gave her a narrow look. "Just for some air?"

"*Hmm.*" Alice smiled slightly. "And maybe for another little look at the hall and green before the police get in the way?"

"You are terrible," Miriam said, but she was already getting up.

§❧

ALICE WAS a little surprised by how readily Miriam had agreed to join her, but she supposed the fact that the culprit had already clearly made their getaway – and the fact that the younger woman was responsible for the donation tin being there to be stolen in the first place – probably had a lot to do with it. What she hadn't anticipated was the fact that the rest of the W.I., fortified by the free wine, were just as eager to accompany them.

"We don't want to destroy any evidence," she pointed out, as the ladies scuffled around pulling on coats and swirling scarves about the place, an upheaval of colour and movement as full of autumn as the drifts of leaves outside.

"We won't," Jasmine said, her nose bright pink. "I've got a very good idea of how to behave around a crime scene, you know."

"And you can just imagine the police, can't you?" Teresa said. "A donation tin? They won't so much as check for fingerprints."

"Probably say we *misplaced* it," Rose added, rather accurately.

Alice gave her an appraising look. Rose had had her own issues with a misplaced body in her freezer in the spring, but even once it had all been cleared up it seemed not to have instilled any confidence in the police in her. Not that Alice disagreed. "Well, let's go and have a look, then," she said. "But we really must try to be careful."

"Stick to the paved paths," Jasmine said, throwing back the last of her wine. "Don't touch anything with your hands – use your sleeve. And ..." She thought about it. "We should probably put our scarves over our heads so we don't drop any hair."

There was more scuffling as everyone wrapped their scarves around their heads with varying degrees of elegance, and Jasmine gave Alice a questioning look.

"We have already been in the hall," she said.

Jasmine looked so crestfallen that Alice pulled her scarf up and over her head.

"Better to be safe than sorry, though, isn't it?" She led the way out into the night, having the absurd thought that they must look like the seven dwarfs, if a bit taller and minus the beards.

"Heigh ho, heigh ho," Gert called cheerfully, so at least she wasn't the only one thinking it. Although she was most certainly the only one not singing it as they followed the curve of the road around the green and toward the hall, its garden softly lit with the solar lamps Gert's aunt's goddaughter's cousin (or something) had sourced for them.

The singing faltered, and Rosemary exclaimed, "The wheelbarrow's back!"

"Is it the same one?" Pearl asked.

"The guy's still in it," Priya said, sounding uncertain. "Do you think they brought the collection pot back, too?"

Without anyone suggesting it, they'd come to a stop, still far enough away from the wheelbarrow that it *could* have been the guy in there, even if the ballgown had been replaced by what looked like a dressing gown, and it was terribly lifelike, too, the way the head lolled and a shoe was hanging off one foot.

Alice took a step forward, and Miriam grabbed her arm. "Don't," she said.

Alice shook her off gently and walked over to the wheelbarrow, her stride slow and careful, and her hand tight on the cane.

But she needn't have worried. The man in the barrow was long past being threatened with canes.

"Oh dear," Alice murmured, and looked around at the rustling, deepening night. "This isn't very good."

The sheet of paper pinned to the man's chest agreed with her.

For you, it said.

3

MORTIMER

Mortimer clutched his tail a little tighter. *"For you?"* he said, his voice sounding weak even to his own ears. "A *body*? Why? Who would do that?" He looked around, as if expecting murderous barrow-thieves to be lurking in the bushes that surrounded the village green, rather than ten ladies, a Pomeranian, a Labrador, a Great Dane, and two dragons slightly shorter than the big dog but somewhat bulkier.

"This is what we need to find out," Alice said.

"Do we?" Mortimer asked, and a scale came away in his paw. He stared at it with a dull sort of horror. *Of course* he was shedding.

"Of course we do," Rose said. "We told you how that police lot talked to Alice. As if she was senile!"

"It wasn't that bad," Alice said. "And I rather think they'll take the body more seriously than a stolen donation tin."

"Oh, they will," Rose said darkly. "But it's *how* they take it."

Teresa put an arm over her shoulder. "It's not in your freezer this time."

"It's still two bodies in a row. That's a pattern."

Beaufort Scales, High Lord of the Cloverly dragons, who had survived the rise of humans and the fading of his kind, triumphed in hunts in which he had been both quarry and pursuer, ancient, tireless protector of his clan and lover of a good cheese scone, was lying on his belly at the edge of the green, examining the hall from the cover of the grass, and now he sat up and looked at Mortimer. "You'll have to have a sniff, lad," he said. "You're much more sensitive to such things."

"I'd rather not," Mortimer said. "Isn't it enough that we got all tangled up with that horrible police officer in the summer?"

"That was almost in Lancashire," Rosemary said, rather dismissively. "Can't expect anything good to come of being so close to Lancashire."

"That's quite true," Carlotta said.

"What, has Manchester moved?" Rosemary asked, and Carlotta sniffed.

"Just because I was born there doesn't mean I'm *from* there. My soul is of the old country."

"You've been to Italy twice. On holiday. If that's all it takes, I'm actually Croatian. Or Greek. Or—"

Someone's mobile phone went off with a cheery little tune, and cut off the argument before it could get any more heated.

"*Jasmine*," Priya said. "I thought you were the one who knew how to act around crime scenes!"

"Quiet, it's Ben," she said, waving at them all in a vague shushing movement.

Mortimer was quite happy to shush. As pleasant as the long grass of the green was, with its soft song of shifting stems and drowsy whispers of the slow, seasonal drift into hibernation, there was *a body* across the road. In a *wheelbarrow*. And everyone seemed to think he and Beaufort should somehow know who left it there, but they weren't psychic. They hadn't even planned to be here tonight, but he'd had an inkling. A scratchy, irritating sense at the back of his mind that had made him so restless Beaufort had suggested a bit of a fly would sort him out. And, of course, they had ended up here, more in the hope of ginger cake than for any other reason, and now there was a body with a worrying note on it, and they were hiding in the bushes with the full complement of the Toot Hansell Women's Institute, and he was shedding. He might now know the reason for the scratchiness, but it hadn't helped anything. He closed his eyes and listened to Jasmine.

"We're not *interfering*," she was saying into the phone, rather indignantly. "Someone stole the guy and left a body in a wheelbarrow outside the hall. That's not our fault!"

There was pause while she listened, and Mortimer watched her face growing pinker. She looked rather scratchy herself, so at least one of the W.I. were having a reasonable reaction to this. A body! Again!

"Of course we haven't moved it. What do you take me for, Benjamin Shaw?"

"Ooh, full name. Bad sign, that," Teresa said. "I always know things have gone too far when Pearl uses my last name."

"I never," Pearl said, then amended, "Well, only when you deserve it, anyway."

Jasmine waved at them again, more sharply this time, and said into the phone, "Whoever's on the phones tonight completely dismissed Alice when she called about the theft. If you're not going to listen to people, then, well. That's your problem."

Another pause, then she said, "Well, I know a stolen guy's not the same as a body, but it's still someone reporting a crime! *And* the donation tin was gone, and we don't know if it's come back or not because there's a *body* in the *barrow!*"

"Jasmine," Alice said. "The donation tin's not really an issue now. Ask Ben if there's anyone on the way, otherwise we shall have to do something about the body. We can't just leave it there for someone to stumble across."

There was an explosion of noise on the phone that suggested Ben had heard Alice and was disagreeing violently. Jasmine held the phone away from her ear slightly and said, "Stop *shouting*," at a volume that was quite near shouting herself.

A moment later she hit disconnect and looked at the little group sitting in a hollow made from the weight of their own bodies in the long grass. "He says someone's coming to secure the scene, and DI

Adams is in the middle of something but is coming as soon as she can."

"Very good," Alice said, and stood up, wading to the edge of the green to look both ways along the road. Then she turned back and said, "There's no one around, but I think we should at least put a tablecloth or something over him. Anyone could walk past."

"That's interfering with a crime scene, though," Jasmine said. "And we already agreed we couldn't go back in the hall for anything in case we disturb some evidence."

"That's very true," Alice said. "But in that case we need to keep people away. We don't want someone else coming along and muddling things up."

"You're right." Gert rolled to her feet. "Come on. A couple of us on the road in each direction will do it."

Alice nodded and looked at the hall again. "And shall we take another look, perhaps? See if we recognise him?"

"I'd rather not," Miriam said.

"Or me," Rose added. "I don't want to get a reputation for turning up dead bodies. People ask questions."

"I was speaking to Beaufort and Mortimer, mostly," Alice said, smiling. "They're hardly going to contaminate a crime scene."

"I might shed on it," Mortimer said.

"Try not to, lad," Beaufort said, padding over to join Alice. The grass whispered around him, reflecting in his glossy scales and turning him into a strange winged alligator wading through tropical swamps. "Or at least pick them up if you do. I know we seem to be rid of that nosy journalist sort, but one never knows who else is sneaking about."

Mortimer shivered so hard his scales hissed against each other, a little susurrus of alarm. "Wouldn't it be better to just look from here? I can see quite well."

"Can you smell anything, though?"

"No," he admitted. And he didn't want to. Death was rarely a pleasant thing to catch a whiff of. Sometimes it was merely sad, the simple animal scent of things gone to rot, filled with the quiet melancholy of time passing and life fading. Other times it was wrapped about with so much sorrow and regret that all sense of its true nature was lost, and the futility and pain of it crushed the heart. And at others … well, at others it was like this. All hurt and rage and horror, drained of colour, and even from across the road he thought he could catch creeping threads of aching disbelief. He didn't want to smell it up close.

Beaufort looked at him for a long moment, and Mortimer braced himself for the High Lord to give him one of those *do buck up, lad, and be a proper dragon* speeches that he was certain were always coming, but the old dragon just said, "Never mind, then. I'll take a little sniff myself. How about you check the green, see if you can find anything here?"

Mortimer had the sudden, unmistakable sense that he was letting the side down, but before he could reconsider Beaufort was slipping across the road, his scales taking on the deep, night-dark grey of the tarmac while Alice hurried next to him with her hands tucked into the pockets of her jacket.

"Is no one else going?" Gert asked.

"We'd best not," Jasmine said. "If Ben's anything to go by, the police are *very* grumpy at the moment."

"So unreasonable," Priya said, and Jasmine looked at her gratefully.

MORTIMER WAITED a little before leaving for his sniff around the green. Miriam was sitting cross-legged on the grass next to him, twisting the hem of her skirt in her fingers and frowning at the hall. She wasn't quite looking at the barrow, and she smelled of buttercups in spring storms, fragile and resilient and shot through with raw yellow alarm.

"Are you alright?" he asked her, as quietly as he could. Dragons aren't really made for whispering, though, and everyone else, who had been getting up to take their positions on the road, looked at her.

"Miriam?" Gert said. "You're looking a bit pale."

"It's this cold," she started, then shook her head. "No, it's not. It's the *body!* Of course I'm pale! Who leaves a *body* for us? And with a note like that? Is it a threat? It has to be a threat. Who's threatening us?"

"And stealing our guy *and* our donation tin," Priya added.

"I really don't think that's relevant," Teresa said.

"Well, it's hardly a fair swap, is it? A guy for a dead body?"

Miriam just twisted her skirt a little tighter, and across the road Alice called, "Are we going to block the road? I think three at each end to be safe, then the rest of us can make sure no one comes through the green."

"Come on," Gert said, offering Miriam a hand. "Come and stop cars with me. It'll make you feel better."

"I'm not sure how," Miriam said, but let herself be pulled to her feet. "It feels like the sort of night when one gets *hit* by cars." Everyone looked at her doubtfully, and she managed a smile. "I just mean it feels very ... strained."

Mortimer had to agree. The whole night *did* feel very strained, but that was what one got when there were bodies lying about the place. "Do you want to come with me, Miriam?" he asked. "I could use some company."

Miriam hesitated, and Gert said, "Good plan. You can do your touchy-feely thing, Miriam."

"I'm not *touchy-feely,*" she said, frowning. "I'm just a little Sensitive."

Mortimer could hear the capital S, and knew she was talking about the way she seemed to sense small changes in the world, dark days in sunshine and luminous moments on grey days. It wasn't unlike the emotional traces dragons perceived as scents, he supposed, if a little less targeted.

"It might help," he said. "I don't think I'm at my best, to be honest."

Miriam straightened the front of her coat and said, "Well. We've enough people for the road, don't we?"

"We do," Gert said, and headed off the green.

"Try not to stand in anything important," Jasmine said as everyone else followed, and a moment later Miriam and Mortimer were alone in the long grass.

Miriam smiled, but it was a shaky affair. "Where do we start, then?"

Mortimer watched the ladies spread out along the road, Teresa already shouting an enthusiastic *stop* to a dog-walker who was wandering along the pavement, then looked up at her. "I suppose we check the duck pond first. See if Nellie's seen anyone."

"Good plan," she said, and waved for him to lead the way.

Mortimer turned and slipped into the long grass, trying not to let his wings get too caught up as he padded in the rough direction of the pond, half-heartedly searching for scents as he went. Miriam followed, not talking, and he could smell the gentle anxiety on her, orange puffs of sadness and jagged yellow notes. He still felt he probably *should* have gone with Alice and Beaufort – and the fact that he couldn't seem to change his scales from an anxious grey meant he'd have been better camouflaged on the road than he was in the overgrown green – but, by the same token, he had no desire to sniff any dead bodies. It was hardly a daily occurrence, but it had become an awful lot more common since meeting the W.I. Dead bodies, and persons of ill intent, who actually smelled much worse, and the whiff of all sorts of deceit and subterfuge, a certain amount of which actually came from *within* the W.I.

He swallowed a sigh before he could set any of the long grass alight. They'd been lucky so far, to not be discovered. Humans, for the most part, had no concept that the world was still populated by creatures of myth and legend, although one would think they might question where the myths and legends came from in the first place. But long centuries of hiding by magical Folk, and humans' capacity for self-deception, meant that very few did question it, even when Folk were standing right in front of them. Still, getting involved in police investigations really was pushing their luck. Police are *supposed* to see things other people don't.

"Feeling sorry for yourself there, with your tea parties and fireside treats?" A voice cut through his thoughts, and Miriam gave a little squeak of surprise. Mortimer had to hold in a belch of alarmed flame – it was impossible to see very far at all in this grass, and he hadn't really paid attention to how far they'd come. "Oh, woe, to be a modern dragon," the voice added with a snicker.

"Hello, Nellie," Miriam said.

"Got any frogs?"

"Not on me."

Mortimer pressed through a final screen of long grass and found his front paws on the rocky edge of the duck pond. A pale, skinny creature with bulbous eyes crouching on a rocky island in the centre of the pond stared back at him, her lank hair curling over her forehead and a fish head in one webbed hand.

"Hello, Nellie," he said.

"Having a bad night, are you?" she asked, and nibbled on the fish head.

"There's a *body*," he said, lowering his voice.

"Again? I wouldn't be hanging around with that W.I. lot. Bad for your health, they are."

"Excuse *me*," Miriam said. "You were quite happy to sit in my pond last Christmas."

"That was an emergency," Nellie said.

Mortimer eyed a goose that was strutting along the edge of the pond, its neck a pale, half-formed question in the dark, and said, "It's not the W.I.'s fault, you know. Stuff just happens."

"Dead people stuff," Nellie said, a little indistinctly.

Mortimer kept his eyes on the goose, partly so it didn't have a chance to sneak up on him, and partly because Nellie was thoroughly enjoying her fish head and the slurping noises were bad enough without having to watch. "Have you seen anyone come through here?" he asked. "They would've had the body in a wheelbarrow. At least in one direction," he amended.

"Oh, sure," she said. "Someone was through with a barrow earlier. Claudius gave them a bit of a fright."

"Claudius?" Miriam asked.

Nellie nodded at the goose, who was evidently actually a gander. "He didn't like the barrow. Think it was the squeaky wheel."

Mortimer wasn't sure geese – or ganders – liked *anyone*, and he was actually a little disappointed Nellie *had* seen someone, since that meant he was going to have to ask follow-up questions, and all he really wanted was some ginger cake. But he'd only have to come back and ask again later, so he said, "Was there a body in it? The barrow?"

"Not a proper one."

"It was improper?" Mortimer wondered if that meant it had been undressed or something. He wasn't quite sure what an improper body was.

Nellie snorted, and finally dropped the remnants of the fish head into the pond, retaining a bone to pick her teeth with. "No, it was a fake one. You know, for the bonfires."

"That was our guy," Miriam said. "Did the barrow come back again, with an actual body?"

Nellie gave her an amused look. "Not past the pond. Not after Claudius objected. Plus it's hardly the terrain for wheelbarrows. This long grass is brilliant. No one's been by to bother me for *ages*."

So they'd taken the barrow away with the guy, then put it back later with the body. It was all most odd, and seemed like an awful lot of effort to go to. Mortimer opened his mouth to ask Nellie if she'd seen the wheelbarrow driver, but before he could she pointed into the dark and said, "They left them, though."

"I can't see anything," Miriam said, peering in the direction Nellie was pointing. Mortimer, with his prismed eyes collecting the faintest scraps of light, could see somewhat better, but all he could make out were what appeared to be two small, sad ghosts, pale grey scratches in the night.

"What are they?" he asked.

"Herons," Nellie said. "They're going to eat all my bloody frogs."

"They took the guy and left *herons?*"

"Yeah. Came past with the herons in a box, dropped them here, then next thing they're running back again with the guy. *Humans*."

Mortimer and Miriam exchanged glances, and he said, "Did you see what they looked like?"

"Heron-dumpers," Nellie said, with a little sneer in her voice.

Mortimer nodded, trying to convey just how seriously he took such things as heron-dumping. "Did you see what they were wearing? Or notice if they were male or female or anything?"

Nellie shrugged. "Female. Had big curls like yours," she said, nodding at Miriam. "Thought it was you, in fact, but without the tie-dye and skirts. All greens and browns, she was."

"They looked like me?" Miriam asked, her hands clutching the front of her jacket.

"Pretty much. But you humans all look a bit alike." She dug a particularly large morsel of fish out from between her teeth and gave a nod of approval. "Looked more like you than most, though. Think she might be the one who was sneaking around putting the chains back up in the summer. Still had a bit of a grassy whiff to her."

Mortimer looked up at Miriam, wanting to ask if she was alright, but she was staring fearfully around the green as if waiting for her doppelgänger to pop up, and before he could say anything at all, the gander screeched so close to his ear that he almost plunged snout-first into the pond. Miriam gave a yelp of alarm, staggering away, and Nellie cackled in delight. Mortimer scrabbled in the long grass, trying to back up, and swallowed a whimper as he felt a scale hook on something and rip free.

The gander hissed, head bobbing and weaving, and Mortimer shot Nellie an imploring look. "Call it off!"

"He's not a *dog*," she said, still laughing. "Go, Claudius! No heron-dumpers or dragons in our pond!"

"Get off!" Miriam shouted, waving her arms wildly at the gander, but it ignored her completely. It reared up, wings beating furiously, and Mortimer decided he'd done quite enough information gathering for one night.

"Miriam, run!" he shouted, then turned – not without difficulty, and snarling one toe painfully in a knot of matted grass roots as he did – and plunged back toward the road, Miriam taking great swinging strides ahead of him with her skirt gathered up in both hands. They didn't slow until the cries of the gander and Nellie's laughter had faded behind them, and the road was at their feet.

"Are you alright?" Alice called from by the hall.

"Just a goose," Miriam called back, and Alice nodded with understanding. Miriam looked at Mortimer, her face pink with exertion and that floating scent of anxiety tight as broken shells around her. "They looked like me," she said.

"But it wasn't you," Mortimer pointed out.

"No," she agreed. "But the herons? And the hair? Dressed all in greens and browns and had something to do with the chains this summer? Who does that sound like?"

Mortimer stared at her. "Your sister," he said.

"My sister," Miriam agreed, and pressed a hand over her heart. "But she wouldn't hurt anyone. She *wouldn't*. It's not what she does. She protects things."

Mortimer didn't reply. He was thinking of Miriam's sister when he'd first seen her, sitting in a fallen tree and shouting about death to the establishment. She hadn't *seemed* violent, but sometimes one doesn't mean to be. Sometimes accidents happen, and then one turns to those one trusts for help, because what else is there?

"She wouldn't," Miriam said again, with a tremble in her voice, and Mortimer sat back on his haunches to put one heavy paw on her arm.

"I believe you," he said.

Miriam nodded. "I wonder if the police will?"

And he couldn't answer that. Not truthfully.

4

DI ADAMS

D I Adams gingerly hit answer on her phone and held it as close
to her ear as she dared. Her disposable gloves were smeared
with things that she didn't really want to consider too much, and
getting it on her phone was bad enough. She didn't want to accidentally end up with cow effluent in her hair as well. Cow effluent, and
worse. But her phone said *DCI Taylor*, so she also couldn't not answer.

"Adams," she said.

"It's Maud," DCI Taylor said, somewhat unnecessarily. "How are
you getting on?"

DI Adams looked around the old cowshed, which was lit by a wash
of portable spotlights that were having the unfortunate effect of
warming the muck that coated the ground, releasing ever more
fragrant gases. DC Genny Smythe and a couple of uniformed officers
were wading through it, trying to avoid the deeper bits where there
was serious risk of an inundation over the top of one's wellies. Somewhere in here was a stash of stolen jewellery, according to a source,
but she was starting to have strong suspicions that their source was
taking the mick. And she was going to be expressing her deep disapproval of such things if she got her hands on him.

"Nothing yet," she said.

"Who've you got there?"

"DC— Genny," she amended. The whole first names thing was still tricky to remember. "Plus Graham and Liv. We've got lights up, but it's a nightmare."

"Hit pause, then," Maud said. "Tell them to seal the scene until tomorrow, and get yourself over to Toot Hansell."

"Oh, God. What now?"

"The W.I. have a guy thief and a body."

DI Adams pressed a hand to her forehead as if to ward off the inevitable headache to come, then gagged. Not at the stink, as she was fairly sure she'd lost her sense of smell entirely an hour or so ago, but at the thought of what she'd just rubbed on her face. "*No,*" she mumbled.

"It's got to be better than sifting through excrement," Maud said.

"I didn't mean—" she started, then stopped. She had, a little. "Can I get a shower first?"

"I'd get yourself over there, Adams. Colin's just been called to some country house that's had its peacocks or macaques or what have you stolen, and I'm not bloody well going near the W.I."

DI Adams thought the DCI's stance on that was quite reasonable. "More stolen animals? Second lot since summer, isn't it?"

"Yes, I think we can safely call it a spate now," the DCI said. "And I'm going to put you on the case instead of Colin, given his mum's into all that daft animal liberation stuff. Bit too close, I think. He can take on your missing jewellery. But right now you can get to Toot Hansell and get started, then swap notes later."

"Fair enough," she said, looking around the fragrant shed, then added, "Are there ever any cases around here that don't involve animals?"

"Yes – a body in Toot Hansell. Get a move on before the W.I. decide to spruce up the crime scene or something."

"On it," she said with a sigh, and hung up. She stared at the phone for a moment, not wanting to put it back in her pocket. There were ... *bits* on it. Which didn't bode well for her face.

~

LUCAS, who served as both coroner and lead crime scene investigator, took a noticeable step back as DI Adams leaned over the body. "Rough day, Adams?"

"Someone told us the jewellery from that theft over toward Grassington was stashed in a semi-disused cow shed." She examined the man in the barrow carefully. He was wearing a dressing gown and what looked an awful lot like a cravat, like the star of some '70s sitcom.

"Was it?" Lucas asked, not coming any closer.

"We've not found it yet." The victim still had on a signet ring of the sort favoured by the type of people who wear cravats, and a paler strip of skin on his left wrist indicated both that he'd been off somewhere sunny recently, and also that his watch was missing. "Any idea on cause of death?"

Lucas moved close enough to adjust the man's head in one gloved hand, pointing at matted blood in his thinning blond hair. "Likely blunt force trauma. He's got a good whiff on him, too."

DI Adams tried to sniff the air in the general vicinity of the wheelbarrow and immediately regretted it. "All I can smell is cow shed."

"Me too, currently," Lucas said, and gave her a crooked grin when she scowled at him. He was a slight, dark-haired man with an affection for Brit-pop and cartoonish death T-shirts, and as much as she still felt that any self-respecting police station should have access to more than one person to process crime scenes, DI Adams couldn't fault his work. He was *fussy.* "You should step back," he said now. "If you drop old manure on him it's really going to mess up my results."

"I like how you say *should,* as if you're just making suggestions," she said, stepping back obediently.

"Some of us use this thing called civility, Adams. You should try it."

"I'm very civil," she protested, and a uniformed officer who was guarding the edge of the scene gave an audible snort. "I heard that," she called, and he turned the snort into a very forced cough, making an apologetic gesture.

"I'm almost done," Lucas said, approaching the body again now that DI Adams and her lingering aroma of cow sheds had moved away a little. "There's not much to be seen. He wasn't killed here, obviously, and at this point it's hard to even say if he *was* killed. The whiff that's not manure is some heavy-duty alcohol. But I'll know more once I've got him back to the morgue."

"So accidental death but someone just decided to drop him on the W.I.'s doorstep?"

"Maybe he was having it off with one of them and his other half bopped him on the head."

DI Adams inclined her head. "Interesting theory. And the guy?"

He gave her a blank look.

"The DCI said there was a missing guy, too."

Lucas looked from her to the body and back again. "He doesn't have it."

"I can see that. But is there any sign of it?"

"Of the guy that isn't there?"

DI Adams nodded at the wheelbarrow. "This is the sort of thing a guy's usually in, right?"

He shrugged. "I was more concerned about the dead body."

"But did the barrow come from the guy? Did they steal the guy so that they could use the barrow?"

"Figuring that out's your job," he said, and made a shooing motion at her. "Now go away before you bring the flies around."

DI Adams had a strong urge to make a face at him, but just because she felt like a kid who'd fallen in something nasty was no reason to act like one. She looked around and spotted Dandy lurking on the edge of the green across the road. He'd got here, then. Her mostly invisible dog – mostly as in the only humans who seemed to be able to see him were herself and a certain annoying journalist – had accompanied her to the cow shed, poked his nose around the door, and promptly taken off in the opposite direction. Not that she blamed him, but she'd thought a dog might be less fussy. And just as she had no idea how he could be mostly invisible, she also had no idea how he got from one place to another, but she wasn't surprised to see him here, even if he hadn't come in the car with her. Dandy seemed to have his own relationships to time and space, including as it related to his size. Currently he was Labrador-sized, if Labradors were covered in masses of long grey dreadlocks.

The door to the village hall stood open, yellow light washing out, and DI Adams walked up the little, flower-edged path to it with a creeping sense of déjà-vu. Her first case in Toot Hansell had started in the village hall too, with a murdered vicar. It had also been her first encounter with the Toot Hansell Women's Institute, and she allowed herself a moment of sympathy for the naïve and invisible dog-less person she had been then. Not that she felt much more equipped to deal with ladies of a certain age now than she had then, but at least she had some idea of what to expect. *Some.*

The hall was set up for a meeting, folding tables pushed together in the middle of the floor and surrounded by chairs. Plates containing the last few slices of cake and tarts, and a handful of lingering biscuits (plus one plate that was very full of what might've been intended as millionaire's shortbread, coated with caramel of a disturbing tarry shade that was currently oozing onto the table, carrying a flood of dusty crumbs with it) were arranged in an alarmingly neat line, and catering-sized pots of tea were being decanted into mugs and splashed with milk and sugar.

"We need more cake," Miriam said, moving a couple of golden, oaty biscuits from an otherwise empty plate onto another that held one lonely macaroon. "This is a terrible show."

"Sandwiches," Teresa said. "We can nip home and rustle some up."

"I've got some sausage rolls in my freezer," Rose said. Her short-cropped hair was a vibrant red with orange tips, presumably in honour of the season. "You know, heat-and-eat type things. Be perfect."

"I've got a lasagne," Carlotta said. "I was going to do it for dinner tomorrow, but I can heat it up now. Keep everyone going."

"Is it your grandmother's recipe?" Rosemary asked. "Handed down from the home country?"

"It's a Jamie Oliver one," Carlotta said, and Rosemary laughed.

"Tot?" Gert suggested, taking a bottle from her voluminous handbag. "We could all do with one. For the shock, like."

"What's that smell?" Jasmine asked, just as her yappy little mutt started growling. Everyone turned to look at the door, and DI Adams put her hands in her coat pockets with a sigh.

"You're not catering a crime scene," she said.

"What've you been up to, then?" Rose asked. "Farmyard duties, was it?"

"Yes," DI Adams said. "But that's quite beside the point. No one needs to make sandwiches, or fetch a lasagne. You don't even need to *be* here."

"But we found the body," Jasmine said. "We even secured the scene!"

DI Adams looked at her for a long moment, watching the other woman's cheeks grow even pinker than they already had been. And it wasn't due to any sort of warmth in the hall, although there was a little fan heater labouring away in one corner. It couldn't do much in such a big space, especially as Pearl's Labrador was sleeping directly in front of it. DI Adams thought she could smell singed dog hair over the stench that seemed to have become embedded in her clothes.

"This is a police matter," she said. "Has someone taken your statements?"

"They have, DI Adams," Alice said, emerging from the kitchen with a cafetière in one hand. DI Adams caught a glimpse of green scales before the door swung shut again, and swallowed a sigh. Of course the dragons were here. *Of course* they were. "But we rather thought you might want to talk to us yourself."

"You did not," DI Adams said, with rather more feeling than she intended, and felt her own cheeks heating up as the hall fell silent. Then Teresa burst into delighted laughter, and a moment later even Alice was smiling, if a little more circumspectly.

"Coffee?" she offered, and DI Adams sighed.

"I may as well," she said. "And I imagine you've got theories, haven't you?"

"We think they used the spare key," Jasmine said. "It doesn't look like they broke in, so they must have used it. You might be able to get some prints."

"I think I could have figured that out myself," she pointed out, accepting a mug of coffee from Alice and breathing in the rich, bright scent of it. Or as much as she could over the stink of cows.

§.

TEN MINUTES LATER, once Pearl and Teresa had taken mugs of tea and the remainder of the cake to the police outside, DI Adams sat at one end of the row of tables while the ladies of the Toot Hansell W.I. huddled around the other. She knew she couldn't take it personally, not when she could *still* smell herself, despite whatever tolerance she'd built up in the cow shed.

"The dragons?" she asked, pitching her voice low.

"Eh?" Rose said.

"What?" Gert asked.

"Sorry?"

"Pardon?"

The query was repeated throughout the group, all of them looking at DI Adams quizzically, except for Alice, who said, "Staying out of the way, Inspector. Nothing to worry about."

DI Adams had her own thoughts on that. In her experience, the dragons were nearly as much to worry about as the W.I. themselves. And the combination was disastrous. But she just nodded, and in a louder voice said, "Tell me about finding the body."

About five people started talking at once, and Alice said, "*Ladies.*"

Everyone subsided except Jasmine, who hugged Primrose a little closer and said, "Why can't one of *us* tell what happened? I'm the one who knows the most about police investigations!"

DI Adams gave Jasmine a startled look, and wasn't surprised to see Alice doing the same. But the W.I. chair said, "If you would prefer, Jasmine."

"I would," Jasmine said, shooting a look at the hall door as if expecting someone to walk in and tell her to stop. "Should I start with the boiler? That was the first thing, then the guy in the wheelbarrow, or maybe the donation tin in the barrow, or both really, but either way the barrow vanished, then when it came back it had the body in it."

"Sorry, it vanished?" DI Adams asked. "While you were here?"

"Just before," Teresa said. "Someone took it and the guy across the green. Rose saw them, but she didn't realise it had been stolen. We tried to find them when we realised that the donation tin was still in with the guy, but we were too late."

"And you think the same person took the guy and left the body?"

"They used the same barrow, at least," Alice said. "Nellie said someone came past her pond and dropped off a couple of herons, then came back again with the guy in the barrow. She didn't see them after that, but they may well have taken another route when they brought the body to the hall. The gander chased them away from the pond, apparently."

"Nellie?" DI Adams asked.

"The sprite."

"Of course," DI Adams said, and rubbed her forehead. Her eye wasn't twitching yet, so that was something. "And this is what, the W.I. guy?"

"For Bonfire Night," Jasmine said. "We do penny for the guy to raise money, and the tin was still in with him."

Miriam mumbled something, staring at her mug, and Pearl patted her arm. "We forgot," she said. "Miriam and Carlotta and I were at the market with the guy this morning, but we forgot to take the tin out."

"*I* forgot," Miriam said, and Carlotta shrugged.

"We should have noticed. We knew you were poorly."

"How much was in the tin?" DI Adams asked. "I'm assuming it's not really penny for the guy these days."

"A lot," Miriam said to her mug.

DI Adams took another mouthful of coffee and wondered what *a lot* was. This being the W.I., she doubted anyone managed to walk past with their wallets intact. "And it's definitely the same barrow out there now?"

"Pretty sure," Gert said. "I got it from my cousin's niece's lad. Nice quality, that one."

"And the barrow was outside?"

"Inside," Jasmine said. "That's why they had to have used the key to get in."

DI Adams nodded and said, "Did Nellie see anything other than the barrow and the guy?" She was really hoping she wasn't going to have to interview the sprite. It wasn't just how one got around putting mythical creatures into an official report. It was the fact that someone had mentioned a gander. She'd already had one run-in with Toot Hansell's wild waterfowl population, and she had no desire for another. And no matter what DCI Taylor said, geese were animal-adjacent, at the very least. She wasn't sure about sprites.

"Miriam?" Alice said gently. "You and Mortimer spoke to her."

"She said all humans look a bit alike," Miriam said, still not looking up. Her cheeks were violently pink.

"What else?" DI Adams asked.

"Nothing. She didn't say anything. She was eating a fish."

"That doesn't seem very relevant, Miriam. What else?"

"Nothing," Miriam whispered again.

"Why do I feel you're not telling me something?"

Miriam hunched over her mug further, and Alice said, "That's rather unfair, Inspector. You know Miriam wouldn't have anything to do with it."

"You're in the middle of a crime scene, yet again," DI Adams said. "And I'm very aware that you're all rather skilled at withholding the truth when you see fit."

"*So rude,*" Priya said, and Rosemary and Carlotta tutted in alarming unison.

DI Adams tried not to think of her grandmother's disapproving face, which was very close to the expressions the ladies were wearing, and kept her gaze on Miriam. She had a scarf pulled up to her nose, and while it was undeniably chilly in here, she'd never known any of the W.I. to let anything hamper their tea drinking. "Miriam?" she said.

"I know you wouldn't have anything to do with the body. But did you see anything on the green? Or did Nellie give you any other details?"

"No," Miriam managed, her nose wrinkling at her tea.

"Lower the scarf so I can hear you properly."

"She's had a cold, Inspector," Alice said, and in DI Adams' imagination her granny folded her arms and tutted.

"Even so." She watched Miriam lower the scarf reluctantly. Her face was blotchy and her nose pink, and she gave DI Adams a wary look that flitted away before she could make eye contact. "Miriam? What do you know about the guy?"

"Nothing," Miriam said, but her voice was too high. "I made a terrible mistake and left the tin with it, but that's all I know."

"And are you sure Nellie didn't say anything else?"

"Nothing! Nothing at all!"

"Are you sure?"

"Yes! Why would she tell me anything? She set a goose on us. A gander, actually! And she said all humans look alike, so she's a terrible witness."

"All humans look alike, do they? So she thought the barrow thief looked a little like you, perhaps?"

"I didn't say that," Miriam whispered.

DI Adams didn't reply straight away. She was flipping through the connections in her memory, the ones that spread out from each person like a spiderweb, binding them together. Miriam was Collins' aunt. Collins' mum was certainly into *daft stuff*, just as the DCI had said, and while there had been no proving it, the council were pointing at her over the mower incident earlier that year. DI Adams had first encountered her hiding in a tree and flinging table condiments at people in protest against hunts, so the mowers certainly sounded on-brand. "Has your sister been around recently? Judith?"

"Rainbow," Miriam said. "She prefers Rainbow now. And no. I mean, I don't think. Why would she be? We're not drilling oil in our back yards or anything."

"She always comes and shouts at everyone at this time of year, though," Priya said. "Telling us to check for hedgehogs in the bonfire, as if we don't already."

"She gets very heated about people putting their heating on, too," Teresa added. "Using fossil fuels and ruining the environment. But what are we supposed to do? Freeze?"

"Fossil fuels are pretty bad, to be fair," Gert said. "Dead dinosaurs and all that."

There was an alarmed scuffle behind the kitchen door, and DI Adams wondered just how closely related to dragons dinosaurs were.

"That doesn't mean she had anything to do with the ... *guy*," Miriam said, frowning at the women.

"Of course not," Rose said. "No one's saying that."

DI Adams took another sip of coffee then said, "What was this about herons, then?"

Miriam shook her head. "I didn't even see them."

"Are they something Rainbow might have?"

"Why would she have herons? It's not as if she has a pond!" Miriam's voice was too high again, and she pulled her scarf up hurriedly.

DI Adams waited, watching the women, then when no one said anything else she said, "Alright. The body, then. No one recognised the victim? Since I'm sure you all had a good look?"

There was a half-hearted murmur of denial, and Alice said, "He's not from the village. We said so in our statements."

"That's it? That's all you have?" She could hear the scepticism in her own voice.

No one answered, then Pearl said, "Maybe he was one of the thieves, and it was some sort of argument over who got to drive the barrow that went terribly wrong."

Everyone stared at her, and Teresa patted her hand. "We've not had dinner," she said to DI Adams. "It makes her go a bit funny."

DI Adams leaned back in her chair with a sigh and said, "Well, I think that's enough for now. Everyone go home."

"But the hall," Jasmine started, and DI Adams shook her head.

"Go home. I'll look at your statements and see if there's anything more I need. No one go hunting bloody thieves, alright?" *Or murderers,* she wanted to add, but didn't. It was no use telling them, anyway. They'd all do exactly what they wanted. Just like always.

She sat there as they trailed out the door, smelling cow excrement and thinking of dead dinosaurs, and wishing she'd taken the job in Southampton instead. Even if it did have bridges.

5
MIRIAM

"I really don't think it *is* Judith. Rainbow, I mean," Miriam said to Alice, as they walked back through the near-dark lanes. The streetlights were put out at midnight in an effort to help the wildlife as much as possible, but even now, with a couple of hours still to go, the lamps were infrequent and the shadows between them deep. "I mean, I know the person Nellie saw *sounded* a little like her, but it couldn't be. Not the *body*. Not even the donation tin. That's not the sort of thing she'd do."

Alice made a *hmm* noise, and Miriam sighed. She was very grateful that the ladies had agreed not to mention to DI Adams that Nellie had a very vague description of the heron-dumper. And it *was* very vague. The whole big hair thing was highly questionable coming from someone who only had a few lank strands the texture of pond grass.

The problem with Rainbow was that she was so *adamant* about everything. It wasn't enough that she'd done the almost obligatory teenage protests – she'd turned it into a career. She'd been employed by at least three different activist groups (climate, animal welfare, and land protection, respectively) and had been fired by all of them for being too inclined to improvise. Rainbow had claimed she was merely embodying the groups' spirit of anarchy in action, but it hadn't convinced any of them to allow her to rejoin. Miriam supposed you couldn't really have an anarchic organisation. It seemed contradictory.

"She wouldn't," she said again. "Not a donation tin. She'd be more likely to top it up than to steal it."

"I imagine so," Alice said, her tone not indicating whether she was really imagining that or not.

"And the body of that poor man definitely isn't her. She's not a murderer."

"It does seem unlikely," Alice agreed, which wasn't the same as saying it wasn't possible, but Miriam supposed that was the best she was likely to get out of the older woman. Alice had a rather different perspective to most regarding what she felt people were capable of, Miriam had discovered. And while she was *fairly* sure Alice hadn't really killed her husband – definitely not the first time, and probably not the second time either – Alice did appear to harbour suspicions that anyone was capable of murder, given the right circumstances. Or wrong, depending on how one looked at it.

"I'm going to call her," Miriam announced, digging in her bag for her phone. "We need to sort this out."

"You're going to ask her if she's either stolen a guy and a donation tin or murdered someone and dumped the body on our doorstep? Or both?" Alice asked, smiling. "I think that might be better face to face, don't you?"

Miriam sighed, and let go of her phone. "You're right. I had another paracetamol while we were waiting for DI Adams. It was a very silly idea. I can never think straight after I've had paracetamol."

"I think we shall just do as the inspector suggested and get some sleep," Alice said, coming to a stop outside Miriam's gate. "I'll call you in the morning."

"Alright," Miriam said, squeezing the bridge of her nose. The paracetamol really did make her feel quite peculiar. "This can't actually be to do with us, can it, Alice? It must just be an accident, the body outside the hall. Surely. I mean, I know there was a note, but ..."

"I'm sure you're right," Alice said, and gave her arm a squeeze.

"Good night, dear." She walked off down the road with her back straight, the light from the houses glinting on her pale hair and reflecting off the silver handle and bands of her cane. Miriam watched her go until she was around the corner, then looked at the front door of her little cottage, promising the warmth of the AGA and the comfort of her own bed.

Then she turned to the old green VW Beetle that was rusting peacefully at the kerb, and crouched to take the key out of the exhaust pipe. It wasn't much of a hiding place, but it was easier than taking the key inside with her. Somehow it would never be in the bowl where she was sure she'd left it, and it'd take her at least an hour to find it. And if it took her that long to find, she'd never take the car out at all.

She took a moment to reflect, as she coaxed the engine into life, that maybe that wouldn't be such a bad thing, this time, at least.

❧

ONCE THE CAR WAS RUNNING, grumbling roughly and coughing grey smoke from the exhaust, Miriam put the heating on as high as she could, and took her phone out. She tried Rainbow first, intending to find out where she was, but it went straight to messages.

"This is Rainbow's number, and you can leave a message if you like, but I won't get it, because the mobile phone companies are just another example of how The Establishment—"

Miriam hit the disconnect button with a huff of irritation. Rainbow was evidently in the middle of one of her periodic protests against all forms of modern communication, and there was no telling how long it might last. She called their younger sister Maddie instead. Maddie had given over a corner of her rambling, gently decaying country estate to Rainbow, who had settled in and made herself a semi-permanent encampment. She and an eclectic rotation of weekend enthusiasts and true believers made soap and organised protests and occasionally wandered over to Maddie's house to shout that she was a pawn of capitalism, which Maddie mostly ignored, as long as they didn't do it in front of the guests.

The phone rang half a dozen times, and Miriam was just wondering what sort of message to leave when Maddie answered.

"Miriam? I'm just in the middle of a ghost tour! I've had to hide in the loo, which isn't very spooky."

Miriam wasn't sure the ghost tours were meant to be spooky for Maddie, as she was the one running them, so she just said, "It's only quick – is Rainbow at the camp, do you know?"

Maddie sniffed. "*Judith* has decided the camp's too comfortable and mainstream. Some of the new recruits put in solar showers and phone charging stations, and it's not in the spirit of things, apparently."

Miriam shivered, and poked the car's heating, but it was up all the way. "I'd think solar showers would be a jolly good idea."

"Well, you know Judith. She's stormed off and left them to it."

"Do you know where to?" Miriam asked.

"Somewhere around the tarn near Malham, I think. Sorry, Miriam, I have to go – I need to set the chain-rattling going in the library."

The phone went dead, and Miriam looked at it for a moment, then sighed and put the car in gear. Malham. Up in the high fells. It wasn't a drive Miriam relished at the best of times – she didn't relish *any* sort of driving at any sort of time – and the night-time trip through the winding roads had her hunched over with her nose almost touching the wheel, peering through the windscreen as she followed the cone of the headlights through one energetic curve after another, hemmed in by drystone walls to either side and the wild, wide expanse of star-torn sky above.

It seemed to take a terribly long time, although when she checked her phone it had only been about half an hour when she pulled into a lay-by on the side of the road. To her left the land rose in great craggy outcroppings of rock, climbing into the darkness as if in search of the sky, but across the road to her right a rough, deeply rutted lane was signposted for the tarn. It wended through a copse of still-green trees, and as she took a torch from the glovebox and got out of the car she could see the light of a fire beyond them, holding back the night. She quite likely had the right place, then, and she wasn't sure if she felt happy about that or not.

"Shall we come with you or just follow closely?" a deep, rumbling voice asked, and Miriam yelped, clutching the front of her coat. She spun around and for a moment saw nothing, then movement on the outcroppings above caught her eye. She peered a little more closely, and the outline of winged shapes perched among the rocks swam slowly into focus. Even when one expects dragons, they can be very hard to spot.

"You scared me half to death!" she said. "What're you doing?"

"We went to meet you at your house," the deep voice of the High Lord said. "Then we saw you drive off and thought we may as well follow."

"At least the inspector didn't see us," a second voice said. Mortimer. "And that awful dog of hers was staying away."

"She did know you were there, though," Miriam pointed out.

"But we didn't have to talk to her," Mortimer said. "I'm sure I shed more when I talk to her."

Miriam made a sympathetic noise. "Have you been trying that hemp cream? It should help."

"Gilbert ate it," Mortimer said, and even his voice sounded grey. "He said he thought it was something else, but I can't imagine what."

"I see," Miriam said, who could imagine. "Well, I'll make you some more. And just tell him it's *hemp*, not … not whatever he thought it was."

"What are we doing here, then?" Beaufort asked, and Miriam watched the bulk of his form detach itself from the rocks and drift soundlessly to the ground. He landed lightly, and looked up at her with starlight pooling in his eyes, setting them glittering in the night. "What are you up to, Miriam?"

She sighed. "I need to make sure my sister didn't touch the barrow. Because the person Nellie saw sounded a little like it could be her, so she *might* have, and that makes her a suspect. I can't keep *anything* from DI Adams"—Mortimer made a sympathetic sound—"but if I know Rainbow didn't have anything to do with the body, that she maybe just took the guy for her own reasons, then I can forget all about it."

"You could simply tell DI Adams and let her sort it out," Beaufort said.

"No. If DI Adams investigates her, then there's going to be ... things." Miriam waved vaguely, encompassing a wide range of Rainbow's favoured activities, very few of which were strictly legal, rather a number of which involved substances that weren't quite hemp, but none at all that Miriam felt her big sister should be arrested for, even if she was very annoying at times. "I'm not getting Rainbow in trouble if she hasn't done anything." And if she *had* for some reason taken the barrow, then Miriam would just explain that there had been some complications – hopefully without mentioning a body – and find out where the donation tin had ended up, if nothing else. She wasn't sure she'd have felt quite as accommodating to Rainbow a couple of years ago, but that had been before Rainbow and her assorted companions had helped the W.I. raid a farm in which Alice's not-dead husband had been up to dastardly developer-type things. And while they hadn't actually needed to rescue Alice in the end, Rainbow had been prepared to face attack dogs and some very unpleasant men in order to help, and Miriam had felt rather more fondly toward her ever since.

"Well then," Beaufort said. "Let's get over there. What's the plan?"

"That you don't come with me," Miriam said. "I don't need protecting, you know."

Beaufort blinked at her. "Of course you don't. But this is an investigation. All paws on deck and all that."

"Remember Rainbow's friend Barry?" she said. "He could see you two. We don't need a repeat of that."

"Definitely not," Mortimer said. Barry had been rather taken with the dragons, and Miriam had a feeling Mortimer was almost as alarmed by a naked man who kept trying to cuddle him as he had been by the monster hunters in the summer. "We'll stay hidden, won't we, sir?"

Beaufort gave a low rumble that seemed to be agreement. "Good point on Barry. He was rather awkward. But we'll make sure we're close enough to hear everything, maybe have a sniff around."

Miriam figured that was as good as she was likely to get with the High Lord in investigating mode. Plus she rather liked the idea of them being around, even if she didn't imagine she'd be in any danger whatsoever from Rainbow. There was just something very reassuring about having dragons handy.

And she couldn't quite forget that note on the body, either.

THE TRACK to the fire was rubbled and uneven, and Miriam took her time picking her way along it, even with the help of the torch from her car. She'd only recently and with great reluctance put her flip-flops away for the season, and she still didn't quite trust herself in boots. They were very comfortable, but also felt very *large* after a summer of bare feet as often as she could manage. She glanced around occasionally as she walked, but the dragons were keeping their word on staying hidden, and in the leaning trees she could see nothing beyond her pool of light. It wasn't a terribly big pool, either. She hoped the batteries were alright. She couldn't remember when she'd last changed them.

She'd been able to hear a guitar as she started her walk, but it stopped as she got closer, and a silence rose up around her, wary and waiting. It grew and swelled, filling the space between the trees, until she could barely breathe for it. She squinted at the fire, but it didn't seem any closer, and finally she called out, "Rainbow? Are you there? It's Miriam."

There was no answer, but the fire went out with a furious hiss, and suddenly Miriam's torch was the only thing holding back the dark. She stopped short, her heart too loud in her ears, and wished again that she hadn't had any paracetamol. She clutched the torch with both hands, pointing it in the direction where the fire had been. The dark felt too deep, the night too heavy, the silence suffocating against her ears and yet full of furtive movement.

"Hello?" she tried again, and her voice threatened to close up on the word. She stumbled in a circle, her small pool of light faltering and barely lighting the trees to either side. There could be anything beyond it. "Rainbow?"

Still no response, but she almost thought she could hear whispers, too low to be heard properly yet alarmingly close in the night. The light of the torch made her feel suddenly like a target, a lure dangled in the depths of the darkness, and she switched it off, biting down on her breath and trying to hear past the roar of her pulse in her ears. Nothing. Not even a whisper of wind in the branches of the trees. Silence and darkness, true dark high up here on the fells, far from towns and villages, just her and the night and the things that inhabited it. Just—

She closed her eyes, opened them again, and whispered, "Mortimer?"

"Here." His voice was even lower than hers, close to her side, and she reached out a shaking hand to encounter the hard smooth lines of his scaled spine.

"What happened?" she whispered.

"Beaufort's looking," he said, and she thought he was stopping himself from saying any more.

She thought of deep winter fells and said, "It's not goblins, is it?"

"Definitely not," he said, so firmly that she knew he'd been thinking the same thing, and then there was a whisper of claw on stone and he added, "Beaufort's here."

"It's alright," the High Lord said, his voice a rumble of comfort Miriam could have wrapped herself in. "I thought it might be a faery circle or some such thing."

"Ugh." Miriam shuddered. She had encountered faeries once, and she didn't fancy meeting them again, especially not out here. "What happened, then?"

"They seem to have found themselves a cave of sorts," Beaufort said. "They ran in and shut the door."

"What sort of cave has a door?" Miriam asked. "One you can shut, anyway?"

"A human one," Beaufort said, and she heard the slither of his tail as he turned and padded away. "Come on. You can knock on it and see what happens."

"Oh, good," Miriam said, fumbling the torch back on. "That sounds like a wonderful plan."

๛

THE FIRE WAS STILL SMOULDERING, and a red plastic bucket lay on its side next to the stones that ringed it. Miriam moved it away, in case there were any hot coals that might melt through it, then scanned the area with the torch beam. Discarded metal tumblers, a couple of toppled canvas camping chairs, and a half-empty bottle of dubious-looking ale were scattered about the place, along with someone's wet socks sitting on top of a cool box.

"Ew," she said, finding herself still whispering. Even with the dragons, it was unsettling out here. The trees cut her off from the road, and beyond the fire she was aware of the vast emptiness that would be the tarn, the faintly metallic smell of hard water drifting to her. If she turned the torch off she imagined she'd be able to see the starlight reflecting on its surface, serene and endless.

She checked around again, then said, "I don't see a cave."

"It's here," Beaufort said, and patted a boulder. She stared at it. It wasn't very impressive. Just a large rock, really, smooth and featureless.

"Um," she started, and the High Lord moved aside, showing her a round, spoked wheel like one imagined on the doors of submarines. "*Oh*. It's a bunker!" She looked around. "Who'd put a bunker up here?" It wasn't anywhere near any old army outposts that she knew of, and it was hardly a place of strategic importance. But people did do odd things. There were all sorts of hideaways pocked around the country, some left over from wartime, others built by rich and anxious landowners, or resourceful DIY-ers.

"Shall I open it?" Beaufort asked.

"Best not." She shooed them away, set the phone down next to her, grabbed the handle, and twisted. It turned easily, then abruptly stopped, wrenched out of her grip, and turned back the other way. Miriam snatched her hands away with a little *ooh* of surprise. "Rainbow!" she shouted. "It's just me! Open up!"

There was a pause, then a man's voice, muffled behind the door, said, "There's no Rainbow here."

"Isn't this her camp?"

There was pause, as if the man were considering that, then he said, "Why?"

"I'm her sister," Miriam said. "I want to talk to her."

"Well, you can't."

"Can you come out so I can talk to you properly?"

"No."

"Why not? It'll only take a moment."

"We don't talk to tools of the establishment."

"I am *not* a tool of the establishment!"

"Of course you'd say that," the man in the bunker said.

Miriam glared at the door, then went and got one of the canvas chairs. "Fine," she said. "I'll wait." She sat down and crossed her arms over her chest, staring out into the night.

After a while, as the torch's beam illuminated the rubbly ground and night birds started to call in the trees again, Beaufort said, "Miriam, how long are you going to wait?"

"Until Rainbow turns up," she said. "Or until they come out and tell me where she is." She shifted in the chair a little, and wished she'd brought the old blanket from the back of the car. It was much colder out here than it had been in the hollow that formed Toot Hansell's valley.

"I see," Beaufort said, and sat down next to her, his scales radiating heat. "I suppose we'll just wait too, then."

"Only if you want to," she said, then she switched off the faltering torch and leaned back in the chair, flanked by dragons, and watched the slow turn of the endless stars, as they glimmered over the antics of dragons and humans just as they had when the High Lord had been young.

6
ALICE

Alice cut the salmon into bite-sized pieces, placed it on a saucer, and put it on the kitchen table. A large tabby tomcat with ragged ears looked at it, looked at her, and said, "Salmon? *Again?*"

"You know most cats make do with packet food," she said, putting the kettle on to boil.

"Only because their humans don't know any better."

"Could we try that?"

Thompson gave her a narrow-eyed stare. "You don't mean that."

"I do," she said, setting up the teapot. "Talking cats has not been one of my favourite discoveries."

"You preferred the goblins, then? Or the faeries?"

"They didn't criticise my catering, commandeer my car, or get hair all over my bed."

Thompson made a scoffing noise that was only partly muffled by the piece of salmon in his mouth. "I'm a delight."

"You're something," she said, and took her tea through to what had once been the dining room, turning the kitchen light out as she went and ignoring the cat's hiss of protest. He wasn't the one paying the power bill.

She settled herself into one of the comfortable chairs that nestled next to the coffee table and flicked on a side light. The walls loomed above her, lined with shelves to the ceiling. The shelves themselves were crowded with books of every sort, from travelogues and cookbooks to treatises on philosophy and psychology and a fat collection of crime tales and thrillers, as well as everything in between. She also had a growing section on mythology and folklore, particularly as it pertained to the British Isles. She wasn't sure it was very useful, as nothing mentioned talking cats or the cake-based needs of dragons, but it couldn't hurt.

She picked up a tablet from the table, found a set of reading glasses, and poked the device into life. It gave her a low battery warning and she grumbled, then went to find the charger, her hip twinging as she pushed herself out of the chair. She'd been out in the cold too long, waiting on the green for the DI to come. She could feel the stiffness setting painful teeth into her joints, and when she sat back down she pulled a throw off the chaise longue to tuck over her lap.

"Comfy," Thompson said, jumping up next to her and putting a paw on her legs. "Nice material."

"It is, and it doesn't need cat hair," she said, poking the tablet again. It opened an internet browser obediently.

"I'm basically a hot water bottle," he said, stepping onto her lap and turning in a circle. "Plus, my purring's very healing. There was a study."

Alice scowled at him. "Oh? I have grave doubts about any studies involving cats these days. Now that I know you can *suggest* things to people."

Thompson looked at her and blinked lazily. "Look, dogs get all the good press because they're all so *love me, love me*. We need all the help we can get."

Alice sniffed, but returned to the tablet. She was just happy Thompson had never tried to *suggest* anything to her. She didn't think. Apparently it was some form of cat-hypnosis, and was used to ensure humans didn't remember any encounters with the magical Folk of the world. Alice was a little unclear on just how such things worked (and it certainly wasn't in any book she'd found, even the most obscure ones), but it seemed that a cat council called the Watch policed the divide between humans and Folk, and were apparently fierce enough in enforcing it that even dragons didn't fancy getting on the wrong side of them. Thompson, despite being Watch, was fairly lax about his responsibilities, particularly since Beaufort had fished him out of the river when he was a kitten (in which life, Alice wasn't sure, as it appeared cats really did have nine of them). He seemed to expend most of his energy in the village making sure no one else caught a whiff of dragons, which Alice rather approved of.

Of course, this meant Thompson should probably have tried *suggesting* dragons didn't exist to the W.I., but it seemed that once one's mind was made up, suggestion didn't work particularly well, and the side effects could be disastrous. Although Alice wondered if *suggestion* could also be used to convince one to spend an inordinate amount of money on fresh fish. An awful lot of it seemed to be ending up in her weekly shop without her being quite clear on when she decided to buy it.

"Whatcha doing?" Thompson asked, craning his head up to look at the tablet. "'Guy thefts'? You looking for murderous guy thieves?" Alice had told him about the events of the evening while she'd prepared his dinner.

"I'm trying to see if there's been a spate in the area."

"Murders? Or guy thefts?"

She scrolled down, looking for a news site that seemed reputable. They were harder and harder to find, it seemed, every headline loaded with exclamation marks and superlatives. "Donation tins being snatched, or guys stolen. A *spate* of murders seems unlikely."

"The Guy Fawkes murders," Thompson said, and started grooming his paws. "Could be a serial killer type thing. Goes in, kills the home-owner, and takes the nearest guy."

"In this case they took the guy and left an unidentified body," Alice said.

"Unidentified? I thought you knew everyone around here."

"I mostly do." She abandoned her guy theft search. There were a lot of opinion posts and letters to the editor bemoaning the fact that, rather than doing penny for the guy, people were running around stealing each others' firewood and guys or burning them ahead of time, apparently in competition to have the best display for Guy Fawkes. An awful lot of people seemed to think this was terrible behaviour and signalled the oncoming downfall of humanity, and Alice wondered if none of them had ever heard of Mischievous Night, or had ever been teenagers themselves. But none of it was very helpful to her, and she tried *donation tin thefts* instead.

"So they wheeled your bod in from somewhere else?" Thompson asked, shifting his attention to a back paw, his leg sticking straight up in front of the tablet. "Interesting."

"He was rather well-dressed, too," Alice said, pushing the cat's foot away. There were thankfully few articles involving the theft of donation tins, and nothing local or recent. She tried looking for missing persons instead. "He was wearing *loafers.* I've not seen anyone in this area wear loafers."

Thompson wrinkled his snout. "Wouldn't they be kind of scratchy?"

"Not if they're well made, I imagine." There were no missing people locally, and she couldn't bear the idea of sifting through the nationwide ones, with their terrible photos of young faces smiling out of a safer past. She went onto the Toot Hansell Facebook group instead, but no one was reporting any missing guys, or rumours of missing people for that matter on there.

"They look scratchy. Big, scratchy sponges on sticks. Do they use the sticks, too?"

Alice looked at him finally. "Sorry?"

"Like the one in your shower. How would you wear that?"

"*Loofah,*" she said.

"Yes."

They looked at each other for a moment, then she said, "I can't find anything about any of it. No stolen donations or missing people. And I suppose some teenagers or something *might* have stolen the guy, but it doesn't explain the body."

"What about the hippy sister? The one you said Nellie might've seen?"

Alice looked back at the tablet, then started poking through the Facebook group photos. It had been early summer when there had been the whole wildflower incident, and that post about the chains had popped up. If she could find it ... but there were too many posts about people collecting jam jars, or giving away late courgettes, or complaining about speeding cars, and she gave up fairly quickly. She tried looking through Miriam's friends instead, but though she found a profile for Rainbow, it was set to private.

She regarded Thompson. "I doubt she's a killer. But accidents happen."

"Especially around you lot," the cat said.

Alice closed the app and pulled up Miriam's last message, which had been a dancing squirrel she'd apparently sent to everyone in her address book. She typed *Are you still up?*, set the tablet down, and picked her tea up again. "I would like to know where the guy went. That might give us some idea of who's behind this. There was only the body in the barrow when it came back."

"Doubt there was any room for both. Not with sponges and sticks everywhere."

Alice sighed, and picked up the tablet again as it dinged.

I'm up! There was a smiley face after it, and Alice decided it was easier to call. Miriam was far too fond of emojis. It made attempting a proper conversation rather vexing.

HALF AN HOUR LATER, Alice walked briskly down the path toward the tarn, a large torch in one hand, her cane in the other, and a pack containing two tightly rolled sleeping bags, a Tupperware full of cheese scones, a thermos of tea, a first aid kit, two more torches, and some extra gloves and hats on her back. Thompson trotted ahead of her, tail up.

"This is more like it," he said. "It's all been very calm since the whole witch in the valley thing."

"She wasn't a witch any more than I am."

Thompson looked back at her, his eyes luminously green in the light of the torch. "You live alone, talk to a cat, carry a scary stick, and see magical beings. You'd absolutely be stake fodder."

"I wish I didn't talk to a cat," she said, then they came out of the trees and the powerful beam of the torch spotlighted Miriam huddled in a canvas chair, Beaufort and Mortimer curled close around her.

"Alice!" Miriam said. "You really didn't have to come."

"We can't have you running about the moors on your own," Alice said, setting down her bag and getting the thermos out. She handed it to Miriam and looked at the bunker door behind her. "They haven't come out?"

"They say Rainbow's not in there, and no one's coming out until I go away."

Alice knocked on the door briskly while Miriam poured herself a cup of tea into the lid of the thermos and sipped it, both hands wrapped around the plastic.

"Hello," Alice said, raising her voice. "This is quite enough now. You need to come out. It's cold out here."

"It's cold in here too," an aggrieved voice came back. "We can't even light a fire."

"So come out and light one," Alice said. "We only want to talk to you."

"I told that other woman – Rainbow's not here. And we don't want to talk to you."

"Why ever not? I've brought tea and scones."

There was silence behind the door, and Alice wondered if they should have let them stew for a little longer. She was banking on this being one of those old, homemade bunkers that were really nothing more than holes in the ground, with no option for any home comforts. Someone was going to need the loo at some point, if nothing else.

"Are the scones homemade?" the first voice called, and a new one talked over them. "*No. We're not coming out. Leave, alright?*"

"We just want to know about the guy," Alice said. "Did you take it?"

"A *guy?*" the new voice demanded.

"Yes. From the village hall in Toot Hansell. It was stolen."

"Oh, so you immediately think anyone who doesn't adhere to your limited nine to five life must be guilty? Why would we steal a *guy?*"

"I'm sure I don't know," Alice said, stepping back as the handle turned on the door. It cracked open a little, and a young man with a khaki green knit hat pulled down low over his forehead peered out, scowling. He had a scruffy, ginger-hued beard, and he looked from Miriam to Alice, then checked the campsite behind them before he spoke.

"Guys don't concern us," he said.

"No? What about donation tins?"

His scowl deepened. "We'd *never* touch a donation tin. That's the very antithesis of who we are." He looked back inside as someone said something, and sighed. "*Fine.*" He clambered out, revealing a tall, lean frame in heavy-duty outdoors gear. "Where are those scones?"

Alice patted her bag. "Everyone come out. I have plenty of tea, too."

A second man appeared in the bunker's hatch, looking from Alice to Miriam, who waved cheerfully. His face was skinny and angular, with grey stubble on his chin and cheeks, and grey hair dangling under his grey hat, making him look particularly pale against his fluorescent yellow work gear. He climbed out slowly, blinking in the torch light, and Alice handed the first man the Tupperware full of cheese scones. He took it, his gaze still shifting suspiciously between her and Miriam, then scanning the shadows beyond the circle of the torch. Alice smiled at him, hoping the dragons were well hidden.

"Why's there a cat?" he asked, pointing at Thompson, who was sitting next to the dead fire. Thompson yawned, exposing sharp white teeth.

"I can't seem to get rid of him," Alice said, which was true enough. "Alice Martin." She swallowed the *RAF Wing Commander, retired,* that threatened to follow of its own accord. She doubted these men were too fond of anyone who might be associated with authority. "And you are?"

"Simon," said the scraggly-haired man, grabbing the Tupperware off the younger man and snatching a scone out. He managed to get half of it into his mouth in one bite, and said around it, "Tom, these are amazing."

"Tom," Alice said, examining him more closely. "We've met, I believe. You were with Rainbow at the manor house. You and ..." She searched for the name. "Jemima."

Tom flinched slightly, then said, "Yeah, I've been working with Rainbow for a long time."

Alice forgave herself for not recognising him straightaway, even though she was normally very good with such things. He'd been quite a skinny thing when she'd last seen him at Maddie's house, swathed in grubby, second-hand waterproofs and wielding water balloons full of cranberry sauce. At some point in the last year and a half he'd grown into his lanky frame, and evidently updated his wardrobe as well. It all looked rather new and well-branded, and his shoulders were testing the limits of his black jacket.

"Is Jemima still around?" Miriam asked. "She was with Rainbow when we saw them last summer. Her and Ronnie."

Tom shrugged. "Ronnie's nerves got the better of him. He moved to Cornwall to make cheese or something. Jem's doing other stuff." He cleared his throat, and took a scone. "Why did you come all the way out here looking for Rainbow?"

"I'm her sister," Miriam said. "I don't need a reason to look for her."

"At midnight?"

"It wouldn't be midnight if you'd talked to me when I first got here," she shot back.

"We told you she wasn't here."

"Are we having scones?" someone else asked, and a woman in a lilac ski suit that looked like it had been the height of fashion in the eighties put her head around the bunker door. She sighed when she saw Alice and Miriam. "Oh. It's *you*."

"Hello, Harriet," Alice said. "I thought I hadn't seen you in the bookshop for a bit." Harriet had been a stalwart member of Rainbow's group for as long as Alice had known of it, but she was also the owner of Toot Hansell's bookshop, which she maintained was basically a charity, so it didn't count as bowing to capitalism. Alice knew this because she'd had to listen to Harriet telling her at least once a month when she went to the shop looking for new reading material.

"I needed a change," Harriet said now, taking a scone and inspecting it suspiciously. Simon gave her an encouraging smile, still chewing. "The bookshop gets very *same-y*. Are these vegan?"

"No," Alice said, handing out plastic tumblers and topping them up with tea. "Is anyone else here?"

"No," Tom said, taking a tumbler. He sniffed it warily, then took a sip. "Told you, Rainbow's not about. Probably gone back to the main camp."

"She took Barry to the hospital," Harriet said, still holding her scone as if unsure what to do with it. "He …" Tom coughed sharply, and she hesitated. "He gets so cold," she finished.

"He wouldn't if he'd wear some bloody clothes," Tom said.

"We can't all afford fancy-pants merino underwear from New Zealand," Harriet shot back, and they glared at each other. "We've been doing this together for *ages,* and we have to look after Barry. You don't like it, go and set up your own group."

"I've been here ages too," Tom said. "You lot are that bloody stuck in your ways. You've getting soft and *old*—"

"Excuse *me*," Miriam said, and snatched the Tupperware off Simon as he made to hand it to Tom. "I'll just take that, shall I? Would be a bit *soft* to be taking food from people."

"Aw," Simon said, and Miriam relented, handing the box back to him.

"You can have some."

"We're not holding food to ransom, Miriam," Alice said, then looked back at Harriet. "Have you been into the village tonight?"

"Which one?" Tom asked. "Bloody rashes of them about the place, all light pollution and noise and cars. Not to mention the farms and what they do to their animals."

Harriet wrinkled her nose in an expression that suggested she at least half agreed with him, but didn't really want to.

"Toot Hansell," Alice said.

"Not been anywhere," Tom said. "See any car about the place?"

Alice had wondered about that. "How did you get here, then?"

"Rainbow brought us, but she took off again. Her and Barry. To the hospital, before you start getting any ideas about them being thieves."

"Do you have any way to contact them?"

"No. We're off phones. Too easy to track." He grabbed the Tupperware off Simon and snatched two scones out before shoving the box at Alice. "Go on back to your tea parties, ladies. Stick to what you know."

"*Really*," Miriam said, and Alice spoke over her.

"I suppose we will. Come along, Miriam. We'll find your sister elsewhere." She put the lid back on the Tupperware and returned it to the bag as Tom crossed his arms and glared at them both.

"You've become very unpleasant," Miriam said to him. "You were much nicer when I first met you."

"Dreadfully sorry I can't fit your social mores," he said.

Miriam frowned. "You should give back those scones if you dislike tea parties so much."

Tom just looked at her, then took a large bite of one, chewing slowly.

"*So rude,*" Miriam said, and Alice turned for the path to hide her smile. She couldn't disagree with Miriam's evaluation of Tom. Apparently he'd grown a large chip on his shoulder to go with his bigger frame.

"What the *hell—?*" Tom yelped, and Alice looked back to see Miriam shaking the thermos lid out primly while Thompson huffed in delight.

"Terribly sorry," Miriam said. "I was just getting rid of the leftovers. But those trousers must be waterproof?"

Tom stared at her, his shoulders hunched and tense, and somewhere on the edge of the torchlight Alice could hear the dragons shifting, in warning or preparation. Then Harriet snorted laughter and said, "Course they are. Bloody waterproof and windproof and all the other proofs too. Not git-proof, though."

"Oh, sod off," Tom said to her, finally looking away from Miriam, and Harriet made an *ooh I'm scared* expression, waving her hands on either side of her face.

"Sorry," Simon whispered, handing Alice his own mug. He was standing a little too close, his gaze intense. "We're not meant to be here, see. It's kind of private property, if you hold with that sort of thing, which is why we hid. Rainbow's been a bit—"

"*Simon!*" Tom shoved the other man, sending him stumbling sideways. "Bloody amateur hour, I swear." He looked at Alice. "Go on, then. Get out of here."

"*Rude,*" Miriam said again.

"Come on, Miriam," Alice said. "We've done all we can here. Do tell Rainbow we were by."

"Don't you want to leave a calling card?" Tom asked.

Alice gave him a small smile of the sort she'd had to use a lot over the years, a little indulgent and a little pitying, then turned and led the way down the rough and broken track, back to the lay-by where their cars sat waiting patiently under the coverlet of night.

Alice waited until they were across the road, then said, "Are you quite alright, Miriam? Throwing tea at people?"

"It's the paracetamol," Miriam said. "It really doesn't agree with me."

"I think it might, actually," Alice said, and waved for her to get in her car. There was no point discussing anything here, and certainly no point trying to talk to dragons. She'd been able to hear the soft shift of stone on stone flanking them all the way from the camp.

Someone was most definitely watching.

7

MORTIMER

Mortimer watched the man crouching in the cover of the trees as the two cars left, Miriam first with a little backfire and a cough of black smoke, and Alice behind her rather more smoothly. The High Lord sat next to him, and their scales were flushed to deep grey night shades, rendering them all but invisible in the darkness. Certainly invisible to Tom, who settled himself in and waited, eating his way steadily through Alice's scones. Mortimer wished Miriam had snatched them off him a little more quickly, since no one that rude deserved W.I.-standard scones, but the tea-throwing had been impressive enough. Beaufort had gone quite a curious shade trying not to laugh about it.

No one moved for a long time, and as the sound of the cars faded, the night quieted still further. The trees whispered to each other softly, and somewhere a night bird cried, but there was nothing else, and Mortimer pressed a paw to his stomach. It was the thought of the cheese scones. He could feel a rumble coming on, and there was nothing he could do to stop it. He tried desperately to think of something else, *anything* else, but he could even hear Tom *chewing*, and that wasn't doing anything to help. A little spasm of hunger gripped him, and he reminded himself that he'd eaten two whole pumpkins and five roast potatoes this morning, and they had actually been rather good, even if Gilbert's cooking efforts were still a little hit and miss. He seemed to have mastered pumpkins quite well, but potatoes were another matter, and always ended up either blackened and charred, or still somewhat raw inside (and occasionally both). They apparently needed a more judicious application of heat than the young dragon had so far managed. But both the slightly crunchy potatoes and the pumpkins had been good, and *he wasn't hungry.*

The rumble started up, a slow roll in the pit of his stomach, and he wondered if he should just run for it. Tom would certainly hear him if he moved, though, and that might be all it took. The young man seemed suspicious enough that he could be open to seeing more than the average human, and often it was the smallest slip that brought down empires. Never mind their problems with the body – it'd be dragon hunts all over again if they were actually spotted. And humans could be so careless with lives, even other human lives, despite how short they were. They were careless with their *own* lives at times, letting them slip away almost without noticing, while they waited for … something. For some ideal moment that never arrived, or could never be returned to, or some distant goal they were so busy running toward that they missed all the beautiful and fragile and heroic life they passed on the way. To be so casual with their own lives, they certainly wouldn't worry much about a *dragon's.*

Mortimer clutched his belly with his front paws, desperately willing it not to growl, and someone shouted from the direction of the bunker.

"Tom?" the other man, the one called Simon, shouted. "You coming or what?"

"Yeah, coming," Tom yelled, just as Mortimer's belly gave a little warning grumble. Tom had stood up, and now he looked around, his frown visible to dragons' vision, better in the night than most creatures. But after a moment he turned and walked back to the camp, and Mortimer's belly gave a growl that was as much relief as it was the thought of cheese scones.

"Oh, that was *awful*," he whispered. "I thought he was never going to leave!"

"He seems a most unpleasant man," Beaufort said. "But that doesn't make him guilty of anything. I didn't see any sign of the guy or the donation tin lying around the camp, did you?"

"No," Mortimer said. "And I didn't smell anything that seemed familiar, or even particularly guilty." Just those ever-present scents of worry and weariness and exhaustion that seemed to follow so many people through life. Although there was something sharper and tighter about Tom under the whiff of strong deodorant, a glint of cold clear water on an even colder night.

"A shame we couldn't get into the bunker. They could have all sorts of things in there."

"That's why you need a cat's skill set," a new voice said, and they looked around to see Thompson padding across the rough ground to join them. "I checked it out."

"Anything?"

"The sort of stink a dog would be proud of."

"Unpleasant but unhelpful," the High Lord said. "Anything else?"

"Nothing useful. A bit of a stash of cans and water, and some blankets and so on. A bunch of tools in a big bag were about the only interesting things I could spot."

They looked at each other for a moment, then Beaufort said, a little doubtfully, "Well, I suppose they could have used one as a murder weapon."

"Most humans have them, though," Thompson said with a yawn. "I wouldn't get too excited."

Beaufort sighed. "We may as well go after the ladies, then. There's no point waiting here if there's nothing to see."

Thompson gave a fluid shrug, and Mortimer tried very hard not to say anything else, but he couldn't help himself. A *dead body* had been left outside the village hall. Outside the W.I. meeting. It wasn't the time for not being thorough.

"What if Rainbow comes back? We're pretty sure there's no one around *now*, but what if she arrives later, and the evidence is in her car, or she says something about the body? Or if they go to meet her? We should keep an eye on them."

Beaufort gave him a curious look, then grinned, his teeth glinting in the starlight and making him magical and terrible all at once. "I'm very impressed, lad."

"I'm not," Mortimer said. "I'm really, really not."

Thompson gave another shrug. "I'll stay. You two can't be bombing around the neighbourhood where anyone can see you."

"We're hardly going to be seen tonight," Beaufort said.

"Sure, but how likely is it that anyone's coming back now? It'll probably be morning by the time anything happens, and you crashing about the fells and into Toot Hansell once it's getting on for the day's a bad plan. At least give me *some* deniability if the Watch check in."

"We hardly *crash about*," Beaufort said, and Thompson just looked at him. Mortimer supposed that, to a cat, most people crashed about.

"Put it this way," the cat said. "I could go and keep an eye on the W.I., but I can't eat anyone who decides to add another dead body to the list."

"I've never eaten anyone," Beaufort said. "It's terrible slander, the eating people thing. It's all that *Saint* George's fault."

"You're right, it makes much more sense," Mortimer said to Thompson, before Beaufort could get too worked up about Saint George. Even all these centuries later, it didn't take much. "And you can get back quicker than us, too."

"Yeah, shifty-shifty," Thompson said, and yawned again.

"Are you even going to stay awake?" Beaufort asked.

"Have a little faith," Thompson said, and then he was gone, stepping sideways into a shift, the strange movement that carries cats out of the world and back in again somewhere else entirely, passing through unseen dimensions peopled by unknown beasts. It's how they appear in locked rooms and unused buildings, cabinet meetings and houses of worship, fish markets and seats of power. Cats are always where they mean to be, or certainly claim that they are, and shifting is how they get there.

"I'm not sure I do have faith," Beaufort said. "Cats are always so *casual*."

"I heard that," Thompson said from somewhere to their left, and gave a huff of cat laughter.

The dragons waited for a moment longer, but the cat didn't say anything else, and there was no telling if he was still there or not. The unmoving air didn't even carry a scent to them, and finally Beaufort said, "Well, lad. We may as well go."

Mortimer followed the High Lord as he slipped onto the road, lumbering a few strides straight down the centre before his wings caught the air and he spun skyward, suddenly weightless and effortlessly graceful. The camp and the tarn fell behind them, the stars stretched above them, and they angled toward Toot Hansell where it burrowed unseen into the folds of the hills, encircled by waterways and entwined with secrets, hidden but not unnoticed.

❧

THEY TOOK THEIR TIME RETURNING, and with how long it had taken the scone thief to leave, it was late when they got back to Toot Hansell. The majority of the houses they silently swept over were dark, even the streetlights slumbering. Miriam's was lit, though, her heavy-paned kitchen windows letting light wash across the garden outside as it slowly faded from its summer of riotous growth to a wilderness of fallen leaves and rotting vines. As they padded up to the door, Mortimer stood in both a puddle and something that squished unpleasantly between his toes and was probably a forgotten courgette. The scent of woodsmoke and quiet, gentle lives drifted on the night, and the little stream at the bottom of the garden, where they'd landed, chattered its secrets to the mossy banks.

The door was ajar, and Beaufort glanced at Mortimer, his eyebrow ridges raised.

Mortimer gave a little shrug. There was no scent of distress or fright, just a whiff of farmyards that must have been drifting over from the fields on the other side of the village, as to this side was just the stream, then deep forest and the tangled mess of wild lands beyond that washed up to the dragons' mount, hidden by old magic and ancient charms.

Beaufort knocked warily, and the door swung open so quickly he was caught with his paw still raised.

Mortimer's snout wrinkled, and he said, "Oh, *no*."

"Oh yes," DI Adams said, and waved them over the threshold. "Do come in. What have you been up to? Stalking innocent hikers? Foisting dead rabbits on unsuspecting bystanders?"

"That was three summers ago," Beaufort said. "I have learned much more about modern humans, and you have learned more than enough about dragons to know it was a compliment."

"It was squishy," DI Adams said, causing Mortimer to check his paws. He seemed to have left most of the mud and rotting vegetation behind, but he thought it was better that they were in the stone-flagged kitchen rather than Miriam's little living room. The living room carpet was already worn and stained, but it didn't need the addition of dead courgettes.

"What have *you* been up to?" Beaufort asked. "You're rather fragrant."

"I'm asking the questions," DI Adams said, and checked the garden before pulling the door partly closed.

"Did you turn anything up?" Alice asked the dragons.

"No," Beaufort said. "Thompson's keeping an eye on things, though."

"Stop," DI Adams said.

"There is some use for cats, then," Alice said, and went back to making coffee in a delicate-looking glass jug.

"Did you not hear me? *Stop.*" DI Adams glared at them all.

"Is the coffee wrong?" Miriam asked. "There's so many types. And the grinds! Grounds? How does one know?"

"The coffee's fine," the inspector said. "*You* lot, however—"

Alice clicked her tongue as she poured the coffee into a mug. "DI Adams, really."

DI Adams folded her hands together. She still hadn't moved from by the door, and the reek of her clothes was drowning any other scent Mortimer might have caught from her, but the way her mouth twitched down as she looked at the floor suggested a flare of embarrassment.

"I'm sorry. It's been a long day."

"Come and sit down," Miriam said, waving at the kitchen table and its creaky yet sturdy old chairs. "It's so *late*, too."

"I better not. You'll never get the smell out." DI Adams opened the kitchen door a little wider and took the mug of coffee from Alice, her fingers dark and smooth against the pale green ceramic. "Thanks."

"Where's your dandy?" Beaufort asked, looking around curiously. "I didn't even see him in the garden."

"He's not come near me since this," she said, waving at herself. "Bloody animal. What use is a magic dog that runs away if things get a bit whiffy?"

"To be fair, you're *very* whiffy," Miriam said. "Would you like a shower?"

DI Adams just looked at her, the mug halfway to her lips.

"Sorry!" Miriam grabbed a cake box and pulled the top off, thrusting it at the inspector. "It's the paracetamol talking. Well, other than the shower. That still might be a good idea. *Sorry!*"

Alice handed a large soup mug of tea to Beaufort, who had settled into his favourite spot next to the AGA, then held another out to Mortimer, who took it gratefully. Although he wasn't quite sure how it was going to taste, given the all-pervasive reek.

"She's been like this all night," Alice said to the inspector. "Don't take it personally."

"Good to know." DI Adams took a piece of parkin. "What have you been up to, then? And don't say nothing. I saw both your cars come back from *somewhere* at near enough midnight, and I may be tired, but I'm not so tired that I think you're just going to ignore a body on your doorstep. Even when *the police*"—she waved at herself—"specifically tell you to."

"It was my fault," Miriam blurted. "I was worried it maybe *was* Rainbow. Not the body, not *that*, but the herons. Which meant you might be looking for her in case she'd seen anything, and the thing is ... the thing ... well, if you went after Rainbow you might find ... other stuff."

"Other stuff?" DI Adams asked, around a mouthful of parkin.

"Not bad stuff. Just maybe not entirely, completely, a hundred per cent legal stuff, even though it might be in other places, well, *is* actually, you know, because laws are different, and laws might change here too, you know, almost definitely really, and lots of people aren't *exactly* within the law, and—"

"Miriam," DI Adams said.

"Yes?"

"Breathe."

"I'd rather not. You really do smell. *Sorry!*" Miriam grabbed her mug and gulped from it, giving Alice a desperate look over the rim.

Alice chuckled softly and took a sip of tea. "We haven't found Rainbow, but we found some of her associates, and they claim they haven't been anywhere near Toot Hansell, and have no interest in guys or donation tins. And given their moral convictions, I doubt they're murderers, so you can probably discount that one."

"Oh, can I? Good to know," DI Adams said, setting her mug on the worktop. She took a notebook from her pockets and flipped it open, finding a page to scribble on. "Other than the herons, was there any particular reason you thought Rainbow might've been around?" She had her eyes on Miriam, who shot an anxious look at Mortimer. DI Adams shifted her attention to him. "Mortimer?"

"Um," he said, and examined his talons. They were looking a bit chipped. He needed to sharpen them.

"The note?" DI Adams suggested. "Was the writing familiar?"

"No," Miriam said. "It was all scrawly, like writing with your wrong hand."

"It was," DI Adams agreed. "So ...?" No one answered for a long moment, and the inspector picked her mug up again. "This is very disappointing," she said, and Mortimer saw Miriam's shoulder's sag. "Very disappointing indeed," the inspector repeated.

"Would you incriminate your family?" Alice asked.

DI Adams tipped her head slightly. "I would if it involved a dead body."

"She *wouldn't*," Miriam said firmly, straightening up. "The herons are possible, but even if she had anything to do with the guy going missing – which I still don't think she did – she wouldn't kill anyone. I know her."

DI Adams sighed. "Fine. Where's this camp?"

"Out past Malham," Alice said. "They have a bunker."

"Thompson checked it," Beaufort said. "Apparently there was nothing incriminating in it."

"Well, if the cat says so," DI Adams said, going back to writing.

"That Tom was unpleasant, though," Mortimer said. "He followed you to the cars, you know."

"I suspected," Alice said, and DI Adams frowned at her.

"Please stop doing things that result in unpleasant men following you around."

"That's victim blaming," Miriam said, then got up hurriedly. "I have scented candles. We should have scented candles. I'm going to get some. And ... and ... *stuff*." She rushed out of the room, and DI Adams looked at Alice.

"Paracetamol? Really?"

"I think she should take it more often."

"I think I should test her for any of these not-illegal-in-other-countries things her sister seems to have an interest in." DI Adams took a sip of coffee, but Mortimer could hear the hint of a smile in her voice.

"Mortimer didn't recognise any scents at the camp as being from the hall or the green," Beaufort said. "Did you, lad?"

"No," Mortimer said. "I don't think so. But it's not like dog scents. They don't stick the same, and if someone was just really quick into the hall and out again, I'd probably miss it, unless they were feeling something very intense at the time." Dragons smelled emotional traces rather than physical scents, the soft blooms and quiet explosions of thought and feeling that every creature leaves like smudged fingerprints on the world. They were unpredictable, and difficult to place, but they could be recognised if one had a sensitive snout, even tracked if the person was experiencing a particularly strong emotion. Mortimer wasn't sure he'd keep his sensitive snout if he had to smell DI Adams for much longer, though.

"Well, I'll talk to them," DI Adams said, and looked at Miriam as she came back into the room brandishing an armful of candles and little terracotta pots that she deposited on the table. "Where's your sister, then? I do need to talk to her."

"I don't know," Miriam said. "Honestly. She wasn't at the bunker, Maddie hasn't seen her, and Rainbow's gone off phones, apparently."

DI Adams nodded, and drained her mug. "Well, you've done plenty, alright? No more chasing around the countryside in the night. Especially not with that note that was on the body."

Miriam shivered violently, but Alice said, "It didn't seem threatening to me. I think it was more someone asking for help."

"With a *dead body?*" DI Adams said. "Really?"

"Is that so much less likely than it being a threat?"

Mortimer found himself very much in agreement with DI Adams as she shook her head.

"Enough," she said. "No more getting involved. If you can discover the whereabouts of your sister, that's something I'd like to know, but you don't contact her and you don't do anything else." She looked at Miriam. "I promise it'll only be to find out if Rainbow saw anything, assuming she dropped the herons off. We've got no other witnesses, so it'd be really helpful."

"Alright," Miriam said, and edged across the kitchen, holding a pot of cream out at arm's length, as if afraid the stench rising off DI Adams might pounce on her. "Here. Lavender cream. It'll help with the smell."

"Thank you," DI Adams said, taking it, and turned to the door. "Tell me what you hear from the cat, alright?" She stopped, hanging her head slightly. "*Tell me what you hear from the cat.* My DCI in London called me a *rising star*, you know that? A fast-track career, she said. In the Met. The *Met.*"

"We're very lucky, then," Beaufort said. "Imagine if we didn't have you here!"

"Imagine," DI Adams said, and headed out the door, pulling it shut behind her. After a moment Miriam opened it again.

"Shall we go into the living room?" she said. "Just until it airs out."

"Excellent idea," Beaufort said, and followed Alice, who was already hurrying out of the room.

Mortimer looked up at Miriam. "Has the paracetamol worn off yet?"

"I don't know," she replied. "It might be that cold, too. It was a really bad one."

Mortimer nodded. "So you're still going to look for Rainbow?"

"Of course," Miriam said. "It's not the same as looking for a murderer."

She led the way into the hall, and Mortimer followed a little glumly. It *wasn't*, but it was still investigating. And he was going to need some paracetamol himself if this kept up.

8
DI ADAMS

D I Adams stared at the ceiling. She was clean, her clothes already on the second round of washing, her hair still damp in its wrap, and she was thoroughly slathered in Miriam's lavender cream, which was strong enough that she thought one of her eyes might be twitching. Dandy had crept in to join her, but the scent of the cream had sent him into retreat, and he was currently lying by the bedroom door. She could see the glint of his red eyes in the darkness like glittering LEDs, somehow both alarming and reproachful.

She flopped over, shoved her pillow into a better shape, and squeezed her eyes closed. She had nothing she could be working on right now, no confirmed ID on the victim, no leads on how he'd got there or where he'd come from, or even on where Miriam's sister might be. She'd gone back to the hall after talking to Miriam and Alice, collected a constable, and headed for Malham tarn. It had taken them half an hour of poking around in the dark, but they'd found the bunker and the remnants of the fire. The ashes were cold and the bunker was empty, so the W.I. had well and truly scared them off. They'd put some tape over the door and told Lucas, but it was rather low on his list of priorities, considering the body. She sighed and kicked the duvet off her feet. She needed to sleep. She couldn't do anything until morning, or rather *later* morning, since it had been almost four by the time she'd run out of hot water and forced herself out of the shower.

But she couldn't sleep.

She sat up and looked at Dandy. She couldn't really see him, but the glimmer of his eyes raised up, so he was evidently looking back at her.

"He wasn't robbed," she said. "Sure, his watch was gone, but his ring wasn't. He's not from the village, otherwise *someone* in the W.I. would have recognised him. Why leave a complete stranger outside their hall? And it had to have been for them. I mean, it's the *village* hall, sure, but it was their meeting slot." She'd checked with Alice on that, and while the W.I. met at each others' houses for the most part, once a month there was the village hall meeting, which was where new members or inactive members or visitors or people who wanted to talk to them for whatever misguided reason could always find them. It was where they had official meetings, to organise fêtes and markets and what have you. So they would have been there, if not for the broken boiler. They would have been there while the barrow and the dead man were left on the doorstep, and DI Adams couldn't see it as a coincidence, not when she knew just how good the W.I. were at getting themselves in the middle of things. But if it had been a message, it was a very ineffective one, since no one knew who the dead man was. There seemed to be no connection to him at all.

She couldn't claim to know the W.I. perfectly – no one knows anyone perfectly, even when they think they do – but they had all seemed as bewildered and concerned as anyone could be expected to be. She'd have liked it if they were a bit more *unsettled*, but it seemed they were getting far too comfortable with dead bodies.

So the dumped body *could* be a coincidence, but that seemed unlikely. Was someone trying to frame them? Also very badly done if so. No one who had ever encountered the W.I. would imagine they'd be anything less than ruthlessly efficient at disposing of bodies. Although, if one knew that, then suspicion almost inevitably swung back to the W.I., because who would ever expect them to be so careless as to just leave a body on their doorstep?

With that thought DI Adams flicked the bedside light on and swung her legs off the bed. She wasn't going to get any sleep if she was lying here thinking about all the ways the W.I. could hide a murder. She padded barefoot to the door, snagging her hoody off the bottom of the bed as she went. Dandy got up, his eyes hidden behind his dreadlocks, and followed her down the stairs, a matted grey shadow. He watched with his ears as pricked as they were able to be as she set the coffee machine up.

"You can't have any," she told him, and he tipped his head at her. "Completely sure that dogs shouldn't have coffee," she added, tapping the old grounds out into the bin.

Dandy whined.

"Sure, you may not be a visible dog, but you're still a *dog*." She looked at him. "Aren't you?"

He just stood there without confirming or denying the statement, radiating disappointment. DI Adams took her favourite mug from the draining board then stood staring at the sink for a moment, wondering about the stolen jewellery. She was almost sure it wasn't in the cow shed. Odds were it had been a false tip, just someone messing with them, but she was going to have to send Genny back out there tomorrow. They couldn't risk the fact that the stolen goods might actually be in there somewhere. Hidden under a couple of decades worth of cow effluent.

A crash made her jump, almost dropping the mug, and she spun around to find the bin on its side on the floor. Dandy was nowhere to be seen, but a trail of coffee grounds led to the locked back door, which he'd no doubt navigated in the same mysterious manner he did any other obstacle. She stared at the bin for a moment, then put her mug under the spout of the machine and switched it on.

"Bloody dogs," she muttered.

It was only as she was picking up the rubbish, which smelled a lot better than most of the previous day had, that it occurred to her it was Collins who was going to need to sort out the cow shed, because DCI

Taylor had said she thought his mum might be behind the wildlife thefts, so he couldn't be on the case. She paused, listening to the familiar, comforting sound of the coffee rumbling through the machine, and wondered about Rainbow's long history of protests. Wondered if there had been anything more than the usual clashes with security guards or police. Any sign that she – or the group – might be violent.

She checked her watch. Interesting or not, it was going to have to wait a few hours.

&a.

DI COLIN COLLINS arrived at the station almost two hours earlier than he usually would, and wandered into the office he shared with DI Adams, setting a cup of takeaway coffee on her desk. She looked at it, then at him.

A big man with close-cropped hair and a round chest, he took a sip of his own coffee and said, "Five text messages by five a.m., and one missed call at exactly six-oh-one when I was in the shower. Good night, was it?"

DI Adams pointed at Dandy, who was sprawled in the middle of the floor, all four legs in the air and the pale of his belly exposed. He panted at Collins. "He knocked over my bin to steal my coffee grounds. *Three times.*"

"I can see why you needed to text me." Collins sat down, taking a sip of his own coffee. "Maybe you should just let him have the coffee grounds."

"I'm pretty sure they're not on a dog's recommended diet."

Collins pointed in the same general direction Adams had, although Dandy would had to have been twice his actual size to be in line with his finger. Which, to be fair, Dandy had been at least that the only time Collins had seen him. Apparently when Dandy was angry enough and large enough, *everyone* could see him. "Your average dog is visible and not of variable size."

"True," DI Adams admitted, and picked up the mug, sniffing it gratefully. She'd already had too much this morning, but she was going to need it. Never mind the lack of sleep, there was the W.I. to deal with. "Have you heard from your mother recently?"

"My mother? I thought you were on the Toot Hansell case." The fact that Collins had chosen a career in law enforcement did not exactly sit well with Rainbow. It also seemed to make Miriam a bit nervous, to be fair, but DI Adams wasn't sure if that was down to her presence rather than Collins'. It was quite possible.

"I am, but DCI— Maud said she suspected Rainbow was behind the animal thefts, or might at least know about them, so I should take that on."

Collins nodded and watched her, waiting.

She scratched the nape of her neck. "And someone robbed the barrow with a guy and its donation tin out of the Toot Hansell village hall, then brought it back with a body in it. Which the W.I. obviously found."

"Obviously," Collins said. "And you think Mum might be involved how?"

"I'm not sure," DI Adams admitted. "But your aunt's all twitchy. Plus there were herons."

"Pardon?"

"Two herons dumped in the pond on the village green. The sprite's upset, apparently."

"Of course she is." Collins took his phone out and scrolled through it, squinting for a moment before fishing his glasses out of the desk drawer. "We don't have a full list of what was taken from the collection yet. The homeowners are on holiday in the Seychelles or something and I haven't been able to get hold of them."

"Nice for some."

"Indeed." He inspected his phone then said, "There were birds taken, but no specifics just yet."

"*Hmm.* Miriam and Alice were running about the Dales last night looking for your mum, since Miriam doesn't want me to find her in case I question her about anything other than what she might have seen while engaged in heron-dumping."

"She has a point," Collins said. "Herons aren't much to pin a murder charge on."

"I think she's more worried about what not entirely legal substances I might find."

"Ah," Collins said, and went back to his phone. "Last message from Mum was a few weeks back saying that she was casting off the shackles of technology, and that if I wanted to get in touch I'd need to send a message to the Toot Hansell bookshop." He hit dial, listened for a moment, then shook his head. "Not in use. She does this every now and then."

"Great." DI Adams got up. "I'm off to the bookshop, then. I've got no witnesses, no CCTV because Toot Hansell doesn't do such things – or not anywhere useful, anyway – and a body in the morgue that hasn't even been identified yet. I'm not saying your mum killed anyone, but if she did steal the guy or scatter bloody herons about the place she might've seen something."

"I'll come," Collins said, putting his phone away. "Mum might be more likely to talk to me than you."

"Really? She called you a filthy pig last time."

"It's a term of affection."

"Sounded like it."

"Besides, she's more likely to call you that. Have you even showered?"

DI Adams glared at him, then grinned as he tripped over Dandy and fell into the wall with a yelp. "Serves you right," she said, and patted Dandy, who had jumped up when Collins fell over him. The dandy looked up at DI Adams, his tongue lolling out of his mouth, and she decided that the coffee grounds were a small price to pay.

❦

THE ROADS out to Toot Hansell were quiet and clear, the sky high and tautly blue above a landscape that was still wearing a dusting of frost. The sun wasn't warm enough or high enough to burn it off yet, and DI Adams turned the heating up as she drove.

"Where are you on the wildlife case?" she asked Collins, who had settled back in his seat and was watching the landscape with a sort of benign interest.

"Pretty similar to the previous one. One of those big old houses that still refer to their wildlife collections as *menageries*, and somehow get hold of all sorts of species that are only marginally legal, if that. Cameras were shot with paint guns, and the person who did it was wearing a zebra onesie and a mask, so not much to go on there. We recaptured a couple of warthogs and two actual zebras, plus the parrots refused to leave the heated aviary, because they're not silly. There's still five antelope, a bunch of monkeys, some flying squirrels and three emus missing, though."

"Emus?" DI Adams checked the fields involuntarily, as if she might spot flightless Australian birds shivering next to the drystone walls. "Poor things."

"Don't feel too sorry for them. They won the emu wars, after all."

"The what?"

"The Australian government tried to wipe them out because they were kicking down fences and eating all the crops. They sent out soldiers and machine guns, but the emus were too quick. The soldiers gave up after three days when they realised they were just wasting ammunition."

"I'm on the emus' side here," DI Adams said, revising her image of shivering birds to proudly strutting ones instead.

"Sure, but you don't want a kick from one."

"They're dangerous?"

"Only if they're threatened, really, but still not great to have them running about. Strong legs, big claws, that sort of thing."

DI Adams wrinkled her nose, then said, "Do you think your mum's behind it?"

Collins shrugged. "If she's not involved, there's a good chance she'll know who is. I'm fine with you taking the case, Adams. Particularly as you've already done the dirty work on the jewels."

DI Adams made a face. "You should probably double-check."

"Oh, no. I have great faith in your skills."

DI Adams picked up her mug, found it empty, and set it back down with a sigh. "I'll send you all the notes." She glanced at him. "If we do find Rainbow at the bookshop, you've got to step out. You're not messing up my case."

Collins turned to peer into the back seat. "This is your fault, you know. I think the whole coffee ground incident has made her worse than usual." He waved his hand in Dandy's general direction, and Dandy licked it. "Ugh. That's never not going to be weird."

"Don't do it, then," DI Adams said.

"I should have got you more coffee."

THE BOOKSHOP NESTLED in the middle of a row of terraced houses, the bay window that overlooked the village square still dark and the pale blue door firmly shut. There were lights on in the apartment above it though, and DI Adams knocked heavily on the door while Collins stood back, surveying the square. With summer lost beyond the shortening days and drifts of dying leaves, and Christmas still too far off for festive lights to be appearing, the whole place felt a little dull and faded. The baskets of flowers on the lamp posts trailed dead foliage, and the tarmac glistened with melted frost. The grey stone of the buildings rendered the square almost dingy, despite the brightness of the shop windows that framed it. Even the little well with its steeply angled roof looked a little derelict and abandoned.

DI Adams knocked again, and this time the door was pulled open by a young woman with her hair pulled back in a tight ponytail. She frowned at them. "We don't open till ten."

"DIs Adams and Collins," DI Adams said. "Can we have a word?"

The woman gave a large sigh. "What's Dad done this time?"

"Dad?" DI Adams asked.

"Simon Brown. Or is it Harriet you're here about? Have they chained themselves to a tree again? Or glued themselves to a motorway?"

"Neither," DI Adams said. "Can we come in?"

"Sure." The young woman turned away from the door, letting them into a small alcove with chipped paint on the walls and worn carpet on the floor. A door marked *Private* lay open onto a hallway, revealing two closed doors and a glimpse of a kitchen at the other end. Stairs climbed out of the hall and an eclectic mix of crookedly hung paintings and photos and prints lined the walls. Rather than heading for the kitchen or the living room that DI Adams assumed must be behind one of the closed doors, the young woman pulled the *Private* door to and locked it, then pocketed the key and turned left, leading them straight into the bookshop. "It's warmer in here. The heating barely works anywhere else."

The bookshop wasn't large, but it made up for it by being exceptionally crowded. Shelves ran from floor to ceiling on every part of the walls, and where windows interrupted them, the shelves continued above. More books were stacked on the floor, and freestanding shelves turned the place into a maze of aisles and angles, all of it scented with paper and old ink and lost stories. There was no carpet in here, just a floor of old, worn wood, and exposed beams divided the white-painted ceiling above.

"Do you want a cuppa?" the young woman asked.

"Not right now," DI Adams said, although she did. But there was such a thing as too much coffee, and she was fairly sure the one Collins had brought her had had about four shots in it. "Are your dad or Harriet around, then?"

"No, they'll be off doing something adventurous." She made *adventurous* sound vaguely unpleasant.

"Do that a lot, do they?"

"It's their *lifestyle*." There was an impressive level of disapproval in her tone. "That's how I ended up here. I was planning a gap year anyway, and Dad came up with the idea of me running the shop for Harriet." The young woman looked around the cluttered space, and DI Adams wondered if she'd already taken some gap years before starting here. She looked older than the average uni student, but it might also be down to the rather fussy slacks and blouse combo she had going on under her firmly buttoned cardigan.

"How's that going?" DI Adams asked.

The young woman made an irritated noise. "I was meant to be able to keep the profits, but I've had to bail them out six times already."

"For protests?"

"Yeah, all over the place. Art gallery in London, port in Southampton, royal residence in Scotland. Suppose they're getting some travel in."

"What was your name?" Collins asked.

"Sorry – Daisy Greenhalgh," the young woman said. "That's Daisy spelled D-a-i-g-h-z-e-e, for whatever reason my mum had in mind at the time – good painkillers, I assume – but I prefer not to spell it that way if I don't have to."

"Got it," Collins said, scribbling in his notebook.

"Do you know if your dad's friends with someone called Rainbow Harmony?" DI Adams asked. "Also known as Judith Ellis?"

"Oh, sure," Daisy said. "She's the one always getting them into the messes *I* have to clean up." She straightened the crisp white cuffs of her shirt where they showed under her cardigan. "It's very irresponsible."

DI Adams managed not to glance at Collins, who was concentrating on his notebook. "Do you have any idea where Rainbow is right now?" she asked.

"No," Daisy said thoughtfully. "I did see her van last night, though. I was trying to sort out some orders, and it went through the square."

"Do you remember when?"

"Six-ish, I suppose. Why? She hasn't done anything really foolish, has she? I don't want my dad mixed up in things."

DI Adams made a vaguely reassuring noise as she scribbled in her own notebook. That would fit with when the W.I. had been terrorising the pub, and therefore when the body had turned up. "I'm sure he's fine. Can you get in touch with him and Harriet? We need to speak to them too – they're not in any trouble at this point, though."

"At this point," Daisy said with a sigh, taking a phone from the pocket of her trousers "Honestly, one doesn't expect to have to babysit one's father. Or his *girlfriend*."

"I suppose one doesn't," DI Adams said.

Daisy dialled, waited a moment, then said, "Morning, Dad. Are you coming by the shop today? Only I can't get into the safe. I need the emergency key from Harriet." She listened, then said, "Well, yes, tell her I do need to, because all the change is in there. Okay. Okay, see you then."

She hung up and looked at the inspectors. "They're coming by in about an hour."

"Right," DI Adams said. "Thank you."

"No problems. If I'd told him the police were around they'd have vanished for another six months. And I really need Harriet to show me how her accounting system works. It makes *no* sense." She hesitated. "I always knew Rainbow was going to get him into trouble. She *seems* so nice, but she's very over the top about things."

DI Adams and Collins looked at each other, then DI Adams said, "Well. We'll wait for Harriet and your dad, then."

"I'll put the kettle on," Daisy said, then looked past the inspectors as the door snicked open. "Oh. Hello. We're not open yet."

DI Adams turned around, already knowing who she'd see.

"Hello, inspectors," Alice said, smiling at them both. "Fancy meeting you here."

"Fancy," DI Adams said.

9

MIRIAM

Miriam gave Colin a little wave, trying not to make eye contact with DI Adams. "Hello, dear."

"Hello, Aunty Miriam," he said. "What're you doing here?"

"I wonder," DI Adams said. Her normally carefully secured hair had sprung a few stray curls, and her voice had an unfamiliar rasp to it that suggested she'd either taken up smoking or had had very little sleep. Miriam could smell lavender from across the shop, though, so at least the farmyard scent had been drowned out somewhat.

"Are you looking for Harriet?" the young woman behind the counter asked. She had a round, open face, and was dressed so tidily that Miriam took her orange hat off hurriedly. She patted her hair and had a sneaking feeling that taking the hat off hadn't actually improved matters.

"Not Harriet," Alice said. "But has Rainbow been around at all?"

The young woman glanced at DI Adams, then said, "Not for a bit. I have a few messages for her, but that's all."

DI Adams folded her arms as she examined Alice and Miriam. "This seems quite a lot like you're not following explicit instructions I gave you last night."

Colin snorted, and the young woman gave him a curious look. "Do you need a tissue?"

"No," he said, then added, "Sorry."

DI Adams ignored the exchange. "You're not meant to be getting yourself involved in anything," she said, and Miriam looked at the books on the coffee table so that she didn't have to meet the inspector's gaze.

"We've merely popped into the bookshop to see if anyone knows where Rainbow is," Alice said. "You did say that you wanted to know, so it seemed like a reasonable step to take."

It was the exact same reasoning she'd used to get Miriam to agree to come down here, and Miriam was currently regretting that agreement. It was bad enough that they were, once again, walking a very fine line when it came to DI Adams' instructions, but she was also still embarrassed every time she thought about how rude she'd been the night before. She should *not* have had any paracetamol, and especially not when everything had already been so stressful. It had been a very poor decision.

"Well, if it's all in hand," Miriam said, looking at Alice hopefully. Alice just looked back at her, eyebrows raised. "We could go?"

"You can stay right there," DI Adams said. "Daisy here has called Harriet, and she's coming by soon. She might be more likely to talk to you two than us."

"Hang about," Colin said. "That's my aunty. Don't be putting her in the middle of your investigation."

"I'll be right here," DI Adams said. "I'll be able to hear everything."

"She didn't want to talk to us last night," Miriam mumbled.

"She might have if Tom hadn't been there," Alice said. "He was quite hostile, but Harriet and Simon were fine." She looked at Miriam. "We can at least try."

"Aunty Miriam?" Colin said. "You don't have to."

Miriam very much wanted not to, but both Alice and DI Adams were looking at her expectantly, and she could still feel the weight of the inspector's disappointment from last night, which had been *horrible*. Plus she was feeling far too hot, yet again. She unzipped her jacket and pulled it off, fanning her face with one hand. "Why is Rainbow always such a *bother?* Nothing's ever easy with her."

"I'm glad it's not just me," Daisy said, sounding as if she were mostly talking to herself, but when Miriam looked at her, the young woman was watching her almost as intently as DI Adams.

No one else said anything, and Miriam frowned. "*Alright.* Fine. We'll wait for Harriet."

"Well done, Miriam," Alice said.

Miriam didn't feel it was well done at all, and she had a headache starting in her sinuses, but she wasn't going to have any more paracetamol. She didn't dare.

THERE FOLLOWED A VERY strained hour in the bookshop. After a muttered conversation with DI Adams, Colin went outside to watch for Harriet's arrival, just in case Rainbow was with her but didn't come in. DI Adams vanished down one of the aisles, and when Miriam peeked around the shelves she saw the inspector sitting on the floor with her head leaning against a shelf, snoring softly. Her hand appeared to be hovering above her lap, so evidently the invisible dog had made himself comfortable too.

The shop was very quiet, no music playing, and it was still too early for much activity in the square. Alice browsed the non-fiction sections, amassing a little stack of books that she carried to one of the chairs tucked among the shelves and sat down to read. Daisy made tea, then returned to the computer, and the place fell deeper and deeper into dusty, sleepy silence. Miriam had the absurd notion that they'd all been caught in a moment of time, like insects preserved in amber, and would be held here forever. She could hear the deep-sea roar of silence in her ears, and even the click of her throat as she swallowed her tea was impossibly loud. She concentrated on breathing as quietly as she could, but finally gave up and wandered over to the counter.

"Hello," she said, and Daisy gave her a puzzled look.

"Hello," she said. "Do you want another tea or something?"

"No, no. How are you finding it, then? The bookshop?"

Daisy looked around at the cluttered shelves. "It's alright," she said, and went back to the ancient computer. There were glittery fairy stickers on its casing that looked nothing like the faeries Miriam had encountered.

"Oh, good. Um … did you do anything fun this summer?"

"I worked here."

"No nice trips?"

"No." Daisy frowned at the screen. "In what world is vegan cheese a business expense?

"Maybe it was for sandwiches," Miriam suggested.

"We've no license for sandwiches. And when it comes to staff meals, tea and biscuits are reasonable, if a bit of a stretch for a place this size. But tell me anywhere that provides *vegan cheese* for staff."

"Um," Miriam said. "Did you study accounting at uni?"

"Art history," Daisy said, and pointed at the screen. "*Socks.* That's a receipt for *socks*. Does she think no one's going to look at this stuff? Honestly, I don't know how she's kept the place running." Her voice was clear, carrying through the silent shop. "She's not taking enough money for it to make any sort of sense that I can see. Does she have another income?"

"Not that I know of," Miriam said. "People give her books, though, so she wouldn't have to buy many."

"The problem is more she doesn't sell any. Where's the rent coming from?"

Miriam didn't have any answer to that, so she just made a sympathetic noise then retreated to a chair by the window. She did her own accounts for her tarot and herbalism business, and she had no desire to think about them too much. And socks *could* be business equipment. One had to keep one's feet warm, after all.

Harriet arrived silently, emerging from a back door tucked in the corner behind the counter with a pot of oat yoghurt in one hand and a spoon in the other. She was still wearing her ski suit, but had taken her hat off to reveal two heavy plaits of white-blonde hair.

"Hello, Daisy, love."

"Hello, Harriet," Daisy said, looking up from the computer. "Your accounts are a complete mess, you know."

"I have a system," Harriet said, waving vaguely, and noticed Miriam and Alice in the chairs. "You two again?"

"We thought you might be a little freer to talk here," Alice said, setting her books down and getting up.

"What, so you can pass information on to your little police buddies?" Harriet pointed her spoon at Miriam. "I know Colin's your nephew!"

"He's Rainbow's son," Miriam said, joining Alice by the counter. "And you trust *her*."

"She's not all respectable citizen like you," Harriet said, managing to make *respectable citizen* sound like a horrifying skin condition that likely involved oozing sores. Miriam looked down at her green velvet skirt, brown woollen tights, and red leaf-motif boots, then at Alice.

"I imagine it's all a matter of degrees," Alice said, and looked at Harriet. "We're trying to help. Someone left a body outside the village hall last night—"

"A *body?*" Daisy and Harriet said together. Harriet put an arm around Daisy's shoulder, pulling her close as if to protect her from the very idea, and Daisy leaned away, her eyes on one of Harriet's plaits and her nose wrinkled.

"Whose body?" Daisy asked. "What happened to him?"

"We don't know," Alice said. "But—"

"Then why are you looking for Rainbow?" Harriet asked, her voice rising. "Just because she chooses not to be tied to your conventional way of living—"

"Someone saw her," Miriam said, her face hot. She wasn't sure if it was being accused of being conventional *and* respectable in the space of five minutes, or the lingering effects of the cold, but she was *very* tired of this. "And we're only trying to help. We know she hasn't done anything, but she might have *seen* something. And that poor man! Just *left* there in a barrow! It's not right."

Alice put a hand on her arm, just lightly, and smiled at her, then looked at Harriet. "As you can see, we're very upset. And the sooner we can make sure Rainbow didn't see anything—"

"Or take our guy," Miriam added. "That wasn't right, either. The donation tin was with it."

"Yes," Alice started, and Harriet interrupted her.

"Again with the donation tin," she said, scowling. "We'd *never* do that!"

"We thought it might have been an accident," Miriam said. "That you needed the barrow for the herons or something."

"Not us," Harriet said, releasing Daisy, who straightened her cardigan carefully. "Nothing to do with donation tins, guys *or* bodies, and you can tell Colin that, too." She peeled the top off her yoghurt pot, dismissing them.

"We'd still like to talk to Rainbow," Alice said.

"You can *like* all you want," Harriet said, and at that moment Simon burst through the door behind her, his hat off and his hair dishevelled.

"*Police brutality!*" he shouted, waving wildly behind him. "Bloody pigs! This is a *trap!*"

"*What?*" Harriet yelped, and rounded on Daisy, who flattened herself to the wall, hands raised.

"They asked me to! And it's Rainbow they want, not you!"

"We need to go!" Simon grabbed Harriet's arm, pulling her toward the door, and DI Adams emerged from the aisle of books, her hands out in a placating gesture. Harriet gave a little shriek and hurled the pot of yoghurt at her, then turned to flee. DI Adams ducked the pot and broke into a run, swerving neatly around the counter and stepping to block Harriet's path. Simon gave a yelp of alarm and tried to push DI Adams away, and Daisy grabbed his arm, shouting, "Don't! They're *police!*"

Alice pulled Miriam back, away from the counter, as Colin barrelled through the door behind it. He pulled Simon away and pinned him lightly against the wall, while DI Adams managed to get the spoon off Harriet, who was laying about with it wildly.

"*Pigs!*" Simon shrieked. "You've got no grounds for this!"

"You threw a pie at me," Colin said, wiping some grey-ish meat off the front of his jacket.

"You were harassing me!"

"I said *excuse me sir,* and you threw a pie at me."

"Is that meat?" Harriet asked, sniffing curiously. "That's meat. *Simon!*"

"That's really not important right now," he said, not looking at her.

"You said you were vegan!"

"Neither of you are, going by all those scones you ate last night," Miriam said, and Alice gave a startled little chuckle.

"Well, vegetarian, at least," Harriet said, scowling at her. "We were hungry!"

"And I was hungry now," Simon said.

"There are other options, Simon."

"Enough," DI Adams said, and looked at Colin. "Any sign of your mum?"

"No, just this one." He examined Simon from close range. "You were at that protest with her in Leeds last month."

"The one against dairy farming," Harriet said. "You *liar.*"

"I can hate the industry but still enjoy the product," Simon protested. "There's plenty of people farming meat and dairy in a small-scale, sustainable way."

"Oh? And you checked that with the bakery, did you?"

"*Enough,*" DI Adams said again.

"Says the oppressor," Simon snapped.

"Yep, that's me. Now why don't you tell us where Rainbow is before I get *really* oppressive?"

"Never," Harriet said.

"Well," Simon started, and Harriet twisted in DI Adams' grip, kicking him. "*Ow!* I mean, what she said. We don't sell out our comrades."

Daisy rolled her eyes so hard that Miriam thought her own might start watering in sympathy. "You could ask Barry," the young woman said. "He's in hospital, so you can find him easily enough."

"*Daisy!*" Harriet clutched her chest. "How *could* you? How did you even know? You weren't—" She stopped abruptly. "How *did* you know?"

"Dad told me," Daisy said. "And they're *police*. It's withholding evidence if I don't tell them."

Harriet glared at Simon. "She's *your* daughter."

"I know," he said, rubbing a hand over his hair. "Kids today."

"What hospital?" DI Adams asked. "When?"

Daisy looked at her father, and when he didn't answer she shrugged. "He just said Barry hurt his hand or something last night and Rainbow took him to the hospital. She'll have to pick him up again, won't she?"

DI Adams nodded. "Well done. I'm glad *someone* around here is cooperative." She pointed at Alice and Miriam. "Stay," she added, and headed for the door, Colin jogging after her.

There was silence for a moment, then Harriet said to Daisy again, "How *could* you?"

"They're trying to solve a murder," Daisy said. "They're not going to care if Rainbow's protesting something."

"We have to warn her," Harriet started, then stopped again, tugging on her plait. "I mean, if we knew where she was, of course."

"If we did know, we should tell the police rather than get ourselves arrested," Daisy pointed out.

Harriet frowned at her. "I'm very disappointed in you."

"Oh no," Daisy said.

"*Daisy*," Simon said. "Don't be rude." He turned to Harriet. "She's right, though. If Rainbow's innocent, she'll be fine."

"I'm going to find her," Harriet said. "I'm not letting her take the fall for this. Rainbow would *never*."

"Alright," Simon said, taking Harriet's hand. "If that's what you want. I'll come with you."

"Wait," Daisy said. "Harriet, I'm sorry. I shouldn't've been rude. But let the police take care of Rainbow. I don't want you two getting dragged into it."

Harriet shook her head. "If Rainbow's in it, we're all in it. That's how it works."

"Dad," Daisy said, her tone pleading.

"We have to go," he said, giving her a quick kiss on the cheek. "We'll be back."

Daisy looked at Harriet. "At least tell me how to get into the safe. The combination won't work and I can't get the change out."

Harriet raised her hands. "I don't know. It's old, and it jams up sometimes. There's a master key somewhere."

"But *where?*"

"Somewhere! Check the kitchen drawers."

"*Which* drawers?" Daisy's cheeks were pinker than they had been even when the DIs had been tussling with Simon and Harriet, and Miriam had the passing thought that she really was passionate about accounts and might have missed her calling.

Harriet ignored her and looked at Simon. "I still can't believe you ate a pie."

"I really like them," he mumbled. "Should we find the safe key before we leave?"

"There's no time," Harriet said, already heading for the door.

"Harriet," Daisy started.

"Oh, just use your eyes, Daisy." Harriet vanished, Simon jogging after her, and Daisy followed. Miriam could hear her asking about the key again, then the back door slammed and the shop fell silent. A moment later Daisy reappeared, looking put out.

"*Do* you know where Rainbow is?" Alice asked. "She's Miriam's sister. She'd rather like to know."

Miriam nodded unhappily. She *would* rather like to know. Everything was shaping up to Rainbow being framed for the body in the barrow, and there had to be someone else involved. There *had* to be. But Rainbow was never going to help herself by hiding from the police. Maybe if Miriam could just speak to her, she might listen. Maybe.

"I don't," Daisy said. "And I hope my dad doesn't either. I don't want him dragged into some murder investigation. The protests are bad enough. And assuming Rainbow's not a murderer, I'm sure it'll all be fine. The police know what they're doing."

Alice and Miriam exchanged glances. Daisy was so *sure*. And very trusting of the police, which Miriam found most odd. She didn't think she'd ever been that trusting of the police, except when it came to Colin. The younger generation always seemed to oppose the generation before, though, so perhaps this was just part of that.

She wondered where Rainbow might go, if it wasn't back to Maddie's or out to the bunker. What other place might be a haven. Miriam thought about it for a moment, then said, "Thank you so much, Daisy. We should go, Alice."

Alice looked at her, then nodded. "Yes, we should. Are you alright here, Daisy?"

"Yes," the young woman said, looking around. "I think I can manage to clean up a yoghurt pot before the flood of two or three customers turn up."

"Oh. Well, good luck," Miriam said, for want of anything better to say, then headed for the door. A moment later they were out in the chill of the day, a sneaky wind biting her legs even through the heavy wool of her tights.

"Well?" Alice asked.

"I might know where she is."

"Not at the hospital, I take it?"

"Not if she's worried about the police. Poor Barry, though! We should really check on him."

"We can do that later," Alice said. "Do you want to call Colin?"

"No," Miriam said. "DI Adams looks very twitchy. I thought she was going to do something terrible with that spoon."

"She does look as if she could use some sleep," Alice agreed. "So where are we going?"

"Not far," Miriam said, twisting her fingers together.

Alice smiled, and Miriam wasn't sure if she liked the approval in it at all. Things seemed to be coming to a bad pass if she was withholding information from her own nephew and Alice was being *approving* at her.

"Come along, then." Alice led the way to her car where it waited patiently in one of the parking spots in the centre of the square, and

Miriam followed, wondering if one could rebel against oneself. She seemed to be acting most oddly at the moment, and today she couldn't even blame the paracetamol.

She was just getting in when Alice said, "Harriet doesn't seem to be making much progress."

Miriam looked up as she buckled her seatbelt and saw Simon and Harriet standing near the bakery. Harriet had a thumb out, smiling hopefully at the few cars that were passing, and Simon was talking to her, his entire body shaped into a plea. "Does anyone pick up hitch-hikers these days?"

"Only if they know them, I imagine." Alice pulled out, taking a route out of the square on the opposite side to the bakery.

They didn't talk until they were on the road out of town, houses cut off behind them by the wash of soft green fields and their hems of drystone walls. Then a deep voice said from the back seats, "You were rather a long time. What did you find out?"

"That Rainbow is missing," Miriam said, looking into the back at Beaufort and Mortimer, still half-hidden by the old blanket Alice had laid over them. "And Harriet insists the guy was nothing to do with them, which I do believe."

"But you have a plan?" Beaufort asked.

"I don't know," Miriam admitted. "But we'll find out soon."

"So where *are* we going, Miriam?" Alice asked. "You're being most mysterious."

Miriam sighed. "To the old house."

Alice looked at her. "Your family home?"

"Our great-aunt's. It's a ruin now, really – she wouldn't let anyone but her do any work on it, and she owed so much money that the bank took it back when she died. She didn't have any children herself, but we used to go there some summers if Mum and Dad were too busy. It was always a bit strange, and she could be very odd, but I liked it. She's the one that taught me how to do the tinctures and things. Rainbow was furious when the bank took it, and squatted there for quite a while. I don't even know who owns it now, if anyone. But that's where she'll go if she's stuck. I'm sure of it."

"And you didn't tell Colin this?" Beaufort asked, eyeing Miriam.

"He already had a lead," Miriam said, her cheeks suddenly too hot. "And she's my *sister*."

"Well done," Beaufort said. "I'm very impressed."

Miriam leaned into the back and looked at Mortimer. He stared back at her, then gave a not-very-reassuring smile. "I'm sure you know best," he said, in a tone that suggested he wasn't very sure at all.

10

ALICE

The drive to Miriam's great-aunt's house took less than half an hour, but it was down a curious maze of unfamiliar, narrow roads that Alice had never encountered before. It never failed to astonish her, after so many years of living here, how there could still be places that remained so quietly and resolutely invisible. The lawless, simple magic of hills and fells and dales and old, deep valleys, she supposed.

She parked in front of a high stone wall, pulling off the tight little lane as well as she could. There wasn't much room – where there had probably once been wooden gates there was now temporary fencing which had been in place long enough to sprout a hedge of brambles that encroached eagerly on the road. Miriam had already got out, and was making a lot of hand signals that Alice assumed were meant to communicate how close to the wall the passenger side was, but which mostly looked like Miriam was fending off an attack of sandflies.

She switched off the engine and got out, then opened the back of the little SUV for the dragons. Across the road was a low drystone wall with a jumbled field of rock and grass beyond it, the sort of land that was fine for sheep but too rough and weathered for much else. On this side the wall that framed the gate was solid and tall, pinning back a tangle of trees that leaned hungrily toward the road, searching for space, and she could see very little beyond the fencing. They'd left the last cluster of houses ten minutes behind them, a strange, silent jumble of hard walls and small windows, turned jealously away from the road and guarding its secrets. There was no sound of traffic, not even the ever-present bleating of sheep, just the chatter of birds and the whisper of wind in the trees. It seemed a very long way from Toot Hansell.

"Ooh, that's better," Beaufort said, ambling into the middle of the road and shaking his wings out. "It's not the most comfortable method of travel."

"It is the most unobtrusive, though," Alice said, untangling the blanket from Mortimer's spinal ridge and folding it up.

"Are we alright here?" Mortimer asked. Even once they'd left Toot Hansell and found quieter roads he'd stayed mostly hidden under the blanket. Alice wondered if she should introduce him to paracetamol. It really had done Miriam a world of good.

"There's no one around," Miriam said. She was looking at the tops of the trees beyond the gates with a resigned expression on her face. "Not out here, anyway."

Alice walked out into the road and followed Miriam's gaze. A small trail of smoke was being dragged apart by the wind, coming from deeper in the trees. "Is that the house?" she asked.

"I think so."

"Well, then." She examined Miriam. The younger woman looked a little pale, and was chewing on her bottom lip. "I'm sure we can clear all this up as soon as we talk to Rainbow."

Miriam looked at her. "What if we don't? What if she actually *did* do something? I mean, not deliberately, but maybe by accident? I should have told Colin. Why didn't I tell Colin?" She scrabbled in her coat pocket, fishing out her phone, then gave a little whimper of frustration. "No signal. Of *course* there's no signal. No one even lives out here!"

Alice nodded thoughtfully. "Do you think your sister could murder someone, Miriam?"

"No," she said immediately, then sighed. "Or, maybe? I don't know. If they were the head of an oil company she might."

Alice wondered if the inspectors had identified the body yet. It had certainly been a well-dressed corpse, what with the loafers and the cravat. And most people didn't bother with such things as monogrammed pyjamas anymore. Or maybe it was one of those things which had come back in an ironic way she wasn't aware of yet. She didn't think she approved of either the original or an ironic revival. No one needed their initials on anything except legal documents. Not once one was past the stage of losing one's clothes at school, anyway.

Aloud, she said, "Well, as neither of us is the head of an oil company we should be perfectly safe. Come on. We'll go and see what she has to say for herself."

"I suppose it's the only thing to do," Miriam said, in tones that indicated she thought they were about to hand out a prison sentence themselves. "Although—" She grabbed Alice's arm and stared at her with wide eyes. "What if she's being forced to act against her will? The guy and the note and all that? And someone else is holding her here, just waiting for us to come along?"

"I rather doubt we're the target of such an elaborate scheme," Alice said.

"Besides, we shall be right behind you," Beaufort said. "It'll be perfectly safe."

Miriam gave him a dubious look. "What about Thompson? We still haven't heard anything from him. He didn't even tell us that Harriet and Simon had left."

"That is odd," Alice agreed, pushing down a twist of unease in her stomach and keeping her voice level. "But he is a cat. They seem quite fickle."

"I probably wouldn't say that to his face," Beaufort said. "But yes."

Alice gently shook Miriam's grip off and tucked her hands into her pockets. "There really is only one way to get to the bottom of this, and that's to talk to your sister. So how do we get in?"

Miriam sighed so deeply that Alice thought she could actually see the air reverberating around her, then said, "Well, there's no getting through here, but there are other ways into the woods. Plus if Rainbow's been using it she'll have to have made a bit of a path. We'll just have to poke around a little."

"Off we go, then."

&

IT DIDN'T TAKE them long to find it. Mortimer was the one who sniffed it out, muttering that someone else was evidently using hemp cream, because the scent of it was all over one patch of wall. Alice had an idea that it was likely not hemp he was smelling, but she didn't point that out, just joined him as he carefully hooked his talons into a pallet, liberally decorated with old branches, that was leaning against the high wall. He lifted it out of position to reveal a crumbled section of wall, and beyond it a faint trail that had been trodden into the long grass and rough ground.

"Well spotted," Alice said.

"Can you smell anything else, lad?" Beaufort asked. "All I've got is a whiff of anxiety and that cream that makes me sneeze."

"Tiger Balm," Miriam said. "Someone's got muscle aches." She said it as if it were a dire indictment, and Alice gave her a curious look.

"Is that so bad?"

"Rainbow doesn't like Tiger Balm. She always said it was too synthetic and arnica was better."

"Maybe someone else is here with her, then."

"Or maybe she's gone rogue," Miriam whispered.

"I hardly think the use of Tiger Balm indicates a sudden descent into immorality."

"She *really* hated Tiger Balm."

Alice nodded. "Well, we shall be careful."

"We should," Mortimer said. "They're more than anxious. They're angry, and scared, and lots of other things as well." He shivered, his scales rippling softly and deepening to a darker grey. "There's been more people through than just Rainbow. And it's hard to tell them all apart."

"That's not surprising, if they've been using this place as a camp," Alice said.

"I'm not sure she would," Miriam said. "It's … well, it's always been special to her. She thought it was one last wild place, you know. The woods."

"Well, I imagine that if she's hiding out someone will have dropped her off," Alice said. "And that may be who Mortimer is smelling. But we shall soon see." She stepped over the remnants of the wall and set off down the path, using her cane to help her over the rougher bits. Although it was mostly to have it handy in case Rainbow really wasn't the only person here.

The path led them in a gentle meander into what had probably once been a fruit orchard, petering out in the patchy grass that coated the ground between the heavy, gnarled trunks of well-spaced trees. Fallen apples and pears were slowly being reclaimed by the earth, and the scent of their rot filled the air with a sweet, not unpleasant tang. Some rabbits scattered in alarm, and birds watched them pass from the branches, tiny eyes bright and sharp.

"I don't much like them," Miriam said. "They're paying too much attention."

"They're birds, Miriam," Alice said. "They're just making sure we're not going to eat them."

Miriam shook her head, hugging her arms around her body. "I don't like it. Aunty T's place never felt like this. This is *creepy*."

"It is," Mortimer said. He was still the same deep grey as the road outside, and looked like a boulder on the move. "Something doesn't feel right here."

"Nonsense," Beaufort said, before Alice could. "You're both letting your heads get the better of you. It's just an old place that's lost its guardian. It's sad and a bit grumpy, but that's all."

Alice wondered if that was actually helpful, but it stopped Miriam and Mortimer complaining, so it was something.

But even Alice had to agree, as they emerged from the trees, that the house itself *was* a little creepy. It had probably once been surrounded by rough, wildflower-dotted lawns and capacious garden beds overrun with sturdy vegetables, the sort of place that had never been manicured but was practical and easy to care for, and where everything had its place. A wooden shed off to the left had collapsed into a pile of shattered timber, overgrown with weeds and nettles, and a small stone building to the right that had probably once been an outhouse, by its shape, was just a crumbling, roof-less shell. Dandelions nodded in its empty doorway. Ahead of them, the house squatted fiercely over its secrets, stone walls half-swallowed by old ivy and its small windows turned to empty, glaring sockets. The roof sagged dangerously, and patches of slate tiles had vanished, leaving behind gaping holes. It looked as though some large beast had been taking bites from it.

Oddly, the door was whole and closed, and a torn, laminated sheet of paper pinned to it still held a few traces of ink. No doubt it was a condemnation, or no trespassing sign, or something similar.

"Oh," Miriam said softly. "It *is* sad."

Alice made a small noise of agreement. Such things are always sad, places that still existed as whole and full of life in one's memory revealed to be broken and unmagical things when encountered in the world. Time takes away the truth of a place, she thought. Because this wasn't the truth of this old house. Not this rotting shell. The truth was wild girls racing barefoot through long grasses, and apples eaten too green and tart as lightning storms, and scabbed knees from climbing trees and muddy clothes from damming streams, and watching for shooting stars in the short summer nights, and a freedom that seemed as if it should stretch on forever. She reached out and put her hand on Miriam's arm, and Miriam gave her a startled look. She couldn't think of what to say, so she said nothing, and after a moment Miriam smiled at her.

"There's no one been in this way," Beaufort said, inspecting the front door. "Shall we carry on around?"

"I think you two should probably be a little circumspect," Alice said. "If Barry's here he'll certainly see you, and while Rainbow is *aware* that there are magical creatures about after the farmhouse debacle last summer, we really don't want to have to spend a lot of time explaining things."

"*Debacle*," Miriam said. "You mean when we mounted a daring rescue mission after your not-dead husband kidnapped you?"

Alice looked at her. "Have you been at the paracetamol again, dear?"

Miriam sighed. "I think it's the lingering effects of the cold."

"Ah. I was going to say, you should take them more often," Alice said, and gave her arm a final squeeze before releasing her and heading for the corner of the house.

The combination of old vegetable plots run to rot and creeping ivy and tangled weeds meant that there wasn't much indication of a path, but Alice picked her way over the uneven ground, using her cane to test for loose rocks, and checking in the windows as she went. There weren't a lot of them – old houses tended to keep them small and scarce to keep as much of the heat in as possible in the winters. These were all glass-less and empty, revealing nothing beyond them but empty rooms with dusty, leaf-strewn floors and cobwebs for curtains.

But as she approached the back corner of the house she caught a whiff of woodsmoke and stopped, looking at Beaufort, who had been padding next to her, navigating the rough terrain with considerably more ease than she was. He raised his eyebrow ridges, and she pointed to the cover of the trees, frowning slightly. He wrinkled his snout, giving her an alarming glimpse of worn but impressively large yellow teeth, then slipped away, his scales taking on multi-hued greens and browns and greys that made even her dragon-ready eyes a little confused. Mortimer followed, and then there was just her and Miriam, standing in the ruins of the crumbling, long-deserted garden and smelling the remnants of someone's campfire.

"What if it's not Rainbow?" Miriam whispered. "What if it's someone else? We didn't see her van or anything."

"Then we are merely reliving some childhood memories," Alice said. "They'll have no right to be here either, you know."

"Wait a moment," Miriam said, and hurried back the way they'd come. Alice waited, resisting the urge to tell her to hurry up, but a moment later she was back, hefting a large branch over her shoulder with some difficulty. "Ready."

Alice decided not to tell her that there was a spider crawling off the branch onto her hair, and instead edged quietly around the house into a back yard that was considerably clearer than the front, a patio of broken flagstones banishing the weeds to their edges and cracks. The back door was open, and a woman leaned in it, weighed down by a heavy outdoors coat and with her hands wrapped around a metal mug. Her curly, grey-streaked hair was roughly tamed into a short plait, and her face was sprinkled with freckles and the memories of sun. She jerked upright as she caught sight of Alice, and yelped as tea slopped out of the mug onto her fingers.

"Bloody *hell*— What're you doing here?"

"Rainbow!" Miriam exclaimed, hurrying past Alice. "There you are! What on *earth* is going on?"

Rainbow looked from Miriam to Alice, and sighed, her shoulders slumping. "Miriam. I seem to be in a bit of a pickle, love."

"That's understating things," Miriam said. "You were seen near the village hall, and then there was a *body*, and the stolen guy and the donation tin— What are you *thinking?*"

Rainbow frowned. "I didn't steal any donation tin. I can't believe you think I would!"

"It was in with the guy," Miriam insisted. "When you took the barrow."

"Oh," Rainbow said. "Well, I just needed the barrow. I left the guy by the post box, so maybe the tin's still with him."

They stared at each other for a long moment, then Miriam said, "Why did you need the barrow?" Her face was very pale.

"I ... I didn't do it," Rainbow said, her knuckles white on the mug. "The body. I absolutely did *not* kill anyone. I wouldn't. I *couldn't.*"

"But did you leave it at the hall?" Alice asked.

Rainbow inclined her head, a wordless admission.

"*Why? Why* were you at the hall with *a dead body?* What did you *do?*" Miriam demanded, and Rainbow scowled at her.

"What did I *do?* Seriously? You actually think I killed him?"

"Well, maybe he was mistreating seals or something!"

"I still wouldn't kill anyone!"

"You brought us the body," Alice said. "You left the note for *us.*"

Rainbow bit her lip, then nodded.

"Where did it come from?" Miriam asked.

"I don't know." Rainbow's voice was low. "I really don't. It was just … it was in my van. I went to the hospital to drop off Barry because he somehow managed to break his bloody hand, and when I got back to the van it was just *there.* Someone put it there, and I don't know who, or how, and I didn't know what to do, and I couldn't go to the police because they're *police,* and—"

"You could've gone to Colin," Miriam said. "He'd have sorted it out."

She shook her head. "He's my son. It's a conflict of interests. And I don't trust any of them, anyway, even him. But you lot are always poking around in things. I thought you could deal with it."

"*With a dead body?*" Miriam's voice had become uncomfortably high, and Alice glanced across at the trees, expecting to see the dragons rushing to the rescue. They weren't visible, though, and she looked back at Rainbow.

"You have to go to the police now," she said. "It's only making things worse, not doing so."

"No. I can't."

"Why not?" Miriam demanded. "You haven't done anything *that* bad. Just protests and so on."

Rainbow screwed up her face, then shook her head. "No. They'll pin it on me. And there's … other stuff going on that I need to figure out."

"What other stuff?" Alice asked.

Rainbow hesitated, examining the two women.

"If you want us to help you, you need to tell us what's happening," Alice said, keeping her tone level.

Rainbow tapped her fingers on her mug, then apparently came to a decision. "Alright. That's fair." She sighed. "I think my group's compromised. There's been thefts."

"Herons?" Miriam asked, and Rainbow frowned at her.

"The herons were *liberated,* not stolen. No, this is other stuff. Bits of art and things going missing while we're getting the animals out. It's not what we're about, and the damn police'll pin it all on me, see if they don't."

"And you think the same people who're doing that are responsible for the body?" Alice asked.

Rainbow nodded. "Has to be. All about bringing me down and undermining the cause, isn't it?"

Alice thought a dead body indicated something rather more serious than undermining the cause, but all she said was, "Do you have any leads?"

"I'm figuring it out. Just keep the police off my back and deal with the body, okay?"

"*How—*" Miriam started, and at that moment there was the unmistakable sound of a fist on the door at the front of the house.

"Police," a familiar voice shouted. "Open up."

"What— Was this you?" Rainbow said, her face suddenly as white as her knuckles had been. "Did you *bring* them here?"

"No," Alice said, then ducked as Rainbow hurled her mug of tea at them. Miriam swung the branch with admirable accuracy and sent the mug flying back toward her sister, but Rainbow was already bolting down the garden, dodging rocks and roots and undergrowth.

"*Judith!*" Miriam shouted, and raced after her.

Alice looked at the broken ground and at her cane, then turned to face DI Adams as she came around the side of the house.

"Which way?" the DI asked, and Alice pointed wordlessly. The inspector took off at a run, and a moment later Colin appeared around the opposite corner of the cottage.

"Thought that was your car out front," he said.

Alice decided to take it as a compliment regarding their investigative abilities rather than the disapproval it was evidently intended to be.

11

MORTIMER

M ortimer wasn't quite sure why they were chasing Rainbow. Alice had specifically told them to keep a low profile, and here they were racing after Miriam's fleeing sister, and Beaufort ... Beaufort took one almost casual bound and latched a talon into the hood of Rainbow's jacket, bringing her to a violent stop. She yelped as she lost her footing and fell back, crashing into the High Lord and sliding to the ground as he released her. She rolled over, panting, and stared up at him.

"What—"

"Rainbow!" Miriam sprinted toward them, her branch abandoned and her hair dishevelled. "Why are you *running?* You're making things worse!"

"Because someone is *framing* me, Miriam! Can't you see that? If the police catch me then they'll definitely charge me, and that body was in my van. Anyone who did that is sure to have figured out how to make it really look like I did it, and probably the thefts too." Rainbow shot another look at the dragons, but it was a panicky, confused thing, and Mortimer supposed that she was in too much fright over running from the police to have much concern left for dragons. "You have to let me go."

Miriam hesitated, and DI Adams shouted from the direction of the house, "Judith! We just want to talk!"

Mortimer caught a flash of movement to the side, and there was the dandy, moving light-footed and easy through the undergrowth, his grey dreadlocks obscuring his eyes and his tongue rolling pink and long between his white teeth. Miriam shivered as if she felt the creature, even if she couldn't see it, and hissed. "Alright! Go! Just hurry up about it."

Rainbow didn't hesitate. She rolled to her feet and sprinted off, her head down and one arm up to protect her face from the lash of the tall weeds.

"Miriam," Beaufort started, then both dragons jumped as Miriam fell to the ground and grabbed her leg.

"*Ooooh!*" she wailed. "I think I sprained my ankle! Or broke it! I might've broken it!"

DI Adams dodged past a tree and came to a stumbling stop next to Miriam. "Which way did she go?"

"I don't know! She pushed me over, and *ohhhh* my ankle!"

The inspector looked at her with a curious expression, then at the dragons. "*Which way?*"

Beaufort *hmm*ed, and Mortimer dug his talons into the ground beneath him. He *wanted* to help, but this was Miriam's sister, and if she wasn't going to say anything, he wasn't either, even if he could feel his tail tightening in alarm so fiercely it was almost painful.

DI Adams made an irritated sound, then shouted, "Collins! Come and help your aunt." Then she was gone, weaving through the tangled undergrowth as well as she could and whistling for the dandy as she went.

"Are you alright?" Mortimer asked Miriam.

"Yes," she started, and was interrupted by Colin, crashing toward them through the overgrown garden.

"Aunty Miriam? Are you hurt?" Colin crouched next to her with an unhappy expression on his face, and Mortimer could smell deep orange threads of worry twisting around him in the still air, littering the place with the scent of broken flowers.

"Oh, yes. It might just be twisted, now I think about it," Miriam said, still clutching her leg. "It was the fright, you know."

Mortimer looked at Beaufort, who nodded. They turned away, paws soft on the treacherous ground, and padded back toward the house, keeping to the shadows and watching for more police, but there was no one else to be seen, just Alice standing on the overgrown patio with her hands in her pockets and her cane leaning against her leg.

"All clear?" Beaufort asked.

"I haven't seen anyone else," she said. "Did Rainbow get away, then?"

"DI Adams is chasing her," the High Lord said, and both he and Alice gave the house a speculative look that made Mortimer give a little yelp of horror. They looked at him.

"No," he said. "We can't. Besides—"

"Besides, there's a police officer here now, and you'll all behave," Colin said, emerging out of the cluttered garden and helping Miriam onto the patio. "You shouldn't have come here. It could have been dangerous."

"We are talking about your mother," Alice said. "And we have dragons."

"Doesn't change the facts of the case," he said, and there was a tightness in his voice that made Mortimer shift uneasily. He wondered if humans shed when they got anxious, too. Not scales, obviously, but maybe hair? Although, given how short Collins' hair was, it'd be hard to tell.

He blinked, then looked at Beaufort and whispered, "Can dragons shave their scales?"

Beaufort looked at him blankly. "Do you mean polish them? It used to be quite a thing in my youth. We'd all try to get the most reflective surface possible, then use them to dazzle each other when we were flying. And, of course, dazzling knights and making them fall off their horses was always quite entertaining." He thought about it. "Although possibly not very sensible. It was after old Guillaume made the king fall off in front of some visiting ladies that the knights started getting a bit anti-dragon. The king had to be helped up. His armour was *very* ornate."

Mortimer couldn't quite bring himself to explain that he was worried about losing scales rather than making a feature of them. It felt very anti-dragon, and not for the first time he wondered if he was really suited to life as a Cloverly dragon. He was sure there must be some less adventurous dragons out there. Maybe he'd been swapped as an egg, and somewhere a dragon who dreamed of dazzling knights and enthusiastic investigating was being forced to live a blissfully quiet life in the furthest reaches of some remote and untravelled forest, mastering the art of baked potatoes and roast pumpkins. Perhaps in Canada. He had the impression that there was a lot of remote and untravelled forest in Canada, and he experienced a moment of wistfulness, as if he were homesick for somewhere he'd never been.

"Thank you, dear," Miriam said to Colin as he guided her across the uneven paving stones. "I'm sure it'll be fine. It's an old netball injury, you know."

Colin and Alice gave matching snorts, and he said, "Netball injury, Aunty Miriam?"

"*You* don't know," she said. "Maybe I played a lot of netball at school."

"I suppose you weren't able to catch Rainbow," Alice said.

"I was … I was trying to do just that," Miriam said. "To convince her to talk to you." She nodded at Colin, and he sighed again.

"You don't have to lie to me. And as Adams is likely still chasing down my mother – a phrase I wish I'd never had to say – you need to tell me what's going on."

"She didn't do anything," Miriam said immediately. "She's being framed."

Colin rubbed a hand over his head, short hair rasping against his palm. "The evidence isn't looking good, Aunty Miriam. The barrow was wiped clean, but we got some fingerprints off one of the victim's shoes. They're a match to her."

Miriam frowned at him. "Even if she put the body in the barrow, it doesn't mean she killed him."

Colin shrugged, the movement oddly stilted. "The evidence is the evidence. And it's not my case."

"Do you have a murder weapon?" Alice asked.

"No. We're still looking for that, and Mum's van," Colin said. "I don't want to think she'd do this either, but she has been getting steadily more extreme. You know that, Aunty Miriam."

"Well, yes," Miriam admitted. "It used to be just chaining herself to the odd tree. Now it's blockading motorways and vandalising art."

"One's tactics must change as one's enemies do," Alice said, almost to herself, then smiled when Colin gave her a startled look. "It's still a long way from murder."

"Exactly," Miriam said, and frowned at her nephew. "A *long* way."

There was a flicker of movement in the corner of Mortimer's eye, and he swung his head to find the dandy standing over him, panting softly. There was the faintest glint of red visible in the region of his eyes, and Mortimer scuttled sideways until he bumped into Beaufort. The dandy examined Mortimer, then dropped a saliva-streaked ball in front of him. Mortimer stared at it. What was he expected to do with that?

"I lost her." DI Adams emerged out of the overgrown garden looking thoroughly put out. There was a leafy twig sticking out of her hair and mud on her trousers. "It's a bloody wilderness out there, and I need a *proper dog* to help me find anything." She glared at the dandy, who ignored her and nudged the ball toward Mortimer with his nose.

"Sorry," Miriam whispered.

"Yes. Glad your ankle seems to be better," she said, and Miriam promptly sat down on the ground.

"A little, yes."

"How did you end up here?" Alice asked. "What about the hospital?"

"Barry was sedated," DI Adams said shortly. "Apparently he hasn't got out of the habit of wanting to take his clothes off, and it was sedate him or restrain him, but when they tried restraining him he was *disruptive,* whatever that means. So there's no point seeing him until he's awake. But then Collins remembered this place, so we decided to swing past here instead, and who do we find?" She glared at Alice and Miriam, then at the dragons. Beaufort gave her a toothy grin, and Mortimer pushed the ball toward the dandy, who promptly rolled it back again.

"We thought she might be more willing to talk to us," Alice said. "Much as you thought of Harriet at the bookshop."

"And we thought the ladies should have some backup," Beaufort said. "Just in case there was any unpleasantness."

DI Adams scowled. "That's why none of you should be here. In case of unpleasantness."

"She didn't do it," Miriam said from the ground. "She's being set up."

DI Adams spread her hands. "That's for us to figure out. And it's made a hell of a lot harder when we can't get hold of her." She sighed, screwed her eyes shut, then added, "And *did* she talk to you?"

There was a silence, in which Alice stared at the sky and Miriam looked at her feet, and Mortimer wondered if he should volunteer the information that the body had been left in the van at the hospital. But if Miriam wasn't going to, it hardly seemed like his place. Miriam was being oddly dragonish about the whole thing, and he assumed it had to do with the fact that Rainbow was family. She'd been much the same when Alice was kidnapped, and he had noticed that humans, just like dragons, had many definitions of family, and only some of them related to whether you were hatched from the same nest.

"If I may offer some assistance," Beaufort started, and DI Adams held a hand out, the index finger up.

"I do not want assistance from any of you. In fact, after your performance just now, Miriam, I'm considering you may possibly be an accomplice."

Miriam gave an alarmed little squeak, and grabbed her leg as if it really was paining her.

"I say," Beaufort started, and DI Adams did the same hand gesture. It was surprisingly threatening, considering she was substantially slighter than even a Cloverly dragon, and could hardly arrest him.

"Collins, you're out too," she said.

"Really? Now?"

"She's your mum. You can't be on this investigation."

"I know, but I brought you here," he protested. "I—" he stopped, examining her, then shook his head and sighed. "Fine. You're right. I'll go back to the jewel thefts."

DI Adams nodded, started to say something else, then stopped again. Mortimer caught a tightening in her, a scent of burnt toast and worry, and he thought the dandy did as well. The creature picked up its ball and trotted over to flop down at her feet. DI Adams looked at him, then said, "Alice, Miriam, go home. Call off the W.I. and stay out of it."

"Of course," Alice said, with perfect sincerity.

"*No,*" DI Adams said. "Really stay out of it. If you don't I'll arrest you as accomplices. Interfering in an investigation is the least of it."

"Steady on," Colin started, and DI Adams interrupted him.

"No," she repeated, looking as if she wanted to do the hand gesture again but thinking better of it. "Just get everyone packed off, will you?"

He sighed, and raised his hands. "Alright. Come on you two." He held a hand out to help Miriam off the ground.

"*Everyone,*" DI Adams said, looking at the dragons.

"We can fly," Beaufort pointed out.

"Not in the middle of the day over my crime scene you can't. There's not going to be another bloody Yorkshire Beast drama on top of everything else."

"Come on," Colin said. "Adams is right. None of us should be here." He glanced at Adams and said, "I'll get everyone off the property, but we'll have to leave to call this in. There's no signal."

"Of course there isn't," she muttered, and turned to stare at the house as Colin herded Alice and Miriam away. Beaufort turned to follow, and Mortimer scuttled after them, thinking that DI Adams must be getting even more scary than she had been previously if Beaufort was going to listen.

They made it to the front corner of the house before Beaufort stopped. Colin hadn't looked back, and the High Lord lifted his chin toward the window above them. Mortimer shook his head violently. The High Lord tipped his own head slightly, then jumped up and scrambled through the window somewhat inelegantly, his scales leaving deep scrapes in the crumbling plaster of the frame. Mortimer stared after him, then looked for Colin again. He was ushering Alice and Miriam ahead of him through the apple trees, still not looking around, although he must have heard the grating of scale on stone. Alice was resolutely looking the other way too, but Miriam glanced back and gave him a tiny nod.

"*Really?*" Mortimer whispered, then jumped for the window, following the High Lord into the shadowy, damp-scented interior. He wasn't sure that he liked the new, dragonish Miriam. She was making him feel out-dragoned.

INSIDE, the low autumn light was dim and distant, and the scent of deep earth and old growth was replaced with the lingering memory of wood fires and quiet evenings and gentle, small magics couched as much in the comfort of ritual as in power. Plaster was crumbling off the wall in patches, revealing the laths beneath, and the ceiling had collapsed here and there, leaving piles of rubble below. Mortimer followed Beaufort as he crept to the doorway and peered around it, then slipped into the hall beyond. The faint scent of burnt toast and weariness drifted from a room toward the front of the house, and for one horrifying moment Mortimer thought Beaufort was just going to walk straight into it, no matter how scary DI Adams was being. But instead he slipped back into the room they'd started in, and looked up at the ceiling.

"*No,*" Mortimer whispered. "We're too heavy. It's already falling in!"

"Just step on the beams, lad," Beaufort whispered back, crouching back onto his haunches. He launched himself up, wings folded tight to his body, scattering a little spray of debris as he squeezed through the gap. It rained onto the floor at the volume of a landslide, as far as Mortimer was concerned, and he threw a glance wildly over his shoulder at the door to the hall before lunging after the High Lord.

The attic space was cramped and cobwebby, and Beaufort was perched on a heavy beam like an upside-down bat, his wings wrapped around himself. Mortimer scrambled to balance the same way, and he'd barely managed to stop wobbling about the place when he heard the scuff of a boot below him. He peeked down and spotted the dandy, nudging his ball around in the rubble. Then the top of DI Adams' head appeared, and he leaned back as she looked up. He held his breath, but she didn't shout, and when he dared take another peek she was scratching the dandy behind the ears. Evidently the shadows within the broken roof were deep enough to hide two dragons with their scales bleached to the colours of old slate.

"Really?" DI Adams mumbled, apparently addressing the dandy. "I thought I was going to find Miriam faking a broken arm this time." She glanced around, then vanished again, and the dandy looked up at them. His dreadlocks fell away from his eyes, revealing that dreadful red, then he picked up his ball and wandered off.

Mortimer took a shivery breath and looked at the High Lord, intending to say that they should get out while the getting was good, but Beaufort was already creeping away over the rafters, moving silently and steadily toward the front of the house. Mortimer swallowed a sigh and followed, because it was that or sit here and pretend to be a bat, and he wasn't sure the actual bats that were hanging in the corner were going to appreciate that. They were already shifting and muttering fretfully.

The cottage was only small, and it was a matter of moments to make their way across the rafters to crouch above the room DI Adams had returned to. There were gaps in the ceiling where the plaster had failed, and Mortimer settled himself to peer through one. DI Adams had pulled on a pair of blue latex gloves and was crouched next to an inflatable mattress, peering into a backpack and taking things out one by one.

A knitted jumper in such a jumble of colours it looked as if it had been made from half a dozen end bits of wool. A pair of heavy-duty socks. A pouch that smelled strongly like the hemp cream Miriam had given Mortimer, and which made DI Adams give a little snort that sounded half-amused.

Dandy leaned on her arm, snuffling at the pouch, and she moved it away from him. "Coffee's bad enough," she said. "You're not starting this as well."

The dandy looked at her, his head on level with hers where she crouched in the middle of the room, and huffed. DI Adams grinned and scratched his head again, pulling him into a one-armed hug, and Mortimer caught a strange silvery purple thread of melancholy comfort rising from her. He looked at Beaufort, wanting to say that they shouldn't be spying, that this was her business, not theirs, but the High Lord's gaze was still fixed on the room. He wasn't moving.

Then DI Adams said, "Huh," and Mortimer looked back down. She pushed the bag away and rocked back on her heels, looking at Dandy. "Nothing there," she said. "How about you, can you smell anything?"

Dandy tipped his head slightly, and for one moment Mortimer thought he was going to look up, but he just pushed the ball to the inspector and stepped back, waiting.

"You're no help at all," she said, but picked the ball up gingerly and headed for the door. "Come on."

A moment later the room was empty, and Beaufort looked at Mortimer, his eyebrow ridges raised. Mortimer shook his head violently, disturbing a bat he hadn't realised had been perching on him, and gave a little hiss of alarm.

"We won't fit," he whispered. "The hole's too small."

"Then we'll go back to the other one," the High Lord said, and grinned toothily in the darkness. "Come on, lad." He turned back into the darkness, and Mortimer sat there staring at the room below while the bat returned to his wing and clambered along it, chittering anxiously.

"I know," he said to it. "I really do."

1 2

DI ADAMS

D I Adams picked her way back to the road, Dandy investigating the trees with the ball still held firmly in his mouth. He'd acquired it when they'd encountered some hairy, yappy little thing while running in the woods around Skipton Castle a couple of weeks ago. The dog had taken one look at Dandy loping toward it, given an astonishingly ear-piercing howl, and taken off in the direction of the car park as fast as its excruciatingly short legs would allow. Dandy had come to a stop and watched it go, his head tipped curiously, and the dog's owner, a rotund man in a wool coat, had glared at DI Adams furiously.

"You *scared* her!" he bellowed.

"I'm just running," DI Adams said.

"Well, *don't*." He ran after his dog, looking quite short-legged and hairy himself, and Dandy and DI Adams exchanged looks. Then Dandy had picked up the dog's discarded ball and trotted on, and DI Adams had decided she wasn't going to wrestle him for it. There were too many other early morning runners and dog walkers for her to start playing tug-of-ball with an invisible dog.

Now he seemed to want to take the damn thing everywhere, and DI Adams was just waiting for it to turn up in the middle of a crime scene, casting confusion over everything. At least no one could see the ball while he was holding it, although PC McLeod had got a terrible fright when Dandy dropped it at his feet. DI Adams had had to pretend she'd thrown it at him in some sort of impromptu team-building thing, but hadn't been prepared for when he picked it up and found it covered in very visible – and feel-able – Dandy slobber. Now the PC seemed to be avoiding her even more than he had previously, which she would've thought was impossible without one of them actually quitting. Not that she could blame him. Team-building was bad enough, even without the slobbery ball.

Collins was standing on the side of the road, his jacket zipped to his chin and his scarf pulled up almost to his nose, a woolly hat tugged down to meet it and leaving just a narrow gap to peer out of.

"I thought I was meant to be the soft southerner," she said to him. "It's not that cold."

"It bloody is when you're just standing around like a numpty," he said, pulling the scarf down a bit so that he could talk. "And you locked the car."

"I didn't want anyone stealing it."

"Out here?" He waved at the empty lane, and she had to admit that the odds were against it.

"Everyone get off, then?" she asked.

"They did," he said. "And no sign of any other vehicles."

"Alright," DI Adams said, and checked her phone. "Still no signal. I'll radio in for Lucas, and I need a team to start searching the woods, too."

"You won't get the station from here," Collins said. "We're in a right dip." He rocked on his heels. "We'll have to drive out to find a signal so we can call it in. Or just I can go, since I can't do much here and have a jewel problem to deal with."

"Right," she said. "Going to walk, are you?"

He looked from her to her car. "Seriously?"

"You're not driving my car."

"Did your mum not teach you about sharing?"

"I have two brothers. I protect what's mine."

He gave her an amused look. "So we're both going, are we? Leaving Mum free to run off whenever she feels like it?"

"She already can," DI Adams said with a sigh. "I know there's a wall, but this can't be the only way into these bloody woods."

"There is that," Collins agreed. "But I'd like to hear you explain to Maud that you left the entire place wide open because you didn't want to let me drive your car."

DI Adams scowled at him, but she couldn't put as much feeling into it as she wanted to. Not when it was his mum's van that had been in the square last night, and his mum who was currently hiding out in the woods, giving every indication of being guilty of a lot more than just possession of the little pouch of weed she'd found in the house.

She fished in her pocket and held her keys out as he grinned broadly. "If you put her in a ditch I'll tell the entire W.I. that you prefer supermarket sausage rolls to theirs."

"You wouldn't," he said, grabbing the keys and clutching them to his chest.

"I would. *And* that you said their cakes were dry."

"I will drive like a pensioner," he said.

"Don't do that. Look how the pensioners we know drive. It's terrifying. Just drive like a normal person borrowing someone else's *very precious* car."

"I'll send coffee with Lucas. I think you need it."

"I certainly do when someone else has my car," DI Adams said, and watched Collins get in, fiddling with the seat and the mirrors, then went to get her heavy high-vis jacket out of the back, along with her baton. Just in case. A moment later he'd pulled away, waving cheerily out of the window, and she yelled, "*Both hands on the wheel!*"

COLLINS ARRIVED BACK before Lucas did, coffee-less. DI Adams was frowning at a new scattering of rubble on the inflatable mattress in the bedroom when he shouted from the garden, and she went out to meet him.

"That was quick," she said.

"I just went far enough to get a signal and phoned in. Barry's awake but just keeps shouting that he has the right to remain silent, and apparently the whole ward wishes he'd exercise it. Lucas is on his way. *With* coffee," he added. "But I also got an ID on the victim. I think we need to swap some notes." His voice tightened on the last words, his shoulders high and braced as if against the wind.

DI Adams nodded, and looked around the garden. "Let's go to the car, then. It's too bloody cold out here, and your mum's not going to come back this way anyway."

He nodded and turned away without answering.

They walked back to the car silently, the wind gusting and eddying around them and setting the lingering leaves chattering. Dandy ranged alongside them, long-legged and somehow insubstantial even to Adams' eyes. Collins didn't talk, and she took the keys from him to let them into the car. It was still warm from his drive, and she rubbed her hands on her legs to take the chill off them.

"Well?" she said, as he took his notebook out and rested it on one knee.

He flipped over the pages, although DI Adams was quite sure he knew what was on them. Collins was big and relaxed and gave off an air of general affability, but she'd never seen him miss much. "The dead man's name was Alistair Lowell. Took us a while to find out because he was meant to be in the Seychelles."

"Ah," DI Adams said.

"Yes. When we finally got hold of the Lowells to tell them about the theft of their animal collection, it turned out that they'd had a rather nasty falling out, and while Lissy Lowell stayed on—"

"Lissy Lowell?"

"Short for Alissa."

"Alistair and Alissa Lowell?"

He gave her a reasonable approximation of a smile. "I know. She stayed on in the Seychelles, but Alistair came back early."

"So the house should've been empty, but Lowell was lurking around sulking."

"It'd seem so," Collins said. "So I'm guessing …" He trailed off, then continued more firmly. "Judith Ellis' group went in to snatch the birds and animals, thinking there was no one there. Alistair Lowell interrupted them, someone panicked and bopped him on the head, and now they've got a problem."

DI Adams nodded, scrawling in tight little circles on her notebook, blooming off into sudden spirals. "Why take the body to Toot Hansell?"

"Who knows? Still panicking?"

"Panicking is dropping everything and running, or dumping the body somewhere like here where we probably would never have found it."

Collins didn't answer, and after a moment she looked at him. He was gripping his pen tightly, but his face was calm when he shook his head. "I don't have an answer to that."

DI Adams nodded. "My point is, your mum's a suspect, but something here's not adding up. Either way I'll find her, but I don't think we can jump to her being a murderer."

Collins loosened his grip on his pen, laying it on his notebook. It promptly slid off and onto the seat, and DI Adams managed not to shout at him to grab it before it marked the cloth. "I've always been worried about this," he said. "That something would get out of hand, a protest or what have you, and she'd hurt someone."

DI Adams leaned her head back against the seat, then shifted again with a small sniff of annoyance as her bun put her neck at an awkward angle. "Did you adjust the seat?"

Collins pointed at himself, then at her, his eyebrows raised.

"Yeah, yeah." She hesitated, then said, "We can be reasonably sure she took the body to the hall. Her van was seen in the area, and Miriam's being very weird, so I think she knows something else. But why take it to the W.I. and risk being seen? Why leave the note? Especially when us connecting the dots with the wildlife thefts was only a matter of time."

"I can't be on this case, Adams. You said it yourself."

"I know. I'm just saying …" she looked at him, then shook her head and handed him her notebook. "Take photos of the jewel case notes. And give me yours."

He handed his notebook over without question, and she was just hovering her phone over the first page of notes when Dandy put his paws on the window and panted at her, his breath steaming the glass.

"What?" she asked.

"What?" Collins asked, looking up. He blinked at the window when Dandy licked it. "Huh."

"No, *stop*," DI Adams said, pushing the door open. Dandy dropped away, panting up at her. "What're you doing?"

He danced away a couple of steps.

"If this is about that bloody ball ..."

He took a few more steps and whined.

"Back in a moment," she said, and shut the car door, jogging after Dandy as he loped back toward the house.

DI Adams took her baton from her pocket as she emerged from the rotting orchard, Dandy ghosting ahead of her. There was no sign of anyone around, no glimmer of movement inside, just the hollow eyes of the windows staring back at her. She expected Dandy to go straight for the house, but he bypassed it, angling into the heavy undergrowth beyond.

"Where're you going?" she asked, her voice low, and he glanced back at her, red eyes glinting, then kept going, melting into the shadows. "Great," she mumbled, but followed, because she was here now, and surely he wouldn't be taking her for a run just for the fun of it?

Ten minutes later she was seriously reconsidering that. The route Dandy was taking in pursuit of whoever – or whatever – had caught his attention indicated that he was using some sort of as-a-dandy-runs navigation rather than anything a human could use, and she was scrambling around bushes and over roots while he *whuff*ed at her impatiently.

She persisted, though, right up until the moment her foot sank alarmingly deep into a muddy patch that she seriously suspected might be quicksand, and she almost lost her boot as she jerked backward.

"Dandy," she hissed at him. "I'm not finding anything in this. It's pointless."

He looked at her, his stance somehow eloquently disappointed.

"If there was someone here, I'm not going to catch them," she told him. "Not at this pace. I'm going back." She struggled away from the suspected quicksand, hoping she could find her way to the house via the trail of broken stems and scuffed earth, and wondering if she should've packed a pocketful of breadcrumbs. Eventually Dandy drifted past, still with his ball in his mouth. She scowled at him. She could really use some dandy skills in this terrain.

By the time she got back to the car there was an unmarked white van parked behind it, taking up too much of the road to enable anyone to squeeze past, and she was hot, sweaty, and had torn the pocket of her coat on a bush.

Lucas was talking to a uniformed officer, and they stopped as she pushed through the gap they'd opened in the fencing and walked over to join them. Lucas leaned into the van and came up with a thermos mug, which he handed to her wordlessly.

She took it in both hands and took a deep sip while they watched her. It was still mostly hot.

"Is it alright?" Lucas asked.

"Fine," she said.

"Colin said two double shots from the posh coffee place. I thought he was taking the mick, to be honest."

"It's that sort of day."

He looked her up and down, then said, "Looks like it. I hope I get to do your autopsy. That level of caffeine on the heart should be pretty interesting."

She stared at him. "I'm younger than you."

"Yeah, but …" He waved at the mug.

"Where's Collins?" she asked.

"He took my car," the uniformed officer said. She had her jacket zipped up to her chin, and she looked slightly put out. "Said he needed signal urgently."

"Alright." DI Adams looked around. "Is this everyone?"

"Myself, Liv," Lucas said, nodding at the uniformed officer, "and Ben's in the van."

"What's that?" Ben Shaw, Jasmine's husband, peered around from the back of the van. "How much of this stuff do you need, Lucas?"

"All the lights," he said. "I'll sort the rest." He looked back at DI Adams. "I'll ask, then, since you're not volunteering. Why do you look like you've been rolling in hedges?"

"I thought I saw someone," she said. "But the undergrowth was too thick. I lost them." She shot Dandy a reproachful look, although, to be fair, it hadn't been his fault. Whoever had been there – *if* there had been someone there – had probably been long gone by the time she got back to the house. It was her fault for leaving it unguarded. "House is all yours," she added, heading for her car. "I need to have a look at something."

"You're welcome," Lucas said, and she almost choked on a mouthful of coffee.

"Bollocks. Sorry, Lucas. Thank you."

"We'll talk about that whole civility thing again later," he said, but he winked at her as he headed for the back of the van to load up.

DI Adams sighed, and slid into the driver's seat of her car. She couldn't even say he was wrong.

The GPS took its time loading up, and she looked for Collins' notebook while she waited, but he must've taken it with him. Hers was tucked into the console between the seats, though, so that was something. Annoying not to have his notes, but not important for now. For now, she wanted to know what other routes led in and out of this place.

A moment later she was looking at the little blue arrow of the car, mired in a thin line of grey road. She zoomed out, watching the woods take shape as an arrowhead pinched between the road and farmland. There were no other official roads marked, and the GPS didn't show any tracks, but if there was farmland, there were gates, and there were ways to get to them. Someone could come from any direction.

She needed a better map. She had a decent hiking route one on her phone, so she picked it up, opened the app, stared at the featureless screen, then threw the phone down and swore loudly enough that Dandy barked in her ear.

"Shut *up*," she shouted back, and he huffed in disproval just as a slightly worried face leaned down next to her window. She opened the door, almost knee-capping Ben.

"What?"

"Sorry," he said. "Am I interrupting?"

"No. If I had internet you would be, but currently you're not, because this *rural idyll*"—she waved wildly—"is completely cut off from the modern world, and therefore modern policing, and what am I supposed to do? Start walking around with a magnifying glass?"

"Sorry," he said again, and Dandy chose that moment to drop his ball. It bounced damply into Adams' lap and she jumped, knocking it out of the car. "Ah— Shall I get that?"

"No," she said, and took a gulp of coffee. "What is it?"

"Lucas says can you come to the house, please."

"He's found something already?" she asked, swinging out of the car and stashing her phone in her pocket.

"More a complication."

DI Adams had already started for the gate, and she stopped to look at him. "A complication?"

"That's what he called it."

"Awesome."

&

LUCAS WAS STANDING outside the front door of the house when she got there, clad in white disposable coveralls with his goggles still on and the hood of the suit pulled low to meet them.

"What's happened?" she asked as she hurried across the rough ground.

"We need wildlife rescue," he said.

"Why?" she asked, managing not to look around for Dandy. He'd been in the car with her, and as good as he was at ignoring the physical properties of walls, he couldn't be in two places at once. She didn't think. Of course, it could be the dragons, which would be potentially even harder to explain.

"Bats," Lucas said.

"Bats?"

"Yeah, you know. As in Dracula?"

"*Vampire* bats?"

"Well, not quite Dracula, then. Regular bats."

"And?"

"And we're disturbing them. We can't work in the house until we know they're not a rare variety or we'll have bat conservation and the RSPCA and who knows who else on us."

DI Adams looked past him at the empty windows of the house, and caught a little scrap of deeper darkness fluttering past it. "*Bats?*"

"Yep. Plus they're kind of messy, and that's not helping anyone." He half turned, showing her a deposit on his back. "Definitely not doing anything for my crime scene."

"Well, that's just bloody fabulous," DI Adams said. "What do we do?"

"Find a phone signal and call someone to sort it. Until then we leave everything sealed off and don't disturb them. They'll go back to wherever they were hiding. Must've been all the lights and movement that flushed them out."

DI Adams thought of the clatter of small stones she'd heard earlier, when she'd first gone into the house. She'd found Dandy and his ball pottering around in a pile of debris, but it was debris that had fallen from the ceiling. "Suppose that would make sense," she said. "The lights, I mean."

"Yeah." Lucas dusted his hands off and looked around. "I can have a look outside, but that's it."

"Go and call it in," she said. "Ben can keep an eye on the house. I'll take Liv and start on a search in the direction Ellis went."

"Are you set up for that?" Lucas asked. "No phone means you can't call for help if you get lost."

"We've already wasted too much time with this place being in a bloody hole as far as mobile reception," DI Adams said. "She's only getting more of a chance to get away on us. Besides, we've got the radios. We can keep in touch with each other, at least."

"Suit yourself," he said with a shrug. "I don't fancy poking around these hills in the dark."

"It's not *that* late."

"It will be soon," he said, and grinned at her.

DI Adams snorted and checked her torch. At least they'd be *doing* something.

13
MIRIAM

M iriam sat in the passenger seat of Alice's car and watched the drystone walls pass at an unnecessary velocity, barely even giving a whimper of protest when they met another car coming the opposite way up the lane and Alice braked sharply. They squeezed past each other, Alice muttering, *"Do* pull over. Your car's not that big," and then they were off again, whipping around corners and bobbing over rises, and still Miriam didn't even ask why they were in such a hurry, or if there was any possibility that they could slow down long enough for her stomach to catch up. She just stared blankly out of the windscreen, and tried to get her racing thoughts to calm down. She wasn't having an awful lot of luck.

"Miriam?" Alice said finally. "Do we need to stop? Only I'd prefer you weren't ill in my car. Muddy dragons are quite enough to deal with."

"We don't even have them," Miriam said. "We left them behind."

"They are dragons, dear. They'll be perfectly safe."

"Like they were in Eldmere?"

Alice pulled abruptly into a little passing bay, tucking them close to the wall and its growth of old moss and weeds. A sheep looked at them blankly from the field beyond, then went back to cropping the grass. Clouds were coming in from the west, a heavy grey cast expanding silently across the sky, and Miriam pushed the button to wind her window down, breathing in the cold, green-scented air and wondering why it was so much less satisfying than using a handle to *actually* wind the window down.

"Miriam?" Alice said. There was no impatience in her tone, and when Miriam looked at her, the older woman's face was set in an unfamiliar and deeply serious expression. It took Miriam a moment to realise that Alice was probably being sympathetic, but she didn't seem to have the right angles for it. "What do you want to do?"

"Me?" Miriam asked.

"Yes, you. It's your sister who's wanted by the police, and your nephew who's in a rather unpleasant situation. This is entirely up to you. We can walk away now and let DI Adams sort it out. We know she's an excellent detective, and very fair, so she will do her job the best that any police officer could. We can leave it with her."

Alice didn't add *or* at the end, simply stopped there, but Miriam heard it anyway. *Or we can Get Involved again, and possibly end up as accomplices, and maybe make things worse for Colin and Rainbow, and risk the dragons being exposed, and us arrested, and DI Adams will start getting an eye twitch again and likely carry through on her threat to arrest all of us.*

She watched the sheep, not answering right away. It was alright for sheep. They just toddled around the fields, eating grass, basking in the sun, and watching silly humans rush all over the place with their dramas and concerns. Of course, they also stood out there in the rain and sleet and snow, and their lambs got eaten, and they were herded around by dogs and wrestled by humans to be shorn or wormed, and every now and then some careless walker would let their own poorly trained dog chase them all over the place, so there were downsides too. Although Miriam was fairly certain they didn't have to worry about family members being accused of murder.

Alice still hadn't said anything further, and when Miriam shifted in her seat to look at her, the older woman gave a small smile and said, "I'm not terribly good at this, Miriam. Would you like a hug?"

Miriam stared at her, then gave a very small laugh. "No, I don't think so. Thank you, though."

Alice nodded. "Probably for the best. Very awkward, are hugs."

"Not really," Miriam said. "I mean, not if you don't *make* them awkward."

Alice *hmm*ed. "Maybe one has to be more accustomed to them."

"You should practice more, then," Miriam said, and Alice looked so unimpressed that Miriam laughed again, a little more easily this time. "I shouldn't recognise you, if you were good at hugs."

Alice inclined her head in acknowledgement. "I think I shall skip the practise, then."

"Yes." Miriam looked back at the sheep, but it had resumed grazing, the brief alarm at their arrival passing. "I don't think Rainbow killed anyone. Not even by accident. She's always believed in non-violent protest. No harm to living creatures. She used to cry if she stepped on a snail by accident and broke its shell. I remember her trying to superglue one back together when we were little, which didn't work very well at all."

"What about the flood in the meat processing plant?" Alice asked. "That one near Manchester you told me she was involved in. Those security guards could have drowned in binding agents or whatever it was. That seems very careless if she's really worried about not hurting anyone."

Miriam shook her head. "It was wastewater from the processing. And the guards weren't meant to be there. They were meant to be on rounds, but they'd skipped them because it was too cold. I'm quite certain. My sister may be many things, but she's not a murderer."

Alice nodded. "Alright. So you would prefer to leave this with DI Adams? If Rainbow is innocent, she'll find the truth."

Miriam thought about it. A large part of her was very firmly in favour of just that, because wasn't that what the police were for? To find the truth? And DI Adams might be somewhat terrifying, but she was also fair, and Miriam thought she really would do her best to find out what was going on. But there was also the fact that Rainbow was acting terribly guilty by running off, and all evidence was pointing at her so far. And there was the question of the thefts Rainbow had mentioned too, which could only be an added complication. And all of that meant that even a very good police officer might be misled.

"No," she said, as firmly as she could. "Rainbow asked for our help, and I think she needs it. Someone's doing a very good job of framing her, and we need to find out who."

Alice looked at her for a long moment, then leaned over and gave her a hug that truly was very awkward, and not just because both of them were still wearing their seatbelts. "Then that is what we shall do," she said, sitting back and starting the engine.

"As simply as that?" Miriam asked.

"Of course. When one puts one's mind to it, anything is possible."

"Not really."

"Well, not *anything*," Alice admitted. "But many things, especially when one has the support of one's friends."

"That makes them sound rather like accomplices."

Alice shot Miriam an amused look as she pulled back out onto the road, but she didn't disagree.

By the time they arrived back in Toot Hansell, the full force of the Women's Institute were gathered in Priya's living room, packed into the sofas and perched on dining chairs carried in from the next room, and a light in the garden shed indicated that Priya's husband Guneet had already made himself scarce (in theory to work on bespoke bird houses that he sold on Etsy, but in reality, Priya had confided in Miriam once, to drink home-brewed whisky with his friend Norman from over the back fence, after which they inevitably got a little teary and spent all their time making tiny model animals for their grand-kids. She'd only had to drive them to the hospital once each for stitches, though, so she felt it was fairly harmless). They had been more than halfway back to the village by the time Miriam had had enough phone signal to make a call, but no one could ever accuse the W.I. of an inability to mobilise quickly.

As she let them in, Priya peered into the dull afternoon, rendered drab by the heavy clouds, and said, "Where are Beaufort and Mortimer?"

"We're not sure," Alice said. "But they know not to come here." Priya had two cats, and though not all cats were part of the Watch, any cat could be. And it was certain that the Watch would take a rather dim view of dragons taking tea with the Women's Institute, let alone getting involved in human investigations. So far Thompson had things in hand – or paw, Miriam supposed – and none of the other village cats seemed inclined to cause trouble, but it was one of those things that it was best not to push, such as by inviting dragons into the parlour while the house cats were snoozing on the hearth.

"Peaches and Zuzu are in the bedroom," Priya said, and Miriam looked past her to see a ginger cat with a disgruntled expression staring back at them.

"I don't think they are," she said.

Priya turned around and put her hands on her hips. "Peaches! I told you to stay upstairs. Jasmine has her dog here."

Peaches looked even more disgruntled, if that was possible, and stalked toward the kitchen.

"Never mind," Alice said quietly. "This is human business anyway."

The noise level in the living room was high enough that Miriam would've been surprised if the cats had made it over the threshold, everyone holding forth at once about the body and the broken boiler, and apparently lending equal weight to both.

"The council are saying *we* can't request a replacement," Rosemary was saying. "As if it's not our hall too!"

"I'm telling you, I can source one," Gert said. "My nephew's sister-in-law's cousin—"

"You said it was your sister's brother-in-law's ... something, before," Carlotta said. "Which is it?"

"I can't keep track of all of them!"

"But it's irrelevant. We can't even *get* to the hall," Rose pointed out. "The police still have it all taped off. And did you see the pyjamas on the body? He was filthy rich. They'll make a right fuss over that."

"That could be very bad for Toot Hansell," Jasmine said. "Rich people getting murdered on our doorsteps."

"Only if we want rich people here," Gert said, and Rose pointed at her, nodding.

"But it is a *murder*," Rosemary said. "That's bad for everyone."

"And what are we meant to do for Bonfire Night?" Teresa asked. "Never mind not being able to use the hall – at this rate everyone'll be too scared to come out."

"I'll ask Ben," Jasmine said. "The least he can do is tell us when we can get back into the hall and start getting back to normal. But honestly, he's *such* a grump at the moment—"

"Men always are," Pearl said.

"Tea?" Priya asked Alice and Miriam, raising her voice to be heard over the chatter. "Or something stronger?"

"Something stronger," Alice said, surveying the room.

"Best not," Miriam said, although she rather fancied it. But she also wanted her wits about her if she was going to be looking for whoever had framed her sister. If it all got too much she could always resort to paracetamol, after all.

She was just squeezing onto the sofa next to Teresa and Pearl when there was a shout from the kitchen, followed by the clatter of dishes, some feline yowls, and hysterical yapping.

"Oh *no*," Jasmine said, and leaped up, rushing to the door just as Primrose came racing in, still yapping. Jasmine scooped her up and stood to face Priya, who had followed Primrose in. "What happened?"

Priya folded her arms with a scowl. "She stole my cats' dinner, and they expressed their displeasure."

Jasmine examined Primrose. Miriam couldn't see any injuries from here, but the younger woman said, "Her nose is scratched!"

"She *stole* my *cats' dinner*."

They glared at each other, then Jasmine deflated. "I'm sorry. She's terrible sometimes."

"Sometimes?" Priya said, but then she sighed and shook her head. "You really need to train her better, you know."

"I know," Jasmine said, and Miriam thought she looked more upset than just a misbehaving dog accounted for. Apparently Priya thought so too, because she put one arm around the other woman's shoulders as they turned back into the room and hugged her gently, careful to avoid getting too close to Primrose.

"Rum toddy?" she suggested.

"That might help," Jasmine said, and went to sit down, keeping a firm hold on the dog.

Pearl looked from Martha, snoring softly with her head on Teresa's foot, to Jasmine, then said, "Martha once stole an entire Sunday roast from my sister's kitchen."

Jasmine looked at her. "*No.*"

"Yes. We've not been invited back since, have we, Teresa?"

"To be fair, I think that was more due to you telling her to stop asking when you were going to meet someone because I was right there. She didn't seem to like that much."

"Or it might've been due to my niece telling her to stop being such a fascist when she got a bit funny about it," Pearl said, and they both laughed. "Still," she added to Jasmine. "The stolen roast definitely didn't help."

Priya returned with a tray of large, very full glasses, followed by Rosemary and Rose toting two big teapots, an assortment of mugs and a jug of milk. There were already plates of nibbles out on the table, a slightly random assortment given the last-minute nature of the gathering. There were the promised heat-and-eat sausage rolls, several bowls of peanuts and crisps, some spring rolls that were also of the heat-and-eat variety, a collection of brightly coloured dips, and a jumble of biscuits that had the look of being the last left in a number of different tins, but no less enticing for that. Miriam was suddenly *very* hungry, and she piled a few of the sausage rolls and spring rolls on a side plate before settling back in her seat.

"Right, then," Gert said. "Rainbow's being set up, you said on the phone?"

"Definitely," Miriam said around a mouthful of sausage roll. "She's not a killer."

"But she was seen with the body at the hall," Rose said.

"She dumped it there," Miriam said. "But she didn't kill him. Someone planted the body in her van, and when she left the hospital after dropping off Barry, she found it."

"So someone sneaked it in at the hospital?" Teresa asked. "Surely there'll be CCTV footage, then."

"Possibly," Alice said. "But we're not going to be able to get it."

"I can," Gert said. "My sister-in-law's aunt's in ... well, let's say IT. She can find it."

Carlotta looked like she was going to say something, then just shrugged and took a large swig of her drink, wincing.

"What about Colin?" Jasmine said. "He can just ask for the footage."

"He's been taken off the case," Alice said. "Too compromised, with it being his mother. And he wouldn't share it with us, even if he could get it."

"Leave it with me," Gert said.

"We could just tell DI Adams," Pearl said. "She'd have to investigate all leads."

"She'll just tell us to pull our necks in," Rose said. "I say we do it Gert's way."

"I rather agree with Rose," Alice said. "Or at least we tell her *after* we've seen if there's anything that can help us on the tape."

"Tape," Jasmine said with a giggle, and took another sip of her drink. Her nose was very pink.

"Or disc, or whatever it is these days," Alice said. "We don't even know if there's anything there that will help us – I doubt whoever put the body in the van took any risks that they could be identified, since they've been quite clever so far."

"I'll get on it," Gert said, pulling her phone out.

"What else?" Priya asked. "What other leads do we have?"

"Rainbow thinks it might have been someone in her group," Miriam said. "Apparently someone's been stealing things when they've been setting the animals free, and she thinks it's all an attempt to undermine the cause."

"The cause of releasing non-native animals into the countryside where they can become pests or die horribly because they're not adapted to the environment?" Rose said.

"Well, yes. But I imagine Rainbow thinks it's better than them being in cages."

Rose made a non-committal sound, and Jasmine said, "What do we know about her group, then?"

"There's Harriet from the bookshop, her new boyfriend Simon, Tom who was at Maddie's last year, and Barry," Miriam said.

"Was Tom the skinny lad following the young posh woman around?" Rosemary asked.

"Yes. He's not so skinny now, though. And he's *rude*."

There was a general mutter of disapproval at that, and Alice said, "That's hardly evidence of guilt, Miriam. Simon's the newest group member, so it would be good to know when these problems started. It might give us something to go on."

"Well, we know where Barry is," Pearl said. "And he's *Barry*. He's the least likely to be up to anything terrible. If we can speak to him we might be able to get some more information."

"Isn't he the one that seemed to object to clothing?" Carlotta said. "I'm not sure he's the best option, really."

"I didn't know you Italians were so prudish," Rosemary said.

"It's less prudishness than aesthetics," Carlotta replied. "He's a bit past the stage where anyone wants to see him naked."

"He'd probably say the same about you."

Carlotta acknowledged that with a shrug, then said, "We'll go and see if we can get into the hospital. W.I. doing the rounds caring for the sick and all that."

"Well done," Alice said. "We have a couple of other possibilities, too. There's the camp Miriam and I went to last night—"

"And kept all the fun to yourself, too," Rose said. "So rude!"

"I was just going to go on my own and talk to Rainbow," Miriam said. "Beaufort and Mortimer followed me, and then Alice brought me tea."

"Just as bad," Rose said. "*I* could have brought you tea." But she was smiling as she said it, and Miriam took another sausage roll. They were rather tasty. The spring rolls, on the other hand, she'd pushed to the side of her plate. They *looked* nice, but inside was a nasty mix of congealing oil and a squishy substance that tasted mysteriously of orange cordial.

"There's also the bookshop," Alice said, ignoring the exchange. "Rainbow's group seem to be using it as a bit of a base to get messages and so on, and I think we should keep an eye on it to see who turns up."

"Daisy was a bit strange," Miriam said.

"She was just worried about Simon. Her father," Alice added, by way of explanation to the rest of the group.

Miriam took a handful of crisps and dipped one into a bright orange hummus of some sort, not replying. She still felt there had been something strange about Daisy, but she couldn't quite put her finger on it. And she had to admit that the young woman had been very helpful, so it was probably nothing more than the unfamiliarity of a new generation, that dislocation when one's cultural touchpoints weren't shared, or perhaps even known.

"What about Rainbow herself?" Pearl asked. "Do we know where she is?"

"In the woods behind my aunt's house," Miriam said, huffing a little. The orange colour was evidently from a generous application of chillies. "It's proper old forest there, and she's familiar with it. I think she can probably stay hidden for quite a while."

"Unless they bring dogs in," Rose pointed out.

There was silence there for a moment, while everyone considered it, then Jasmine said, "Where are the dragons?"

"In the woods as well," Alice said. "They stayed behind when we left, so they'll find Rainbow and keep an eye on her. I assume they'll wait until it's dark, then fly out and update us."

"If they find her, we can get her out," Teresa said.

Everyone looked at her, then Alice said, "That's more than doing a little investigating, Teresa. That's harbouring a suspect. Obstructing a police investigation. Aiding and abetting."

Teresa nodded, and looked at Miriam. "Are you sure she's innocent?"

Miriam took a deep breath, but she didn't need to think about it. "I'm sure," she said.

"There we go, then."

All eyes turned to Alice, who nodded. "Alright," she said. "As soon as the dragons are in touch, we make a plan to get Rainbow out."

"And in the meantime we're off to the hospital," Carlotta said, checking her watch. "We'll get there just before visiting hours are over."

"No texts," Alice said. "Voice calls only, and keep them to a minimum. We don't want to leave any evidence of any of this."

A murmur of agreement went around the room, and Pearl patted Miriam's knee. "We'll sort all of this out," she said. "Don't you worry."

And Miriam thought that they truly were accomplices now, but that maybe that was what all the best friends were. Accomplices in life.

14

MORTIMER

Beaufort led the way back across the fragile ceiling, and Mortimer and his newly-acquired bat followed, the dragons keeping to the still-sturdy beams that spanned the space. Their wings were tucked as close to their bodies as possible and Mortimer's tail was cramping from trying to hold it high and stop it dragging on the plaster. The bat kept up a steady commentary of barely-audible chittering, and Mortimer wondered if it had rabies. Bats did sometimes, he thought. If he got rabies no one could expect him to take part in investigations. Although he supposed that was being a bit extreme.

They made it back to the room they'd started out in without anyone falling through the ceiling or being bitten, and Beaufort poked his head through the hole and peered around cautiously. He looked at Mortimer, and said in a low voice that nevertheless reverberated around the space, "It looks all clear, lad."

"Are you sure?" he asked. "What if DI Adams is just outside? Or the dandy?"

"The dandy seems quite alright with you."

"I'm not alright with *him*," Mortimer protested. It wasn't just those eyes. The dandy's scent was strange, wild and fierce and distant, connected to the world in remote ways that even dragons couldn't quite grasp. It was like smelling starlight in water, burning with a heat that froze the senses.

"You just stay put. I'll have a little look around." The High Lord dropped easily through the gap in the ceiling, landing softly with his wings flared slightly for balance and bringing a little shower of dislodged plaster with him. He grinned up at Mortimer, looking far too happy to be creeping around a crime scene, then slipped out of the window.

Mortimer waited, happy to be still and quiet for the moment. There had been altogether too much rushing about and climbing in and out of cars and worrying about murders over the last day. The tight, dark space felt at least somewhat safe, even with the tickling dust and scent of bat guano drifting about the place. At least no sharp-eyed police officer was likely to stumble on him up here.

Then Beaufort put his scaly head over the windowsill and whispered, "Come on! No one's here."

Mortimer had very little desire to *come on,* but he shook his wings gently and whispered to the bat, "Off you go."

The bat protested, clinging on a little more tightly, and Mortimer sighed. It'd let go soon enough when he got out into the light, dull though it was. He hooked his paws over the gap in the ceiling and slid carefully through, still clinging to the rafters with his back paws so that he didn't crash to the ground. And just as he reached the point where gravity got hold of him and pulling himself back up was next to impossible, he heard the scrape of the kitchen door, and quick soft footsteps on the creaky boards of the hall.

"Go back!" Beaufort hissed at him, and Mortimer *pulled* with his back legs, feeling the rafters crunching warningly under his grip and sending another little patter of fallen plaster to the floor of the room. The footsteps in the hall paused, and Mortimer gave one desperate heave and vanished back into the shelter of the attic, clutching the beams with all four paws and trying to make himself as small and invisible as the bats clinging to the inside of the roof space. They were shifting and chittering anxiously in the wake of his return, and his would-be passenger was winging in circuits around him, complaining about being dislodged.

The footsteps started up again, slow and careful, and paused in the door to the room. Their owner didn't speak, and after a moment they moved on. Mortimer stayed where he was, willing himself not to breathe too loudly and the ceiling not to give way. The bats stretched and closed their wings, muttering angrily. One detached itself and landed on Mortimer, clambering up his spine, and his previous companion dived at it. They screeched furiously at each other, the sounds vanishingly high even to his ears, and he hoped again that neither of them bit him. That was all he needed, a bat bite. Now he'd thought of it, he really didn't fancy rabies. Even if it did get him out of investigating, the side effects wouldn't be worth it. Although, could dragons actually get rabies? He hadn't heard of it, but that would be just his luck.

One of the bats – he wasn't sure if it was the original one or if the other had won the perch-on-the-dragon contest – chittered into his ear in a friendly manner, and he tried, very carefully, to flick it off, but it had a tight and slightly painful grip on his scales. There was no sound from below, no footsteps or sign of the person who'd passed the room. He couldn't even smell them over the scent of bat guano. The second bat was climbing up his flank to meet the first, and Mortimer tried to take it gently in one paw to pull it off. It promptly bit him. He managed to bite down on a squawk of surprise, but not on a little jump. His tail thumped the ceiling between the beams, and a patch of plaster sheared off from around the hole and plunged to the floor below, his tail going with it. He lurched away, hauling his tail back up again, and crashed into the under-side of the roof while running feet sounded in the hall below.

The bats screeched in a chorus of alarm as their home shook around them, and suddenly the whole loft space was filled with wildly fluttering leathery wings and soft round bodies, bumping into the roof and Mortimer and each other before dropping through the hole and flooding out into the light, still screaming in fright.

Someone else screamed as well, and a moment later the kitchen door banged open. Mortimer collapsed against the beams, and would have stayed there for the next hour, or at least until his legs stopped shaking, if a hiss hadn't come from below.

"Good job, lad! Now *hurry!*"

So Mortimer wrenched his talons out of the beams (he'd been clinging on even more tightly than he'd realised) and plunged straight out of the hole without thinking about it too much. Bats were darting and squeaking around the room, complaining to each other, but he ignored them and followed the High Lord out of the window and into the cool green quiet of the garden beyond. A moment later they were plunging into the trees, leaving the ruins of the house behind them, and for one moment he allowed himself to feel that things were going to be alright. That he'd escaped, and no harm was done.

Then he realised his paw was stinging and he held it out to the High Lord. "I've been bitten!"

Beaufort slowed down enough to look at his paw. "You have. What on earth did you say to them?"

"I didn't say anything," Mortimer protested, and wondered if he really could get rabies. He'd have to watch for foaming at the mouth. Erratic behaviour wasn't exactly going to be a warning sign, otherwise half the Cloverly clan had had rabies for the past three years.

He swallowed a sigh and followed Beaufort as they headed deeper into the woods. At least there were no police out here. Rabies *and* police really would've been far too much to deal with. Although …

"Where are we going?" he asked.

"We're following a zebra," Beaufort replied.

"*What?*"

BEAUFORT DIDN'T STOP, or circle back to the road. He just kept heading deeper and deeper into the woods, which were rich with mulch and damp, heavily tangled roots plunging deep into the earth, and mushrooms blooming in the shelter of the trees. Birds called cautiously, question and answer, and moss and lichen blanketed the rocks.

Mortimer caught the scent of running water somewhere just out of hearing, and the quiet paths left by wild things, and it soothed the harsh edges of the day at least a little. There was the heavy musk of a badger sett, and the soft damp whiff of foxes, and the trees were old and thick-set and rich with lost stories. He could have happily walked here for a very long time indeed, but he doubted that was the High Lord's intention, especially given their pace.

He took a shaky breath, then said, "Beaufort, sir? Did you really say zebra?"

Beaufort glanced back at him, grinning toothily. "Not a real one, lad. Someone in a costume."

"Well, I thought it must be," Mortimer said, although he hadn't really thought any such thing. He hadn't had time. "Ah … why?"

"Why are they in a suit? I don't know. It looked warm, though."

"Oh. That's nice. Why are we following them?"

"Because it was them who came into the house," Beaufort said, in a tone that suggested Mortimer was being a little slow on the uptake. "I couldn't see what they did from outside. Could you?"

"No," Mortimer said, not adding that he'd mostly been trying not to catch rabies at the time.

Beaufort stopped suddenly, looking around, then said, "Can you see any sort of trail?"

Mortimer, who hadn't really been paying much attention to the route they'd been taking, examined the tangled undergrowth. They had veered off from the house, heading deeper into the woods and away from the road, and the ground was a mix of leaves and dirt that should have left at least faint traces of anyone who had passed through. "Um," he said. "Is this definitely the way they went?"

"I'm not sure," Beaufort admitted. "I saw them go into the trees, but then I went back for you, and they could easily have doubled back."

Mortimer's scales gave a tingling yellow flush of shame, and he said, "Sorry."

"Not at all," Beaufort said, then held up a paw. "Listen."

Mortimer cocked his head and caught the crumple and crunch of bracken underfoot, then a sharp curse in a familiar voice.

"Dammit, Dandy," DI Adams said, somewhere unseen among the trees. "I can't see *anything* in this."

There was no response that Mortimer could hear, but the soundtrack of snapping twigs and dislodged stones and swearing continued, and the dragons looked at each other.

"What now?" Mortimer asked, his voice low. "If she and Dandy are chasing the zebra, we can't. The dandy will find them before we do. *And* find us."

Beaufort *hmm*ed. "True. It's still too light for us to fly anywhere, though. And the ladies will have gone by now." He looked around, putting one paw on a fallen tree trunk and its cargo of rot and new growth, his snout raised to the hidden sky.

"So ...?" Mortimer asked.

Beaufort gave him that toothy grin again. "So why don't we try to find Miriam's sister?"

"You mean the one we just ran down and who is likely terrified of us?"

"We didn't *run her down*. We just intercepted her getaway so that Miriam could talk to her."

"I don't think she seemed very happy about that idea."

"Well, no," Beaufort admitted. "But she shouldn't be out here alone. Especially not with mysterious zebra-suited intruders about the place. What if that was the murderer?"

Mortimer couldn't quite suppress a shiver, and he glanced over his shoulder before something else occurred to him. "What if *Rainbow's* the murderer? We'll be walking right into her hands!"

Beaufort examined him. "You do remember you're a dragon, lad?"

"Well, yes," Mortimer said, not feeling very dragonish at that particular moment. "But still."

"There's no *but still* about it. We shall find her and talk to her, and if she is the murderer we shall take her into custody, and if she's not we shall figure out what's going on."

"We can't take her into custody, Beaufort. We're not police."

"Citizen's arrest, then."

Mortimer was fairly sure that still didn't extend to dragons, but there was no use pointing that out. The High Lord was right. Rainbow had already seen them, more than once, and if she was as innocent as she said then she needed help. Particularly out in these woods. Humans weren't made for such deep, wild places. Places with long memories, that had watched as their fellows had been crushed under the weight of human progress, torn down for fuel, or to build houses, or simply because they were inconvenient. Places that had seen their rivers poisoned and filled in, their wildflowers replaced with crops, their birds rendered homeless and hunted. Woods like this weren't friendly to those who could carry a flame. Mortimer could even feel eyes on himself. Dragons had been known to be careless with their breath on occasion, after all.

"Alright," he said. "Let's find her, then."

"Well done, lad," Beaufort said. "You're excellent at this, you know. I was just about to cause a distraction outside the window when you set all those bats off. Very quick thinking."

Mortimer decided not to tell the High Lord it had all been down to the bat biting him. It had worked, after all.

THEY CIRCLED BACK to the house and picked up Rainbow's scent where they'd left her earlier. Like her sister, she was light upon the land, but where Miriam left a faint trace of calm violet smudges run through with cheesy puff orange anxiety, Rainbow left something green and moody and gnawed at the edges with long slow grief. It was hard to pick out among the trees' own ancient concern for the lost, and it made Mortimer think that perhaps Rainbow had less to fear from the woods than others might have. It didn't make it safe for her, though.

"She can't have gone far," Beaufort said, as they padded along her trail. "It's hard enough getting through here on four paws, let alone two."

Mortimer made a small mumble of agreement, his own paw still smarting from the bat bite (its fangs were apparently small enough and sharp enough to get in around the edge of a scale), and concentrated on following the trail.

It led them deeper and deeper into the woods, plunging away from the house into old, wild forest until they met a brook that chattered over mossy rocks and between green-clad banks, forming tiny natural pools and shimmering cascades as it made its way to lower ground. There were scrapes on the rocks where the moss had come off, following the route of the water, and even with the rich brown dampness and the sharp electric scent of the water drowning all else, those scrapes were as good as arrows saying *this way!*

They found Rainbow sitting on the bank only a few minutes' walk further on, and stopped at a reasonable distance from her.

"Hello," Beaufort said. His scales glittered in muted greens and golds in the dim light filtering through the trees, and he looked carved from the world around him. Mortimer looked down at his paws, expecting anxious grey, and discovered he was wearing his own deep purples and royal blues, which was rather nicer than expected.

Rainbow jumped, scrambling to her feet, and stared at them. "Hello," she said after a moment.

"We're friends of Miriam," Beaufort said.

"You're dragons," she said.

"That too."

"I told Barry he was bonkers, going on about dragons."

"Not so much."

She nodded. "I thought something was up after the farmhouse thing, but I didn't think you were actual *dragons*. I didn't really see you up close, and it's a bit jumbled in my head for some reason."

"That does happen," Beaufort said. "Call it a defence mechanism."

Mortimer thought it was more to do with Thompson and his suggestions, but that was too much to explain.

"Oh. Good. I thought it might be from … well, it doesn't matter. Good to know I'm not going dotty, anyway."

They stared at each other for a moment longer, then Beaufort indicated himself. "Beaufort Scales, High Lord of the Cloverly dragons, and my friend Mortimer."

"Hi," Mortimer said. He had a bit of a warm flush going in his chest over *friend*. He supposed they were, at that, even if he still struggled to think of the old dragon as anything other than the High Lord.

"Rainbow Harmony," Rainbow said. "Um, Protector of the Earth and Warrior for Peace."

"Very nice," Beaufort said approvingly. "Not sure about the Warrior for Peace bit, but I understand the sentiment."

Rainbow nodded. "What d'you want?"

"To help. We're investigators."

"Investigators?"

"Yes. With the W.I."

There was silence for a moment, then Rainbow said, "A lot of things actually make much more sense in light of that."

"I imagine so," Beaufort said. "So what can you tell us?"

Rainbow looked from one dragon to the other for a moment longer, then said, "Alright. Look, I'm being framed. I didn't kill anyone, and I'm not responsible for the thefts that have been happening, either."

"Of course not. Who would want to frame you, though?" Beaufort asked.

Rainbow sighed. "When it was just the thefts, I thought it was someone in my group. People lose sight of the cause sometimes, and what we do doesn't exactly pay the bills. But murder's a step too far. It's got to be part of something bigger, probably to do with The Government."

Mortimer nodded. "I don't trust them either. They have *Tasers*."

"Yes! And the lot of them are in the pockets of the oil companies. It's all about the money." She tapped the side of her nose.

Beaufort made a thoughtful sound. "But how would framing you for murder help them? If it was the government, surely they could just call you a threat to national security and lock you up?"

Rainbow hesitated. "Well, yes, but then it makes me a martyr. This way I look like the bad guy."

"That's so sneaky," Mortimer said, and he could feel the colour draining from his scales. "How awful!"

"They're the true enemy," Rainbow said.

"It still seems a bit sloppy," Beaufort said. "Why didn't they have someone ready to catch you when you had the body? You were able to get rid of it, after all."

"Well, they're not perfect."

"Are you sure there's no one else?" Beaufort asked.

"Oil companies themselves. Big Pharma. They're just as bad."

Mortimer blinked. "But you took Barry to the hospital."

Rainbow waved one hand dismissively. "One does what one has to do. He needed more than some tinctures." She looked momentarily worried. "I wonder if anyone's been to check on him? He's all on his own in there."

"Anyone else?" Beaufort persisted. "Someone closer to you, perhaps? There was someone in the house just now. In a zebra suit. Who might that be?"

Rainbow stared at him. "In a zebra suit?"

"Yes, we tried to follow them but there was a bat incident."

She shook her head, a quick short gesture. "No. That can't be right."

"It wasn't. One bit me," Mortimer said, and she gave him a puzzled look.

"No, I mean the zebra suit. That's Harriet's. She wasn't meant to come here. Unless she needed to warn me about something, I suppose."

"She could have been wanting to do that," Beaufort admitted. "We didn't see what she did. And we may have scared her off. Purely accidentally, of course."

Rainbow chewed on her lip. "She was probably trying to tell me they're onto me." She took a deep breath. "So now they'll be after her, too. I need to find her."

"They?" Beaufort asked. "The police?"

"No, whoever's behind it all. The Government. They're so *sneaky*. They'll use any method they can to silence us, you know. Infiltration. Bugs." She looked down at her clothes, scowling. "And if they've found me here ... I bet they've planted trackers on me. I'll lead them straight to Harriet, straight to *everyone*. Oh, those sneaky—" Her words were lost as she hauled her jacket off without bothering to unzip it.

"I might have rabies," Mortimer offered, by way of solidarity over bugs, but Rainbow wasn't listening. She didn't stop until all her clothes were in a pile on the edge of the stream, then she looked at the dragons.

"Can you burn those for me?"

"Yes?" Beaufort said.

"Good." And she took off at a run through the trees, flashing pale as a thought through the heavy trunks. The dragons watched her go, then looked at each other.

"At least she didn't try to hug us like Barry," Mortimer pointed out.

"She's going to freeze, though," Beaufort said. "And we couldn't even find the zebra, or Harriet, or whoever it is. How's she going to?"

Mortimer bundled the clothes together and said, "Should we take them to her?"

"Too late," Beaufort said, tipping his head, and Mortimer followed suit. Somewhere beyond the trees he heard the slam of a car door and the rev of an engine.

"Oh dear," Mortimer said. "She found her just like that?"

"It sounds like it," Beaufort agreed, and looked up at the sky. "Maybe they had a meeting place set up. Do you think it's too light to follow them?"

"*Yes*," Mortimer said, so forcefully that Beaufort gave him a surprised look. "Sorry," he said. "But there's police."

"I'm sure you're right, lad," Beaufort said, still looking slightly nonplussed.

Mortimer examined his paw and wondered if the rabies was taking hold.

15

ALICE

One should never underestimate the abilities of women of a certain age, Alice thought. Especially the ones who seemed the most harmless. Those were the sort of women who could distract a person with a gentle word and a smile, perhaps a request to get something from the high shelf in the supermarket, and while one's back was turned they'd steal that last, coveted cheesy bread loaf from your cart, or the cart itself, or possibly the entire store.

Or, in this case, a patient from behind the back of a police officer.

"I'm sorry, Carlotta," Alice said into her phone. "I think I misheard you."

"Ugh, the signal's always so bad out here. I said, we've got Barry."

"How have you *got* Barry? You called me before and said there was a police officer guarding his room."

"Well, yes, but that's why we thought we'd better get him away. We'd never have been able to talk to him with the police there. And it's not as if he's dangerous or anything."

Rosemary's voice rose over the hands-free in the car, a little distant, as if she were turning to look into the back. "Do keep your pants on, there's a good chap."

"They're scratchy," a male voice said, indistinctly.

"We'll get you some nice soft ones when we get there," Rosemary said.

"Carlotta, I'm not worried that he's dangerous," Alice said. "I'm worried about the police arresting you."

"Oh, don't worry about that," Rosemary said. "It just so happened that I had a little moment of panic where I thought someone had stolen my bag, and the nice young officer helped me find it again. He was *very* patient, and not even upset when it turned out I'd just put it down in the waiting room and wandered off with a cushion instead. Barry likely escaped while the officer was helping me."

"This wasn't part of our plan," Alice pointed out.

"Well, no," Carlotta said. "But poor Barry was very unhappy in there. They restrained him when he kept taking his gown off, and sedated him just because he wouldn't stop singing 'Money Money Money'. It's not right. People's music choices are their own business."

Alice decided her house was strictly off-limits to any fugitives, especially ones with a taste for Abba, and said, "So what are you doing now?"

"We're on the way back. We thought maybe he could stay with Gert. She's got a good firm hand with people, and Rosemary's John won't know what to do with a nudist. He gets all pink and flustered if he sees someone's knees. We could go to my place, but my Bertie might bite something delicate, so it doesn't seem safe."

Bertie was Carlotta's parrot, who had a wide and varied vocabulary. Alice imagined it could become even more varied with the introduction of Barry. "I shall leave you to call Gert, then," she said. Gert's vocabulary was also wide and varied, and she didn't feel like dealing with it right now. She had more things to worry about.

"Shall do," Carlotta said, cheerfully enough, and Alice hit disconnect on her phone.

"What's happening?" Miriam asked. "Did I hear that they've taken Barry out of the hospital?"

"That does seem to be the situation, yes," Alice said.

"DI Adams isn't going to like that," Miriam said.

"No, I rather think not," Alice agreed. They had retired to Miriam's house, it being the most likely place the dragons would return to. Jasmine and Priya, meanwhile, had gone to park somewhere strategically distant (and before the phone signal vanished) from the woods near Miriam's great-aunt's house, so that they were handy to collect Rainbow if she emerged, but hopefully not so close that the police noticed them. Rose and Gert had gone to keep an eye on the camp near Malham, Rose because she was still put out that she hadn't been invited the night before, and Gert because she had a certain presence that might persuade Tom to behave himself if such a thing were needed. Pearl and Teresa were watching the bookshop in case anyone turned up there, although they'd already called to say that there was a note on the door declaring it was shut due to technical issues. Alice wondered if that was the fault of the ageing computer or the recalcitrant safe.

Miriam went back to brewing more tea. Priya's rum toddy offering had been some of Guneet's homebrew, a detour from his usual whisky, and the general consensus had been that it was not a recommended detour, and that a lot of good tea was needed to get rid of the taste.

"What do we do?" she asked. "We get Rainbow back here, and now we've got Barry too, and what then?"

"We keep them safe and we try to figure out who might be framing Rainbow," Alice said. "Then we present our evidence to the police once we're ready."

"You make it sound so easy," Miriam said.

Alice made a thoughtful sound. "I don't feel it should be *that* hard. How many enemies can your sister really have?"

Miriam didn't answer, and after a moment Alice added, "Well, who would go to these lengths to frame her?"

"Oh. Yes, I suppose that's a good point," Miriam said. "It's *quite* excessive, isn't it?"

Alice nodded, tapping her fingers on the table, then said, "I've changed my mind. We'll get Carlotta and Rosemary to bring Barry here."

"*Here?*" Miriam squeaked. "In my *home?*"

"Just so we can interview him."

"But what if he's naked?"

"You have seen naked men before, Miriam."

"That doesn't mean I want one in my kitchen." She got up. "I'm going to get some towels. At the very least he can sit on a towel."

"Most sensible," Alice said, and picked up her phone.

&

THE ARRIVAL of Barry was marginally preceded by the arrival of the dragons, whose scratchy knock on the door was instantly recognisable. Miriam rushed to open it, and let the High Lord and Mortimer into the kitchen. They trailed in, damp with a misty, persistent rain that had started up as the afternoon drew on, bringing in an early dusk.

"You're very early," Alice said. "We thought you'd wait until it was properly dark to risk flying." She tried not to sound reproving, but it really was very silly of them. The last thing they needed were dragon sightings. A murder was more than enough to deal with.

"We stayed in the cloud cover," Beaufort said. "And we felt we should get back sooner rather than later."

"What's that?" Miriam asked. She'd put the kettle back on, but now she stopped with the teapot in one hand and pointed at Mortimer, who had a bundle tucked into the crook of one foreleg. "Are those *clothes?*"

"Ye-es," Beaufort said. "Also the reason we thought we should get back fairly quickly."

"What happened?" Alice asked.

"Rainbow thinks The Government is after her," Mortimer said, in a near-whisper, as if he thought The Government might be lurking nearby.

"That doesn't explain the clothes," Miriam said, taking them from Mortimer. "These are Rainbow's." She gave them a horrified look. "Did something *eat* her in those woods? Are there eating things out there? *Goblins?*"

"There are eating things everywhere, but no, they didn't," Beaufort said. "She said there were bugs in her clothes, took them all off, and asked us to burn them."

"I asked if it was rabies, but I think it was a different sort of bug," Mortimer said. "I might have rabies, though, on account of the bats."

Alice decided she couldn't follow that line of reasoning right at the moment. "So she's in the woods naked now? That seems foolish."

"No, we heard her get in a car," Beaufort said. "Quite possibly with Harriet."

"She left with Harriet?" Alice asked.

"We're not certain. We saw someone in a zebra suit, but couldn't catch up to them. Rainbow seemed to think it was Harriet, so we thought maybe they had a meeting place arranged."

"That sounds quite likely," Alice said, inspecting the clothes as Miriam laid them over a chair. "Miriam? Do you know much about the roads out there? Is there another way to reach the house?"

Miriam went back to the tea. "There never used to be, but that was a while ago."

"Some things grow rapidly," Beaufort said, and Alice heard the words he didn't say. That some things are lost even more quickly, such as wild old woods and the hidden, fragile places of the world.

"Did you see the car?" she asked the dragons.

"She was in it and away before we realised what she was doing," Beaufort said. "We'd have had to be under the cloud cover to follow, and it was still too light."

Mortimer made a small noise that suggested there had been some rather strenuous pleading on his part to get the High Lord to come to that conclusion.

"Entirely the right choice," Alice said, pushing down her disappointment, and at that moment there was another knock at the kitchen door. "And we do have another lead."

"Wonderful!" Beaufort exclaimed, and Miriam opened the door to admit Rosemary, Carlotta, and Barry, who was wearing a hospital gown under a large red wool coat, his knees knobbly and exposed beneath it. He had a cast on one arm, the coat's sleeve hanging loose on that side.

Mortimer retreated to behind the kitchen table, and Miriam said, "Hello, Barry. You're very welcome here, but this is a clothing-compulsory house."

"Aw," Barry said, but he went to the table docilely enough and helped himself to a piece of plum cake. "Yum," he said, and waved at Mortimer. "Hello again."

"Hi," Mortimer said, and shuffled around the kitchen table a little further.

"He seems very calm," Alice said.

Carlotta nodded. "I had a little of Priya's homebrew in my flask. Just in case of the cold, you know. It seems to agree with him."

"I'm glad it agrees with someone," Alice said, who thought she could still taste it at the back of her throat.

Miriam sorted out more mugs and more tea, and in very short order they were seated at the kitchen table, all four of them and the dragons looking at Barry. He was working on a second piece of plum cake, and had a couple of jam thumbprint biscuits on the side of his plate. He was still wearing the big coat and seemed unconcerned by their scrutiny.

"Barry," Alice said. "Can you answer some questions for us?"

He screwed his face up. "Like the police questions? They were so pushy and impatient. So *angry*."

"They were angry at you?" Miriam asked. "That's not right."

"Not at me. Just in general." He waved vaguely. "I think the world makes them angry."

"Well, *we're* not angry," Rosemary said.

"No," he agreed. "You're friendly." He shot Alice a wary look. "You're a bit angry, though."

"I'm not," Alice said, before she could stop herself, and Barry looked back at his plate, hunching his shoulders.

"Barry," Miriam said, leaning forward and folding her arms on the table. "I'm Rainbow's sister."

"I know," he said to his plate.

"I'm trying to make sure she's safe. Can you help me?"

He looked up without raising his head. "I don't know."

"If I ask you some things, will you answer them if you can?"

He gave a little shrug, still hunching forward, and then said, "Can I play with the dragon if I do?"

Miriam looked at Beaufort and Mortimer. "Of course," Beaufort said, in a hearty voice.

"Not that one," Barry whispered. "He's *jolly.*"

"Oh no," Mortimer mumbled, hunching almost as much as Barry. He looked at Beaufort, then at Miriam, then sighed. "I mean, yes?"

"Nice dragon," Barry mumbled, his cheeks going pink.

"Nice person?" Mortimer offered, his scales as deeply grey as the kitchen floor. Alice wondered just how much fun Barry was going to have playing with an anxious dragon, but she didn't say anything. She merely sat there trying to look as un-angry as possible, and hoped Miriam would ask the right questions.

"Alright," Miriam said, still in that gentle voice. "Do you want some more tea before we start? Or more plum cake, perhaps?"

"Yes," Barry and Mortimer both said, and Barry gave the dragon a luminous smile through his straggly beard. Mortimer bared his teeth back in what was likely meant to be an answering grin, but looked a lot as if he had stomach problems.

Carlotta got up and went to the kettle, and Rosemary shared out the cake, and Alice tried to keep her face in a neutral expression and not to look too obviously impatient.

"We think Rainbow's in some trouble," Miriam said to Barry. "Someone may be trying to frame her for a crime."

"Oh, I know," Barry said.

"You know?" Miriam glanced at Alice, who raised her eyebrows. The body had been in Rainbow's van *after* she'd dropped Barry at the hospital. Had someone told him?

"Yes. The thefts."

Alice dug her fingers into her mug to stop herself leaning forward, and just smiled encouragingly. Or tried to, anyway. Barry was still avoiding looking at her.

"What can you tell us about the thefts?" Miriam asked.

"It was fancy stuff," Barry said.

"What sort of fancy stuff?"

"From the houses," he said, waving vaguely. "Art things and pretty pieces."

"Which houses?"

"The ones with the fancy stuff."

Alice could feel her toes actually curling in her shoes as she resisted the urge to slap a hand on the table and demand he talk sense. That or shake him. Shaking him would be *very* satisfying.

But Miriam only smiled and watched Carlotta set a mug of tea in front of him, then said, "So Rainbow didn't take this fancy stuff, but someone's trying to make it look like she did?"

He nodded, and said around another piece of cake, "We only care about the animals. The animals are important, you know? And the birds. I like birds." He stopped, looking at Mortimer wistfully. "Can you sing?"

"No," Mortimer said.

"That's a shame. Because you're like a bird otherwise."

"Am I?"

"Just with scales instead of feathers. Like a dinosaur. They were birds."

"Barry," Miriam said, pulling his attention back to her. "Rainbow said someone was stealing from the same houses you set the animals free from. Is that right?"

He nodded, slurping his tea.

"Did you ever see anyone in the group with some of this fancy stuff?"

He shrugged, a tight small movement, and stared at his tea.

"Barry?"

"No. I don't know. I can't say. I ... I don't want to go back to hospital."

"You won't have to," Carlotta said, topping his tea up. "You're very safe here." She looked at Miriam, who nodded and tried another tack.

"Do you know anyone in the group who likes fancy stuff?"

He considered it. "Tom likes fancy clothes. He didn't used to, but then Jemima got a posh boyfriend who has fancy clothes, so then Tom wanted fancy clothes too."

"Oh? When did that happen?" Miriam asked.

"When Jemima got a boyfriend," Barry said, his tone making it clear that should be obvious. "But she left the group anyway, to be The Establishment. Which was okay because Simon joined, so we still had enough people."

"Enough for what?" Miriam asked.

"For everything. The protests and the animals and all of it." He took another bite of cake.

"And the fancy stuff?" Miriam tried again. "Did that start happening after Simon joined, perhaps?"

Barry chewed slowly, then took a long drink of tea, and fussed with his plate. "It's very bad. A week or a month or something after we free the animals, *boom*. Fancy stuff gets stolen. It makes it look like us, and it undermines the cause if people think we're in it for the money." He looked around the table, his eyes wide and brown and earnest. "And we're *not*. It's for the animals. And the birds. For the Earth."

Alice wondered if that was true for everyone. It had to be quite the temptation, if you were breaking in somewhere anyway. And every revolution had to get its funding from somewhere. But the body was a whole step further.

Miriam looked at her, and Alice made a little *carry on* gesture with one hand. Miriam looked at her blankly, then Rosemary said, "But who do you think might do that, Barry? Who might want the fancy stuff? Do you think it's Tom?"

He frowned at his plate, then picked up a jam thumbprint and wedged it into his mouth whole. "Don't know," he said indistinctly. "It's usually The Government. They do all sorts of bad things."

"That is what Rainbow said," Beaufort agreed.

"It seems a little … *small scale* for the government, though," Carlotta said. "Surely they'd frame you for something bigger. Blow up a power plant or something."

"We'd *never*," Barry said. "That's how people get hurt. We don't hurt people."

Alice thought the body rather disproved that, but the question was which part of the *we* had done it.

"And what about ..." Miriam hesitated. "As well as the thefts, there was ... um ..." she trailed off and mouthed, *the body*, as if Barry was a toddler she didn't want hearing bad words.

"Eh?" Rosemary said.

Barry sighed. "I miss the old stuff. Living in trees to protect them. Camping out in fields to stop them being dug up. Taking boats out to barricade ports. It's all changed now. Videos and social media and so on. *Going viral.* It's all got to be filmed or it doesn't mean anything. And everyone's always telling me to put clothes on because it ruins their pictures." He looked at the women seriously. "The human form is very natural."

"It certainly is," Carlotta said, and offered him another piece of cake.

"And we've got all these *new* people too, with their power packs and solar batteries and *stuff*. What sort of alternative living is *that?*"

Alice looked at Miriam, and mouthed, *Tom?*

"How long ago did Jemima get a new boyfriend?" Miriam asked.

Barry shrugged. "A bit ago."

"Did the thefts start after that?"

"Oh, yes," Barry said, biting into the cake.

The women and the dragons looked at each other.

"I'm calling Rose and Gert," Alice said, taking her phone out. "See if they've seen him out at the bunker."

"Can we tell DI Adams now?" Miriam asked. "Surely this is proof?"

"It's only to do with the thefts, not the body," Alice said. "And we don't even know if he's definitely responsible. It's a shaky link."

"Can I play with the dragon now?" Barry asked.

"One more question," Alice said, as gently as she could, and Barry looked at her, although he seemed to be making eye contact with her left ear. "What happened to your hand?"

"I broke it," Barry said, his voice flat.

"How?"

He looked away, his face pale and set. "I fell."

"How, Barry?"

He shook his head, and tears trembled in his eyes. "I *fell*. I didn't mean anything. I just *fell*."

Alice looked at the other women around the table, and at the dragons, but no one said anything, and after a moment she said, "Did you bump into anyone when you fell?"

"I'm not meant to say," he whispered. "I didn't think I did, I thought it was the door, and then the door hit my hand so hard it broke it – my hand, not the door – so I don't understand how I hit anyone else, but I'm not meant to say." He picked up a napkin and wiped his nose almost delicately. "I promised," he added.

"Even dragons?" Beaufort asked, and Barry gave him an uncertain, wide-eyed look, then shook his head.

"No one," he said, his voice painfully low. "Or they might keep me in the hospital forever, and make me wear clothes all the time, and never see the sky."

No one spoke for a moment, then Alice hit dial on her phone. Rose answered almost immediately, and Alice didn't bother with niceties. "Is there anyone at the bunker?"

"We haven't seen anyone," she said. "But they could be inside."

"Any vehicles?"

"None I've seen."

"Stay away from it," Alice said, because there was no guarantee Simon wasn't responsible, or even Harriet. Or at least involved. "Even if you see someone, no contact at all, understood?"

"Got it," Rose said. "Inside job, was it?"

"Quite possibly. Call me the moment you see anything." She hung up and looked at the little group at the table. "We very much need to find Rainbow again."

"Can we call Colin, at least?" Miriam asked. "It is his mother."

"He's off the case," Alice pointed out. "He'll only pass it on to DI Adams, and we can't waste time while she makes a fuss over the Barry situation."

They all looked at Barry, who mumbled, "I'd like to go outside now. This is a lot of *inside*, and the hospital was all inside, and it's making me feel quite sick."

Alice thought that might actually be the four slices of plum cake and six jam thumbprints, but she just said, "Mortimer, how about you and Barry go outside?"

Mortimer got up slowly. "I'm not frolicking," he said. "I don't frolic."

"I love frolicking," Barry said brightly, and got up so quickly he almost knocked his chair over. Mortimer followed him out into the garden with his head and tail low, and Alice pointed her phone at Miriam.

"Call Pearl and Teresa and see if they can have a peek in the bookshop windows. I'm sure they can think of an excuse if need be." She looked at Carlotta and Rosemary. "Can one of you call Gert and see if she found out anything on the CCTV? I forgot to ask."

"Of course," Carlotta said, pulling her phone out.

"I'll make sure Barry doesn't get his cast wet," Rosemary said, pulling her coat on. "Or harass poor Mortimer too much. That dragon's going to be bald by teatime at this rate."

"Who're you calling?" Miriam asked Alice.

"If Rainbow's gone, Jasmine and Priya may as well come back. Other than you, they're the best out of all of us on computers, and I want to see what they can find out about Tom and the thefts."

Miriam made a small noise that was half flattered, half relieved, and picked up her phone.

From outside, Alice could dimly hear Barry shouting as she pulled up Jasmine's number.

He was enjoying his frolic, if nothing else.

16

DI ADAMS

DI Adams was having serious doubts about her decision to proceed with the search for Judith Ellis without a full team. She had two torches, the compass and GPS on her watch, a waterproof jacket, her trousers tucked into her boots, and the radio clipped to her lapel, but this was ... unpleasant. The trees were heavy-trunked and surrounded by vast, sprawling masses of roots, and scrubby undergrowth grabbed at her legs, and rain dripped off the canopy and down the back of her neck. It was still daylight, but beneath the trees it was dim enough that she was using a torch to probe the shadows, searching for a glimpse of life.

"Inspector?" PC Liv Byrne called from probably only about twenty metres away on the other side of the stream they were following. DI Adams could barely even see the glimmer of her torch in the shadows of the trees.

"Constable?" she called back. "Have you found something?"

"Um ... no. It's just ... these woods are really thick, aren't they?"

"It's pretty heavy undergrowth," DI Adams agreed. "But let's stick to radio silence." Even though they weren't on the radio, but the same thing applied. There was no reason to warn everyone who was out here that they were coming. Although the cracking of broken twigs and clatter of disturbed stones underfoot was probably more than enough of a giveaway.

"Sorry," Liv said, and then there was quiet but for the sound of their own steady progress.

DI Adams waited until she was sure Liv couldn't see her, then whistled as loudly as she dared. The sound of Liv's movements stopped.

"Was that you?" the PC called after a moment.

"Yes, sorry. I was going for bird sounds, you know. As cover."

There was a long pause, then Liv said, "I don't think that's going to work."

"No," DI Adams agreed. "My mistake." She wondered how quickly that would get around the station – the city cop from down south whistling in the woods. But it had worked. The long-legged form of Dandy drifted through the trees to her like a woodland spirit, and offered her his ball. "I don't want it," she whispered, and he pushed it against her thigh. She swallowed a groan, took the slobbery ball, and put it in her pocket. "Time to earn your keep, magic dog," she said, keeping her voice low and listening to make sure Liv was still ploughing steadily onward. Dandy tipped his head at her. "Help me find Rainbow. The one who ran away before." Dandy tilted his head in the other direction, the dreadlocks over his eyes shifting to give a flash of those luminously red eyes. DI Adams took a woollen hat she'd found in the kitchen out of her pocket and held it out to him. "Her. Find her."

Dandy snuffled at the hat, then took it delicately in his teeth and swallowed it in one gulp.

"*No—*"

"DI Adams?" Liv called. "Did you say something?"

"Just tripped over. It's fine," she called back, and glared at Dandy, dropping her voice. "You weren't meant to *eat* it, you over-sauced poodle."

Dandy's tongue lolled out of his mouth, and she was almost certain he was laughing at her, then he turned and headed into the woods, angling off in a slightly different direction to the one she'd been

taking. She watched him go, unsure if there was any point in following, and he stopped, looking back at her over his shoulder, then
pointed his nose in the direction he was going before looking back at
her again.

"Fine," she hissed. "But if you're taking me to a stash of hats and
balls, I'm shaving you. I swear it." She switched off her torch and
started after him, keying her radio and keeping her voice low. "PC
Byrne, I'm heading"—she checked her watch—"roughly north-north-
east. I've found a bit of a trail."

"Copy," came back almost immediately. "Shall I follow you?"

"No, keep on the stream and see if you come across anything that
way. This could be nothing."

"Copy that."

Radio silence fell again, and over the crunch and squelch of her
own footsteps DI Adams could hear birds calling, warning each other
about the intruder in their midst, and the chatter of the shallow
stream falling away to her left, and the patter of slowly building rain
on the leaves above them, and all the myriad noises of a forest as light
fades and the night waits its turn. Dandy led her on, making no
allowances for her dearth of legs and excess of height (compared to
him, anyway), and she followed as quietly and carefully as she could,
which wasn't very on either count. She could already feel scratches on
her hands and a couple on one cheek stinging. Bloody countryside.

It felt like they'd been going for at least half an hour, but which her
watch told her was actually less than ten minutes, when Dandy
stopped, his head lifting as he stared into the steadily darkening
woods, his ears coming to half-mast. DI Adams crept up to join him,
the unlit torch still clutched in one hand and the other touching the
baton in her pocket for a little reassurance. He didn't look at her, just
kept scanning the trees ahead of them, waiting for something to show
itself. DI Adams was about to nudge him and tell him to keep going
when there was a flash of movement in the dimness to their left. They
both turned to it, and a moment later a deer of some sort stepped
delicately through the undergrowth, its coat deeply shaded and scored
with vibrant white stripes, and its dark eyes wearing a pale mask. Its

ears were almost comically large, but its horns were larger still, chunky and pointed. It shook its head irritably, dislodging a clinging twig, then picked its way on. Another followed it, and three more, their flanks painted with those long stripes amid dark fur that rendered them almost invisible in the deep shadows. If Dandy hadn't sniffed them out, DI Adams was quite sure she wouldn't have seen them.

Only once they were swallowed entirely by the trees did Dandy start forward again, and she followed, frowning to herself. Stripes weren't usual for deer, were they? Or horns, for that matter? Antlers she'd heard of, but these had been long straight things. She was hardly an expert in such matters though, and it was also the least of her worries right now.

She went back to concentrating on keeping up with Dandy and not tripping over something and sending herself headfirst into a tree trunk. There'd be time to wonder about deer species later. Right now, she had to find Judith Ellis before the Toot Hansell W.I. took it into their heads to get any more involved.

THE NEXT TIME DANDY STOPPED, DI Adams peered around expectantly, waiting for more deer to drift across the path. She could still just about see where she was going, and she rather fancied another look at the creatures before she had to turn her torch on and scare off everything within a half-mile radius. But this time Dandy was looking up, and she followed his gaze curiously. She couldn't see anything, and when he gave a very small growl at the back of his throat she decided the time for discretion had passed. Perhaps Judith had ensconced herself in the branches? It made sense. She was well-known for chaining herself to them, after all.

DI Adams flicked on her torch and pointed it at the tree, fully expecting to see either a lady of a certain age in camouflage gear, perching up the tree like she was reliving her childhood, or, more likely, a squirrel. Dandy was very keen on them, and had a disconcerting habit of chasing them *up* trees, meaning she had to ignore a Labrador-sized dog prancing around the branches in the park, and occasionally falling out of them when he misjudged his weight. She was becoming more used to it, though, and as no one else seemed to see him, she doubted it was too much of an issue.

Instead, the torch reflected on a pair of large eyes and an even larger set of teeth, which snarled at them in the instant before the creature they belonged to vanished. DI Adams and Dandy both gave matching yelps, and she added, "What the hell was *that?*" although there was no one around to answer her. The radio crackled almost instantly to life.

"DI Adams? Is everything okay? I thought I heard something?"

"I'm fine," she said, although her heart rate was so high that her watch was going to have conniptions in a moment. She turned in a circle, playing the torch over the undergrowth, just in case there was something else toothy creeping up on them. "There seems to be some unusual wildlife in here, though."

"*Yes,*" Liv said instantly. "Monkeys!"

"*What?*"

"There's *monkeys!* They threw stuff at me. Ellis must be the one robbing the animal collections, and stashing them out here." The excitement in her voice was audible.

DI Adams took a deep breath. Bloody Judith. She might not be W.I., but she was at least as troublesome. "What's she playing at? Monkeys can't survive out here, surely?"

"I don't really know," Liv said. "There's those ones in Japan that swim in hot springs to stay warm."

"Didn't realise this was the hot spring capital of the north."

Liv didn't answer, and DI Adams wondered what she could say to make it clear she was just tired and over-caffeinated, not having a go. Before she could think of anything, her radio crackled into life again.

"Adams, Lucas."

At least he was back. Maybe they could make some progress now. "Go ahead," she said.

"I sent a photo of those bats to a mate of mine at the Institute for Tropical Disease Research."

"Not liking the sound of that."

"No, it's just her speciality is diseases in bats, so she's familiar with them, and the RSPCA told me to call the Bat Conservation Trust, and *they* told me there was no one nearby so to call the RSPCA, so ... looking for solutions at the moment. Anyhow, my mate says they're not native."

"Does that mean you can go back in there?"

"No, it means we have to contain them because they can't be loose here."

DI Adams turned again, checking for teeth and eyes, but there didn't seem to be anything lurking nearby. Dandy was standing to attention at her side, though, and he'd grown up to the size of a Great Dane, which she wasn't particularly reassured by. Not if it meant there were things out there he felt he needed to be that large to deal with.

"So when can that happen?" she asked.

"I've got someone trying to roust the RSPCA lot," he said. "But it probably won't be till tomorrow with that many bloody bats. There's a couple more bodies and a dog handler on the way, though, so maybe we can turn up your fugitive anyway."

Dandy started to growl, low and steady, and DI Adams shone her torch in the direction his nose was pointed. She couldn't see anything, not yet, but the dog's head was low and his teeth were bared. If he'd been able to raise his hackles under that heavy coat, she was sure they'd be up.

"I don't think it's a good idea tonight," she said, keeping her voice low. "PC Byrne, make your way back to the house immediately. Lucas, bring PC Shaw and meet her."

"Copy," Liv said immediately, and DI Adams turned her radio right down, silencing Lucas in the middle of asking what was going on. Silence fell around her, just the steady growling of Dandy, slowly rising in volume. Her heart ticked up again, and she took a long, slow breath. He wasn't looking up into the branches, so either this was something new, or it had come down to the ground.

Dandy swung his head to the right suddenly, his growl morphing into a snarl as he glared into the undergrowth. It was moving. Or there were more than one.

DI Adams exercised her vocabulary in some imaginative ways, and took a slow step backward. Something in the bushes to her left grunted, a deep and disdainful sound, and she swung the torch toward it. A new sound came from her right, a resonant drumming that set the skin on her arms crawling, and she panned the torch back again, thinking of trolls and goblins and monsters, Black Dogs and Barghests and Shellycoats and drivelling, ravenous Red Caps, her heart going too fast and the fading day sharply delineated in dim light and shadow. She took another step in retreat, and Dandy stopped growling abruptly. He grabbed her hand in his mouth, tugging her in another direction. Deeper into the woods.

"Oh, bloody brilliant," she whispered, but he could see more than she could out here. Could smell and hear better too. She freed her hand, took her collapsible baton from her pocket and snapped it out, the weight reassuring in her hand. Dandy watched her raise the torch to her shoulder, then took a step in the direction he'd been pulling her.

DI Adams nodded at him and followed his lead, walking slow and careful, her back prickling. She couldn't tell if she was imagining things or not now – grunts and hisses in the undergrowth, the scraping of big claws on rocky ground, and that strange, deep drumming, alien and echoey. Dandy let her go past him then followed on silent paws, his growling starting up again and every now and then hiking into a snarl at the movement of unknown bodies in the dark.

She couldn't place the noise. Other than Dandy, there was no growling, no snarling. Just those almost judgemental grunts and disdainful hisses, and the sense of movement in the trees. She wondered what else Judith had dumped in the woods. What had Collins mentioned? Emus? *War-winning* emus? Emus that could kick down fences?

Even as she thought it there was movement behind her, the scrape of hard claws on stone, accompanied by a medley of hissing and grunting. She spun, the torchlight flooding over round grey bodies and curving necks capped by small heads and glaring eyes. Three of them, tipping their heads one way then the other, advancing on huge feet armed with horrifying talons. They stopped as the torchlight hit them, and the moment stretched long and still. One hissed almost questioningly, darting its head forward, and another took a cautious step toward her, lowering its head a little. It gave a hopeful grunt, and the third rushed forward suddenly, shaking its feathers enthusiastically. DI Adams yelped, jumping back, and Dandy's snarl all but shook the air. The bird stopped so suddenly it staggered, and abruptly all three were looking at Dandy instead of her.

Dandy lowered his head, the snarl giving way to a threatening growl as he put himself between the birds and DI Adams. The hissing changed tone, the grunts becoming fiercer, and DI Adams held a hand out to Dandy.

"Heel," she whispered to him, and he made no move to do so. Not that she had really thought he would, but it was worth a try. She took a step forward instead, grabbing a handful of the heavy dreadlocks that hung from his shoulders. "It's okay," she said, not sure if she were addressing the birds or the dandy. The birds shuffled warily, their heads darting as they looked from her to Dandy, and she was having trouble looking away from their feet. They were disproportionately large, each toe crowned with a vicious-looking claw.

She took a step back, tugging Dandy with her, and the birds followed. Dandy's growling hiked up a notch.

"It's okay," she said, retreating another step. The birds matched it. "We're not going to hurt you."

One of the birds made that creepy drumming noise again, and she had the feeling it had moved past judgemental into simply laughing at her. She risked a glance around, looking for a distraction, or a way out, and the birds surged forward. Dandy ripped out of her grasp as he plunged to meet them.

"*Dandy, no!*" DI Adams shouted. The first bird reared up, neck moving like an entirely separate beast, and aimed a vicious kick at Dandy. He slipped past it, quick and lithe, and nipped at the bird's standing leg, bouncing away without making contact. The bird staggered sideways as it lashed out again, colliding with the second emu and sending it off-course. The third sprinted at DI Adams with a hiss of fury, neck stretched long and beak aimed straight at her, then tripped over a stray root and sent itself stumbling even as she threw herself out of its path, skidding to her knees on the rough ground and rolling up again.

"*Dandy!*"

He ignored her, dancing between the other two birds. They hissed with rage, kicking out in great deadly sweeps with those terrible claws, feet sweeping so close to him that they parted the heavy locks of his hair. She started to shout again, but a closer hiss reminded her that she still had one emu intent on her, so she waved the baton at it threateningly. It snaked its neck in a manner that was horribly reminiscent of an oversized goose and grunted, squinting against her torchlight. She risked another glance at Dandy, just in time to see a kick make glancing contact with his shoulder. He yelped, a startled, almost betrayed sound, and skittered away.

"*Hey! Leave him alone you overgrown* **chicken drumsticks!**" DI Adams bellowed. She lunged forward to put herself between him and the emus, waving her arms and baton in the vague hope that making herself look bigger might help. The third bird's grunt took on a note of triumph behind her, and the other two emus turned their attention to her. She had one moment to imagine getting kicked simultaneously by three dinosaur descendants who didn't look like they'd actually descended all that far, then as they rushed her she dodged sideways. She stumbled on the rough ground, dropping her torch and baton and catching herself on her hands. The movement turned into something that was half fall, half cartwheel, and completely inelegant, but effective. Dandy *whuffed* a deep-throated warning, and hurdled her as he charged the beasts.

She came to her feet again in time to see a scrum of colliding emus and Dandy emerging from the other side of it, dreadlocks flying.

"Dandy!" she shouted. *"Heel!"* She didn't wait to see if he'd deign to obey, just sprinted for the tree the big cat had been in, hoping it wasn't still there. Pounding feet and furious hisses rushed in behind her and she jumped, grabbing a low-hanging branch and muscling herself up onto it gracelessly, boots scrabbling at the trunk for purchase. A searing pain on her calf almost sent her back to the ground, but she jerked her leg away and hauled herself out of reach, the bark rough and wet and utterly beautiful under her palms, thanking whatever small forest gods might be out there for the fact that she'd taken a beak to the leg rather than a foot to the face.

"Dandy!" she shouted again. "Come *on!*"

The emus swung toward Dandy, trapped on the other side of the clearing with the light of the dropped torch sending the birds' shadows looming over him. DI Adams yelled, something fragmented and incoherent that was both a plea for Dandy to move and for the creatures to leave him be, but they ignored her. They surged toward the dandy, and big as he was, he went down under the combined onslaught of lashing beaks and triumphant grunts and those terrible, brutal, feet.

"Dandy?" DI Adams managed, clutching the branch beneath her. The word came out in a wheeze, breathless and uncertain, and her stomach rolled over heavily. The emus were milling around, and she couldn't tell if they were trampling him underfoot or if they were readying themselves for another attack. She swallowed hard, trying to make sense out of the fractured shadows, and there was a soft *whuff* from above her. She jerked her head up so fast that her neck twinged painfully, and met Dandy's red eyes. He was back to Labrador size, perched on the next branch up like a misshapen owl, and he panted at her, his tongue lolling.

"Oh, you ..." She couldn't decide how to finish the sentence, so she just reached up a little precariously and he licked her hand. "Are you hurt?"

He whined, but without much feeling, and settled himself more comfortably. She supposed there wasn't much she could do now anyway, so she scrambled into a more secure position, ignoring the pain in her calf. She watched the emus for a moment, rendered monstrous by the torchlight as they shambled around below the tree, then turned her radio back up.

"Lucas, Adams."

"Adams! What happened? You went off air."

"Small problem with a … what's the collective noun for emus?" she asked.

There was silence for a moment, then, "Did you fall and hit your head?"

"No. I'm in a tree, and I think there was a big cat in it earlier but it seems to be gone now. I'm more worried about the emus. Can you get someone out to find a phone signal and call the RSPCA again?"

More silence. Finally Lucas said, "You're not joking."

"Ask Liv about her monkeys."

"There were definitely monkeys," Liv said immediately. "And I think something was following me on the way back, at least until Ben and Lucas met me."

"Might've been the big cat," DI Adams said.

Lucas came back on, still sounding faintly bemused. "Yes, fine, I will go out and call the RSPCA again. Not sure how set up they are for emus and big cats down at the local rescue centre, though."

"Tell them they're just going to have to come up with something," DI Adams said. "And get me another coffee, and call Collins and tell him his mum and her animal liberation efforts are a menace to society. Or certainly to police operations."

"Fair enough," Lucas said. "Sit tight."

"Not much choice on that," DI Adams said, and leaned back against the tree trunk. Dandy panted down at her. "Good dog," she said after a moment, and he wagged his tail gently, then whined. She reached into her pocket, found his ball, and tossed it up to him, then they sat there and watched the emus grunting and stomping, and hoped the big cat didn't come back.

⁊⁊

AFTER A WHILE she took her notebook out and leafed through it by the light of her phone, wondering what Collins had rushed off for. But whatever he was up to, what she had right now was one dead man presumably killed in a wildlife break-out gone wrong, which she wasn't exactly looking forward to putting in an official report. She also had a suspect wandering around a patch of woods in which big cats and emus had apparently established their territory, which seemed like a bad combination, and likely to lead to a second wildlife break-out-related death. Although, she added to herself, wildlife rather than … *other things* made an improvement on some of her recent situations.

She looked at Dandy. "Thoughts?" she said, and he panted at her. "You're a rubbish partner."

He whined again, and her radio crackled into life. "Adams, Shaw."

"Go ahead."

"Are your emus still there?"

She peered down. "I don't see them."

"Alright. What direction did you take from the house? Liv and I are coming in after you."

She considered telling them to wait for more backup, but it was starting to rain, and the roughness of the bark that had been so comforting before was biting her skin through her trousers. Plus her calf was aching and she wasn't sure what sort of germs emu beaks carried.

"Hit the stream and turn left. My torch is on the ground, but start shouting when you get close."

"Copy."

The radio went quiet, and she looked at Dandy. "Can you keep an eye on them? Maybe make sure no one gets kicked?"

He gave a little whuff, and melted down the tree to disappear into the dark. DI Adams shivered. The night was suddenly a lot colder.

MIRIAM

Miriam's kitchen door swung open, and Jasmine hurried in looking pink and breathless, with Primrose tucked under one arm. "We're here!" she announced to the room at large. Priya padded in after her rather more circumspectly, rain dripping off the hood of her pink waterproof coat.

"Hello love," Rosemary said. "We were just making tea."

"What's happening?" Jasmine asked, setting Primrose on the ground and dropping a bag on the table, then trotting back to the door to hang her coat up. "We've got our laptops, and our waterproofs and our wellies, so we're ready for whatever we need."

"Wonderful," Alice said. "I take it you didn't see anyone of interest while you were looking for Rainbow?"

Jasmine took her phone out of the bag and waved it at them. "I took photos, but it was just the police, I think. They didn't see us, though. We were quite well hidden."

"*Quite well hidden,*" Priya said, peeling her coat off. "My poor car's all mud and leaves and scratches now, I'm sure of it."

"But Ben— I mean, no one saw us," Jasmine pointed out. "It was worth building a decent hide."

Priya glanced at her but didn't say anything, and after a moment Miriam said, "Jasmine, dear, is everything alright?"

"Yes. Why?"

"Well, you keep saying Ben's very grumpy at the moment, and you seem quite worried about him seeing you." Miriam decided not to add that Jasmine was also twisting the sleeve of her jumper so hard it was unlikely to go back into shape any time soon.

"I just don't want to get him into trouble," she said. "The ... we reflect badly on him sometimes, you know. Or I do, I suppose, because of what we get up to."

There was silence in the room, then Alice said, "Beaufort, would you pop out and see how Mortimer's getting on?"

"*Hmm?*" the High Lord said. "I'm sure ..." he trailed off, looking at the women, then said, "I'm sure that's a very fine idea." He padded out the door, and Carlotta put a mug of tea in front of Jasmine, then handed another one to Priya.

"*Reflects badly* on him?" Miriam said, before anyone else could. She wasn't sure she was the best person to be talking, since she was the only one in the room who had never been married, and hadn't been much inclined to anything else, either, as the whole romantic to-do seemed like *such* a fuss, but she was too annoyed not to. "Is that what he's been saying?"

"He just means ... I mean, he wants a promotion, of course, and ... well, if we keep meddling in investigations ... or if I do, really, it's the whole guilt by association thing and he's really fed up and he says I should quit the W.I." The last words came out in a rush, and no one spoke. Miriam plucked at the front of her jumper, getting some air moving. She was suddenly *very* hot indeed, and she didn't quite trust herself to speak. And to think she'd *liked* Ben! Here he was being another silly man about things.

"And what do you want to do?" Alice asked. Her voice was very calm.

"Well, of course I don't want to quit, but I don't want to upset him, either. He's really *so* grumpy." Jasmine sighed. "It's irritating. He's just never happy about *anything* at the moment, and he's even being horrible about my food." There was a different sort of pause this time, and she looked around at them. "I know it's terrible. But he always used to say he loved it, and now he barely eats it. He doesn't even pretend. He used to take leftovers for lunch, and I know he threw them out, but still. It was the thought." She fiddled with her sleeve again. "It feels like I can't get anything right."

Priya put an arm around Jasmine and leaned her head against hers, then said, "You do so many things right. If he's so fussed about his silly meals, let him make them."

Jasmine gave a startled little laugh. "Well, I mean, I *could*, but he works and I only—"

"Cook, do everything at home, and work who knows how many hours with that online customer service thingy," Carlotta said. "Which they don't pay you enough for, by the way."

"People really are very rude," Jasmine said, a little wearily. "Someone called me a stuffed pigeon the other day when I couldn't give them a refund because they lost a button off a shirt they bought three years ago. I'm still not sure how insulted to be."

"Plus you do all the W.I. social media and accounts for free," Alice said. "I don't know where we'd be without you."

Jasmine made a small noise but didn't answer.

Rosemary slid the half-empty plate of cake across the table to the younger woman. "I think it sounds like he needs a little shake up. If he doesn't like your cooking, stop cooking for him. Tell him to get a takeaway on the way home. If he wants to be grumpy, leave him to stew in it. And whatever you do, *don't* stop doing the things you love, or that matter to you."

"Oh," Jasmine said quietly. "I mean, I love the W.I. of course, but ..."

"There's your answer, then," Carlotta said.

"Is it?"

"Whatever you love, do more of it," Priya said, nodding firmly. "Life is far too short and far too complicated to be lived without joy."

"Just like that?" Jasmine gave a little smile, trying to make a joke of it, and Miriam's heart squeezed.

"It's never quite just like that," Alice said. "But it's very doable, especially for someone as capable as you, Jasmine."

"I'm not, really," Jasmine said, and Carlotta swatted her with a tea towel. "*Hey!*"

"I'll do it every time you say that," she said.

Jasmine looked at Miriam, who smiled. "I'm afraid I'm not much help, dear," she said. "The whole husband thing is a bit of a mystery to me."

The younger woman snorted. "To me, too. And I've been practising for ten years."

"Oh, you amateur," Rosemary said, but she was smiling. "Give it another twenty and there'll be no question about you doing exactly what you like."

Miriam shrugged. "I just don't know why one needs to wait that long."

"Some of us quite like our husbands," Priya replied. "Most of the time, anyway."

"I *do* like Ben," Jasmine said, her voice a little wobbly.

"Well, there are always solutions," Alice said. "One way or the other."

Everyone looked at her, and Miriam was quite sure she wasn't the only one thinking about Alice's missing husband again.

"Um," Jasmine said, and poked her bag. "Okay?" The wobble in her voice was more pronounced, and Priya hugged her, pulling her into a tight and easy embrace that squeezed a little sob out of the younger woman. Miriam hurried to join them, and even Alice placed a careful hand on the younger woman's back, rubbing it gently, and for one moment the warmth of the kitchen held an even warmer knot of entwined arms and whispered words, hearts and heads pressed close in a magic that was fiercer and deeper than anything the world outside could hold – or withstand.

"You can always get another one if you have to," Carlotta whispered into the wild quiet. "I've had three."

"Things you love?" Jasmine asked.

"Oh, no. Husbands," Carlotta said.

"That's how they do it in the old country," Rosemary said, and a little wash of laughter wrapped around them, bright and light and easy.

❧

JASMINE AND PRIYA sat at the kitchen table, each with their laptop open, Alice peering over Jasmine's shoulder.

"I'm glad we have some young people to do this sort of thing," Alice remarked.

Jasmine snorted. "I'm not really sure I qualify as young people anymore."

"No comment," Priya said, not looking up.

"Well, you're younger than me," Alice said, straightening up. "And I've no patience with poking around the internet. I always seem to end up in places I have no desire to be."

"I *used* to be the cool aunt," Jasmine said, her fingers clattering on the keyboard. "But my nephew sent me a TikTok vid with a crying laughing emoji the other day, and it was just a blank screen. I'm too scared to ask him if there was meant to be a video there, or if the blank screen is some new thing that I don't understand, so I just sent a crying laughing emoji back." She looked up. "I think I've lost all credibility."

"The cool aunt phase never lasts long," Carlotta said with a sigh, and reached across the table to pat her hand. "You're still young and cool to us, though."

"I'm sure that makes you feel much better," Priya said to Jasmine, and she laughed.

Beaufort, who had come cautiously back in the door with rain dripping from his wings, said, "What's TikTok? Is that some sort of clockmaker convention?"

"It's videos," Priya said.

"Of clocks?"

"Mostly people."

"With clocks?"

Priya hesitated. "I want to say no, but the odds are there's a whole hashtag in there that probably is clocks, or people with clocks."

"It would seem most odd if there wasn't," Beaufort said. "Quite a misrepresentation, really."

"Carlotta, did you reach Gert?" Alice asked. "Did her nephew's aunt's ... oh, I don't remember. Did they get anything on the CCTV?"

"Oh! Yes," Carlotta said. "Sorry. The footage from the hospital CCTV wasn't very helpful, apparently. Rainbow's van was parked in some very quiet corner of the car park, and the video hasn't picked it up well. But she said it looked like an SUV of some sort pulled up next to it, and there's a glimpse of someone who might be in a costume at one point, but that's it."

"A costume?" Beaufort asked. "Perhaps a zebra suit, such as at the house?"

"She didn't say."

Alice nodded thoughtfully. "And Rainbow thought that was Harriet."

Miriam frowned. "Surely not *Harriet*. She and Rainbow have been friends since ... well, school, at least."

"Someone else could've taken the costume," Rosemary said. "Those onesie type things are usually one-size-fits-all."

"I imagine anyone could have access to it," Alice agreed. "Or it could be an entirely different suit. It doesn't help us."

"Tom's been working with Rainbow for quite a while," Jasmine said, and Miriam leaned in to look over her shoulder. She was scrolling thorough Facebook photos of a motorway protest, and paused on one. A skinnier Tom glared angrily out of it, one arm slung over Rainbow's neck and the other gripping a sign that read *Burn the Rich*.

"It used to be eat the rich," Miriam said, almost to herself. "It seems more eco-friendly than burning."

"Waste of resources, really," Rosemary agreed.

"What else is there, Jasmine?" Alice asked. "Is Jemima in any of them? Tom's ex-girlfriend? Quite a skinny thing, blonde dreadlocks."

"I remember," she said, clicking through. "It doesn't look like she's been around – or at least in photos – for six months at least, though."

"Can you tell anything about Tom's clothes? When did he start buying expensive gear?"

Jasmine frowned and kept clicking through the photos. Miriam looked away, blinking slightly. The speed she was going at was enough to make one feel quite ill.

"Not much on Rainbow's page, and Tom's is private, but a few months ago his profile pic changes from him and Jemima, to just him looking ... well, look." She turned the computer so everyone could see. Tom grinned back at them with his arms folded across his chest, posed carefully to show off his biceps. He wasn't wearing enough clothes for Miriam to be able to tell if they were branded or not.

"Definitely a post-breakup revenge picture," Carlotta said. "On the beach looking all happy with life."

Rosemary made an agreeable noise. "His beard is much tidier, too." They both leaned a little closer to Jasmine. "Can you make that photo bigger?"

"You think he's robbing places to get a lifestyle that makes Jemima jealous?" Priya asked, sounding sceptical. "That seems a little extreme."

"Bad break-ups can do all sorts of things to people," Carlotta said.

"The private animal collections have been being targeted for longer than a few months," Priya said, going back to her screen. "Someone's been hitting them up and down the country every couple of months since the end of last winter from what I can see." She looked up. "I know it's an assumption that it's all Rainbow's group, but it seems like a *reasonable* assumption."

"I should imagine," Alice agreed. "What about thefts? Have they been happening at the same places?"

"I'm looking now."

Jasmine had left Tom's profile and gone back to Rainbow's group's page, much to Carlotta and Rosemary's disappointment, and now she said, "I think I've found Simon."

Miriam leaned in now that the screen was free of naked torso. "And that's Daisy next to him. His daughter." She was half turned away, as if about to walk off, but it was unmistakably her, in a pretty white wool hat and matching scarf.

Jasmine clicked the photo, and frowned. "Neither of them are tagged. But I can try doing an image search for each of them."

"Do that," Alice said. "Interesting that she's in a protest photo. She didn't seem too keen on it."

"Maybe she was there to spend time with Simon," Miriam said. "Or to make sure he didn't get into trouble."

"I thought you said she was his daughter," Priya said.

"Yes, but she seemed like the more responsible one," Miriam said, and Alice nodded agreement.

"It's not a protest photo," Jasmine said. "Or I don't think so. It looks like they're just on a day out or something." She pointed at someone in the background. "That looks like a school field trip."

Alice leaned over the screen, squinting, then said to Jasmine, "Where is it?"

"It doesn't say. But there's animal cages, see?" She pointed at the background again, although Miriam couldn't see much more than a slightly out of focus monkey of some sort. "I think it's been uploaded by accident. Maybe it was a reconnaissance mission of one of the collections or something." She'd gone quite pink, her eyes bright.

"Oh, well done, Jasmine," Alice said. "When was that photo from?"

Jasmine *hmm*ed, then said, "February of this year."

"That's before the first theft I've found so far," Priya said. "First non-animal theft, anyway."

"What sort of things do they steal?" Miriam asked. "Does it say?"

Priya poked the computer a little more, then said, "There's not a lot of detail. Small bits of art, and jewellery, things like that."

"I suppose that would be rather easy to put in one's bag or something," Carlotta said. "No one would even know."

"Art?" Miriam said. "What sort of art?" Something about that seemed important, but she couldn't think why.

"Fairly expensive stuff," Priya said. "Not the really silly stuff that would be noticed straight away, but this here says a miniature portrait of a Marquess' pig in a tutu painted by the Marquess' mother would be worth a hundred and fifty thousand at auction."

"And that's not really silly?" Rosemary asked, which got her a murmur of agreement, although Miriam wasn't sure if she meant the portrait or the price.

"We should ask Barry about this photo," Alice said. "He may remember where it was. Or if anyone was particularly interested in the house rather than the animals when they were there."

"Ooh, good idea," Rosemary said. "And also we should see if there are any other photos of Tom."

"Particularly with his shirt off," Carlotta said, and they grinned at each other.

"I think Mortimer would be the person to ask Barry," Beaufort said. "He seems to have a way with the poor man."

"Excellent idea. Let's do that." Alice looked at Miriam. " And I think we need to go back out to the bunker. Rainbow may have gone there to hide out."

Miriam shivered. The very idea of the bunker was quite horrifying. "Even after the police have been there?"

"After the police have been there is the perfect time," she said. "One wouldn't expect them to come back."

"Alright. And Barry?"

"We leave him with Carlotta and Rosemary. They're quite capable of dealing with him."

"A shame he doesn't have a nice chest," Carlotta said, and Rosemary murmured agreement.

Miriam sighed. She didn't like the idea of going back out into the wilderness of the moors, as the rain and darkness deepened, and the night grew cold and chill, up there among the rocks and stones and twisted, wind-torn trees, but this was her sister. Sometimes one just had to get on and do what was needed.

"Fine," she said. "I'll get my coat. But first I'm calling Colin."

"He's not on the case," Alice said.

"DI Adams, then," Miriam said, picking her phone up.

Alice looked as if she was about to argue, but then she just nodded.

"You're right, of course. It's all very circumstantial, but it's information that may help."

"Probably don't tell her about the CCTV, though," Priya said.

"Or Barry," Jasmine said.

"Or mention the zebra at the house," Beaufort said. "We were meant to have left, after all."

Miriam looked at them all. "So what *can* I tell her?"

"That Tom's been buying expensive items, and Rainbow knew about the thefts, and they may be connected to the body," Alice said. "And that the thefts started not long after Simon joined and Tom changed."

Miriam frowned at her phone. "That really is very circumstantial, isn't it?"

"But it is something," Alice said.

"Civic duty and all that," Carlotta added, and went to get her coat. "We'll bring Barry in."

Miriam started to dial, then changed her mind and switched to a text message. She didn't think she'd remember what she could and couldn't say if DI Adams got sharp with her. She hit send, then looked up at Alice. "Does anyone have Harriet's number? Maybe we should try calling her?"

An expression of mild horror crossed Alice's face, as if she couldn't imagine why she hadn't thought of that, then she said, "I think I do. Tom said they'd all given up their phones, but let me try." She picked up her phone from the table, putting it on speaker while Carlotta and Rosemary paused at the door, and a moment later a message clicked on.

"*Hi, it's Harriet. If you need the bookshop, call the landline.*" She reeled it off. "*I am no longer shackled to modern technology, and refuse to allow The Government and Big Business to track me, so I'm not checking messages. Fight the power! Have a nice day. Bye.*"

Alice hung up, and no one spoke for a moment, then Rosemary and Carlotta headed into the rain, pulling the door shut behind them. Priya and Jasmine went back to their laptops, and Miriam checked her message to DI Adams. It was sitting there with one tick on it, showing it had sent but not been received, and she had the irritated thought that modern technology was all well and good when it *worked*.

"Do you really think Rainbow will be at the bunker?" she asked.

"It's hard to say," Alice said. "But if Rainbow knows the police have been through already – and I imagine she will do, especially if it was Harriet that picked her up – I would think she'd feel it was quite safe."

"But what if it's the others there instead?" Miriam asked.

"We shall just have to be very careful," Alice replied, and Miriam thought that seemed about as helpful as modern technology was being at the moment.

She put the kettle back on as the door opened and Rosemary and Carlotta came in, ushering a sodden dragon and a bedraggled man ahead of them. She hoped neither of them had hypothermia. That would be all they needed.

18

ALICE

A lice tried not to be impatient. She would have liked to have left by now, but Miriam was making cheese toasties, sliding them out of the pan and onto the dragons' plates, where they vanished almost before she could get the next one started.

There had been a lot of fussing around when Mortimer and Barry had come in, as Barry had lost both his red wool jacket (which Carlotta had loaned him) and his hospital gown, and Mortimer was dripping and dejected. But Miriam had found a dressing gown and some pyjamas that fit Barry well enough, even if they were a little short in the legs and arms, and since Gert was still at the bunker Rosemary and Carlotta had taken him off to Carlotta's house, despite the risks posed by naturism and parrots.

Mortimer had tried to ask Barry about the photo before they left, but to no avail. Barry had taken one look then sat down in the corner with both hands over his head, and started to chant softly, "No hospital, no hospital, no hospital." He'd still been chanting when Carlotta and Rosemary had led him away, and Mortimer was currently steaming softly next to the AGA, eating his way steadily through the remaining plum cake, while Beaufort sat next to him, sampling the sandwiches with every evidence of satisfaction.

"I wish we could be sure Rainbow was at the bunker," Miriam said. "Rather than just stumbling in there."

"I wish we could, too," Alice said, and looked at Jasmine and Priya, both still tapping at their laptops. "But we shall just have to work with what information we have. Have you found anything more about Simon?"

"I found his Facebook account," Jasmine said. "But it's not been active for a few years. Just people posting happy birthday on his wall and him not responding. He must be off social media."

"And Harriet? Any sign of him on her Facebook?"

"There's nothing at all on hers. She has the bookshop page, though, which is quite busy."

"That's probably Daisy." Miriam put a final sandwich in the pan. "She seems terribly efficient. *Terribly.* I was scared she might ask me about my accounts."

Jasmine looked up and said, "I did say I could help, you know."

"I know," Miriam said. "But it's just …" She waved the spatula vaguely. "I mean, it all works out."

"Not if anyone decides to look into it," Jasmine pointed out, and Miriam made an uncertain noise, then dropped the last sandwich onto Mortimer's plate.

"That's all my bread," she said. "Will it keep you going?"

"Marvellous," Beaufort said. "I think this is something we should try at home, don't you, Mortimer?"

Mortimer wrinkled his snout slightly. "I'm not sure how that would work. The potatoes are challenging enough."

Alice clapped her hands before anyone could get too distracted by the issue of dragon cuisine. "We should get started," she said. "Jasmine and Priya, you'll keep looking into things?"

"Of course," Priya said, not looking up, and Jasmine nodded, a little less enthusiastically. Alice had an idea that the younger woman wasn't entirely convinced by the relationship advice that had just been doled out to her, which was understandable. Some things could only be learned by living, and all one could hope was that one had friends around to make sure the lessons were softened a little when they came.

She nodded at Beaufort. "You'll check the woods by the old house and see if you can track the car?"

"We will," Beaufort said. "We may be able to figure out if it really was Harriet in the zebra suit, too, if Mortimer can get a good whiff of them."

Mortimer made a dubious noise.

"Good," Alice said. "We need to find Rainbow as soon as possible. Because there is a risk that if it wasn't Harriet who met her ..." She trailed off, suddenly aware of Miriam washing the pan with rather more concentration than was necessary. "Well, she may have been detained," she finished, which still didn't sound terribly good, but it was the best she could do.

"Kidnapped, you mean," Miriam said to the sink.

Or worse, Alice thought, but just said, "There is that possibility."

"We'll find her," Beaufort said. "With all of you on the trail, as well as us? There's no chance that we won't."

"Yes, but she's in a car," Mortimer started, then looked at Miriam and said, "Which makes no difference at all."

"Well done," Alice said, and patted Miriam carefully on the shoulder. "Let's go and have a look at the bunker."

"What if Simon or Tom are there?" Beaufort asked.

"We'll have Gert and Rose," Alice said. "Plus Angelus. They're hardly going to tackle all of us."

Miriam looked from one of them to the other, then sighed. "At least let me try DI Adams again."

"You can do it on the way," Alice said. "Now let's get started, shall we?" She took her coat from by the door and looked at the others with the most encouraging expression she could manage. She very much wanted to clap her hands together, but she had an idea it wouldn't have the desired effect.

"I don't think I've any more cake," Miriam said to Jasmine and Priya. "But there are crackers in the pantry, and cheese in the fridge, and—"

"Do come on, Miriam," Alice said. "I'm sure they won't starve."

"We won't," Priya said cheerfully. "We can always nip home for a bite anyway."

"Tea in the caddy," she called as Alice ushered the dragons out and herded her through the kitchen door. "There might be a packet of biscuits in—" She stopped as Alice pulled the door shut behind them and started around the house. "That was rude."

"It's Jasmine and Priya, Miriam. Not guests."

"I suppose," she said, trailing after Alice. "But I'd hate them to be sitting there hungry and not know they could just grab something."

"No one has ever accused the W.I. of not making themselves comfortable," Alice said, which was one of the reasons she was always a little reluctant to host meetings. She *did*, of course, and no one had ever been through her drawers or poked in her cupboards, and she was sure they never would. But there was just something dreadfully intimate about someone else being *at home* in one's own house, and the W.I. had made an art form of it.

"Are you sure about this?" Beaufort asked as Alice beeped her car open. "We could come with you."

"We will be fine," Alice said. "You two get off, and be careful. There may be a lot of police officers around."

Mortimer made a sad little sound, and held a paw out to Miriam. She plucked a scale from it and said, "I shall keep it safe for you."

"I don't think I can even use it for baubles," he said. "The stress is making them all dry and dull."

"I'll keep it anyway." She tucked it into a pocket in her jacket, and Alice got into the car as the dragons slipped down the garden toward the cover of the woods, where they could take flight without some overzealous dog-walker spotting them. Although anyone who was out walking a dog tonight was very dedicated, Alice thought. The rain had set into a monotonous autumn chorus, too light to have the exhilaration of a downpour, but too heavy to offer the hope of relenting any time soon. The late afternoon creaked and pattered with it, and the street was rendered watery and dull, begging for the lights to be lit already.

"*Are* you sure about this, Alice?" Miriam asked, as Alice started the engine and got the heater running. "What if Tom's lurking around out there somewhere? Or Simon, or both of them?"

"We shall keep a careful watch," Alice said. She hesitated, then added, "I also need to look for Thompson. It's most odd he hasn't turned up. That's been a full day without him complaining about the salmon."

"That seems *very* bad," Miriam said. "What if they've done something awful to him!"

"We shall find out more when we get to the bunker," Alice said, and pulled away from the kerb, the headlights cutting a tunnel into the dreary day. She wasn't at all sure that what they were doing was a sensible idea, but the bunker felt like a stone left unturned, and she wanted to check it. And there really was the question of Thompson, which was weighing on her a little more than she liked to admit. He'd almost been drowned just a couple of months ago through helping her. She hated to think that he might be in trouble again on her account, annoying as he was.

Between the rain and the low light and the ever-present risk of wandering sheep, Alice took the road a little more slowly than she had the previous night, the tarmac unrolling wet and slick ahead of them in the headlights. The wide expanse of sky had been smothered by a heavy freight of cloud, and wisps of murk clung to the peaks and rendered the world distant and silent. There was no one else on the road. It wasn't a day for sightseeing, and it wasn't exactly on a commuter route up here, where the land still seemed to begrudge the lanes, barely allowing them space to run. One had the feeling that the drystone walls were as much to hold the fells back from swallowing the road as it was to keep the livestock off it.

Miriam tried calling DI Adams, but there was no response. Alice was almost sure she tried Colin too, but with no more luck. If they were both at the old house, they'd have no reception.

They were already into the high fells when Rose called, her voice hollow over speakerphone and cutting in and out as the signal grew patchier.

"Hello, Rose," Alice said. "Is something happening?"

"Nothing at all," Rose said, cheerfully enough. "Bunker's a ghost town."

"That seems good," Miriam said.

"It's *boring*," Rose said, and Gert grumbled in agreement over the speakerphone.

"Any sign of anyone?" Alice asked.

"No one," Gert said. "We can only watch the road, though. People could have come and gone on the tracks and we'd never see them."

"Well, we'll know soon," Alice said. "We're on the way out."

"Right. Ah ... have you spoken to Pearl or Teresa recently?"

Alice and Miriam exchanged glances, Miriam fidgeting with the fabric of her skirt and her mouth twisted into a tight line.

"No," Alice said. "Why?'

"We can't get hold of them," Gert said. "Neither of them."

Miriam fumbled her phone out of her coat pocket, scrolling through it as Alice said, "When did you try?"

"I was messaging with Teresa twenty minutes ago," Rose said. "I sent her this video of a llama chasing a cat, and she never replied, so I called her, but she's not answering."

"I see," Alice said, and looked at Miriam.

She put her phone back in her pocket and shook her head. "Both go straight to messages. And Pearl probably forgot to charge hers again, or left it in a drawer somewhere, but Teresa *always* has hers."

Alice didn't answer straight away. She rather sympathised with Pearl's approach, even if she didn't condone it. She wasn't particularly keen on her own phone, or the whole concept of being contactable any time someone felt like it, but she still made sure it was charged and in her bag. It was a useful tool, and while one might not like the direction progress took at times, certain things just had to be embraced. To not do so was to be left behind by the world, and that way lay the sort of fruitless anger and bewildered frustration that blinded one to the good that was bundled in with the annoying.

"Alice?" Rose asked. "Have we lost you?"

"No, still here." She drummed her fingers on the wheel and came to a decision. "You head into Toot Hansell and see if they're around. *Carefully.* Miriam and I will check the bunker then join you."

"Got it," Gert said. "I need to get out of this bloody van anyway. Feels like I've been stuck in here with this one's stinky great dog *forever.* I should've packed a gas mask."

"It's not his fault!" Rose said. "He has a nervous stomach."

"It's certainly making me nervous right now," Gert said. "We'll head off, then, and Rose can get herself a bloody dog-sitter."

"I didn't complain about your egg sandwich."

"It was an *egg sandwich.* Angelus smells like he's been storing eggs in his digestive tract for the last three weeks."

"It is a bit strong, I suppose," Rose admitted.

"You're not far off, then?" Gert asked.

"Five minutes," Alice said.

"Close enough. We'll wave as we pass you."

⁂

GERT AND ROSE DID, indeed, wave as they passed, and there was plenty of time to do so as the road was narrow and Gert's van was rather big, and there were, on occasion, less than tidy edges to the walls, as many a scratched car and punctured tyre could attest.

Gert came to a stop and leaned out the window, looking down at Alice. "Sure you don't want some company?" she asked.

"You haven't seen anyone?"

"Not on the road."

"Then we shall risk it," Alice said. "There's no reason for anyone other than possibly Rainbow to be there."

"Fair enough," Gert said, leaning back into her car. "Keep your phone on."

Alice waved in acknowledgement, and the two vehicles passed on their own ways into the deepening night of the moors.

Miriam had been fiddling with her phone, and now she put it back in her pocket again. "I wish Rainbow would call me, or Maddie. I did call Maddie before, to ask if she'd heard anything, but she was just going on about how the settlement was running a drumming circle that was so loud it completely ruined one of her ghost tours. I suggested that it might add to the atmosphere, but she didn't seem to think so."

Alice made a small noise of sympathy, either for Maddie or the drumming circle. She wasn't sure which was required, but the right noise tended to cover most eventualities. "Here we are," she said, and pulled into the lay-by, switching the lights off and then the engine. The relentless patter of the rain closed in around them, and the windscreen flooded as the wipers stopped.

Neither of them spoke for a little while, then Miriam said, "They wouldn't have seen much from here. Should we be doing this? What if *everyone's* there? Tom *and* Harriet *and* Simon? Or others we don't know about?"

"It's a reasonable question," Alice admitted. "But what if Rainbow's there, and needs help?"

Miriam wrinkled her nose, then took a deep breath and zipped her coat up, taking a torch from the bag at her feet. "Alright," she said. "Honestly, my sister's such a pain."

Alice decided not to feel too guilty about persuading Miriam so easily, and said, "Would you like to borrow a cane?"

Miriam looked at her, a grin starting at the corners of her mouth. "Do you have a spare? I should have brought the cricket bat."

"I do have a spare," Alice said, pulling the hood of her coat up and getting out into the weather. The wind was a wispy, reluctant thing without much strength to it, which was something, but the rain felt as if it could carry on forever, until it swallowed the world. She opened the boot and took out a slim cane of hardened dark wood, handing it to Miriam. She took it, examining the handle, which was carved in an intricate pattern of deeper burnt browns. "Nice balance, that one, and a good heft. Extra strong, too. I checked with the gentleman at the shop."

Miriam looked at her, the hint of a smile blossoming into the real thing. "What did you tell him you were using it for?"

Alice waved dismissively, taking her own cane out and shutting the boot. "I merely said that I needed something that could withstand rigorous use." She paused, giving Miriam a smile of her own. "Although I did have to whirl it around in the shop a bit to check the balance, and I think that may have given me away a little."

Miriam burst out laughing. "What did he say?"

"He asked me to dinner," Alice said, and led the way across the road. "He must've been seventy if he was a day."

Miriam jogged to keep up with her. "But you're not that much ..." She trailed off as Alice looked at her, eyebrows raised. "Interested," she finished.

"No," she agreed. "I very much was not."

The rocky trail was slippery underfoot, and Alice found herself using her cane to steady herself as she walked. The curse of the hip replacement was that, while it worked exceptionally well these days, she was terribly aware of how easily she might find herself needing the second one doing. And falling on the rough ground here was a sure way to it. Miriam padded on easily, sure-footed in a pair of ancient-looking wellies, heavy woollen socks showing over the tops, and every now and then she feinted at the shadows with her cane. It seemed to have reassured her even more than the cricket bat tended to, which was good. Alice was almost certain that no one would be here, but almost was as good as useless. They had to assume there was still a risk the killer – whoever they were – was hiding out in the bunker, waiting to be sure that Rainbow had been arrested and charged. So this was no time to relax.

The campsite, when they reached it, looked as if it had been abandoned for months. The remnants of a fire were still encircled in rocks, but ash dribbled sadly away in the rain, more and more erased with every moment. There were no chairs left out, no kettle waiting to be filled. There was nothing at all to suggest that anyone had ever been here.

Alice picked her way to a cluster of old branches that had been piled in front of the bunker door, hiding both the handle and a few loose strips of police tape. She pushed it unceremoniously aside, and knocked sharply, hearing Miriam's little intake of breath. There was no response, and she looked at Miriam. "Someone's put the branches there to hide it. It's not as if anyone could do that from inside."

"That doesn't mean there isn't anyone inside."

"True," Alice admitted. "But we can't just stand out here in the wet wondering about it."

Miriam shifted her grip on the cane, then lifted it to her shoulder for good measure. "I rather thought you'd say that. Go on, then."

Alice leaned her cane against the rocks, grabbed the handle and spun it. There was no resistance, and she heard the locks disengage. She pulled the door open while Miriam hovered over her with the cane at the ready, and encountered nothing but darkness within. She shone her light down and discovered a hard-packed dirt floor, an old metal bucket in one corner with a couple of scorched pots sitting in it and a crate of tin plates and mugs next to it, and two sets of bunk beds with some boxes shoved underneath. There was also a large tabby cat with tatty ears sitting in the middle of the floor, and he gave them a disgruntled look.

"About bloody time. Bet it wouldn't have taken you this long if I was a damn dragon."

Alice shone the light on him. *"Thompson?"*

"No, it's the sodding Lion King. Get the light out of my eyes."

"Oh dear," Miriam said. "How long have you been there?"

"Forever."

"What happened?" Alice asked, climbing down the short ladder to the floor beneath. It was cold in here, a chill baking off the bare walls, and full of musty, stale air.

"I was poking about in here after you lot left, since the bloody dragons seemed to think it was oh-so-important, but someone shut the door on me. The whole thing's basically a damn cage, so I couldn't shift out until the door opened again."

"And no one's been back?" Miriam asked.

"Oh, they came back in," the cat said, and sighed. "But then I thought I'd eavesdrop a bit, so I hid under the bed. It was all a bit boring, though, and someone had left a really nice fleece down there, so I had a bit of lie-down while I waited. Next thing I know the door's shutting again." He gave Alice a narrow-eyed look. "This is what I get for helping you lot."

"It's what you get for sleeping on the job," Alice said, playing her light across the boxes under the bunks. "Miriam, come and help me take a look at these."

"Really? It looks kind of tight down there."

"It's fine." Alice poked through a jumble of washcloths, half-used bars of soap, and a couple of loose razors, making a face. "Did you at least overhear anything useful?"

"Maybe," Thompson said, grooming himself. "Let me just get over the shock first."

"Why did you have to wait for the door to open?" Miriam asked.

"Can't shift from a cage," Thompson said. "The universe has rules, otherwise there'd be a lot fewer cats in rescues and so on." He thought about it. "Although sometimes it's better than being out, you know?"

Miriam was still hovering at the entrance, and she nodded sympathetically. Alice was about to say that she was glad there were *some* rules that applied to cats, when Thompson's head snapped around, glaring toward the door with his teeth bared. Miriam gave a shriek, vanishing from sight, and there was a painful-sounding thud and a clatter of stones from outside.

Alice jumped up and lunged for the ladder, shouting, "Miriam!" She caught a glimpse of a rain-slicked outdoor coat, the wearer's head turned away, and the door slammed shut with a thud that reverberated in her belly. "*Miriam!*" she tried again, but of course there was no answer, and her shout was half-drowned by the cat's squawk.

Thompson slid sideways across the floor, shaking one front paw out. "Sodding leftover radishes!" he screeched. "My *ear!*" He looked wildly at Alice. "I was bloody halfway into the Inbetween when they shut that. Am I disfigured? Tell me. *Tell me.* Is it awful?"

She examined him. He'd lost all his whiskers on one side, and there was a bare patch on his shoulder. There was also a new notch in his ear, but it was pink and neatly cauterised. "You're fine," she said, and pulled her phone out. Unsurprisingly, there was no signal. "We are, however, trapped."

"*Again,*" the cat said. "Don't suppose you brought any salmon with you?"

She just looked at him, thinking of that awful thud, and Miriam's misgivings – *everyone's* misgivings – and now here they were. Or here Miriam wasn't, more to the point. She sat down on the bottom bunk and covered her face with her hands, and a whisper escaped her, almost against her will. "Oh, no."

"It's not that bad," Thompson said. "I bet some mice'll move in."

19
MORTIMER

It wasn't a pleasant day to be flying. There was little wind, it was true, and the drenching rain and low cloud offered good cover for dragons, but it was also *drenching*. Mortimer felt like his scales might be washed off at any moment.

"Alright there, lad?" Beaufort called. He was gliding effortlessly, the broad span of his leathery wings sleek with rain and flushed with shades of grey, from murky shadow to wispy, foggy tones. He looked carved from the edge of a storm, his neck long and his head high, and the coil of his tail snapped across the weighted sky. He was the sort of dragon poets wrote epics about – probably *had*, in fact – and right now all Mortimer wanted to do was retreat to Miriam's kitchen and curl up in front of the AGA, or, failing that, go back to his own nice dry cavern and see if he could crack the mystery of making a perfect baked potato. Possibly with more cheese toasties on the side.

"Alright," he said, without much enthusiasm.

"Not far now," Beaufort said. "That's the edge of the woods there. I think we stay high for now, see if we spot the road the car would have left on."

Staying high seemed good. Mortimer liked the idea of staying high. Even through the rain and low cloud he could see banks of lights set up at the old house, ahead of them and to the right. There'd be police all over the place, and even Colin hadn't seemed very impressed by them getting involved. And he was the least scary police officer Mortimer had come across. Plus there could still be rabid bats waiting for him.

They followed the edge of the woods where it met farmland, the line of the drystone wall that divided the wild from the tamed forming a snaking join, like the ones Mortimer used when he fused scales together. Ridged yet permeable and infused with strange old magic and even older beliefs. The fields were dull and empty, the land rough and pocked with boulders that had heaved themselves free of the soil, and the nearest house sat in a mire of muddy yard and outbuildings, lights already on and dull in the wet. The road that ran past the house was visible as the far border of the woods, fields shaping the land on the other side of it. The pocket of wilderness was deep and dark and, even under the rain, scented with old fierce things, but it was small. A teardrop of a place, resisting the onslaught of the world.

"There," Beaufort called. He stretched his neck, pointing down and a little to their left with his snout, and Mortimer peered down. It wasn't really a road, and even calling it a farm track was probably stretching the limits of the definition, but it was the only other way into the woods that they'd seen, and it seemed to lead roughly to a spot not far from where they'd last seen Rainbow.

"They couldn't get a regular car down there," Mortimer said. "Not in this weather. It'd get stuck. It couldn't be their van."

"Good point," Beaufort said, dropping lower. "But there was an SUV at the hospital on the CCTV. Maybe they used that." Mortimer made a small noise of agreement, and Beaufort added, "We need to be careful now. We don't know how far into the woods the police have gone."

Mortimer had been trying not to think about that, but he had no problems with being careful. He followed the High Lord as they spiralled down, searching the track for signs of sharp-eyed police offi-cers lingering in the cover of the trees. There was no one to be seen, and a moment later they landed on the long grass that ran up to the drystone walls. Gouges were torn into the earth, and the track had been scoured out by the recent passage of tyres, water pooling in the ruts and turning it to a swamp. Mortimer peered around warily, but there wasn't even a sheep to be seen. Everyone had sought shelter other than two very misguided dragons, it seemed.

Beaufort padded over to where a sagging, padlocked gate marked the end of the rudimentary lane and sat back on his hindquarters, resting his paws on the top to examine the woods beyond. Mortimer followed him, and saw a swathe cut into the trees, branches lopped and trunks toppled. The paler flesh of the trunks were exposed where the bark had been torn away, and the rain washed sadly down it all.

The High Lord sighed. "Lovely old trees these. Poor things."

Mortimer nodded. It wasn't new, the damage to the woods, or not all of it. It was the sort of steady erosion where someone had taken just a little, when spring had been slow to come and winter supplies had run out, and then a little more, when autumn came in too soon, because what was a little when there was a whole wood there? And maybe that was all it was still, a little top-up that felt harmless, but wood burns faster than it grows.

Neither of them spoke for a moment, Mortimer smelling sadness and loss amid the damp wood, then he dropped quietly back to the ground, following the tyre tracks to try to find a scent. There wasn't much to go on, not between the mud and the rain and the lingering grief of the trees. The only other thing he could smell was the whiff of sticky fear that Rainbow had been carrying when they'd found her in the woods, a small creature fleeing from predators. There was no relief in it, but even if she'd known who picked her up, why would there be? She was still running, and until the running stopped there'd no rest to be had.

"Hello," Beaufort said, addressing the trees. "Anyone about?"

There was no reply but the steady patter of the rain, and after a moment the High Lord looked down the track. "Looks like the dryads aren't in any mood to help us out. Shall we walk?"

"What about the police?" Mortimer asked.

"I can't see anyone. Or hear them. We are dragons, lad. We're not very easy to spot."

"Yes, but they use police dogs to track people, you know. What if they have dogs?"

Beaufort looked at him. "We're *dragons*. I think we can manage a few police dogs if we have to."

Mortimer made a doubtful noise, but he padded in a slow circle, investigating the edges of the field as he kept trying to pick up some sense of who had been here. He found a spot where the wheel tracks stopped, and were ground deeper from someone sitting in place then backing up again, and paused. Tight-wound hunger and deep blue worry, the sharp sad tang of citrus going to rot, and raw pink scratches of fright, but it still didn't *tell* him anything. It didn't smell like a murderer, but maybe the murderer wasn't bothered enough by what they'd done to leave any sort of emotional trace. How was he to know what a murderer thought?

"This is useless," he said, lifting his head and staring into the trees. "There's *nothing*. They didn't even have a sandwich and drop some crumbs."

"They did not," someone said, so close in front of him that he scuttled backward with a yelp and collided with the ungiving mass of the High Lord.

"Steady on, lad," Beaufort said, and Mortimer stared at the dryad. She was crouching in the mud just beyond the gate, her rough, gnarled hands pressed to the ground and her fingers dug deep into it. Her mossy hair hung in soft wet hanks around her face, and she grinned at them. There was a soft crackle to her left, and Mortimer peered around to see a broken sapling righting itself, sprouting new shoots, while one of the overhanging trees, which had axe marks in its trunk, started to blossom fresh bark.

"Hello," Beaufort said to the dryad. "Beaufort Scales, High Lord of the Cloverly dragons and investigator. This is my associate, Mortimer."

"Investigator?" the dryad said. "Are you here to investigate who's cutting my trees down? Because I can tell you who. I've been setting the roots to tear down their house, but it's a long process. They don't live close enough."

"That's very unfortunate," Beaufort said. "But—"

"Unfortunate? *Unfortunate?*" The dryad glared at him. "This is the last stand of original forest in the county. Oh, there are other old pockets about the place, but here, deep in my woods, under my protection as I am under hers, is Old Mother. Her roots run to the very heart of the earth. Her branches can spin clouds from the sky. Her—"

"That's very impressive," Beaufort said, interrupting the dryad. Uninterrupted, a dryad can talk about trees – or weeds, or hedges, or dandelions – for an entire night and into the next day without drawing breath. "I can see that it's very important to protect her."

"Yes," the dryad said. "It is."

"So maybe we have the same goal," the High Lord added. "It can't be any good having the police running around in your woods."

"They're scaring the badgers. And they were already nervous enough because of the bloody great cats."

"Bloody great cats?" Mortimer repeated, a little wheezily.

"Yeah, two of them. Spotty one called Claude and a stripy one called Eugene. They seem alright. Not very chatty, though. Just keep complaining about the rain. I mean, what do they expect? It's *autumn.*"

Mortimer thought longingly of Miriam's AGA again, then said, "They're not around here, are they?"

"No, they keep well away from anyone. Apparently someone hoiked them out their respective jungles or whatever and they ended up in an *apartment?* They don't seem very clear on how it all happened, but, you know. It'll be bloody humans up to their usual tricks."

"They're not hungry, are they? They've got enough to eat?" Mortimer checked the edges of the woods warily.

The dryad shrugged. "They catch a few squirrels. And I think they've been raiding some chicken coops around the farms and blaming it on the foxes, who're getting all sniffy about things. Politics, you know."

"Well," Beaufort said. "It seems you have quite the population in there."

"I keep good woods, me," the dryad said, rocking back on her heels and adjusting her hair. "Gaelen. Currently in a male phase, just so you know."

"Pleased to meet you," Beaufort said.

"Hi," Mortimer said, and checked the shadows again. "You've not seen any dogs, have you?"

"Just the dandy," Gaelen said. "And dogs are alright. Know enough not to wee on me instead of a tree, anyway, which is more than can be said for a lot of humans."

Both dragons made suitably outraged sounds, and Beaufort said, "Dreadfully rude."

"*So* rude," Gaelen agreed.

"I wonder if you could help us," the High Lord said. "We just need a little information."

Gaelen nodded. "About the car that was here, I suppose?"

"Yes. Did you see it?"

"Yeah, I came down to see if it was someone chopping my trees up again, but they were just sitting there."

"Just sitting?"

"Just sitting. I kept an eye on them – I mean, I know it's wet, but the amount of people who throw cigarettes out, or eat lunch and dump the plastic bits ... it's ridiculous."

"What do you do if you see them?" Mortimer asked.

"Shove the rubbish back in their car," Gaelen said. "They never see me. It's best if it's some sort of fish sandwich type thing, or eggs. Something soft and smelly, anyway. I can usually mush them into the boot or through a window if they've got them open a bit."

"But this person wasn't eating lunch?" Beaufort asked.

"No. I mean, this track's meant to be private anyway, so on this side the only people are usually the damn wood-thieves. But this one just sat there until the naked one came running out of the woods. Then they drove off together."

"Did you see the driver? Was it a man?" Beaufort asked.

The dryad waved vaguely. "Maybe? I mean, they were human."

"Long hair? Short hair?"

"Hat. The naked one had long hair, though, if that helps?"

Mortimer sighed. Dryads' lives are long and stretched, and their form changes with the seasons and with the trees, while their gender is somewhat undefined and known only to the dryad themself. Traditionally they were always referred to as female, but no one knew if that was because they *were* female, or if it was just because of the connection to growth and fertility and their habit of wearing a lot of flowers. But all of that meant they tended to just define people by species rather than anything else, so descriptions were tricky.

Beaufort looked at Mortimer, and he shrugged, then said, "Did the naked one seem happy to see them? Happy to leave with them?"

Gaelen thought about it. "They seemed surprised, I'd say. Both of them did. But the naked one was quite worked up, and they got in the car smart-ish and took off. And then you lot popped up, which *was* a surprise. Didn't expect dragons in my woods. And would have expected at least a hello, really." He gave them both a severe look.

"Sorry," Mortimer mumbled.

"We were in the midst of an Investigation," Beaufort said, and Mortimer could actually hear the capital I. Gaelen looked, if not impressed, at least accepting of it as an excuse.

Beaufort started to say something else, and Gaelen held up a hand, looking into the bushes.

Mortimer backed away a couple of steps, wondering if dogs or big cats would be preferable.

"Humans," Gaelen said, and then he was gone, swallowed by the woods as if he'd never been there. He could be pressed against the trunk of the nearest tree, or crouched among the weeds, and even dragon eyes would be hard-pressed to see him.

There was a bark in the direction the dryad had been looking, sharp and imperious, and Beaufort looked at Mortimer. "We best be off, lad."

Mortimer didn't need a second invitation. Dogs were plenty to worry about.

They took to the sky without hesitation, climbing for the cover of the low clouds. They stayed high enough that their forms would be lost against the cloud to anyone who looked up, and low enough that they could see as they circled the scar in the edge of the woods. Below them, a police officer in a heavy jacket pushed through the trees, a big, sharp-eared dog leading her. The dog looked up at the dragons and gave one brusque bark, but its handler just walked to the gate and peered each way along the wall. A moment later she was joined by two other officers in uniform, and one in a heavy yellow police jacket with the hood pulled over their head. They did look up, the hood falling back, and while Mortimer was fairly sure they were too high to be seen, he was almost certain DI Adams looked straight at him, anyway.

THEY CIRCLED the woods once more, but there was nothing to be seen from here. Rainbow had gone willingly with someone, and whoever it was had been waiting for her. That was the oddity, since she'd been hiding out. Had she always intended to leave, and her friend had been planning to pick her up? But then why did Gaelen think they'd both seemed surprised? Had the person not been there for her at all?

"The zebra," Mortimer said aloud.

"What's that, lad?" Beaufort asked. They'd swung into the field across the road from Rainbow's house, sheltered by the trees that lined the wall, and were watching the old gate. The fencing had been removed and it had been swung wide open, and a uniformed officer who was standing in front of it, rain dripping from her hood, looked up as a police car drew in. Colin got out, making some apologetic gestures, and as the officer took his place he stood staring at the gates, rubbing the back of his head with one hand before finally walking to DI Adams' car and getting in. How very frustrating it must be, Mortimer thought, to want so much to help someone, yet to be unable to do so. In that he supposed he was lucky. After all, as horrifying and stress-shedding-inducing as their investigations were, they did get to help, even if the question of whether they should be or not was rather murky.

"The zebra," Mortimer said again. "They were leaving, was all. They must've circled back to their SUV or whatever when we lost them. They didn't expect Rainbow to actually come out."

"But why were they here, if they weren't planning to help Rainbow?" Beaufort asked, then answered his own question before Mortimer could. "If it's the same person as from the hospital, it'd be to do something that would make sure the police caught her."

"Yes. Or to …" Mortimer hesitated, then continued. "To find her in the woods and … you know."

Beaufort looked at him. "It's dangerous in those woods, what with big cats and so on."

"Exactly," Mortimer said quietly. "But now she's run out, and they've got her. So they'll just do it somewhere else."

"We need to tell Colin," Beaufort said.

"We're not meant to be here," Mortimer pointed out. "Plus there's too many other police now."

Beaufort made a noise that was very near a grumble, but nodded. "You're right, of course. And if she's gone, then there's not much we can do here. Let's follow the track for a bit, see where it comes out. You never know what we might spot."

Such as a dead body in a field, Mortimer thought, but didn't say. It wasn't much of a plan, but it definitely sounded better than talking to Colin. He looked grumpy even from here.

THE TRACK TOLD THEM NOTHING. Once they were sure no one was watching from the woods they came back down to land in the fields, padding along the ruts with the last of the day's light draining away around them and taking the colours with it. There was nothing to be found but tyre prints, and even those petered out as they joined a track that actually qualified for the name. Mortimer caught the slightest scent of sharp-edged fear on the gate that let them out of the field, but nothing else.

The new track carried them close to the farmhouse, and they slipped past just beyond the yard with their colours melding with the shadows while the dogs barked from the shelter of the sheds. No one came out to look at them, though. Not long after that the track broadened out and tarmac replaced the hard-packed dirt, and they stopped, looking around at the night that was rushing in on the edges of the clouds.

"I don't think there's anything here," Beaufort said, sounding less enthusiastic than usual.

"Me either," Mortimer agreed. "At least no one … no one was thrown out of the car or anything." *No body*, his head corrected, but he couldn't quite bring himself to say it.

"Yes," Beaufort agreed, and shook out his wings, the rain pattering cheerily on them. "Back to Toot Hansell. Alice and Miriam may be back already, and if not we'll go on to the bunker."

"I hope they're back," Mortimer said. "They've had plenty of time."

"I'm sure they will be," Beaufort said, and a moment later they were airborne again, not even needing the clouds for cover as the sky grew darker and the world below drew in on itself, hiding from the wet and deepening night.

THERE WAS a comfort in swinging into the familiar jumble of Miriam's garden, into the wash of light from the kitchen windows and the scent of a deep-rooted, warmly lived life baked into the ground and the walls, oranges and yellows and warm wild greens. They padded up to the kitchen door and Beaufort opened it, pushing it wide.

"She still didn't lock it."

"She really should," Mortimer said. "There seem to be far too many criminals about this village than are reasonable."

Beaufort gave a chuckle of amusement that died mid-breath as he walked into the room.

Drawers and cabinet doors hung open, disgorging their contents onto the worktops and floor, and the pantry door was ajar, revealing emptied tubs of baking goods and a jumble of dislodged tins. The kitchen table still held a couple of mugs and a plate, but one of the laptops was on the floor, emitting a nasty scent of crushed electrics, and muddy footprints trekked towards the hall, two chairs overturned in their wake. The dragons looked at each other.

"Jasmine?" Beaufort called. "Priya?"

There was no answer, and Beaufort started for the hall door, but at that moment there was the slam of a car door from the street, and Mortimer, still on the doorstep, heard running footsteps on the path.

"Someone's coming," he hissed. *"Hide!"*

Beaufort didn't argue, simply followed Mortimer as they fled back out into the night, leaving Miriam's house in disarray and dragons paw prints on the floor, stark as an arrow saying *magical beasts this way.*

20

DI ADAMS

It was a lot easier traipsing around emu- and big cat-infested woods with three other officers and a large, toothy dog, DI Adams decided. Although the presence of the large, toothy dog meant that her own sometimes large and always toothy dog had had to make himself scarce. And while the extra bodies meant that the wildlife had kept its distance, it hadn't helped them find Rainbow. She had evidently made good her escape, and DI Adams wondered, if she'd been just a little quicker, or if Dandy's route had been just a little less Dandy-centric, they might've nabbed her earlier. But wishes and fishes and all that.

She walked back to the house from the gate the dog had led them to, with its rough track and tyre prints and dearth of suspects, trying to ignore the gnawing sensation that she should be doing something *more*. There was very little that could be done right now. The house couldn't be processed until the bats had been removed, which couldn't happen until the bat conservation lot turned up the next day. The RSPCA had said in no uncertain terms that emus and big cats were outside their area of expertise and they were having nothing to do with it, which meant waiting until tomorrow once again, when they could get a specialist team from a zoo in. And until then, even if she'd thought Rainbow or anyone else was still lurking in the undergrowth somewhere, there was nothing more that could be done without risking someone getting taken out by a boa constrictor or a charging emu or whatever else was stashed away in here. The one excursion to try and follow her scent before it was washed away was as much as DI Adams was willing to risk.

"Is that everything, Inspector?" the dog handler asked.

DI Adams wiped rain off her face and nodded. "Yeah, nothing more we can do tonight. I may need you again tomorrow, but that seemed pretty clear, didn't it? She left by car?"

"Betty was pretty certain," the other woman said, patting the dog. "This rain, though – if you do want anything else done, it should be tonight."

DI Adams looked at the big dog, her dark eyes reflecting the torches. Her head was up, and her ears twitched constantly, seeking out sounds. She kept panting, then stopping as she looked around, straining to sort through scents, and every time she looked at DI Adams she bared her teeth. Her handler had brushed it off with "You must've been around a cat," but DI Adams hadn't missed the wary look the other woman had given her. It made sense. She didn't trust anyone Dandy didn't trust either, and she didn't blame Betty for being suspicious. She was pretty certain that Dandy smell wasn't something the average dog was happy with.

"No, go on home," she said aloud. "There's too many random bloody animals in this place. Last thing we need is one of you bitten by a warthog or something."

The handler tipped her head, oddly doglike herself. "Do they bite?"

"No idea. Best not find out." DI Adams waved the woman toward the road and waiting cars, then went to check the house was secure. The doors were pulled shut, the tape stretched over them, and a miserable-looking PC Shaw was standing at the kitchen door with an umbrella in one gloved hand and a thermal mug in the other. "Go and get warm," she told him.

"But the scene," he started, and she cut him off with a wave.

"I don't think it's safe for anyone standing about outside in this place, and the odds of anything being disturbed are minimal. I'm putting a car on the track and another at the gate, and we'll just have to risk it. I'm not writing up a report about how I let someone get savaged by howler monkeys."

He shifted. "I think they're squirrel monkeys, actually. From how Liv described them."

"Good to know," she said, and ushered him off, taking a last look at the house. There was nothing more here. Rainbow was gone. Everything pointed at her, and whether she was being framed or not, DI Adams was going to find her, if for no other reason than to express her extreme displeasure at having to hide in a tree for twenty minutes until Ben and Liv had found her.

She started to turn away, but Dandy appeared in front of the kitchen door, panting at her.

"What?"

He regarded her for a moment, then turned and vanished into the house. She hesitated. Disturbing Lucas' crime scene wasn't going to win her any points, and though he was a lot less picky than some she'd worked with, upsetting any crime scene officer was a spectacularly bad idea if one wanted anything processed in decent time. On the other hand, the bats had already done a good job of messing things up.

She reached over the tape to open the door, and as she swung it wide she saw Dandy's eyes glinting back at her from the shadowed interior.

"Fine," she said, keeping her voice low, and followed him, her hand cupped over her torch to cut the light in the hope that the bats wouldn't get too upset. A few flitted past, squealing distantly, but there was no great flood of them, which was, finally, one thing going the right way.

Dandy led her to the front room, and he looked up at her, then nudged Rainbow's bag with his snout.

"There's nothing there," she said.

He nudged it again, nibbling at the front pocket, and she pushed him away then crouched down.

"This is properly disturbing a crime scene," she told him, but pulled her gloves out of her pocket and tugged them on before slipping her hand into the front pocket of the bag, already inexplicably sure of what she was going to find.

And she found it almost immediately, the metal and glass cold even through the gloves and the leather smooth and supple and strangely alive-feeling. She stopped, her hand lingering, then took the watch out, tipping it to examine the face. It was heavy despite its expensive slimness, and she had a feeling that it would match the mark on the dead man's wrist perfectly.

She looked at Dandy. "It wasn't here before."

He looked back at her, his matted hair falling away from his eyes. They burned in the low light.

"I'm sure of it," she said. "Who put it there? Rainbow hardly came back and planted evidence on herself."

He just panted softly, and she looked around the room, thinking of the fruitless chase after Dandy's ghostly quarry, and wondering what she'd missed. Then she carefully replaced the watch, got up, and picked her way back to the kitchen. She stood there as Dandy vanished into the night, looking at the crate in the corner which was the room's only furnishing. It held a few cans of baked beans, some cuppa soup and some tea, and nothing more. The place was a bolthole, but not a well-used one. Not a *planned* one. It was a fallback, and where does someone go when the fallback fails?

"Family," DI Adams mumbled, heading down what was becoming a well-trodden path through the old orchard. They go to family. She needed to talk to Miriam again. She trudged to her car, and spotted Collins in the passenger seat with Dandy panting over his shoulder. The door was ajar to stop the whole car steaming up, and Collins was hissing, "I can't just pet you. What if someone sees me petting an invisible dog?"

"Or talking to one," DI Adams said, leaning down at the door and making him jump.

"There you are. Your bloody dog keeps grabbing my hand and trying to get me to pet him. I don't think you're giving him enough attention."

"He likes belly rubs."

"I can't see where his belly *is*."

DI Adams peeled off her jacket, dumped it in the boot, then jogged around the car and got in before she could get any more drenched. She sat down and stared at Collins, who wordlessly handed her a thermal mug and an egg sandwich in a slightly crushed box.

"What are you doing here?"

"You're welcome."

She sighed, took a sip of coffee, and sighed again, a little more deeply. "Yes. Sorry. Thank you for the coffee. What're you doing here?'

"Supplying you with caffeine. Bringing you sustenance. Eat the sandwich, by the way. Lucas is placing bets on how many ulcers you have, and I'm starting to worry my guess is on the low end."

She looked at the sandwich. She *was* hungry, now she thought about it. She peeled the packet open and took a bite, then said around it, "None of these things require you to be on my crime scene, or in my car."

"Just helping out a colleague who's trying to arrest my mother."

She pushed Dandy's nose away from her mug and said, "Which is, of course, precisely why you shouldn't be here."

"Granted." He scratched his nose. "But I do have some more info. Plus Barry's gone missing from the hospital, which I think is probably very related, don't you?"

DI Adams didn't say anything for a moment, just took a sip of coffee. It was still reasonably hot, and intensely strong. She was starting to suspect Collins was testing her caffeine tolerance, which was a fool's game. "What's the other info?"

He took out his notebook, and tapped his phone where it sat on his knee. "When I looked at the location of your jewel theft, I recognised the house name. It's where the first of the wildlife collections were broken out of."

DI Adams frowned at him. "That was months ago, though, wasn't it?"

"Yeah. But I went and got some signal and did some digging

around. There's been private wildlife collections hit up and down the country, which we knew, and realised they were likely linked. But we were just looking at them. When I looked a bit further, it turns out there've been thefts from all of the same houses. They're never reported until weeks or even months later, but there's a match for every one. We just didn't realise because they've been in different counties each time, and the connection hasn't been there because of the timing."

DI Adams took a sip of coffee, then said, "Are you saying you think your mother's been robbing these places as well?"

"Not her," he said immediately. "Mum's about as anti-capitalist as it's possible to get."

"Are you sure? Seems that robbing rich people would be a good anti-capitalist move."

"Only if she did something good with the money. Which would mean big injections into the various causes she supports, and I've spoken to as many of them as I could get hold of. No anonymous donations of any notable amounts in the time frames."

DI Adams considered it – not just the thefts, but the fact that Collins really had been checking up on his own mother. She wouldn't dare do that with hers. Her mum would know, somehow, and *just doing my job* would not be an acceptable excuse in any universe. "Maybe she's saving it up for something. Stockpiling it for some grand gesture."

"It doesn't track. If she was stealing, she'd want to make a statement of it. Free the animals, take the goods, send the proceeds somewhere it can be used. Instead the thefts are so quiet that the victims don't even notice until later, because they're too concerned about the animals. Unused silver from sideboards, little artworks from spare rooms, old jewellery that's never worn, just enough cash that it *could* have been misplaced or spent, that sort of thing."

"I'd love to be able to misplace money and not notice," DI Adams said absently.

"Me too," Collins agreed. "But do you see what I mean? It was someone trying to keep it under the radar, and that's not Mum's style. *Nothing's* subtle with her."

"That's a fair point." DI Adams looked at the roof of the car. "But then the murder – you think whoever was doing the thieving was interrupted?"

"Interrupted, panicked, hit them a little too hard and realised the pattern would be discovered."

"So pinned it on someone with a known grudge against the rich."

"Well. More than the rest of us, anyway."

DI Adams acknowledged that with a tip of her head. "So the next question is, of course, which of her Merry Mavericks did the thieving. Any leads on that?"

"Not my case," Collins said solemnly, and jumped as Dandy licked his ear. "*Ugh.*"

"My thoughts exactly, Dandy."

"What, that you'd like to lick my ear? That's harassment, that is."

"No, harassment will be what I do if you don't tell me about what you've not been investigating in this case that's not yours."

Collins didn't answer straight away, and she took another bite of sandwich, then paused.

"Wait – you said Barry was missing. Did the W.I. ...?"

"That I don't know," he said, catching the slobbery ball that Dandy dropped on his lap with a grimace. "But I spoke to the officer who was meant to be watching him, and apparently Barry vanished while said officer was helping a woman of a certain age locate her missing hand-bag, so I think we can make some assumptions."

"That seems reasonable." DI Adams wedged her mug between her legs and pulled onto the road, the dark crushed to the land under the weight of the rain. "What else have you not investigated?"

"I asked Genny to look into Mum's group. On your behalf, of course," he added, when DI Adams looked at him. "The newest member's Simon. No firm dates, but it could tie in. However, going by the photos, Tom's suddenly developed a liking for flash watches and brand-name merino. The proper stuff from New Zealand. Fully kitted out in it, outerwear too."

DI Adams gave a low whistle. One of her brothers had a vaguely named job that earned him pay cheques in figures she tried not to think about, in case she felt obliged to check the legality of it all. He was still as annoying as he'd ever been, though, and at Christmas he usually gave everyone something horrendous like chocolates with his face printed on them. But every now and then random gifts would arrive in the post, such as the merino undershirts that had turned up at DI Adams' door when she'd first moved north. She'd liked them so much she'd hunted out the site to buy some more, but had very quickly decided she'd stick to the cheap itchy versions. She'd seen how much the jackets went for when she was looking, though. It was hardly gear for the impoverished pursuer of an alternative lifestyle.

"I remember Tom from the manor house thing," she said. "He was pretty scruffy then. But maybe he came from money, and has just decided it's too cold to keep up the downtrodden protester appearances."

"Maybe," Collins agreed. "Genny's digging still, but his home address is his parents', and it's a council flat in Seacroft."

"That's some excellent not-investigating."

"I thought so."

"Do we know where he is now?" DI Adams asked.

"No, but I think it might be worth passing by the W.I., since I imagine they'll already have their MI6-level village network on the hunt for him."

DI Adams snorted, speeding up a little as the road widened. "They will as well. Where am I dropping you?"

He frowned at her. "Really?"

"There's still every possibility it *is* your mum. The info's great, but you can't be in the middle of this."

He raised his hands, sighing. "Fine. Yes. But who're you taking with you?"

"Dandy."

"Not how this works."

"The odds of my running anyone down tonight are slim to nil."

"You still can't go on your own. You know that."

DI Adams started to answer, and her phone beeped with a message. "Look at that. Signal!" She pulled up the message service on the hands-free, and a moment later Priya's voice filled the car.

"Alice?" Her voice was shaky. "We're at Miriam's. They've got Pearl and Teresa, and we have to stop. They're—" The line went dead, and DI Adams jabbed the disconnect button, then hit call back. It went straight to messages. She tried Alice instead, and again the message kicked in straight away. Her stomach twisted, and it wasn't the excess of coffee. Or not entirely.

"I've a missed call from Aunty Miriam," Collins said, and leaned forward to poke her phone where it rested in the holder. "So did you. And a text." He scrolled through, and gave a sound that was half-groan, half growl. "They're going to the bunker. They think it's either Tom or Simon, but they're still going to the bloody bunker to look for Rainbow."

"Try calling them," she said to Collins, handing him her mug. "Any of them. And don't put that in the cupholders. He steals it."

"Got it," Collins said, and checked his seatbelt as she accelerated, the Golf clinging to the wet road as it roared through the corners, the rain flooding the windscreen faster than the wipers could manage, but DI Adams didn't slow. The roads were empty, and it might not be far to Toot Hansell, but it was further than she needed it to be right now.

§

SHE BROUGHT the car to a sliding stop just behind Miriam's little green Beetle, which seemed to be melting toward the tarmac in the rain. She swung out without bothering to grab her coat and ran for the house, Collins scrambling after her and Dandy flashing through the garden like the night given form. She glanced back, pointing at the front door and then up, and Collins nodded, already on his way to it with his baton in one hand and his face set and grim.

The path around the house was sodden, water splashing back at her as she ran, and a moment later she skidded around the corner to see the kitchen door standing open, light painted across the path. She shifted her grip on her own baton, the heavy torch in her other hand, and marched to the door, standing to the side as she shouted, "North Yorkshire Police! Show yourselves!"

There was no answer, just the slam of the front door flying open, and she plunged into the kitchen, baton and torch at the ready. Collins shouted, "*Police!*" from the front of the house, and she heard his heavy tread on the hall floor, then running up the stairs.

She moved fast, scanning the room as she crossed it. No one in the corners or under the table. A laptop abandoned on it, and another on the floor, screen shattered. Muddy footprints pointing straight into the house. Footprints, and paw prints. Pantry door ajar, no one inside except a jumble of goods indicating the place had been turned over. She headed for the hall.

"No one upstairs," Collins called, and the floorboards creaked as he jogged back down the stairs.

DI Adams peered into Miriam's big and gently shabby front room with its permanent scent of wood smoke and old candles, and as she did a muffled shout came from the downstairs loo, tucked under the stairs.

"DI Adams?"

She spun back to it. "Priya?"

"We're in here! We're stuck!"

They absolutely were. Someone had sealed them in with the hefty old cabinet that usually lived by the door, collecting hats and mail on top and shoes underneath. DI Adams put her shoulder to it as Collins joined her.

"Ready?" she said, and they heaved together, the cabinet juddering and complaining, and things clattering around inside. It moved easily enough with the two of them, and in two heaves the door was clear. DI Adams opened it to reveal Priya sitting on the loo and Jasmine on the floor, Primrose cradled in her arms.

"Finally!" Jasmine said, scrambling to her feet. "We could barely breathe!"

DI Adams looked around the little space, thinking it must've felt like that. There was just room for the loo and a sink with a tiny window set into the wall above it. The tall end of the little room was taken up by a built-in wardrobe that was spilling coats out of a gap in the door. The lower end, under the stairs, was crammed with boxes and crates, and there was barely room in here for one person, let alone two.

"What happened?" she asked, as they came out.

"Anyone hurt?" Collins asked at the same time.

"That too," she said.

"Primrose could've been," Jasmine said. "She *kicked* her!"

"Monster," Priya said. "In a *zebra* suit!"

"With a mask," Jasmine added. "A woman about my height. White, I think, going by her hands. Um … I didn't recognise her voice." She shook her head. "I'm sorry. I should've noticed more, but she kicked Primrose, and—"

"That's good, Jasmine," DI Adams said, ushering them toward the kitchen. "That helps. Is Primrose okay?" Primrose was currently growling furiously at Dandy, who was investigating the mugs on the kitchen table hopefully.

"Primrose was brilliant," Priya said. "The zebra came in the kitchen door, and we were so surprised that she grabbed Jasmine and pulled her off her chair before we could do anything. Primrose bit her, so she let Jasmine go, and I threw my laptop at her." She grimaced. "I wish I hadn't, now. It was new."

"We made it out of the kitchen and were halfway to the front door before she caught us," Jasmine said. "Caught *me*." She hesitated and took a breath. "She had a kitchen knife. She told Priya to call Alice or she'd stab me."

"But I called you instead," Priya said shakily. "I probably shouldn't have, but—"

Jasmine put an arm around her. "You were brilliant. The zebra took the phone and made us get in the toilet, and we could hear her banging around everywhere." She looked at the kitchen and its open drawers. "Looking for something, I suppose."

"And Pearl and Teresa?" DI Adams asked.

Priya shook her head. "She just said they *had* them, and we needed to tell Alice to keep everyone away. That they wouldn't be hurt as long as we all left them alone."

DI Adams and Collins looked at each other. "And where did you last see Pearl and Teresa?" Collins asked.

"The bookshop," Jasmine said. "They were watching the bookshop. Alice and Miriam went to the bunker with Gert and Rose."

DI Adams nodded, already heading for the front door. "Collins, go after Alice and Miriam. Take Miriam's car if you need to."

"You can't go—"

"I'm not going into the shop. I'll keep an eye on things until backup arrives. Just make sure we're not missing any more W.I., alright? And get an answer out of your aunt about where Rainbow might be."

"Why do I get the hard job?" Collins called after her.

"Because it's all your bloody family's fault," she shouted back, then she was out the door and jogging through the rain to her car, whistling for Dandy as she went. He raced past her, leggy and wild, and for one moment, running together through the night's wild freight of rain, in pursuit of murderers and the lost, she forgot that she hadn't slept for two days and that her fleece was drenched and her calf still stung from an emu injury. For one moment she could have run forever with Dandy at her side.

Then she tripped over a forgotten flowerpot, stumbled, almost fell, and staggered into the gate, barking her shin, and she felt every minute of missed sleep.

But she had a feeling she'd be arresting someone very soon. And that was better than a triple shot of coffee any day.

ALICE

A lice tried opening the door, putting all her weight into twisting the big circular handle, but it was firmly jammed. Whoever had closed them in had secured it from the outside somehow. She turned, shining the torch around the interior, and said, "There's no other way out?"

"Don't you think I'd have taken it if there was?" Thompson said.

"That's reasonable," she admitted.

"Even the vent's got metal grating over it. So unless you've got a shovel with you, I think we're stuck."

"Wonderful," Alice said, and crossed to the bunks, pulling out one of the boxes from beneath. There wasn't much in it – a small pouch containing essential oils, some hairbands, and some plain underwear. A little pocket notepad that contained nothing but a list of the essential oils and varying numbers next to them, like dosages. A foragers' handbook.

She put everything back and turned her attention to the next box, which held a few packets of instant mashed potato, a couple of tins of sliced pineapple, and some toilet paper. She gave the bucket in the corner a resigned look and hoped they wouldn't be down here that long.

But that led to her wondering how long they might be stuck, and that led to thinking about Miriam, and the thud, and how she really should have just left this all with DI Adams. Right from the beginning. If it wasn't for her, Miriam would never have even imagined getting involved in *any* of the investigations they'd been embroiled in, and therefore Rainbow would never have dropped the body off with them, and so none of them would be in this horrible situation. She wondered if Gert and Rose had found Pearl and Teresa yet. Surely they must have? And they'd have tried to call, either way, which meant they'd have realised something had happened. They'd tell DI Adams. She just hoped it would be fast enough.

"Any food in there?" Thompson asked, examining the box.

"Not unless you like pineapple."

"Eh. More of a melon cat."

"In which case, I can't help you." She slid the box back under the bed and pulled the third and final one out. "How come you didn't leave when the police were here?"

"Didn't have time. They literally looked in, then shut the door and left. Not exactly thorough – I barely woke up."

"I'm sensing a pattern," Alice said.

"Yeah, the police are really slack."

She smiled. "I imagine they were looking for Rainbow. There's still tape on the door, so they were probably going to search it properly later."

"That tape works really well to keep people out, I've noticed."

She discovered some water in a flask by the bucket, and poured some into a metal mug, setting it on the floor for the cat. Then she examined the tiny space and said, "Where's that vent? If I can push my phone through to the outside I could send a message."

"You could just settle down for a bit, you know. Have a nap."

"I don't think so."

"Suit yourself." Thompson licked water off his chops, then jumped to the top bunk and put his paws on the wall, nosing at a metal grill that was screwed to the concrete ceiling above it. "See how you go."

Alice climbed carefully onto the top bunk, wincing as she folded herself into the small gap between the mattress and the top of the bunker, and feeling quietly grateful that she'd kept up all the flexibility exercises after her hip replacement. She inspected the grill, then pulled a multitool from the pocket of her coat and set about the screws holding it in place. Even if she couldn't get the phone through it, it was something to do, and she desperately needed that right now. Anything to stop thinking of that awful thud.

The vent came off surprisingly easily. She'd expected the screws would be frozen in place, but they barely complained, and before long she was reaching gingerly inside, the concrete shell rough under her fingertips. The vent went straight up for a very short distance before it turned at a sharp right angle, and as she felt along the bend, her fingers brushed plastic. She frowned, and patted it carefully. Not hard plastic. It felt like a heavy-duty bag of some sort, slickly waterproof. She pressed her fingertips into it, trying to drag it toward her, and it slid grudgingly over the bumpy surface until she could squeeze it down the vent toward her. It bent slightly as she did so, feeling like a book of some sort.

The top bunk was too low to sit on, so she climbed down and sat on the bottom one to examine her prize. It was a small, bright orange dry bag of the sort that kayakers and boaters use, the top rolled down tightly to seal it.

"Oh ho," Thompson said, examining it. "What's this? The ill-gotten gains? A secret tuna stash?"

"Somehow I doubt it's the latter," she said, opening the bag. She pulled out a small book titled *Break the System*, which had Post-its sticking out of it in various places.

"A *book?*" Thompson asked. "Is it an expensive one?"

"I don't think so. It looks new."

"I don't get humans. Who hides a book?"

"Good question," Alice said, opening it to examine the marked pages. She'd expected highlighted passages, some sort of self-published manifesto, perhaps, but it wasn't a printed book at all. It was a notebook, the pages covered with dots and squiggles that she assumed must be shorthand.

She squinted at it. Once upon a time she'd have known how to decipher it, but that had been back in school, when typing and short-hand were the sorts of things one was expected to learn. She hadn't made much effort to remember it past the exams, and this looked very unfamiliar. She wondered if it was a new form she wasn't aware of.

She flipped through a little further, but there was nothing other than the shorthand, which looked less and less like shorthand and more like hieroglyphics the more she stared at it. She looked from the notebook to the bag, frowning. Why hide it? Was it details about the robberies? Descriptions of the houses? A record of the stolen goods?

"What does it say?" Thompson asked.

"I don't know."

Thompson raised himself onto his hindquarters, his front paws on Alice's arm so that he could look at the notebook. "Is that some sort of code?"

"I think it's shorthand of some sort. Secretaries used to use it. Reporters still do, I think."

"Someone's the group secretary?"

"I somehow doubt the group is that formal." She checked inside the dry bag, but there was nothing else of interest. "It being hidden like this makes me think it's to do with the thefts, but it seems a bit silly to put it on paper, even if it is in shorthand."

"Humans are pretty silly," the cat pointed out, snuffling the edges of the pages as she turned them. "And you're really into hiding weird stuff."

Alice kept paging through the book, as much for something to do as in the hope of finding anything she could actually decipher. She supposed it *could* be the details of the thefts, but whoever was doing it was setting Rainbow up rather effectively. Leaving things written down seemed careless.

She rested the book in her lap, considering the possibilities. She was almost as sure as Miriam that it wasn't Rainbow. Rainbow was passionate, but she wasn't violent, and she wasn't a thief. Barry wasn't a threat to anyone except for those who were affronted by the human form. Which left Harriet, Simon, and Tom, and she just couldn't see Harriet being a murderer either. There was the veganism, for a start.

Thompson stretched. "Well, that was exciting. I'm having a nap."

"That's how you got into trouble in the first place."

"Do you have any better ideas?"

Alice looked around the tiny bunker, then went to try the door again. It still didn't budge. "No," she admitted.

"No," Thompson said, and yawned. "So you keep fussing if you like. I'll nap." He curled himself into a compact, comfortable ball on the bunk, his front paws resting on the notebook, and she gave him an irritated look.

Although, to be fair, it wasn't as if there was much else to do. She looked under the bed, wondering if there was anything else to be found, but other than the boxes she'd already checked, it was empty. Besides the vent, there didn't look to be any hidden corners or secret spaces. No trapdoors or—

She looked at Thompson. "What weird stuff do we humans hide?"

He adjusted his position, not opening his eyes. "Notebooks, evidently. Three chocolate bars in a hole in the wall to the left of the door. Some really nasty dried meat called Billy Bong or something inside the top mattress, which I am not yet starving enough to try again. Some miniature bottles in the drain. A key inside that crack on the righthand part of the ceiling."

Alice looked up at the crack. "A key?"

"Yeah."

"How did you find it?"

"Flashy man came back in when everyone else was out and put it there."

"Flashy man?"

"The one who looks like he washes regularly."

Tom. Alice looked at the cat, then gave his head a good scratch. "Well *done*, Thompson."

"What?" He sat up and watched her upturn the bucket so that she could use it as a stool. "Is it for the door?"

She couldn't see anything, and she had to stand on her tiptoes to reach, but when she felt around carefully inside the crack with her fingertips they touched metal almost immediately. She hooked the key out and examined it. It was short-barrelled and multi-branched, and weighty in her hand. "I think it's a safe key," she said.

He blinked at her. "What, like a safe word?"

Alice wasn't entirely certain if the cat knew what that actually meant – or where he'd heard it, for that matter – so she just said, "No. For a physical safe. I should imagine it's the safe where the stolen goods are."

"Great," the cat said, putting his chin back on his paws. "That's a huge help, then."

Alice had to admit he wasn't entirely wrong.

SHE HAD the grill off and her arm stuck as far inside the vent as she could manage, pawing around as she tried to discover if the next turn of the pipe just at the end of her reach was going to deliver her phone to the outside world or simply drop in into some signal-less rain trap, when there was a bang on the door and the handle gave a little wobble. Alice froze, and Thompson gave a hiss of alarm.

Scuffling at the door, as if someone were pulling branches or rocks out of the way, and this time the handle turned more easily, but still not enough to open it. A bit more of a scuffle and the door was pulled wide, light flooding the interior from a powerful torch. Alice raised a hand to shield her eyes, her other arm still stuck in the vent, and a man's voice said, "Hello."

Thompson hissed again.

"That's very inconvenient," Alice said. "I almost had phone signal."

The torch beam dropped lower, and beyond it Alice saw Tom crouched on the threshold, swathed in the sort of waterproof gear that would somehow be warm, breathable, and entirely dry all at once. He played the torch over the bunk beds. "Just you?"

Alice took a breath, and reminded herself that this at least meant Miriam wasn't lying unconscious – or worse – just beyond the door.

And it also meant something else. "You didn't attack her, did you?" she asked.

"Of course I bloody well didn't," he said, his voice sharp. "What the hell – just because I made some changes – *healthy* changes, by the way – everyone thinks I'm the bloody enemy now." He paused, then frowned and added, "Wait – who was attacked? Rainbow?"

"No, Miriam. Rainbow isn't with you?"

"No. I thought she might've gone to you. Well, Miriam." They stared at each other, then he clambered down the stairs. Thompson growled, and he flinched. "Why's there a cat again?"

"There's always a cat," she said.

He gave her a puzzled look, then crossed to the bunk. "Do you need help getting down?"

She shook her head and extricated her arm from the vent. She'd grazed her knuckles, she noted disapprovingly. "Is that your notebook?" she asked, since it was lying right there on the bunk. "I couldn't read it, but I did look at it. I realise that's a terrible invasion of privacy, but it is an investigation."

Tom gave a doubtful little laugh. "When Rainbow said she'd dumped the body on you so you could investigate, I thought she'd been hitting the kombucha a bit hard. Maybe not, though."

Alice climbed down to the floor, painfully aware that Tom was between her and the door. And that she'd left her cane outside. He may not have attacked Miriam, but that wasn't to say he was innocent. "You knew about the body?"

He nodded, taking his hat off and running a hand back over his hair. "Rainbow called me as soon as she found it. I said she should go straight to the police, but she was too worried, what with all the thefts."

Alice nodded slowly. "She talked to you about them."

Tom looked for a moment as if he was going to start going on about people making assumptions again, then he just nodded. "She did. I was the only one she trusted, with Ronnie gone and Harriet taken up with Simon. And Barry's ... Barry."

"What did she think was happening?"

He sighed. "She swung between thinking someone was just in real need of money, to thinking it was some sort of set-up, probably by the government." He spread his hands. "I did ask if she'd looked at the government recently."

Alice looked at the notebook. "And that is yours?"

"Ye-es," he said carefully.

"Is it notes on the crimes?"

"Not exactly."

She peered at him. It was hard to tell in the torchlight, but he seemed to be going somewhat pink. "Oh?"

He groaned. "I was trying to write a book of poetry for Jem. I know, it's pathetic, but she was like *the one*, you know?"

"Not really," Alice said. "And you used shorthand?"

"Um. It's Elvish."

She looked from him to the notebook, then closed it and handed it to him. "And your healthy changes?"

"Jem's seeing some bloody Eton old boy sort. I've been doing a bit of freelance work, and with living at the camp I don't have many expenses." He shrugged. "I thought maybe if I looked more the part ..."

Alice examined him, trying to feel the truth in the words, then decided it didn't matter. Right now, the only thing that mattered was finding Miriam – and that he hadn't been the one behind the thud. *Probably.* "You don't know where Rainbow is now, then?"

"No. She was meant to be holed up at the house, but when I went to check on her there were police all over the place. They haven't found her?"

"We think someone picked her up," Alice said, hoping he didn't ask *how* they knew. "Possibly someone in a zebra suit."

Tom swore softly. "That's Harriet, the zebra suit."

"I imagine anyone could wear a zebra suit," Alice pointed out.

"Well, true. Rainbow didn't want to hear anything against Harriet, but she's *always* broke. And since she and Simon hooked up she's kind of fallen out with Rainbow. Could be he's behind it, or it could be her, or a joint thing. But I can't see how they're doing it. They're both always where they're meant to be when we're on operations."

Alice thought of the Facebook photos of the animal collection, and Daisy turning away. "What about his daughter?"

"Daisy? Never really see her. Bit weird, that, though."

"How so?"

"Well, Simon calls her his daughter, but she's my age. He'd have to have been like fifteen when he had her, max."

Alice frowned. "She looks terribly young."

Tom didn't say anything, just cleared his throat and looked at his hands, and Alice realised that everyone under forty looked much the same age to her these days. She made a small noise of annoyance, mostly at herself, and said, "Well, whoever it is, they likely have both Rainbow and Miriam."

"You didn't see anything when they grabbed Miriam?"

"I wish I had." She sighed. "I was in here, letting out Thompson—"

"Who?"

"The cat."

Thompson mewled obligingly.

"Really, why's there always a cat?" Tom asked.

"He's …. a companion animal," Alice said.

"A *companion* animal?"

"He was in here, anyway," Alice said. "And I was letting him out when someone grabbed Miriam and locked me in. There were no other cars, and I didn't see anyone when we got here, but in this rain they could have followed us up the road and I wouldn't have known."

Tom scratched his jaw, beard rasping under his fingertips. "There's more than one track up here, as long as you've got a decent vehicle. I didn't see anyone."

Alice nodded, thinking of the SUV at the hospital. She imagined that would count as a *decent vehicle.* But all she said was, "They'll be long gone. Where might they take Miriam? Do you have another camp or something?"

"Not that they'd go to. The old house is full of police, and the main camp at Maddie's is too busy for them to pull something like this. I say we try the bookshop."

"You really think Harriet's involved?"

Tom shrugged. "Maybe not, but it's the only place I can think of. Daisy might know where Simon is, if nothing else." He tucked his notebook into the inside pocket of his coat. "Let's go." He looked at the cat. "Ah – do you have a leash or something?"

Thompson hissed, and Alice said, "He'll make his own way," then headed for the ladder. She looked back as she climbed it, and saw Tom glance at the crack in the ceiling, but he didn't move toward it. The key was already on her keyring, zipped into an inner pocket of her jacket, and she was almost sure he couldn't see whether it was still in its hiding place or not. She certainly hadn't been able to.

The night had spread itself over the fells while Alice had been in the bunker, and it was damp and cold and murky, but after being trapped for so long the sky felt wide and glorious, full of the whispering patter of rain on old rocks. Alice took a deep breath, thinking of the bookshop, and Pearl and Teresa not answering their phones, and Gert and Rose trundling back to the village. "I'm calling some friends," she said, taking her phone out. "They might be able to tell us something."

"Good plan," he said, closing the bunker and starting to pile the loose branches back in front of it.

Alice hit call, but not on Rose's number, or Gert's. She called Colin instead, and he answered almost immediately. "Alice? Are you alright?"

"I'm alright," she said, picking up her cane in her free hand. "But Miriam's gone." Her voice wobbled on the word, and Colin swore.

"*Gone?* What d'you mean, gone?"

"We're on the way to the bookshop—"

Tom grabbed the phone off her, making her jump. He'd moved so quickly and so silently she hadn't even registered it. He hit disconnect while she frowned at him.

"That was a man's voice," he said. "What're you doing?"

"Trying to find my friend and her sister," she said sharply.

He looked at the display. "DI Colin Collins? Is that a real name?"

"Yes. And he's Rainbow's son."

Tom groaned and looked at the sky. "Of course. I forgot. But we can't call the police. We *can't.*"

"Why not?" she asked.

He rubbed his mouth, looked at Thompson, then at her, and said, "Rainbow's not exactly a law-abiding citizen. None of us are. I mean, we're not murderers, obviously, but in these cases – in *so many* cases – the police just go for the easiest explanation. The body was in Rainbow's van, therefore she's the murderer."

"I'm sure that can be sorted out."

He hesitated, then shook his head. "That's not the only thing I'm worried about."

Alice examined him, then said, "Tell me."

He took a breath. "The stuff that's been going missing? From what I understand, you'd need specialised contacts to sell it. And people who have those sorts of contacts ..."

"They cover their tracks," Alice said, keeping her voice steady. But she could hear that *thud* again.

"Exactly," he said.

Alice considered it, feeling the rain dripping from her sleeves and running down her hands, and the soft touch of the droplets that missed her hood and splattered her face. Her stomach seesawed gently with the thought of it. *They cover their tracks.* He was right, of course. But it had been too long already since the bunker had slammed, cutting her off from Miriam. There was no time for second-guessing. She held her hand out for her phone. "You might be right. But I'll take that risk. I need to find Miriam."

Tom didn't answer straight away, just watched her. He was standing a little too close, the bulk of him a touch too coiled for comfort, and her stomach turned over in a slow, heavy roll as she thought of the note on the body. *For you.* But surely if this was all to do with Tom, Tom with his Elvish notes and mysterious income and uneasy yet convincing arguments, if it was him and he wanted to be rid of her, she'd never have left the bunker. *Surely.* Unless he needed her to locate the rest of the W.I., scattered and divided in the depths of a dank autumn night—

He handed her the phone. "Alright," he said. "Maybe you're right. Maybe I'm just overthinking."

She took the phone wordlessly, her chest still too tight to trust herself to speak. She hit dial, and it was answered almost immediately.

"Alice?" Colin asked. "What happened?"

"I'm fine," she said. "Like I said, bookshop. It sounds like it may be Simon and Harriet we're after."

"Not we," Colin said. "I'm almost at the bunker. Don't move."

Alice looked at Tom. "He's on the way," she said.

"That's a great help. He should be on the way to the bookshop."

She nodded. "On that, I agree. Come along." She turned and started toward the track, already dialling Rose. It rang once, twice, three times, and her fingers were so tight on the phone that she could feel flares of pain in the knuckles when Rose answered.

"Alice!" Rose said, sounding breathless.

"Rose? Are you alright?"

"Yes, sorry – I just took Angelus for a wee and now he doesn't want to get back in the van."

"Oh. Good." She took a breath, collecting herself as Tom pointed at a battered old Range Rover hidden in the shadows of the trees. She headed toward it. "Any sign of Pearl and Teresa?"

"No. Pearl's car's here, but that's all."

"Alright. We're on the way." She hesitated. "Or I am. Miriam's gone. Someone grabbed her."

Rose was silent for so long that Alice said, "Rose?"

"Yes," she said finally. "No. I heard."

"Keep an eye on things, but don't go near the bookshop. Let me know if you see anything."

"Alright," Rose said, her voice very quiet, and hung up.

Alice put the phone in her pocket and took a moment to straighten her hat, wondering if she should call the others, but there was no point. And she couldn't face saying it again. She *couldn't*.

Tom looked at her as he opened the driver's door. "Are you alright?"

Alice nodded, and looked at Thompson. "If only we had a way to check the bookshop right now."

Tom gave her a strange look, but the cat twitched his ears gently, then meandered away from them. She looked back at Tom. "Alright," she said. "Let's go."

"Your cat," he said uncertainly.

"Oh, no. He doesn't belong to anyone. Cats never do."

"Right." Tom looked like he wanted to say something else, but he just swung into the car, and Alice clambered in on the passenger side, touching her keys, tucked away in an inner pocket, and keeping close hold of her cane.

Because a Range Rover was most certainly an SUV.

22

MIRIAM

Miriam's head hurt, and she wasn't quite sure what day it was. She didn't remember going to bed, actually, and for a moment she just lay there with her eyes closed, feeling a painful throb somewhere in the region of her forehead and wondering if she'd overdone the paracetamol, or the cold medication. Perhaps both. That would certainly explain the churning going on in her stomach. She swallowed hard and touched a hand to her face, surprised to find it damp. That was odd. Was her ceiling leaking?

Then she realised that her hair was damp too, and her knees were stinging, and there was some low arguing going on not far away. She opened one eye a crack, and found that didn't hurt too much, so she opened the other one, and peered around. She was lying on a sofa that was covered in a crocheted blanket made of so many different coloured wools that she had to close her eyes again for a moment to stop herself feeling woozy. She stayed very still, her head slowly clearing even if the pain wasn't.

The bunker.

Alice.

Rainbow missing.

And someone had ... well, she didn't remember that bit, just that she'd been talking to Alice and Thompson one moment, and the next she'd woken up here with a sore head, so she supposed someone had hit her on it. If it had been anything else – a stroke or something awful – she'd be in hospital. And the only likely person to have hit her on the head was the murderer. She swallowed hard, her stomach twisting, and wondered if Alice was here too. She hoped so. She wasn't sure she could face a murderer without Alice.

The arguing slowly swam into some sort of focus as she lay there, the voices hushed but clear.

"But why bring her *here?*" a woman's voice was asking. "What were you thinking? You should have shut them both in and left them, or even just waited for them to go away. Now we've got a situation."

Shut them *both* in. Miriam swallowed a moan of disbelief. Did that mean Alice was still at the bunker? Of course, that was better than her being hurt – or worse – but Miriam had a sudden swell of panic at the idea that she might be here alone.

"That's enough," a man's voice said. "I made the decision that seemed right at the time."

"Really. Bopping someone on the head and dragging her off seemed like the right decision."

"At this rate she won't be the only one I'm bopping on the head."

"Oh, I'd like to see you do all this on your own. *I'm* the one that should be getting rid of baggage around here."

"She's still unconscious. She didn't see me. Calm down."

Miriam decided that keeping her eyes closed was definitely the best move, and not just due to the blanket.

"This is a nightmare," the woman said, her voice getting fainter as she walked away. "A complete nightmare. All I said was see if she's got the key on her. That was *it.*"

"You're not bloody well in charge here," the man said, then his voice became inaudible as there was the click of a door closing.

Miriam waited a little longer, willing herself to appear unconscious, then when there was no sound of movement around her she opened one eye again. She peeked at the room, careful not to look too closely at the blanket. There was a lamp on a side table at the end of the sofa, and in its light she could see the closed door. Other than that, there was a desk piled with files and books and postage bags, a small fridge and kettle in the corner, and a ragged rug on the floor. Definitely no Alice. She opened her eyes properly, and when she still couldn't see anyone lurking about, ready to bop her on the head again, she sat up.

Her head gave a throb of pain, and an involuntary little whimper escaped her, but she caught herself. No time for that. She touched the painful spot gingerly, and found a folded wedge of toilet paper stuck to it. She made a face and removed it to find some blood, but not much. Evidently she wasn't about to bleed to death on someone's '70s-era crochet masterpiece.

No one had shouted when she sat up, and when she craned to look behind the sofa she found there wasn't really any *behind*. Just a hefty collection of boxes, most of them overflowing with books and printouts, and a door with a sink next to it. She stared at the door. It had a deadbolt on it, which meant it was probably an exterior door, and that shook any final wooziness from her. She scrambled to her feet, swayed for a moment, then hurried around the sofa. She tripped over the corner of the rug, bounced off the office chair, knocked over a box that disgorged a pile of old bank statements onto the floor with a startled thud, and grabbed the deadbolt just as the door on the other side of the room flew open.

"*Stop!*" the man yelled, and behind him a woman shouted, "Grab her, dammit!"

Miriam had no intention of stopping or being grabbed. She wrenched the deadbolt open, flipped the old latch, and stumbled out into the dark, welcome chill of the rainy night. But there was no time to savour it. She broke into what her head insisted was a full sprint, but her body seemed less convinced by the idea. She veered left, almost tipped over a low brick wall, recovered, and struggled across a bare patio onto the street, aiming for a streetlight she could see at the end of the alley and willing her legs to work faster. They seemed to be coming under some sort of control, but not quickly enough. There were fast footfalls behind her, and someone grabbed her arm.

"We're not going to hurt you," the male voice said, but Miriam had made no such promises. She spun toward him, flailing out with a clumsy blow that was half punch, half slap, and wishing she had Alice's cane still. She caught the man straight on his nose and he yelped, dropping her arm and jumping back. "*Ow!*"

Miriam resumed her slow-motion sprint for the light, and someone else grabbed her, one hand in her hair and the other seizing one of her arms, twisting it up behind her back, high enough to set off a spark of pain in her shoulder.

"*Stop,*" the woman said behind her. "This is not what we had planned, but you come in, sit down, and behave yourself, and everything's going to be just fine."

Miriam tried to pull away, but the woman's grip was strong, and all she could do was twist a little in place, not even enough to see who she was talking to. "My sister," she managed. "What did you do with my sister?"

"She's fine," the woman said. "But she gave you a key, and we need it."

"She didn't give me anything."

"I saw her clothes at your place. I know she was there, but I couldn't find the key."

"But she wasn't," Miriam said. "The ... we collected her clothes from my great-aunt's house. I don't know anything about a key. And when were you at my house?" She gasped. "Priya and Jasmine! What did you *do?*"

"Nothing," the woman said, and added to the man, "Get me a balaclava."

"Really?" the man asked. "Is there any point?"

"*Yes,*" the woman hissed, then took a breath. "We're still on track. And if this one doesn't have the key, we can use her to convince Rainbow to give it up."

"That won't work," Miriam said, her stomach resuming its slow rolls and making her gulp. "Rainbow doesn't even like me that much."

The man sighed. "You can make this a lot easier, Miriam. Just tell us."

"I don't know anything about a key," she said. "I really *don't!*"

"We'll see," the woman said. "You might just need some persuasion."

Miriam tried to decide if the woman sounded serious or not. Surely no one *really* said things like that? That sort of thing only happened in movies! But she let herself be turned around and guided back toward the house, following a skinny man in a balaclava and a heavy waterproof coat across a small patio enclosed by the low brick walls she'd almost fallen over. She looked around at the row of terraced houses, and craned to look back toward the light.

"Stop that," the woman said.

"Daisy?" Miriam said. "This is the bookshop. And you're not Harriet. And—" she gasped. "*You did art history!* You know art!"

There was silence behind her, then Daisy said, "I bloody said, Simon. I *said* it was a bad idea bringing her back here."

"Oh, you're using names now?" the man in the coat snapped. "Nice, *Daisy.*"

"May as well." Daisy kept propelling Miriam toward the door. "We're just going to have to deal with her *and* her sister *and* bloody Harriet together. This whole thing is a complete mess. You and your *protest groups.*"

"You have done something to Rainbow!" Miriam said.

"Not yet," Daisy replied. "And we didn't want to do anything to anyone, but now you've gone and got in the middle of things, and we've got no choice."

Miriam tried to dig her heels into the ground, slowing her slide toward the door, and yelled so loudly that it set off a throb in her forehead again, "*Help! HELP! Kidnappers! Thieves! Fire! FIRE!*"

Daisy shoved her, hard, and Miriam would have fallen if the younger woman hadn't kept a firm grip on her arm. "Get inside," she hissed.

"I will not," Miriam snapped, and drew a breath to yell again. Before she could, however, there was an officious bark behind them. She craned to see past her captor.

"Seriously?" Daisy said, and looked around. "It's just some old dog.

It's fine." She tried to push Miriam again, but Miriam had managed to get her free hand and both feet braced against the doorframe.

"Martha!" she called. "Martha, fetch help! Good dog!"

The Labrador *whuff*ed softly, then gave a wobbly howl.

"Shut up," Daisy hissed, and Simon pulled Miriam's hand off the doorframe. She jerked away from him, and he grabbed her again.

"That's enough," Simon said, his grip painfully tight. He suddenly seemed vastly different from the pale, pie-eating man of the day before. "Come on."

"Martha!" Miriam called as she was pushed through the doorway. "Martha, *get help! Help!*"

She didn't have time to see if Martha had risen to the challenge. The door was slammed and bolted again, and this time she was bundled through the little office room, into the hall, and up the stairs, shouting the whole way.

"You can't do this! My nephew's a police officer! And I have a cane! A really good one! Plus I know … *people* who can *do things!* I—" She was cut off with a muffled yelp as Daisy paused on the landing to slap gaffer tape over her mouth, then taped her wrists roughly but securely together in front of her. "*Mmmm!*" she said, indignantly.

"At least when this is done I'll never have to deal with village ladies again," Daisy said, and propelled Miriam into a little bedroom equipped with a single bed and an old-fashioned dresser. "Bloody nightmares, the lot of you." She sat Miriam down on the floor and used more tape to attach her bound hands to a radiator, looping it around the pipes and back through her wrists several times. "Don't worry, it doesn't work," she added, as Miriam looked at it in alarm. "This place really is such a dump. Harriet hasn't the first clue about running a business."

"*Hmm,*" Miriam pointed out.

"I have no idea what you're trying to say, and I don't care," Daisy said, and walked to the door, where Simon was lingering.

"Can she breathe?" he asked.

Daisy looked at Miriam. "Can you breathe?"

Miriam shook her head, even though she could. She wouldn't have been able to a few days ago, though, when her cold was in full force, so it was only a small lie.

"She's fine," Daisy said, and pulled the door closed. It was an old-fashioned wooden one, with a round knob and a proper keyhole, and she turned the key in the lock. Miriam huffed air out of her nose, and looked around the room. They hadn't even left a light on for her. There was only the faintest suggestion of streetlight coming in the window, illuminating another glaring example of crochet art spread on the bed, and gleaming on the edges of the mirror on the dresser. Miriam tugged hopefully at the tape attaching her to the radiator, but there was barely any give. She looked around, sighed, and wondered what Alice would do in this situation.

She had a feeling it wouldn't have involved begging a dog for help and being recaptured before she even got off the patio.

MIRIAM SAT THERE FOR A WHILE. *Daisy.* If only she'd worked it out earlier! Daisy who did art history went to the houses and told Simon what to steal. It was quite clever, really. She wondered where Harriet was, and Rainbow, and how Simon and Daisy were planning to *deal* with them. And also – with a sudden sick roll of her belly – which of them had killed the poor man in the barrow.

She lifted her head as the sound of a heavy knock on the door downstairs drifted through the house. She stilled, straining to hear more, and a moment later the knock came again, hard and heavy with the sort of insistence that comes with authority.

Colin, she tried to say, but all that came past the tape was a little *mmmph.*

The knock again, and she strained at the bonds, whimpering. She was on the wrong side of the building, at the back, but if someone opened the door and she could make enough noise...

Voices now, muffled by the bedroom door. She couldn't tell what was being said, but surely, *surely* that meant the front door was open. She screamed against the tape, putting every last gasp of breath into it, and slammed her feet into the floor, lifting them and crashing them down, feeling the old boards creak under the carpet, again and again, her own efforts drowning any sense of what was going on downstairs, but she didn't stop. She didn't *dare* stop, because what if this was her one chance, the only way to let anyone know what was happening?

Her feet were jarring inside her wellies, her thighs and belly aching from lifting her legs and slamming them down again, and she was sweating wildly with the effort, feeling like a child throwing a tantrum, when the door flew open.

"Shut *up*," Simon snarled at her. He'd taken his balaclava off, and his hair was wild. "Stop it! This is *all your fault!*"

Miriam stopped, staring at him.

"You made us do it!" he said, pointing down the stairs. "You *made* us. We've never had to do this sort of thing before! You and all your ridiculous friends, poking your noses in—"

"Simon!" Daisy shouted from downstairs. "Leave her. Help me with the safe. We've got to move."

"You ..." Simon pointed at her, then shook his head. "Dammit. This should've been easy." He slammed the door and locked it, and Miriam listened to him run back down the stairs. Her stomach was playing up again. *You and all your friends.* Who had been at the door? What had they *done?*

She squeezed her eyes shut against sudden hot tears, and wondered if it had been Alice, and where Pearl was if Martha was out wandering the streets. What was *happening?* She slumped forward, fighting for breath around the tears, wishing for dragons, for Colin, for *anyone,* but there was no one. There was just her, and what could she do? Nothing at all, just a silly old woman stumbling into things that didn't concern her and—

There was something digging into her legs, sharp enough to break through her panic. Keys? Could she use keys somehow? No, she'd left the house unlocked— She stopped struggling suddenly, trying to calm her breathing. In slowly, out slowly. In for a count of four, out for a count of four.

There was an argument going on downstairs, raised voices drifting up to her, but she ignored them and adjusted her position carefully, shuffling closer to the radiator, twisting and wriggling. *There.* There was just enough play in the tape Daisy had used to attach her to the pipe that she could get her fingers into her coat pocket. Carefully, now, she thought, shifting gently, her fingers sliding off the slick surface of Mortimer's scale. *Careful!*

And then she had it, gripped fiercely in her fingertips, and she tried to slice the tape on her wrists with it, but she couldn't get the angle. She gave a little whimper of frustration, and forced herself to stop before she dropped it. She needed a different grip. If she could hold it in her teeth ... She set the scale down carefully, and slid herself backward until she was lying face down on the floor, her head pressed against the radiator and her fingers touching her face. It was hard to get the angle, and she had to smush her cheek painfully into the cold metal as she scraped desperately at the tape on her mouth with her fingernails, her arms straining and her hands cramping at the uncomfortable angle, but it was working. *It was working.*

Suddenly a corner was free, and she gave a whispered crow of delight, pinching the curling edge and pulling the tape off with a little hiss of pain. She licked her skinned lips, wincing, then fumbled to pick the scale up in her fingertips. She wedged herself against the radiator again and grabbed the scale in her teeth. The edges were sharp and uncomfortable, but she ignored it and pressed the scale into the tape on her wrists. It was tricky, because she couldn't see what she was doing, so she just swiped and jabbed and hooked wildly, scraping the skin of her arms and jabbing the scale into her lips painfully. But here and there she felt the tape part as she got it just right, or near enough, and she twisted her arms this way and that, trying to get it to tear.

And finally, *finally* it did, her arms popping apart as she strained against the restraints, and she scrambled up with a little shriek of triumph that she had to muffle, pressing her lips together. She started for the door, then stopped. Wait. They'd locked it. Out the window perhaps? She turned back and looked out at the night doubtfully. It was quite a drop, straight onto paving stones, and she didn't feel a broken leg was going to help her much.

She looked at the door again, touching her mouth gingerly where the scale had cut it, and a rough voice said, "What're you up to, then?"

She swallowed a scream and spun back to see Thompson sitting on the windowsill. "What're *you* doing?" she hissed.

"Looking for you. Thought you might need rescuing, but evidently not."

"I can't get out," she said, her voice low. "The door's locked."

The cat jumped to the floor and trotted to it, inspecting the frame, then was gone. She heard a rattle from outside, and some quiet metallic clinking, then he was back, walking across the room to her with the key in his teeth. He offered it to her and she took it, staring at him.

"Hope it unlocks from the inside," he said. "I can't turn it."

"It should," she said, stepping as quietly across the old carpet as she could, wincing when the boards creaked. "These old doors usually do." But her heart was still going too fast as she slipped the key into the lock, and it chattered against the metal.

But it turned. It turned, and then she was out into the upstairs hall, peering down the stairs toward the front door.

"Hang about," Thompson said. "I'll go down first, check it's all clear."

"Alright," Miriam whispered, and stayed crouching there as he padded softly down the stairs, his tail waving gently above him. She lost sight of him as he headed into the hall, and she fidgeted anxiously.

Then he was there, next to her, and she almost fell over, biting back a little scream of fright. "Don't do that!"

"What?" he asked, sounding puzzled.

"Just— It doesn't matter. Is it clear?"

"They're digging around in the back room there. Looks like they're trying to cut the safe out. You can head straight out the front door."

"Good." Miriam got up, then looked at him. "There's no one else here, is there? We couldn't get hold of Pearl or Teresa before. And someone came to the door before, and I think something ... happened. Plus Rainbow and Harriet might be here somewhere too."

Thompson looked at her, then sighed. "You lot can never leave well enough alone, can you?"

"No such thing when it comes to friends."

He tipped his head. "You check upstairs, I'll check downstairs. *Quietly*, mind."

"I can be quiet," she hissed, although she had to admit, as she picked her way carefully down the hall, the house wasn't helping her. Every board squeaked and groaned, and she wasn't sure that simply running wildly across them all mightn't have been just as subtle.

She checked the room next to the one she'd been held in first. It was also a bedroom, if a little bigger and given over to more boxes of books and files. She left the door open and crossed the hall to find a bathroom, empty and faintly grimy. That just left one room, toward the front of the house, and as she headed for it Thompson materialised on the landing.

"Leg it!" he hissed. "Scruffy's coming to check on the noise!"

Miriam looked around wildly. "Leg it *where?*"

"Just hide!"

She lunged through the bathroom door just as the stairs started to creak with a heavy tread, and Thompson gave a loud mewl from the landing.

"What the hell— Daisy, did you get a cat?"

"No. Why would I?" Her reply was indistinct, and the steps on the stairs continued up.

"Puss, puss," Simon said, and Thompson mewled again. There was a pause, then sudden quick steps. A door banged against the wall, and Miriam winced. "*Daisy!*" Simon bellowed. "She's gone!"

"*What?*" Running feet below, and Miriam put her shoulder against the door, bracing it shut, but no one came bursting in. Instead, she heard feet going down the stairs, fast, then urgent voices. She opened the door a crack, peering around it, and spotted Thompson on the landing. He looked back at her and shrugged, and they listened as the back door opened, slammed, and then silence washed in around them.

Miriam crept out and joined Thompson. He looked up at her with luminous green eyes and said, "Your ladies are in the cellar."

"*What?*" She didn't wait for an answer, just ran for the stairs, taking them two at a time. A moment later she was banging on the cellar door. "Pearl! *Pearl!*"

There was a shout from behind the door, then Gert's voice. "We're locked in! Can you find the key?"

"*Gert?*"

"The *key*, Miriam!"

"I'll try," Miriam checked the lock, but the key wasn't in it. She hurried to the shelf that ran along the hall, clattering among old knickknacks and half-used candles and bits of post. Nothing. Maybe there was bowl, she always had hers in a bowl—

"Miriam," Thompson said, and she turned to see him standing on the threshold of the back room, his tabby fur lit by a strange orange light. "We have a problem."

"I know. I can't find the key, and they could be back any minute!"

"No," he said, and looked at her, and this time she caught the crackle and roar of paper catching light. "We're on fire."

23

MORTIMER

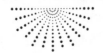

Mortimer had wanted to rush straight out to the bunker, to make sure Miriam and Alice were safe, but Beaufort had shaken his heavy head, and they'd listened outside the door as Priya and Jasmine had told the inspectors what happened. Mortimer had been able to feel the indignant heat baking off the High Lord, and his own wings trembled in the early dark. Then the front door had slammed as DI Adams left, and now the High Lord let out a slow breath that steamed wildly in the garden, and knocked on the kitchen door.

Colin opened it and looked down at them without much surprise. "Did you hear everything?"

"Mostly," Beaufort admitted.

Colin nodded. "I can't get Aunty Miriam or Alice on their mobiles. Do you know where they are?"

"Only that they went to the bunker," Beaufort said. "What about everyone else?"

"Rose and Gert are at the bookshop," Jasmine said, handing a mobile phone back to Colin. "Carlotta and Rosemary are fine, but they've lost Barry."

"*How?*" Colin asked, and Jasmine made a little vague motion.

"I didn't ask. But I can't get hold of anyone else at all."

Colin pocketed his phone and nodded. "You two go home. I'm serious about that. *Go home.*"

Priya and Jasmine looked at each other, then nodded. Mortimer could smell the pale silver threads of fear winding around them, brittle as cobwebs in morning light, and his chest was painfully hot.

Colin looked at the dragons. "Show me where the bunker is. No rushing in – we don't know who's there, or if anything's even happened, and you lot are still meant to ... well, not exist."

"We shall only intervene if strictly necessary," Beaufort said, and Colin sighed.

"I don't know why I waste my breath," he said, and jogged out the door into the rain, shouting as he went, "Priya, Jasmine, *go home.*"

"Do be careful," Beaufort said to the two women.

"I think we might," Priya said. "Just this once."

"Are you two coming?" Colin shouted from the garden, and the dragons turned and ran after him, swift-pawed in the rain.

꩜

MORTIMER NEVER ENJOYED BEING SQUEEZED into the back of Miriam's tiny little VW Beetle, with the road feeling far too close beneath him and the exhaust seeping up to squeeze his throat, but he wasn't quite sure how he felt about flying above it as they raced through the rain-drenched fells, either. Beaufort seemed to be enjoying himself to an almost impossible degree, swooping and spiralling in front of the car, and occasionally dropping so low and close in front of it that Mortimer saw the brake lights come on violently. But the High Lord would just swoop away again, turning lazy loops in the air, then come roaring back, passing low enough over the car to tick his talons off the roof, then speeding off ahead.

Mortimer was desperate to race ahead of the car himself, but not to play. He wanted to rush straight to the bunker, and while he realised that they were as likely to meet Alice and Miriam on the road back (and no one would be able to tell him that they'd done so if he'd gone off on his own), when the fells began to flatten to high moors he did just that. He veered off, not bothering to tell Beaufort, because the old dragon would know where he'd gone, without a doubt. He arrowed straight for the campsite, his eyes narrowed against the strike of the rain, and spiralled out of the sky with his neck arched and his tail coiling behind him. He landed lightly on the stony ground that surrounded the ruins of the fire, casting around for scents before he could even fold his wings, but there was nothing immediate. No one nearby in the shadows.

He growled, the sound a low rumble in his throat, and tried the bunker, spinning the wheel and pulling it open. A wash of scent rolled out to meet him – the warm spiked edges of cat, and Alice's cool green notes of still rivers with murky depths, and a smattering of rage and fright and ragged orange edges of panic. And— He jerked away from the door as something caught his attention, the rain all but smothering the little lash of scent, the emotional traces left behind in the wake of an event.

There. Miriam, comfortable yellows and wistful blues, and then the broken-glass-in-storms whiff of surprised violence. He couldn't see anything, no blood on the ground, no ... no *body,* but something had happened, someone had done something to Miriam, and he'd *known* it, just known it, he should have flown right here, he should have, this was a *disaster,* how had he been so *careless*—

"Hey," a rough feline voice said, and Mortimer spun to see Thompson sheltering under one of his wings – or he had been until Mortimer moved. The cat wrinkled his snout and padded into shelter again as the rain found him.

"What happened?" Mortimer demanded. "Where's Miriam? And Alice?"

"Breathe, dude," Thompson said. "You're getting all smoky, and I don't fancy singed fur to go with my missing whiskers."

Mortimer opened his mouth to say that he had every right to be a bit smoky, and realised he was dribbling dark vapour over his jaws and his chest was so hot that the rain was sizzling where it hit his back. He let a slow breath out, watching the smoke dissipate a bit, then said more calmly, "What happened?"

"Unclear," the cat said. "Alice and myself got locked in that bloody bunker, and Miriam was whisked off by assailants unknown."

"Assailants? They hurt her?"

Thompson tipped his head. "Again, *breathe*. You're very excitable for a dragon, you know."

Mortimer took another deep, slow, breath, then said, "You don't know where she is?"

"No. Flashy Man let us out of the bunker, and Alice has just dispatched me to check out the bookshop, see if she's there."

"But you're still here," Mortimer said, not bothering to hide his impatience.

"Saw dragons incoming and figured I'd see what was happening with you lot first," the cat said. "Might be you knew something."

"No," Mortimer said. "We don't know *anything*. Someone's been into Miriam's house searching for something, though. They attacked Priya and Jasmine."

"The plot thickens." Thompson nodded toward the unseen road. "Alice is that way if you're looking for her. They just left."

"But Miriam?" Mortimer said, as calmly as he could. His chest was heating up again, and he really didn't want to have a singed cat on his conscience, but Thompson was going to have to find a sense of urgency somewhere.

"I'm on the trail. Get thee to Toot Hansell, likely the bookshop. More updates soon." The cat winked at him, then stepped sideways and vanished, leaving a final huff of laughter behind.

Mortimer glared at the space where the cat had been sitting, then puffed a little belch of flame at it, easing the pressure in his chest. Miriam was missing. Someone had attacked her, and now she was missing. He leaped forward, taking to the air in one smooth bound, not even circling back to find the High Lord. There was no time.

He was getting to Toot Hansell.

OR THAT WAS HIS INTENTION. But then there was still Alice to check on, because surely Flashy Man was Tom – it certainly couldn't be Simon – and wasn't he a suspect? And while Colin was quite large, so was Tom. If there was trouble, and Beaufort decided to get involved, it could all get very messy and complicated and just generally impossible. Although it *shouldn't*, he reminded himself. Beaufort was a High Lord, and very good at diplomacy and negotiations and all that sort of thing. But he was also Beaufort.

As he swept back up into the sky, strong wings pulling him effortlessly higher, Mortimer could see two sets of headlights pointed at each other, where Colin had stopped Miriam's Beetle with its nose to the getaway vehicle. Mortimer wavered, his headlong flight slowing. He needed to find Miriam. Anything could have happened! But there was Beaufort, just on the edges of the lights, watching the two cars attentively, and at some point he was going to Get Involved. There was no denying it.

Mortimer groaned, tried out some of the more inventive curse words he'd heard Gert use, and swept back toward the cars, coming to land in the shadows beyond the headlights. He trotted over to join the High Lord, who glanced at him and said, "Find anything, lad?"

"Someone attacked Miriam," Mortimer said. "She's *gone*."

Beaufort nodded. "Alice has just said."

They turned their attention back to the scene in front of them.

"No," Tom said, crossing his arms over his chest.

"You're going to have to come in," Colin said. "You're a suspect."

"You can't arrest me for that."

"I can." He pulled his phone out and poked it. "Only now I can't bloody well get hold of Adams."

"That settles it, then," Alice said. "We shall just have to carry on to Toot Hansell and see if Miriam's at the bookshop."

"*No*," Colin said. "You're going home, and Tom's coming with me."

"I haven't done anything!" Tom protested. "That's police harassment!"

"You don't want to see what it looks like if I have to harass you."

Tom looked at the old Beetle. "I'm not sure it'll carry us both, anyway."

Colin scowled at him. "I'll just bloody well commandeer yours, then."

"Sodding police. Rainbow's right about you. Have you really arrested your own mother?"

"At least once," Colin said.

"Jobsworth."

"This is a murder investigation."

"I can't get hold of Pearl *or* Teresa," Alice said, her voice sharp. "They were meant to be watching the bookshop, but when Rose and Gert went to check on them, they'd gone. There's no time for this. We need to go."

"Again, *police*," Colin said. "What you need to do is go home."

"I really don't think so," she said, and took her keys from her pocket, holding them out to him. "Take my car. Leave Miriam's here. It's far too slow."

"Alice—"

"Miriam is *missing*. I'm not wasting any more time on this."

"We have it in hand, Alice."

"Sure you do," Tom said. "That's why you're out here in your aunt's old banger, on your own."

Colin looked from one of them to the other, then raised his hands in defeat. "I promise I will arrest at least one of you by the end of the night, just to make myself feel better."

"You've been spending too much time with DI Adams," Alice said, shoving the keys at him rather insistently.

"Probably," Colin said. "Get in the car before I change my mind." And he folded himself back into the Beetle, backing out onto the road again as Tom and Alice followed in the Range Rover.

Beaufort looked at Mortimer. "Well, lad?"

"Thompson said he'd update me," Mortimer said. "But he also said to get to Toot Hansell, so I think we should just go. We can't get in the car anyway, not with Tom right there."

"Quite true," Beaufort said, and they watched the Range Rover pull onto the road, heading in the direction of the village. Alice peered out of the window and gave them a very small nod as they passed. Beaufort waved back, then said, "Off we go, then."

"Right," Mortimer said, and this time he didn't hesitate. He arrowed straight for Toot Hansell, his wings tearing smooth streaks through the low cloud and his legs tucked tight to his belly. He could feel the fire still built up within his chest, and smoke drifted from his nostrils to fade in a swirl of turbulence behind him.

They would find Miriam. They had to.

As a dragon flies was a shorter and faster route than any car could take, especially in the tangled folds of the Yorkshire fells, with their ravines and streams and outcroppings of impenetrable rock, and it wasn't that long before they were swooping down on the jumble of buildings that formed the village, the streams and waterways that encircled it turned to heavy dark ribbons by the dull night, and lights scattered across it like fallen stars. Mortimer banked toward the centre of the village, aiming straight for the bookshop, and Beaufort called, "Steady on, Mortimer."

"What?" Mortimer heard the impatience in his own tone and swallowed hard. "I just mean—"

"I know, but there may still be humans out and about. It's not that late. Plus we don't know for sure she's in there. Pub roof." Beaufort swung toward it, his wings angling just so, every movement made with a perfect economy that made his earlier antics over the car seem to belong to a different dragon altogether. His greens and gold were gone, his scales a mottled mesh of greys that seemed to create a seamless transition from the sky to the roof, and he landed lightly, talons scraping across the tiles on the ridge softly.

Mortimer followed, suddenly ashamed that he'd almost rushed off. The old dragon may have seemed like he was taking things lightly on the way out to the bunker, but he never truly did when it mattered. There are so many times in life where there is no choice but to take things seriously, and to survive them one must find joy in the moments in between. The High Lord hadn't survived so many long and treacherous centuries by not knowing which was which. Mortimer should have known that by now.

Below them, a lone man smoking in the shelter of the bus stop on the square stared up at them, the cigarette halfway to his mouth. Neither dragon moved, and after a moment the man looked at the tip of his cigarette, looked up at them, then stubbed the cigarette out in the bin and headed back to the pub. "Bloody counterfeit cigs," Mortimer heard him mutter. "Putting all sorts in them."

"Now what?" Mortimer asked quietly.

Beaufort surveyed the square. The pub was on one corner, and the bookshop was in the middle of a terraced row that ran off at right angles to them, sandwiched between a slightly tatty-looking tea shop and a door someone had painted bright orange and adorned with small bats. There was a low light on in the bookshop's bay window to illuminate a display of vintage children's books, framed with wreathes of autumn leaves. Pumpkins sat below the sill on the uneven pavement, and Mortimer thought wistfully that it'd be quite nice if he could get through a few months with his worst concerns being how many roast pumpkins was too many for a reasonable dragon to eat.

"That's Gert's van," Beaufort said, pointing to a windowless white van parked at the opposite end of the square to the bookshop.

"I don't see them," Mortimer said.

"They're probably in the back." Beaufort checked the square again. "There's no one around. We'll go down and check in with them, see if they've seen anything."

"Alright," Mortimer said, but the High Lord was already on the move, not waiting for an answer. They stuck to the rooflines, skimming them with their talons barely above the mossy tiles, wings moving softly and silently, until they were over the bakery. Mortimer could smell the bright heady scent of yeast, and the satisfied memories of good rises, and the white van was just below them. One final check of the square then they were down beside it, Beaufort knocking on the back doors with one scaly paw.

"Gert?" he whispered. "Rose?"

There was no sound from inside, not even the scuffle of someone moving, and they looked at each other. Beaufort tried the door, and it opened easily, revealing a few stacked boxes of electronics strapped to one side, and a dog bed on the floor.

"This seems bad," Mortimer said quietly.

There was a whine behind them, and they both spun around. Angelus panted at them, his big ears tipped forward. He was trembling, his eyes rolling in fright.

"Good dog," Mortimer said, backing up until he bumped into the van.

"He is a good dog," Beaufort said. "Look how brave he's being! You used to be very scared, didn't you? *Didn't you?*"

"I still am," Mortimer said, and the High Lord looked at him.

"I was talking to Angelus. He's far more scared of you than you are of him, you know."

Mortimer wasn't sure that was really the case, but his attention was caught by a second dog who emerged from behind Angelus, this one plodding forward on slightly bowed legs. "Martha?" he said, and she wagged her tail gently, then flopped to the ground. Angelus whined again, then folded himself down next to her. They both looked expectantly at the dragons, and after a moment Martha staggered unsteadily back to her feet. Her tail waved vaguely, and she looked at the square, back at them, then padded slowly off.

Beaufort and Mortimer exchanged glances, then Mortimer crept slowly out from the shelter of the van. Martha had waited, watching him, and now she set off across the square in the direction of the bookshop, her gait stiff. Mortimer followed, his wings twitching in the knowledge that anyone could look out of a window at any point, or stumble out of the pub, or turn into the square with a blaze of headlights.

But it didn't matter. It was a lead, and they were following it. Whatever that took.

WHAT THAT TOOK WAS A PAINFULLY slow walk around the square, with Angelus panting over his shoulder, to a little lane that ran parallel to one side of the square, and behind the bookshop. They passed Pearl's car parked in the shelter of a skip, Martha barely sparing it a glance, and walked all the way to the back of the shop itself, where she stopped and looked at Mortimer.

"This is not very helpful," he said to her. "We knew she was here."

"We knew *Miriam* might be here, lad," Beaufort said, his voice quiet. "But do you think Martha's brought us here for Miriam?"

"*Oh. Oh no*, but that means—" Mortimer stopped as he caught a whiff of something sharp and hot and spiked with raw metal edges. "What's that?"

"What's what?" Beaufort asked.

Mortimer shook his head, checked the street again, then slipped over the low gate and into the little paved back patio area. A few empty flowerpots were scattered around, gently decaying, and otherwise there was nothing to be seen but two wheelie bins nestled by the fence. He cast around, wondering where Thompson was, and caught ... *there*. Miriam, the bloom of cheese-puff anxiety blossoming into full-blown panic, overlaying two threads of worry and desperation that were unfamiliar yet recognisable in the way that such old emotions so often are. He turned to find the dogs watching anxiously from the road, and Beaufort close enough to him that he jumped. The big dragon could be astonishingly quiet.

"We have to go in." His chest was rumbling with heat again.

"We can't, lad," Beaufort said quietly. "Colin and DI Adams are on the way. We don't want to start messing things up for their case."

Mortimer stared at him. "You *never* say that!"

"This time I have to." The old dragon tipped his head slightly. "One of us has to be sensible."

Mortimer had never wanted to disagree quite so much, but at that moment he caught hurrying footsteps behind the door. "Hide!"

They dived in opposite directions, Mortimer coiling himself behind the bins as they wobbled violently in the wake of his arrival, and Beaufort scampering up the wall and clinging there like a gigantic gecko, which Mortimer wanted to shout wasn't sensible *at all.*

The door flew open and two people hurried out, dragging a third between them, her bushy hair half-tamed by a hat. For one horrifying moment Mortimer thought it was Miriam, but then she spoke, her voice sharp and angry. It was Rainbow.

"What're you going to do?" she hissed. "I heard you with Miriam. She saw you, and she's loose. I bet she's getting the cops in already!"

"No one's going to believe what she says," the man on one side said. Simon. "Say anything to protect her sister, she would."

"And as you'll have fled the country with all the bits you robbed, leaving a dead man behind, that's all the evidence the cops need," his companion said. She was younger, her face pale as they hurried Rainbow out the gate. "Bloody hell – what's with these stupid dogs?"

Angelus skittered backward, whining, but Martha started barking, a deep, sonorous sound that echoed off the windows. Simon aimed a kick at her, and she stumbled away, but not quickly enough, and her bark turned into a yelp as he caught her side a glancing blow. Angelus burst into a volley of hysterical yapping, making little panicked darts at the trio, his eyes rolling, but they ignored him, already unlocking a mud-spattered SUV parked on the side of the lane.

Movement caught Mortimer's eye, and he saw Beaufort slipping up the wall toward the roof. He hesitated, then eased himself out from behind the bins, concentrating on keeping himself in deep grey wall colours, and trusting to the distraction of the barking dogs as he started to climb. There was no way Rainbow was really fleeing the country. These two were, though, and Rainbow would be disposed of, and the world would be left with one less person who cared enough to fight for it. But if Miriam was loose, then she was okay, and Mortimer felt an absurd little swell of pride at the idea that she'd got free all on her own.

The SUV growled into life and pulled hurriedly away, accelerating too fast in the confines of the lanes, Angelus barely getting out of the way before it hit him. Martha watched it go and turned back toward the bookshop, plodding through the open gate onto the patio, heading for the door that was hanging open in the wake of the trio's departure. Beaufort took to the air from the roof, his wings vast and silent as he shadowed the car, and Mortimer slipped over the eaves and into the sky in the same movement.

The car had reached the road beyond the lane, turning away from the square, and Mortimer was about to follow, but he looked back, something pricking and itching at his senses, that same niggling unease as the other day. He looked at Beaufort, but the big dragon was intent on the pursuit. Mortimer swung back suddenly, tightening his wings and arrowing straight along the length of the lane, barely above the houses. His eight-chambered heart was pounding, and it was nothing to do with the exertion of the flight.

He caught the scent as he wheeled over the roof of the bookshop, a raw and violent hunger underlaid with something much more familiar but no less dangerous, a building force coming in too fast. He folded his wings, dropping straight down as Martha started across the threshold, grabbing her in a panicky grip at the same time as trying to be desperately careful with his talons. She gave a puzzled *woof* as he clutched her to his chest, spun to put his back to the bookshop and flung his wings wide, bracing himself. From inside came a vast and hungry *whoomph.*

The pressure wave of the explosion washed heat and glass and horror across the street as the flames painted his shadow long and violent on the patio, and somewhere he could hear Angelus barking, and, even more dimly, someone screaming, and all he could think was, *Did she get out? Did she?*

And there was no one to answer the question.

24

DI ADAMS

D I Adams was halfway to the village square, already on the phone and requesting officers to the Toot Hansell bookshop and hoping that she wasn't overreacting, but at the same time preferring that possibility to *under*-reacting when there were four of the W.I. plus Rainbow missing, when she came around a corner and her headlights washed over someone jogging in a shambling gait straight down the centre of the road. She braked hard, Dandy giving a startled yelp and sliding off the passenger seat into the footwell (for one moment she was distracted, wondering why he didn't fall through things when he was so good at *walking* through them), and came to a stop just behind the jogger. They were barefoot, wearing floral pyjamas, and were currently trying to struggle out of a sky-blue dressing gown printed with cheerful clouds. They didn't look around, just kept pattering onwards.

"What *now*," she muttered, but she couldn't exactly just go around them. This wasn't normal behaviour even for Toot Hansell. It could be a caretaking issue, and ignoring it was one of those things that plenty of officers did, but she'd never wanted to be one of them. Plus, she needed to wait for backup anyway. Knocking on the door of the bookshop without it could end up endangering everyone inside. Assuming they *were* inside, of course, and the W.I. weren't just as carried away as always. She growled at the back of her throat, put the handbrake on and swung out of the car. Dandy was already out, loping around into the jogger's path, where he sat down and panted up at them.

"Hello puppy," the jogger said, startling DI Adams.

"You can see him?" she asked.

"Sure," the jogger said, waving as he tried to go around Dandy. Dandy wasn't making it easy, though, simply sliding into the way again. "He's a big dog."

DI Adams caught herself before she could say, *he's an **invisible** dog*, and circled the man, examining him. "Barry, isn't it?"

He squinted at her. His hair hung around his face in gentle, greying ringlets, and he was breathing hard. He finished wriggling out of the dressing gown and let it drop behind him, then started undoing his pyjama top.

"Hang about," DI Adams said. "It's cold. Keep that on."

"I'm warm."

"You won't be now you've stopped running. I'm DI Adams. We met at Maddie's house last year. At the river."

He looked at her a little more closely, then his face lit up with a broad smile and, to DI Adams' horror, he walked straight up to her and hugged her. She considered shoving him away, but that seemed unlikely to make him cooperative, so she just patted his back awkwardly.

"Hi!" he said, stepping back. "I remember now. You swam with me."

That was one way of describing it. "Good to see you too. Where're you off to?"

He looked around, then leaned a little closer to her and whispered, "I know a secret way."

"A secret way to what?"

"To find Rainbow," he said. "Because she'll be at the bookshop. I tried to say I could find her, but Rosemary and Carlotta said I should have a bath and a lie-down." He frowned. "I don't think they take me seriously."

"No?" DI Adams said, picking up his dressing gown.

"No. So I climbed out the bathroom window. And now I need to go." He gave DI Adams a serious look. "There may not be much time. There was a *dead body*."

"I know," she said, examining him. "What do you know about that?"

He looked at her, his fingers plucking at his buttons, then at Dandy, who stretched his snout up, begging for pats. Barry scratched him behind the ears, smiling. "You're not quite real, are you?"

Dandy *whuffed*, his tail wagging.

"He smells real enough," DI Adams said.

"Not him," Barry said. "You." He sneaked a glance at her.

"Sorry?"

"You're not quite real. With the nice not-dog and the duck and stuff."

DI Adams didn't answer for a moment, her fingers tightening on her keyring. A small brass duck hung from it, shining gently in the night. "What do you mean?"

Barry gave a one-shouldered shrug. "Maybe I mean more real? I don't know. It's confusing."

Well, she agreed with that, at least. And she didn't have time to think about it any further. "*Do* you know anything about the body, Barry?"

He hesitated, then spoke to Dandy rather than her. "I'm not meant to say."

She waited, feeling time slipping slowly away, and willed herself to be patient. He might not be the most reliable witness, but he was a witness. And it was more than she'd had a moment ago.

Finally, still talking to Dandy, he said, "No one notices what I do, really, because mostly I just look after the animals. I like animals. But I watch people, too, because they're not as nice as animals, so you have to watch them very, very carefully. And when Simon started coming to the houses, Daisy would be there too. And she went into the houses, and no one knew she was there because she wasn't meant to be there, because she wasn't in the group."

DI Adams nodded, even though he still wasn't looking at her. *Daisy.* Interesting. "And she took things from the houses?"

"Yes," Barry said quietly. "And I knew I should tell Rainbow, but when I tried Simon interrupted, and then later he told me I'd be put in a hospital and never see the sky or pet an animal again if I told anyone. So I didn't. I *couldn't.*" He finally looked at her, his chin trembling. "I couldn't!"

"Of course you couldn't," DI Adams said. "But it's okay now. Because you've told me, and I'm a police officer, so I can make sure no one puts you in a hospital."

He gave her a dubious look. "I didn't tell you because you're a police officer. I told you because of the not-dog, and you being not quite real. Like me."

"Fair enough," she said, swallowing a sigh. "So what about this secret way into the bookshop?"

"I'm going now. You can come with me if you like."

"Maybe you should come with me. I have a car."

"You're police," he pointed out. "It never ends well when I go with police. But if you come with me that would be okay."

DI Adams wondered if she should be trusting anyone who didn't seem to think she was quite real, but she looked at Dandy, who panted at her and wagged his tail. "Alright," she said, as much to the dandy as to Barry. "I'll come with you. But let's use my car. It's quicker."

"Okay," he said cheerfully, and turned and trotted to her car so quickly that she was left staring after him for a moment. "Come on!"

THEY SKIRTED THE VILLAGE CENTRE, passing the slumbering green with its freight of long dry grass, and the hall with its caution tape removed, looking small and quiet and bereft. Further on was the church nestled among its trees and graves, and as they followed the curve of the road, turning back toward the centre of the village as it circled the green, Barry said, "Pull in here."

"Here?" She braked with a sigh and looked at the building just off the road. "This is a pub, Barry."

"I know," he said, and winked at her.

"Tell me you're not just after a pint."

"No, no, no," he said, shaking his head firmly. "But we need to go in."

DI Adams pulled into the car park, hitting dial on her hands-free as she did. Collins answered almost immediately. "Adams? Where are you?"

"Slight detour. I ran across Barry, and he reckons he has a back way into the bookshop."

There was a pause, then Collins said, "I'm not sure—"

"I know. Where are you?"

"Almost at the bunker."

DI Adams rubbed her forehead. "Alright. Go to the bookshop once you're done. I've called for backup, and I'll be there soon. Keep me updated." She hung up and looked at Barry. "Show me this secret way, then."

"Hurry," he said, and got out, jogging barefoot across the gravelled car park toward the pub doors. DI Adams opened her door and looked at Dandy, who tipped his head, then melted up the path, vanishing through the closed door.

"Guess this is what we're doing, then," she muttered, and scrambled out, pausing to grab her coat, baton and torch from the boot, then hurrying across the little stretch of gravel to the closed door. She let herself into a wash of warmth and golden light. There were lots of standing lamps and uplighters going on, with candles on the tables and throw cushions on the deep sofas by the fire. It still had the lingering ale smell of old pubs everywhere, but it was tempered with the scent of wood smoke and coffee, and a whiff of cooking garlic made Adams' stomach rumble. It was all very atmospheric and cosy, inviting long conversations and slow meals and quiet introspection, and currently a young woman behind the bar was looking uncertainly at Barry as he trotted purposefully across the room toward a door in the corner.

"Um, sir?" she said. "Can I help you?"

"DI Adams, North Yorkshire Police," DI Adams called, fishing her ID out of her pocket as the woman turned toward her. "He's with me. We just need to take a look around."

"Oh. Okay," the woman said, and waved violently to a young man who was leaning over a table. Someone was saying in a bewildered voice that they were sure they'd had four lamb chops, but now there were only two? DI Adams narrowed her eyes at Dandy as he slipped across the room. He licked his chops, wandered past Barry and vanished through the door.

"It's here," Barry said, looked at her. "Where the not-dog went. *Hurry.*"

She joined him and tried the handle, then turned to the young woman. "Key?"

"That's just the cellar—"

"*Key.*"

The young woman grabbed a set of keys from under the bar and hurried over to her, her face pale. "Sorry," she mumbled, opening the door. DI Adams nodded and pushed through, lights coming on automatically as the door opened. She took the steps two at time, Dandy loping ahead of her and Barry padding along behind her, and a moment later they were standing surrounded by stacked kegs and the stale whiff of old yeast. A passageway opened up to her left, and Barry pointed at it.

"That way," he said.

"Really?"

He nodded firmly. "I've been before."

She wondered for a moment just how much time she was wasting, but they were here now. She headed down the passage, racks of wine lining the walls to either side. Dandy stopped to gnaw on the neck of a bottle and she hissed, "Stop that!"

He glanced at her, eyes a flash of reproachful red, then trotted on as the racks stopped and the ceiling dropped down toward the floor, the sides narrowing in. There were some old wine crates back here, but nothing more, and she stopped. Barry walked past her, crouching down to start shifting the boxes.

"Excuse me?" someone called behind her. "DI Adams, was it?"

She turned to see a slim man looking at her a little nervously, one hand resting almost protectively on a wine rack. "Jodie said you'd come down here – is everything alright?"

DI Adams pointed into the narrowing passage. "Where does this go?"

"Oh, *well*," he said, and she realised she might as well have asked her dad to elaborate on the latest developments in home robotics. He had the same enthusiastic lilt to his voice. "The whole town has quite the network of tunnels. Not just priest holes, which are relatively common, of course, but a large-scale—"

"Where does this one go?" she asked, pointing a little more enthusiastically.

"Right into the town square. Used to be that many of the old buildings could access it, but most of the entrances were blocked off. There's only the—"

"Bookshop," she said, and Barry looked back at her, grinning.

The landlord gave her a startled look. "Yes! How did you know?"

"I told her," Barry called, still working on his boxes.

"Barry?" the landlord said.

"Hi Bryan." Barry emerged to give him a hug, which the younger man returned calmly. "Can you let us into the passage?"

"Of course," he said, releasing Barry and taking a set of keys from his pocket. "Odd time of day for sightseeing," he added to DI Adams.

"Bit more urgent than that," she said, taking her phone from her pocket to call Collins. The signal was already gone and she gave a hiss of annoyance. "Keep this clear for us to come back through, alright?"

"Of course," the landlord said, walking forward in a crouch. "I just keep it locked so no one wanders down here by accident. And to try to stop the rats coming through."

"Lovely," DI Adams said, and tried not to gag. Hopefully Dandy could deal with any rats.

The landlord was almost on his knees by the time they reached the door, and DI Adams was walking in weird little crouch that made her thighs ache. But there was a neat wooden door fitted to the passage which made her think of Alice in Wonderland, and he unlocked it, pulling it wide and shivering as Dandy poked his head through from the other side, panting.

"Ugh. Air's a bit whiffy down here."

Dandy shut his mouth with a snap, and DI Adams fiddled with her torch to hide her grin. "Cheers for that."

"Sure." He shuffled aside to let her and Barry through. "Ah ... good luck?"

"Thanks," she said, and looked at Barry. "You stay here."

"No," he said simply.

"Yes," she tried, and he just shrugged and squeezed past her, setting off at as fast a pace as his crouch would allow into the dark. "Bollocks," she said, and followed, the torch lighting Dandy's shaggy form and Barry's curved back, hunched as a goblin.

THE PASSAGE WIDENED AGAIN before they'd gone too far, and they were able to break into a jog, ducking under the lower parts of the tunnel roof as they went. It was surprisingly dry and dusty down here, the walls hard stone shored up in places with old wood whose structural integrity DI Adams rather doubted. Occasionally they splashed through a muddy patch where the walls and ceiling seeped moisture and slicks of slimy growth showed up in her torch, and now and then she felt the passage rise, and roots dangled in veils above her. She didn't see any rats, but with Dandy loping ahead of them she imagined they'd have made themselves scarce.

Every now and then she felt a tremor in the ground, as of something vast shifting in its sleep, and she assumed there were cars passing above her. It was the safest assumption to make, she felt, and she didn't want to think too much about the fact that there were other noises down here with them too, whispers and sighs and things that moved on the corner of her vision. Barry twitched and twisted, looking one way then the other with his breathing ragged, but he didn't slow. They plunged on into the depths of the tunnels.

Theirs wasn't the only route deep within the town. Branches ran off at angles into the darkness, like the veins of some vast plant leaf, some narrow enough that DI Adams doubted she could have fit down them sideways, others so wide that she and Barry could have easily run down them alongside one another. The place was riddled with passageways, and she felt sure there should've been sinkholes and subsidence and all manner of nightmares for builders and structural engineers and so on to deal with, but she'd never heard anyone mention anything. The most suspicious thing she knew of was the bottomless pond that was only bottomless sometimes, which made a lot more sense in the light of the fact the land was basically Swiss cheese.

Barry barely hesitated at the many junctions, though. He just kept on, muttering to himself now and them, and where a fork presented itself he'd hold up a hand, pointing it one way then the other, then choose one without much dithering. Whatever internal map he was following, it was a clear one. DI Adams simply followed, checking her watch now and then. The compass was still working, at least, and while they were twisting and turning a fair bit, overall they were certainly heading back toward the centre of town. She just hoped that Barry's route didn't lead to a dead end, because the GPS definitely wasn't working, and she didn't fancy guessing her way back through all these junctions.

Time stretches in an unpleasant manner when the way's dark and unfamiliar, and there's only the torch beam to carry one forward, but Barry finally came to a stop and looked back at her.

"Are we here?" she asked, keeping her voice low. She was breathing hard from the run, and from the sense of the earth above her.

Barry pointed up a side passage and whispered, "This is it."

"I'll go first." DI Adams squeezed past him and edged into the passage, but she didn't get far before she encountered a barricade of old crates and broken planks, more like someone had just chucked a load of rubbish into the passage than intentionally tried to block the way. She looked back at Barry. "Are you sure?"

"This is it," he said, peering around her. "That's the bookshop cellar."

DI Adams sighed, set the torch on the floor next to her, and got to work.

It was a lot like Jenga, she decided five minutes later. Trying to take something off the top without the whole lot caving in on them. The passage was too narrow for Barry to work alongside her, so he just took each piece she moved and shuffled back down the tunnel with it, depositing it somewhere out of the way then coming back for more. Dandy had vanished, so he was no help whatsoever, and she couldn't see light beyond the barricade to suggest how far it extended. But she kept on doggedly, ignoring the ache in her back and the splinters in her palms, and suddenly she heard scuffling on the other side.

"Dandy?" she hissed. "You've got teeth, give me a hand. Otherwise no more balls for you, I promise it."

There was a pause, then another scuffle, and she jerked her hands away from the crate she'd been about to grab. Rats?

"Dandy?" She whispered it this time. "If that's a rat, please eat it."

A very small whisper came back. "Is there someone there?"

"Rainbow?" she asked. "It's DI Adams."

The voice was a shout this time. "DI Adams! Everyone! It's DI Adams!" There was a sudden babble of more voices beyond the barricade, then, "It's Teresa, by the way. I was trying to find something to use as a weapon."

Of course she was. "Never mind that. Help me get through." DI Adams renewed her assault on the barricade, and now she could hear more voices behind it, and the scrape and bang of wood and junk being dragged away. A moment later there was a sudden, bigger crash, followed by a lot of enthusiastic, smaller crashes that suggested the ladies were attacking the pile-up with very few concerns for its essential Jenga nature.

"Hey!" she yelled. "Go easy or you'll bring it all down on us."

"No time!" someone shouted back. "We need to get out *now!*"

"Rose?"

"Yes – Pearl and Gert are here too. But something's going on upstairs – there's been lots of shouting, and I don't think we can hang around."

"Is Miriam there?"

"No—" She was cut off as DI Adams pulled a pallet away and the last of the barricade turned into an avalanche of splintery wood and exposed nails. Teresa yelped as she was hit in the kneecaps by an aggressive plank, and Pearl grabbed her as she staggered away.

"Anyone hurt?" DI Adams asked, scrambling over the debris into a stone-floored cellar lit by a single bare bulb hanging from the ceiling, the patchily-painted walls stacked with boxes and odd tins of paint and cobwebby ladders and broken picture frames.

"We're alright," Rose said. The side of her face and the collar of her coat were slick with drying blood, and DI Adams stared at her.

"Sure?"

"Sure," she said. "Head wounds always bleed a lot."

DI Adams examined the others. Teresa had a hole in her leggings and Pearl's coat was missing a couple of buttons, but everyone was standing. A pile of torn gaffer tape on the floor suggested they hadn't been waiting around to be rescued.

"Gert?" she asked.

"Here." She was limping down the stairs, her face pink. "Anyone found any Allen keys? I need some decent bloody tools to get through that door. Miriam's looking for the actual key, but they might've taken it."

"They've gone?" DI Adams asked.

"Just a moment ago," Gert started, then there was pounding on the door above and a muffled shout. DI Adams pushed past Gert and ran up the stairs.

"Miriam!" she shouted. "It's DI Adams! Collins should be in the square – go and get him."

"Fire!" Miriam yelled back. "Everything's on *fire!*"

Even as she said it, DI Adams caught a whiff of smoke, and she swore. "Miriam, *get out,*" she shouted through the door. "Get out *now!*"

"But how—"

"*Now!*"

She turned and ran back down the stairs, seeing the women's faces turned toward her, wide-eyed and horrified. Barry crouched in the entrance to the tunnel, looking around wildly.

"Where's Rainbow?" he asked. "Where is she?"

"I'll find her," DI Adams said. "You're all going out through the passageway."

"I need to find Rainbow," Barry insisted, clambering over the debris, and DI Adams grabbed his shoulder.

"No. You're leading them back to the pub. You know the way, right?"

"Right, but—"

"*Now,*" she said, and handed him her torch, then pushed him back toward the tunnel. "I will find Rainbow, I promise. You have to get everyone out. I'm relying on you."

He stared at her, hesitating, then nodded and scrambled back into the passageway. "Follow me!" he shouted.

DI Adams looked at the four woman, who all stared at her uncertainly. "He got us here," she said. "Everyone out. Move it!"

They moved it, DI Adams helping them as they scrambled over the barricade with varying degrees of grace.

Gert was the last to go. "You can't stay," she said.

"I'll be right behind you," DI Adams promised, and Gert frowned, but she followed the others, still limping.

DI Adams sprinted for the stairs, the smell of smoke already filling the cellar and scratching at her lungs.

❧

THE FIRST EXPLOSION took her by surprise, sending her staggering back from the door before she'd even reached it, almost dropping the wrench she'd grabbed off the shelves on the way across the cellar. It had come from the back of the house, an angry *pop* that suggested a gas bottle, maybe for a heater or something similar. Not huge, but not good in a house that was basically a tinderbox. The door wasn't scorching against the back of her hand when she went back to it, even if it was hot, so she kept going, attacking the handle with the wrench. She wished it were an axe, but it was better than nothing.

"*Rainbow!*" she bellowed as she hammered at the door. "*Rainbow, are you out there?*"

"DI Adams!" came a shout from outside. "DI Adams, I can't get out!"

"Miriam?"

"The front door's jammed! I think it needs a key to open it, and I can't make it work, and the back's burning—" Miriam gave a little scream as something crashed, and the ceiling in the cellar shook, scattering plaster and dirt.

"Break a window! *You need to get out!*" DI Adams renewed her assault on the door, concentrating on the handle and trying to smash the lock off. She was aware of Miriam shouting something, but she kept going, swearing under her breath as the stupidly solid old metal just refused to give.

"Easy, tiger," a voice said at about knee-height, and she yelped, missing her blow and almost swinging the wrench right into her own knees. She looked down to see Thompson. "Stand back," he advised, and DI Adams didn't think about it. She bolted down the stairs just as Dandy came flying off the top step, clearing both her and the cat. He skidded across the cellar floor, and the door above exploded out of its frame. Miriam stumbled through, coughing, and Mortimer emerged out of the smoke behind her, glowing with heat, and guided her onto the stairs. DI Adams ran to meet her, and above them the floor gave a sudden, trembling moan.

"Oh bollocks," DI Adams whispered, and Mortimer surged forward, his wings spread.

Dandy barked once, short and sharp, and DI Adams lunged for the passageway, propelling Miriam ahead of her, but there was so much debris in the way, and more plaster was coming off the ceiling, hot and painful as it hit her neck, and the air was thick with smoke, setting her coughing and her eyes streaming, and the crash of the ceiling falling in sounded like the end of the world.

25

ALICE

Tom wasn't a terrible driver, Alice had to admit, but she'd still have preferred to be the one behind the wheel as they slid around the corners, the old Range Rover's big engine grumbling hungrily. She supposed she wouldn't have been much faster, but she'd have felt an awful lot better doing something rather than just being ferried around. Safer, too.

Colin, in Alice's car, overtook them on the edge of the village, and as they came screeching into the square he was already climbing out. His gaze was on the roofline of the terrace the bookshop was situated in, and he was frowning.

"Let me out," Alice said, already undoing her seatbelt.

"At least let me park," Tom protested, but jammed the brakes on as she opened the door. She swung out, ignoring the pinch of pain in her hip, and hurried to Colin. He glanced at her, then back at the sky.

"What's happening?" she asked.

"Is that chimney smoke?" he asked in return, pointing, and at that moment there was the *whoomph* of something small yet powerful exploding at the back of the terrace. Colin swore and sprinted for the bookshop door, Alice behind him. He tried the handle, then banged on the wood, the whole door shaking in its frame. "*Police! Open up!*" There was no response, and he hurried to the display window, cupping his hands on the glass to peer inside. "I can see fire out the back," he said, stepping away. "Call the fire service." He turned and sprinted down the row, deceptively fast for a big man.

Alice already had her phone out, and turned to look at Tom, who was standing beside the car looking as if he didn't know whether to jump back in and flee or run to help. "Start knocking!" she shouted, pointing at the other houses in the terrace. "We've got to get everyone out."

Tom lurched into a run, and she said into the phone, "Yes. Fire. Toot Hansell village square, the bookshop." She tried the door while she waited for them to take details, answering their questions automatically, her heart going too fast. Miriam. Where was *Miriam?*

Tom grabbed her arm and she almost screamed in surprise, rounding on him furiously instead. "*What?*"

"You're too close," he said, pulling her back. "If the window blows out it'll be all over you."

"But Miriam," she started, but she knew he was right so she let him pull her away. Emergency services were still talking to her in a calm voice, and she said sharply, "I don't have time for this. Are they on their way?"

"Yes, Ms Martin, but if you can just stay with us—"

She hit disconnect as Colin came running back down the row, his face smudged with soot. He was carting something in his arms, and as he got closer Alice saw it was Martha.

"She was at the back door," he said. "I can't get in that way, the fire's too fierce already. Keep hold of her, and move back." He set Martha at Alice's feet then ran back toward the cars, and she grabbed the old Labrador's collar, pulling her away as she retreated further from the bookshop. Tom had finished knocking on doors and sprinted to the pub, darting inside. People were starting to emerge, milling around with glasses, all waiting for someone to tell them if they were meant to watch or if they were expected to *do* something, and Colin reappeared with a tyre iron in his hands.

"I need an axe," he yelled at the square in general. "We need to get that door open!"

"I've got one!" the publican shouted, and turned to run back inside.

Colin looked at Alice. "They'll be alright," he said. "I'm sure they will."

She looked at him, nodded, then frowned. "Where's DI Adams?"

He started to say something, and at that moment there was the most terrible explosion, and a roaring wave of heat and glass and painful air pressure washed across the square. Alice ducked, raising her arms to protect her head, vaguely aware of Colin grabbing her and turning her away from the lash of the heat as he put his back to it. Screams and shouts of surprise rang across the square, partly muted by the assault of sound, and when she looked up again with her ears painfully stuffy, the whole front window of the bookshop was gone. Inside was nothing but roaring reds and oranges, the books incandescent as they burned, and smoke and flames running vicious fingers over the brick and glimmering behind the upstairs windows as they shattered in an echo of downstairs. The front door was still shut, blistering and blackening already, and she kept one arm up to protect her face from the heat, catching Martha's collar again with the other as the old dog made to wander off.

Nothing could have survived inside. Not in that.

She swallowed, her throat clicking, and looked at Colin. His face was set, and he looked down at her.

"Are you alright?" he asked.

She nodded, even though she wasn't.

"Good. Keep well away, alright?" He headed back toward the building, where an elderly woman with her hair in rollers and a kettle in her hand had just appeared on the doorstep of the house at the end of the row, looking put out.

The publican of the rough pub with the sticky floors had come out with the axe, dropped it, and run back inside again. A moment later he reappeared with a hose, which he attached to a tap next to the door, shouting at his customers as he did so. Buckets were appearing as more people ran into the square, and without much more direction a chain formed, filling the buckets at the hose then passing them somewhat unsteadily but surprisingly effectively down to the bookshop. The little splash of water into the inferno inside seemed unlikely to help an awful lot, but it was *something*, and there were more and more buckets and more and more hands appearing all the time.

But it was still nothing more than a way to stop the fire spreading. There was no saving anyone inside, Alice was sure of it, but she just kept petting Martha carefully without ever looking away from the bookshop, as if to do so was to give up hope. As if, if she looked long enough, Miriam might come running out of the flames like it was all no more than a magic trick.

The houses on either side of the bookshop on the terrace were already empty, the residents joining in with the bucket chain, and at the fourth house the elderly woman looked at the bookshop, then dropped her kettle and jogged around the side of the building. Before Colin could follow her, she re-emerged, unrolling another garden hose behind her, and some of the pub team cheered and went to join her with their buckets.

Martha licked Alice's hand, and a moment later a cold nose pushed into her side. She turned and discovered a shivering Angelus, his lead trailing on the ground next to him. "Oh dear," she whispered, and used her free hand to rub his ears. "I'm sure it'll all be fine," she said. "Everyone will be fine."

Tom was standing next to her with his hands buried in his hair, watching the burning shop, and without looking at her he said, "Really?" His voice caught on the word.

She frowned at him. "Well, you could *help*." She pointed at the well. "Grab a few more people and get started with that." He stared at her, and she added, "Also some rope and buckets. The winch in there hasn't worked for an awfully long time."

Tom opened his mouth, then shut it again and jogged toward the bucket chain, shouting for people to lend a hand. Alice watched him go, then raised her eyes to the pub roof, hoping to see dragons.

There weren't any.

WHILE A DISADVANTAGE of living in a small village a long way from the nearest fire services was that it took an unfeasibly long time for them to reach an emergency, an advantage was that locals tended to come up with solutions to most problems. The bucket, hose, and well situation had barely managed to settle into a rhythm when a woman came roaring into the square in a rickety, mud-splattered Volvo estate and swung out, her pyjamas tucked into her wellies. She grabbed a clanking tool bag and ran to a metal plate set into the pavement near the well, shouting, "Someone help Gerald with the hose!"

A man had tumbled out of the passenger side of the Volvo with his bald head shining in the firelight, and he wrestled a hose out of the back while the woman clattered around at the hydrant. Colin sprinted toward him, grabbing Tom as he went, and a moment later they had a heavy-duty fire hose unrolled across the square, aimed at the bookshop.

"Ready?" the woman shouted, and the half dozen people who had grabbed the hose shouted back, "Ready!"

There was no dramatic noise to accompany it, no *whoosh* of pressure, simply the hose swelling so fast that one of the men (who had emerged from the pub more unsteadily than most) lost his grip and fell over, then a blast of white water exploded from the end. Colin and a young woman with spiky hair wrestled to keep it aimed at the bookshop, and an impressed *oooh* rose from the rest of the square as the bucketers paused to watch. The fire hissed and spat like an oversized, furious cat, and scraps of flaming wreckage surged into the air, drifting in the darkness like broken stars. Alice tried to see the shape of a dragon in that suddenly released galaxy of destruction, but she couldn't. Not and be sure she was actually seeing it, not just wanting to. Everyone fell still, and the only noise was the relentless water, drowning the flames, and the crumple of collapsing beams.

Alice took a deep breath and closed her eyes for a moment, one hand on each dog, and reminded herself that there was no giving up hope right now, not even with the bookshop a shell in front of her. DI

Adams was terribly clever, and the W.I. were endlessly resourceful, and there were, of course, dragons, even if right now she couldn't see any of them.

When she opened her eyes again, nothing had changed. Of course it hadn't. One didn't change things simply by wishing. It required a little more action.

"Come along," she said to the dogs, and headed across the square, giving the teams of water-bearers plenty of room. It was a slow walk, Martha's gait requiring a little patience, but right now she had no hurry. There would be no going into the ruins of the bookshop to try to figure out what had happened.

They skirted the end of the terrace and went down the little street behind it. Smoke billowed from the bookshop's back door, and the wheelie bins had fallen over, plastic warped by the force of the fire. Alice kept her distance, examining the blackened brick, and wondered what, exactly she was waiting for.

Something else collapsed inside the house, releasing a hiss of smoke and fluttering, flaming pages, and Angelus yelped in alarm. Martha, who had been plodding along next to Alice quite happily, gave a little, welcoming bark, and tottered onto the patio.

"Martha, no," Alice said, hurrying after her to grab her collar. "You'll burn your paws."

Martha just strained toward the shop, and as Alice followed her gaze something moved just beyond the threshold. For a moment she thought it must be furniture crumpling, or an internal wall, because nothing could have survived in there. The house was hollowed out, a molten centre where a thousand different worlds had once dwelled.

Then a snout appeared around the gap where the doorframe had been, scales running with reds and oranges and deep lava streams of burnt black and white-hot glass, and Mortimer said, "Is it all clear?"

Martha gave another happy little yap, and Alice looked around. There was no one she could see, not on the lane or looking out windows. Everyone was in the square, watching the main attraction. "It's all safe," she said, and Mortimer slipped out, a ghost born of flames. His scales seemed liquid in the night, glowing with heat, and the scent of scorched stone rose around him as he padded to the gate and slipped through onto the street, crumbling one post to charcoal where his side brushed it.

"Oops," he said, looking back at it. "I just about drowned in all that water. It's working very well to get the fire out, though."

Alice looked at his paws, where the tarmac was melting around him, and said, "You still seem a little warm."

"I am," he admitted. "I may have got a little upset about all this."

Alice had to stop herself from giving him a comforting little pat on the shoulder, and instead asked the question that she wanted the answer to so much, but also didn't.

"Are they alright?"

"Yes," Mortimer said, and the last of the fire gilded his teeth as he grinned at her, and suddenly the dark wasn't anywhere near as deep as it had been, and the night nowhere as long.

THINGS SEEMED to happen rather more quickly after that, as if the simple fact of knowing that everyone was alright had released the village square from some trembling stasis of uncertainty. The exact details of *how* they were alright, while intriguing, seemed rather less important, Alice supposed. She waved Mortimer off as he slipped up the wall of the nearest house to the roof and took off into the night, shedding soot and charred scales, and leaving behind four very interesting indents in the lane that Alice supposed would just have to be explained by falling debris. She kicked some of the roof tiles that had spilled onto the patio into the road by way of explanation, then made her way back around to the square.

The fire truck had arrived while she had been gone, and the crew were shooing away the volunteers, who seemed fairly willing to give up the task, especially as the owner of the dodgy pub was bringing pints out to everyone. Alice was quite certain they'd be going on people's tabs rather than being free, though. She navigated her way through the crowds and the fire hoses and puddles and abandoned buckets until she found Colin, who was talking to a stocky woman in a firefighter's uniform.

But before she could even pass on Mortimer's message a familiar car pulled onto the edge of the square and DI Adams got out, waving her ID impatiently at one of the fire crew when he tried to shoo her off. Alice took a step toward her, her chest suddenly tight, because even if Mortimer had said everyone was alright, how could he be sure? How could he *know*, when he'd been trapped in the house and everyone else had been ... wherever they were?

DI Adams headed toward them, shouting, "Collins!" in a rough voice, and the passenger door of the car swung open. Miriam got out, her hair even wilder than usual and her outdoor jacket torn on one shoulder, and Alice covered her mouth with one hand, blinking against the smoke, which really was irritatingly persistent.

"Alice!" Miriam exclaimed, hurrying toward her. "Are you alright?"

"Am *I* alright?" Alice asked. "You were in a burning bookshop!"

"Well, yes," Miriam said. "But you were locked in a bunker."

"You're both a bloody liability," DI Adams said. Her hair was loose, all tight curls that softened the angles of her face, and she was liberally daubed with soot and dirt. Her coat and jacket were both gone, and one sleeve of her shirt was rolled up above blistered skin.

"That's a little excessive," Alice said.

"Not really," DI Adams said, and gestured at Colin impatiently as he joined her. "Turns out it's only bloody Daisy and Simon, who are *not* father and daughter. They must still have Rainbow, as she wasn't in the house."

"I don't *think* she was," Miriam said. "And I didn't see Harriet, either."

"They can't have got too far," DI Adams said. "I've called it in – told everyone coming in to block roads instead. We'll get them."

Colin looked at the crumbling bookshop and nodded, then coughed and wiped a big hand over his face, smearing soot everywhere. He gave Miriam a hug. "I'm glad you're alright, Aunty."

"I'm sure your mum will be too," she said, hugging him so tightly that Alice could see her fingers digging into his back. "She *will*."

DI Adams pulled her phone out of her pocket, looked at the display, then grunted and stepped away to answer it. Colin kept one arm around Miriam as he said, "How did you get out?"

"Secret passages, clothing-optional human, invisible dog, fireproof dragon, everything leads to the pub," a rough voice said from below them, followed by a cough. "And a heroic cat, obviously. That pretty much covers it."

"Hello, Thompson," Alice said. "I had rather thought you'd turn up sooner."

"Oddly enough, all the shifting and running around took it out of me a bit."

"I had to carry him," Miriam said. "Can cats faint?"

"*I did not faint.* I may have been mildly overcome by smoke inhalation."

"Smoke tends to stay high," Colin said. "Were you on someone's shoulders?"

The cat growled, but it turned into another cough, and DI Adams rejoined them. "They've already picked up Daisy and Simon. They'd run off the road about half a mile outside Toot Hansell. Stuck in a field with both of them hiding under the car and refusing to come out."

"How odd," Alice said, smiling.

"Mum?" Colin asked, and DI Adams grimaced. Her voice was gentle when she replied.

"No sign of her or Harriet."

"Ah, well," Colin said, and squeezed Miriam in a one-armed hug. "I'm sure they'll turn up."

Miriam nodded, not speaking, and Alice watched the fire team as they drowned the last of the smoke and sparks, and wondered what else was drowning in there. She hoped nothing, but it was terribly hard to know.

Impossible, really.

"Um," Tom said, in the tone of someone who'd been trying to work out how to interrupt for a few minutes. He'd taken off his coat and his face was slick with a mix of sweat and rain, his sleeves pulled up to expose muscular forearms. He was holding his phone in one hand, and he offered it to Colin. "I just got this."

Colin took the phone from him, frowning.

"Honest, just this minute. It'll be a from a burner phone, though. You know what she's like."

"Rainbow?" Miriam asked, clutching Colin's arm.

Tom nodded. "Just now. So she's out."

DI Adams let out a deep sigh and rubbed her hands over her face. "Bloody hell," she said. "You and your family, Collins."

"I know," Colin said with a sigh, and read the text aloud. "*Me and Harriet alright. Got out when the car went off the road, with a bit of help.*" He looked up. "There's about five exclamation marks there."

"Weird," Tom said, but everyone else just nodded. He gave them puzzled looks.

"*Laying low till the heat comes off,*" Colin continued. "*Damn pigs will try to get me for something. You can talk to Colin though, and give him a hug from me. He's not a bad sort even if he is a pig. R.*" He looked up from the phone and sighed again, but it was a relieved sigh, one where Alice could see his shoulders lifting and his back straightening. "Bloody hell, Mum."

"I don't mind giving you a hug," Tom said. "If you want one, I mean."

Colin nodded, but said, "No, you're alright."

Miriam gave him a hug instead. "She did say you were a good sort. That's an improvement."

"I suppose it is," he said, and handed the phone to Tom. "I'll give you my number and you can forward me that text."

"Sure," Tom said. "Only, are you going to arrest me? Because if so you can just keep the phone and I'll get off before that happens."

Colin shook his head, but he was smiling. Alice thought that was something. A smile goes a long way, especially after a day as long and fraught as this one had been.

Miriam touched Alice's arm and said, "Would you mind terribly if I gave *you* a hug? I was very worried about you, you know."

Alice looked at her, and said, "Well, I suppose," and the next moment she was swamped with the damp wildness of Miriam's hair, and the warm homey scent of long summer days and deep winter nights that still ran under the stink of smoke and fear and sweat, and she found she was smiling too.

Which was certainly something.

"I expect chicken hearts," Thompson announced. "For the heroics. Possibly some liver. I've not had liver, but I've heard it's good."

"Did someone say something?" Tom asked, but no one answered, and after a moment he wandered away into the chaos and drifting smoke of the village square, leaving them under the soft, persistent rain in the slow November night.

2 6

MIRIAM

It was almost a week later, and the village hall was warm to the point of being uncomfortable, the windows flung open to allow in frosty autumn evening air. The trestle tables were pushed together in the middle of the main room, and plates of apple and cheese slices and trays of mini-quiches and tubs of sausage rolls and some slightly dubious-looking mini-doughnuts rubbed shoulders with shortbread and tiffin and parkin. Solid tumblers with generous measures of jewel-toned sloe gin were ranged around the table, as were hefty mugs of tea, two soup mugs of the same, and one large coffee mug, which DI Adams was currently guarding jealously against an invisible assailant. Miriam had an idea why, as she'd been halfway to the bin to tip out the coffee grounds when the cafetière was removed delicately from her hands and relocated to the corner of the kitchen. It was spotless when she went back a few minutes later.

But right now she couldn't even contemplate drinking her tea. The grass outside might be crisp and ghostly, but in here she'd already been into the loo to take off the leggings she'd been wearing under her skirt, and was currently barefoot.

"Why isn't the thermostat working?" Gert demanded, leaning into the cupboard to peer at the boiler. "I've turned it right down!"

"Well, it's your cousin's sister's three times removed whatever who fixed it," Carlotta replied. She'd stripped down to a short-sleeved blouse, and looked like she'd quite like to take that off too. "It's probably in upside down or something."

"Nothing to do with me," Gert said, coming back to the table. "The council must've sent out some dodgy parts or something. Alice, you'll have to tell them."

Alice nodded. "I shall. I don't know how they found out about it, though. I didn't have time to call them."

"It was oddly efficient," Teresa said. "Normally takes them forever to do anything."

A murmur of agreement went around the table, and Miriam offered a plate of cheese and pickle sandwiches to DI Adams, who waved them away. She had her jacket off and her shirt sleeves rolled up, a dressing still visible on one forearm. Miriam knew there were burns on her shoulders, too, and that a small section of her hair at the back was shorn short, and she couldn't help feeling a little guilty. She had been the reason DI Adams had stayed in the burning shop, after all.

"Did you recover all the stolen goods, inspectors?" Beaufort asked. He was sitting on the floor at one end of the table, the top of it eye-level with him, which was slightly disconcerting. Miriam wondered if they should try to find some sort of dragon benches at some point.

DI Adams shook her head. "Most of it's long gone. Daisy and Simon had been doing similar things for a long time – they had a carpet cleaning company at one stage, worked for event catering – all sorts of jobs that gave them access to expensive homes. Daisy really had studied art history at uni, and had a good eye for art and jewellery, small items that they could easily pick up and that weren't likely to be missed for a while. Simon had a network of contacts to get them out of the country and sell them in Europe."

"What were their actual names?" Pearl asked. "Would we recognise them? Were they world-famous master criminals?"

Colin snorted, and DI Adams said, "Their actual names aren't being made public yet, so Daisy and Simon work just fine."

"That's got to be a yes," Pearl said with some satisfaction, and Teresa squeezed her hand, smiling.

"So, what – they ran out of places who wanted carpet cleaning and decided to join Rainbow?" Gert asked.

"Pretty much," Colin said. "But also it gave them access to some big collections, and an immediate scapegoat. They were already circumventing alarms and disabling cameras to get to the wildlife collections, so while Simon was working as part of Rainbow's team, Daisy would hide herself nearby. She'd come in once the alarms and cameras were down and grab what she wanted."

"Until it went wrong," Alice said.

"Until it went wrong," DI Adams agreed. "Alistair Lowell was meant to be in the Seychelles, but instead he walked in on Daisy helping herself to some family heirlooms in a sitting room. She panicked and shoved him, and he was pretty inebriated at the time. He fell into the edge of a marble hearth."

A little intake of breath went around the table, and Gert topped up everyone's sloe gin. Miriam covered her glass with her hand. One was *more* than enough, especially in this heat. It was worse than paracetamol.

"Daisy called Simon to help her, and Barry followed," DI Adams continued. "When he tried to get into the room Simon shut the door on him, breaking his fingers – that's why Rainbow had to take him to hospital. He still saw what happened, but they managed to convince him he'd be blamed for it because he's not quite right."

"Bloody cheek," Rose said, and Priya said, "*Exactly.*"

Colin took a scone, a little cautiously. "Why are they orange?" he asked, not looking at Jasmine.

"I bought far too many carrots," Rosemary said. "I did that online shopping again, and I thought I ordered ten carrots, but I got ten *kilos*. Last time it was one Brussel sprout instead of one pack. I think they do it on purpose."

"Or you're just very bad at it," Carlotta pointed out. "We should all be shopping at local markets, anyway."

"Yes, that's exactly where you get your tomatoes at this time of year."

Carlotta dipped her head in acknowledgement, smiling.

"Pass the jam," Colin said to DI Adams, and she did, then helped herself to a scone too, splitting it open to butter it.

"None of it was their usual style at all, from what we can tell," Colin continued. "They were strictly theft, and the death was accidental. They would've legged it straight away, but they needed to get into the safe, and the master key was missing. Plus they wanted to be sure Rainbow was blamed."

"Oh, the *key*," Miriam said. "Daisy was fussing about that when we were in the bookshop."

"The key from the bunker," Alice said.

"They key *I found* in the bunker," Thompson said, from where he was sprawled beneath the overworked radiator. "You're welcome, by the way. But I still have no liver."

"There's pâte," Priya offered.

"It looks exactly like cheap cat food."

"I made that," Gert said.

"Homemade cheap cat food, then." Thompson ignored Gert's frown as he yawned and stretched. "And no one even bothered to get me chicken hearts. I lost my whiskers and singed my tail, and I can't even get a decent meal."

"You're welcome to try elsewhere," Alice said.

DI Adams held half her scone out, away from the table, and it vanished. Miriam put her hand out hesitantly in the same general area, and was rewarded with the warm, woolly pressure of a shoulder against her fingers. She petted it gingerly. It felt warm and a little coarse, and exactly like petting a visible dog, but it also made her feel somewhat strange, as if she were standing on a high cliff looking down at clouds below. It just didn't make *sense*.

"I suppose Rainbow bringing us the body rather complicated things for them," Alice said, sipping her tea.

"It did. For the investigation as well, since you wouldn't tell us you'd seen her," DI Adams said, looking at Miriam.

Miriam face grew even hotter than it already was in the heat. "Well, she wasn't the one you should have been looking for anyway. The body was *planted* in her van! And *we* didn't see her. Plus Nellie really isn't very good at descriptions. She just said she looked like a heron-dumper."

"Although she did say her hair was the same as yours," Mortimer pointed it out.

"It is not," Miriam said, touching her hair. It was feeling quite pouffy, and she frowned. "Rainbow's is longer, anyway."

"So who collected Rainbow at the house?" Beaufort asked. "We couldn't tell from the scents at all, and Gaelen was about as much help as Nellie."

"I don't suppose I'd be very good at telling dryads apart," Teresa said.

"But they're like trees. They'd all be different, surely," Rose said.

They looked expectantly at the dragons, and Beaufort took a gulp of tea then said, "When I was a lad most Folk used to think all humans looked alike. But it's a little lazy to think so, really."

There was a moment of silence, then Colin said, "Daisy sent us to the hospital knowing Barry would act guilty, and hoping we'd then follow up with Rainbow. That gave her time to sneak out to the house and search for the safe key, as well as plant Lowell's watch. She was in the zebra suit, so when Rainbow saw her, she thought it was Harriet. Once she got in the SUV, Daisy tased her—"

Mortimer choked on a sausage roll, spitting bits onto the floor, then swallowed hard and took a gulp of tea. "Sorry," he mumbled. Martha got up from under Pearl's chair and lumbered over to lick up the scraps, then lay down with her chin resting on one of Mortimer's paws. "Hi," he said, and her tail thumped the floor gently.

DI Adams took a bite of the scone and gave an appreciative *mmm*.

"But what was so urgent in the safe?" Gert asked. "Surely they could've just cut their losses a bit earlier."

"About a million worth of jewellery," DI Adams said, and Pearl choked on her tea almost as loudly as Mortimer had on his sausage roll. Teresa patted her on the back fondly, not looking away from the inspector.

"Apparently they decided it was go big or go home time after Lowell," Colin said. "Daisy cleared out the house then shoved it all in the safe, thinking they'd leave as soon as Rainbow was in custody. Daisy had already changed the combination, so she thought no one could get in. But Rainbow had access to the safe too. She swung by to grab some cash on the way to the hospital with Barry, and when she couldn't get in she used the master key. She saw what was in there, changed the combination again, and took the key. She gave it to Tom after she found the body, and he dropped her at the house to hide."

"Because no one talks to the police, apparently," DI Adams said.

"Except Barry. He's your bestie now," Colin said, grinning.

DI Adams frowned, and took a sip of coffee. "We came to an understanding."

"He keeps coming to the station and leaving feathers and old birds' nests and nice stones with PC McLeod," Colin said. "I'm waiting for him to turn up with a jar of tadpoles or something."

"Wrong time of year," Rose said, "Let me know if he brings anything interesting in, though."

DI Adams sighed deeply.

"But what happened to Harriet?" Miriam asked. "Where did she go?"

"Simon and Daisy thought she had the key. Simon got her back to the bookshop after we saw them, and kept her there." DI Adams pointed at Pearl and Teresa. "Your turn. How did you end up in the bookshop?"

"Well, nothing was happening," Pearl said. "And we didn't know Daisy was in on it. I thought I'd just say I was popping by to collect an order. I did have a book on order, you know," she added.

"Not anymore," Rosemary pointed out, and everyone made little regretful noises.

"It's not right, a village without a bookshop," Rose said. "I mean, it wasn't a great bookshop, but it was *our* bookshop."

"We'll have to help Harriet if she starts again," Teresa said. "We've got so many books. We could donate some."

A murmur of agreement went around the table, then Pearl continued. "I went over while Teresa kept watch, and Daisy let me in. But Harriet was in the back somewhere. She heard me and started shouting for me to run, and the next thing I knew I woke up in the cellar all tied up, with Teresa next to me."

"I went after her when she didn't come back," Teresa said. "I thought I'd be able to handle Daisy if it came to that, but I barely got time to knock. She just *went* for me."

Rose took up the story. "When Alice told us Miriam had been taken, we decided we'd go and knock on the door. Tell them we were looking for her."

"Of course you did," DI Adams said, and looked thoughtfully at the sloe gin.

Rose ignored her. "We thought it might make them less likely to … *do* anything. And there were two of us. But we heard Miriam thumping around upstairs, and that Simon blindsided Gert and shoved her straight down the cellar stairs. Daisy hit me with something, and next thing we're all tied up in the cellar together."

"And this," said DI Adams, "is why you stay out of police business."

No one spoke for a moment, then Thompson said, "Do you still think that's going to work?"

"No," DI Adams admitted. "But I live in hope."

"So are Tom and Harriet in any trouble?" Miriam asked. "They were just protecting Rainbow, you know."

"Your family have no idea what law-abiding means, do they?" DI Adams asked Colin.

"We *do*," Miriam said, more indignantly than she meant to.

"So you just ignore it, then?"

Colin sighed and examined the doughnuts, which were slowly congealing in the bottom of their tub, then picked up a piece of apple and cheese slice, the fruit tightly layered and softly brown under a glaze of brown sugar. "Tom's cooperating, and has acquired a posh girlfriend who happens to be a trained lawyer. He'll be fine."

"Oh, that's nice," Pearl said, and Rosemary and Carlotta made regretful noises.

"And your mother, Colin?" Alice asked, fanning herself with a napkin.

"According to the group page on Facebook, she's off having a protest tour of Europe," he said around the apple slice. "With Harriet, who I imagine is waiting for the insurance on the bookshop to be sorted out."

"That sounds fun," Miriam said, then frowned. "Well, in a very Rainbow way."

"Yes, we've left messages telling them they're not going to be arrested, but there's been no response."

"So do you have a good case?" Rose asked. "Even if you don't have the stolen goods?"

"Oh, we have the jewellery," DI Adams said. "They didn't manage to get the safe out of the shop, and it was fireproof. Plus they're trying to pin as much on the other as they can, so it's a pretty tidy case."

"I still can't believe they tried to burn us," Pearl said with a shiver. "That was so scary!"

Teresa gave her a tight hug, and Thompson said, "That was an accident."

Everyone looked at him.

"Not *me*," he snapped. "Gods. Suspicious minds, the lot of you. They were using a gas torch thingy to try to cut the safe open, but when Miriam got free and they thought she'd already made it outside, they decided to run while they could. They just dropped everything, grabbed Rainbow, and legged it. Didn't even turn the torch off."

"And Harriet was evidently already in the car," Beaufort said. "I found her when I intercepted them."

DI Adams made a small *hmm* sound, but didn't say anything else.

For a moment silence fell on the hall, and in the cupboard the boiler gave a hiccough and a muted roar, and they all turned to look at it.

"Is that thing going to blow up?" Thompson asked. "Because I've lost enough fur for you lot already."

"I ... don't think it will," Mortimer said, and everyone looked at him.

"Have you taken a look at it, then, lad?" Beaufort asked. "I didn't know you were up with boilers."

"I'm not," he said, with a small sigh. "But Amelia ... well, she heard everyone complaining about how it wasn't working well, and she thought she'd ... take a look." He looked at his mug. "She's really rather good with things like that, but she may have been a bit overenthusiastic."

The boiler burped again, and the icing on the ginger slice gave up and started to dribble off the sides. Teresa rolled her leggings up to her knees and said, "Can you tell her to take another look? I think she's set the thermostat to *dragon*."

A ripple of laughter rolled down the table, and Alice said, "I suppose it's a good thing we were too busy to tell the council. I doubt they'd think much to dragon repairs."

"Can you try to keep your *too busy* on this side of life-threatening next time?" DI Adams said. "If Barry hadn't known about the whole underground passage thing I don't know if we'd have got to everyone in time."

There was another pause while the assorted humans and non-humans considered that, then Alice said, "We can certainly try, Inspector."

DI Adams sighed, tested her sloe gin, and winced. "I don't know why I thought you'd say anything else."

The laughter that washed around the hall was warm and easy, resting deeper in the bones and closer to the heart than even the dragon-standard boiler in the cupboard could. Outside, the day was clear and bright, polished with frost and crisp with fallen leaves, and it smelled of woodsmoke and warm hibernation and the gentle, silent places where small things sleep. Miriam touched her own burns, already healing with the liberal application of arnica and aloe, and wondered what she would have done differently. Not very much, she thought. Not when it came to friends who were family and family who counted. Other than be faster with her borrowed cane.

"I've made a decision," Jasmine announced.

"Oh?" Alice said. "What's that?"

"I thought about what you said. About deciding what *I* want to do."

"Well done," Carlotta said, patting her on the shoulder. "What is it?"

"I'm going to become a Police Community Support Officer," Jasmine said, her face pink with heat and delight. "I've already applied. Isn't that *wonderful?*"

Priya clapped, and Rose jumped up to hug the younger woman, and a rush of approval washed around the table. Miriam looked at Colin and DI Adams, who were both staring at Jasmine. DI Adams still had a piece of scone in her fingers and it vanished suddenly. She jumped, then wiped her fingers on a napkin.

"Wonderful," she said, and drank her untouched glass of sloe gin.

"Wonderful," Colin echoed, and reached for another apple slice.

Miriam just poured herself some more tea and smiled at Jasmine, and said, "It *is* wonderful," because while she could think of nothing worse than having to wear a uniform and proper shoes and going around being officious at people, she had an idea it would make Jasmine very happy indeed. And nothing in the world was more wonderful or beautiful than seeing one's friends grow into the person they were always meant to be, to find their own path and their own happiness. And it never looked the same for any one person, because happiness has many shapes and forms and colours, and just as one could never entirely understand another's sorrow, neither could one fully understand another's happiness. But one could feel it, and celebrate it, just as one felt and honoured another's grief, because that was what it was to be human, and to be so deeply, beautifully, painfully connected to each other.

Or maybe not *human,* she thought to herself, watching Martha roll over in front of Mortimer, pawing at him gently, and Thompson muttering to Alice, and DI Adams setting her coffee mug on the floor and petting something unseen. Maybe it was simply what it was to be fully, wildly alive.

"Wonderful," Beaufort declared, giving Jasmine a gentle pat on the shoulder. "And just how does one go about becoming a Police Community Support Officer, then?"

There was an understated *splat* as Mortimer dropped a doughnut, going abruptly grey, and Rose laughed and said they should ask Walter if he wanted to join as well. DI Adams leaned her elbows on the table and rubbed her forehead gently while Colin topped up both their glasses, and outside the year continued its slow roll through the rhythm of the seasons, beautiful and wild and fraught with wonder, living and dying and growing again.

And that was also what it was to be alive.

And what a truly magical thing that is.

A BEAUFORT SCALES MYSTERY

THANK YOU

And here we are at the end. Just for now, though. There are more adventures of crime-solving dragons and alarmingly resolute ladies of a certain age to come (not to mention snippy cats and grumpy sprites). Thank you for joining me once again, lovely people. Thank you for your trust, and your belief, and your love for modern dragons. I don't take such things lightly. They are exceptionally precious.

The next Beaufort won't be until late 2024 at the earliest – I'm sorry about the wait, but I find these books demand a certain mindset and energy, and I'd rather take my time getting to them than rush and have the story be anything less that the best I can offer you. So thank you as well for your patience in waiting on them.

But there will be other books in the meantime! Look for the DI Adams series to kick off in early 2024, and if you haven't read *What Happened in London* yet, you might want to pick that up. Be warned, though – it has teeth …

And a final request before you go, lovely people. I'd appreciate it immensely if you could take the time to pop a quick review up at your favourite retailer, or on Goodreads. It doesn't have to be long – "that's where Claude went!" or "I never did trust emus" will more than suffice. But more reviews mean the retailers' algorithms do mysterious, fancy things (technical term there) and show my books to more readers, and more readers mean I can continue to investigate the doings of cats and dragons and report back for as long as possible. So every review is an enormous help. Thank you so much!

And if you'd like to send me a copy of your review, to chat about dragons and baked goods, or ask about anything, drop me a message at kim@kmwatt.com. I'd love to hear from you!

Until next time - read on!
Kim

BEWARE THE SNAP-SNAP-SNAP ...

Baton. Light. Chocolate. Duck.

This is not DS Adams' usual kit. This is not DS Adams' usual case. She doesn't think it's *anyone's* usual case, not with the vanishing children and the looming bridge and the hungry river. Not with the *snap-snap-snap*.

But six kids are missing, and she's not going to let there be a seventh. Not on her watch. And she knows how to handle human monsters, after all. How different can this really be?

So: Baton. Light. Chocolate. And the bloody duck.

Let's be having you, then.

Scan above to find What Happened in London, or use the link below:
https://readerlinks.com/l/3701956/b8

PS: This is a darker story. There's precious little cake and a whole lot of peril, and not a single dragon. So it may not be for everyone. Just so you're prepared!

BONFIRE NIGHT TREATS

Your free recipe collection awaits!

Or any night, really. Or day. Any time you need a little sustenance for investigations, refreshments for hungry dragons, or, well, cake. Because who needs a reason for cake?

Grab your free collection of (almost) W.I.-approved recipes today to ensure you're well-fuelled for all eventualities!

Plus, if this is your first visit to Toot Hansell and my newsletter, I'm also going to send you some story collections – including one about how that whole barbecue thing started …

Happy baking!

Scan above to download your recipe collection, or pop the link in your browser: https://readerlinks.com/l/3699722/b8

ABOUT THE AUTHOR

Hello, lovely person. I'm Kim, and in addition to the Beaufort Scales stories I write other funny, magical books that offer a little escape from the serious stuff in the world and hopefully leave you a wee bit happier than you were when you started. Because happiness, like friendship, matters.

I write about baking-obsessed reapers setting up baby ghoul petting cafes, and ladies of a certain age joining the Apocalypse on their Vespas. I write about friendship, and loyalty, and lifting each other up, and the importance of tea and cake.

But mostly I write about how wonderful people (of all species) can really be.

If you'd like to find out the latest on new books in *The Beaufort Scales* series, as well as discover other books and series, giveaways, extra reading, and more, jump on over to www.kmwatt.com and check everything out there.

Read on!

a amazon.com/Kim-M-Watt/e/B07JMHRBMC
g goodreads.com/kimmwatt
BB bookbub.com/authors/kim-m-watt
f facebook.com/KimMWatt
o instagram.com/kimmwatt

ACKNOWLEDGEMENTS

These books may have my name on them, but they wouldn't be here without you, lovely readers. Your unwavering belief in tea-drinking dragons, crime-solving ladies of a certain age, and the many and varied inhabitants of the Yorkshire Dales (human and otherwise) is what brings these stories to life. They'd be nothing but words on a page without you. So, with all my heart, thank you

Many thanks also to my wonderful friends, both online and off, writers and readers, both and neither, who present me with squirming baskets of plot bunnies, weird little memes, unrepeatable yet hilarious anecdotes, tubs of veggie soup, and the regular insistence that I get off the computer and interact with actual humans. All of these are vital to the happy life of an author, and I love every one of you.

As ever, Lynda at Easy Reader Editing has checked for multiple Barries, tamed the hyenas, rounded up the buffalo, and generally made this book something I'm proud to put out into the world. All good grammar praise goes to her. All mistakes are mine.

Onward to the next adventure, lovely people. Keep finding the magic in the world.

Kim.

ALSO BY KIM M. WATT

The Gobbelino London, PI series

"This series is a wonderful combination of humor and suspense that won't let you stop until you've finished the book. Fair warning, don't plan on doing anything else until you're done ..."

– Goodreads reviewer

🐌

The Beaufort Scales Series (cozy mysteries with dragons)

"The addition of covert dragons to a cozy mystery is perfect ... and the dragons are as quirky and entertaining as the rest of the slightly eccentric residents of Toot Hansell."

– Goodreads reviewer

🐌

What Happened in London (a DI Adams prequel)

"This book will grip you within its story and not let go so be prepared going in with snacks and caffeine because you won't want to put it down."

– Goodreads reviewer

🐌

Oddly Enough: Tales of the Unordinary, Volume One

"The stories are quirky, charming, hilarious, and some are all of the above without a dud amongst the bunch ..."

– Goodreads reviewer

~

More free stories!

The Cat Did It

Of course the cat did it. Sneaky, snarky, and up to no good – that's the cats in this feline collection, which you can grab free by signing up to the newsletter. Just remember – if the cat winks, always wink back ...

The Tales of Beaufort Scales

A collection of dragonish tales from the world of Toot Hansell, as an extra welcome gift for joining the newsletter. Just mind the abominable snow porcupine ...